FRANK

RITES OF AZATHOTH

FIRST EDITION TRADE PAPERBACK

ISBN: 978-1-944703-19-6
LCCN: 2016962142

Book design & typesetting:
David G. Barnett
fatcatgraphicdesign.com

Assistant editors:
Amanda Baird

Necro Publications
necropublications.com

Printed in the United States of America

10 9 8 7 6 5 4 3 2 1

FRANK CAVALLO

RITES OF AZATHOTH

— 2017 —

DEDICATION:

For Kate Morris, because you always wanted one of these and because you roasted marshmallows around a campfire with me in the Okavango when no one else wanted to.

George—
There are no Civil War, JFK or Beatles references in this book—
But I hope you enjoy it anyway—
—[signature]

ACKNOWLEDGMENTS:

Thanks, as always, go first and foremost to my family. I could not have done anything without you.

A special nod to the felony coffee crew—George, Jay, Josh and Jeff—for helping me keep my sanity in an utterly insane place. Thanks as well to Deucey, for the scotch and for letting me bounce ideas off you.

A note of appreciation goes to Lawrence for showing me all around D.C. (I told you some of that stuff would make it into a book someday) and to Tom for coming along on the trip.

To Stormy, thanks for keeping up with me, and thanks for letting me read your stuff back in Windhoek, now I'm returning the favor.

Lastly, to Dave and the folks at Necro, who stuck by me and who tirelessly continue to push my very weird stories on an unsuspecting public, I am eternally grateful.

DAY ONE

"Those who enter here have no more light."
— The Descent of Inanna
Sumerian Text, circa 3500 BC

They came for him at night.

There was no warning. No hint of their intrusion—their attack—until it was almost complete.

There were at least a dozen of them, he couldn't be sure. They broke into his tent in the dark, piling on top of him, seizing his arms and his legs, throwing a burlap bag of a hood over his head and yanking it tight around his throat. He nearly choked right then.

So silent and so fast, he never got more than a foot off the bed before they injected him with something.

He gasped for air, trying to bring voice to his mouth even as the rope constricted his windpipe and his head swam from the sedative. He wasn't trying to scream. He knew that would do him no good. There was no one to hear him. No one else out there with them, isolated and cut off from the world—just as they desired. Just as the Priestess had told them they needed to be.

But still, he struggled. He managed a few desperate words. He demanded a reason. An accusation or a charge to justify the intrusion. He demanded something...anything.

Nothing came back to him. Only a punch to the gut. A shock of pain ripped through his stomach and down into his groin.

They hauled him back up to his feet. He could feel his own great, sudden weight. He was heavy. Laden with iron, shackles locked around his wrists and ankles, joined by a spider web of links that seemed to envelope him. Blind, bound and bewildered—wheezing, tired and aching, he refused to quell his protests.

"The Priestess will hear of this!" he warned. "You can't do this to me!"

They began to drag him; in which direction, he could not tell. But a moment later, he could sense a change in the light, a hint of brightness bleeding through the fabric around his head. He continued to protest, raising his voice out of frustration, out of anger and finally fear.

"I am her second. No one is more loyal!" he shouted. "Valeria will not allow this!"

For a moment, the forward progress halted. Everything fell back into a deathly, horrible quiet. He felt someone come near to him. He could hear breath and feel the subtle warmth of a face next to his own. It was followed by a delicate whisper in his ear, a woman's voice he almost recognized.

"She is the one who ordered this."

That was the moment he knew he was damned.

ONE

INTERNATIONAL SECURITY SYMPOSIUM
HAMILTON CROWNE PLAZA HOTEL
WASHINGTON, D.C.

Diana Mancuso bumped shoulders with a man in a tuxedo. A complete accident. Her apology got all the way out before her glass of Riesling was done spilling onto his jacket. It could not have sounded less sincere; a casualty of having had at least one too many already.

"Not to worry, young lady," he said.

He smiled as he pulled a monogrammed hankie from his pocket and daubed it over the wet-spot. She realized it was the Brazilian ambassador. Typical politician. Always smiling. She knew he was probably cursing her in Portuguese behind his dark eyes.

Even though it wasn't necessary, and not at all likely to do any good, she apologized again. This time, she made an effort to express something like genuine contrition. A moment of eye contact, and a few self-effacing comments. She even offered to pay his dry-cleaning bill.

He declined.

She excused herself, and faded just a little further into the background of the ballroom. From there, positioned with her back to the wall, she was far less likely to expose herself to any more awkward moments. She was also in a perfect spot to watch everyone else at the reception, and to marvel at how they accomplished something that she'd never been able to do.

Even after four glasses of wine, she still couldn't.

She hated the entire ritual, the mindless small talk and hobnobbing. The pretense of friendship and congeniality. Especially because most of the people who were so good at it despised one another.

D.C. was all about appearances. Perceptions. Plenty of smiles and handshakes to go around. Seventeen years at the F.B.I., the last nine of them across the river at Quantico, had taught her at least that much about the nation's capital. Inside the Beltway all the dirty work was done when no one was watching. No one looked you in the eye when they pulled the trigger, or twisted the knife.

Hypocrites and liars, every last one of them.

Diana managed to get the attention of a waitress. She handed over her empty glass and ordered another. The waitress, in her most discreet voice, pointed out that Diana had spilled some wine on her own dress.

"I know. I'm a fucking mess," she answered.

The waitress forced a smile as she handed over a napkin, but she seemed uncomfortable with casual profanity. She excused herself.

Diana didn't spend much time on the stain. She was never going to wear the dress again, and she wasn't planning on staying much longer anyway.

She could almost hear her mother, lecturing her about acting unlady-like. One more reason to hate these occasions, *and these fucking people*. Nights like this made her feel like a little girl again. Awkward and uncomfortable in clothes that didn't completely fit, taking every opportunity to slip her heels off under the table. Even at forty-three, she still felt like the kid sister playing street hockey with her brothers, still felt like the girl in the denim overalls with holes in the knees who hated wearing a dress to Mass on Sundays.

When she saw Richard Norris coming her way, she balled up the napkin and tossed it behind her. Then she ran her hands over her hair to make sure it was still in place. A healthy dose of product had it glistening, tied back in a chic bun. She kept it all one length, cut to just above her shoulders. It hadn't been any longer in the last ten years. She'd dyed it a shade darker than her natural chestnut two days before, the latest round of an endless fight against encroaching grays. For the evening's festivities, she was trying a new look, combing it all back from her face.

She hadn't done that since she was a teenager, since she wore it in a ponytail every day for so many years that her mother—who hated the tomboy look—had threatened to cut it off in her sleep. These days of course, she was wearing it without the ratty Bruins cap that had been the other constant part of her high school wardrobe. As much as she loved *the B's*, it wouldn't have gone with her outfit.

"Would it kill you, Diana?"

Norris's voice broke her out of her spell. He had closed the distance between them without her realizing, vodka martini in hand. Like everyone she'd known since her first day of kindergarten, he almost never called her by her full name.

"What's that?' she said.

She turned toward him, pretending for a moment that she hadn't heard him.

"I said, would it kill you?" Norris repeated. "To mingle, that is?"

Diana rolled her eyes. This happened at least once at every party, dinner or occasion at which there were more than five people in attendance. It was almost as annoying as when people she didn't know would tell her to smile, right out of the blue.

Fuck you, she thought. Norris seemed to see it in her eyes. But she didn't say it.

"Kill me?" she answered. "No. But if that's the best reason you can think of to do something…there are lots of things that won't kill me. Rooting for the Yankees, having a polite conversation with your wife. But I'm not gonna do either of those any time soon."

"The last one might just kill you," he said.

Diana waved past him, over toward Julia Norris. At the moment, she was quite well engaged with a Four-Star General on the other side of the room.

"Well, Chairman of the Joints Chiefs, no less," she said. "Should you be worried?"

Richard Norris grinned as he sipped the last of his drink. He left the olive in the glass.

"Worried about James Krieger? No. Ol' Black Jack talks a good game, but I'll tell you a little secret."

He motioned for her to sidle up closer to him. She leaned in.

"Took some shrapnel in Grenada, right in the groin. They saved one testicle, but he's as limp as a noodle. Could take a whole bottle of the little blue pills, wouldn't do a damn thing, except maybe give him a heart attack."

"No kidding?"

"Even so, I've known Jack Krieger for ages, since we were both at the Point. There's nobody in D.C. I'd trust my wife with more."

"There's a ringing endorsement."

Norris laughed. That put her a little more at ease—for a minute.

Richard Norris was tall, a few inches over six feet. He looked like a movie star in his black tuxedo, every bit the picture of a real-life G-man that one would expect from an Assistant Director of the F.B.I.

The years had been kind to him, remarkably so in fact, for a man edging closer to his fifty-second birthday. He was what the celebrity magazines would have called distinguished, but still damn good-looking in Diana's opinion. He kept himself in terrific shape, ran three miles a day and never smoked a thing. She'd heard that he'd been a top track and field athlete at West Point in the seventies. He still looked like he could compete.

His hair had been blond in his youth, and the transition to silver-gray suited his fair skin perfectly. The fading color was one of his only outward concessions to the decades. Unlike most men his age, he hadn't lost a wisp of it, still as thick and full as a twenty-year old. He combed it back from his forehead in a part that would slip down to his eyebrows every so often.

There weren't a lot of young, single women working at F.B.I. headquarters, but every one of them had talked about that hair at least once. For Diana Mancuso, the number was a little bit higher.

"I'd ask you to dance, but I know that isn't your thing," he said.

He was right. She hated dancing.

He motioned to the waiter who passed by for another martini as he started to walk away.

"Ten minutes. Suite 923," he said.

She knew very well what that meant. He smiled, leaving her with one last jibe.

"You're doing a good job, by the way."

She looked at him cross-eyed as he slipped away from her into the mingling masses of diplomats, military officers and law enforcement professionals from around the globe.

"Holding up the wall," he said. "Keep it up."

Fuck you, she thought again.

TWO

HAMILTON CROWNE PLAZA HOTEL
SUITE 923
WASHINGTON, D.C.

"Same plan as usual, right?" Norris asked.

He was already straightening his bow tie. Diana hadn't even gotten her dress back on yet.

"Oh, fuck me!" she answered.

Norris shot a look across the room, smiling at the obvious humor of her favorite expletive, given their particular situation. Her expression answered for her though, as she glared back at him with a look that said she was not in a mood to appreciate a joke—especially her own.

"I'll head back down first. You follow about seven or eight minutes later?" he continued.

She wasn't paying attention. All her focus seemed to be directed at her dress.

"Hey, are you listening?" Norris asked.

She lifted her head as he came around the bed.

"Do you have any idea how much this cost?" she said. She didn't need to point out what she meant. The huge hole he'd ripped open along the hem of her cocktail dress was impossible to miss. "I told you to give me a second, but you just couldn't wait, could you?"

He rolled his fingers over her cheek.

"I never can," he said.

"Screw you," she said, swatting his hand away, but letting a hint of a smile slip through at her second double entendre in as many minutes.

"I bought this just for tonight, two-hundred and thirty-eight fucking dollars at Nordstrom. Now it's ruined."

"I'll buy you a new one," he said.

He picked up his dinner jacket from the chair and slipped it on.

"You bet your ass you will, but that's not the point, Richard. I have to go back downstairs. What am I supposed to do? Walk around with my hand on my thigh for the rest of the night?"

"Don't you have some safety pins or something?"

"Yeah, right. I always carry a bunch in my purse, you know—for whenever my boss rips half the lace off of the bottom of my dress. If you think your wife won't notice…"

"Okay, Okay. Hey, why don't…"

She cut him off.

"Look, just get outta here. I'll see you back downstairs. Don't worry, I won't be there *too soon.*"

«««—»»»

True to her word, she waited the appropriate amount of time before re-joining the party downstairs. She even made sure to get off of the elevator on the second floor, and take the back stairs to the ballroom. But the trip down the steps only made the gaping hole on her left side bigger. No matter how she pulled on the hem, the ripped lace was still visible. It was only going to get worse. Given that, she figured it might be a good time to make her final exit. She looked at her watch. 11:30 on the nose. It was past her bedtime.

She looked around the hall. The crowd was still every bit as strong as it had been during dinner. For a lot of these people, conferences like this were a big deal, a chance to network with other professionals from all over the world. For her though, it was drudgery, and the third one in the past two years.

Surveying the sea of men in tuxedos and ladies in cocktail dresses more expensive than hers, she fixated on Norris. He was already back in the mix, schmoozing as usual. This time with a handsome gentleman who wore a little white flower on his black lapel. She motioned, as discreetly as she was able, but her wave failed to catch her boss's attention. She was going to have to go over.

Before she could say anything though, before she could muster up a lame excuse about needing to check on her non-existent cat or having to get to the office early tomorrow, Norris pre-empted her.

"Diana, I was wondering where you got off to," he said. His act was so convincing that even she almost believed it. "There's someone here I want you to meet."

Norris lifted his hand in the direction of the man with the flower lapel, who smiled when he saw Diana walking toward them.

"This is Roger Saxon," Norris began. "CEO of Saxon/Lux Inc."

Saxon nodded. Norris turned to his friend to continue the introduction.

"Roger, this is Diana Giuliana Maria Mancuso," he said, taking a peculiar, ostentatious pleasure in pronouncing every syllable of her long Catholic name.

Diana glared at him as he made the introduction. He never got tired of doing that, running through her entire name, including her confirmation name, which not even the most devout Catholic ever used. She wanted to slap him, but his face beamed with such a broad, Tom Cruise smile that it was impossible to stay mad at him.

"Ah-ha," Saxon said, leaning in a little closer. "Irish then?"

"Diana's fine," she corrected. "I am, actually—Irish that is. On my mother's side."

"Obviously," Norris pointed out, still smiling.

She made a deliberate show of ignoring him, squinting a little before turning away from him to face Saxon. He smelled like Old Spice and single malt scotch.

"Kelly's my mother's maiden name," she said.

"I stand corrected then," Saxon said. "Boston, right? The North End maybe?"

She nodded, more than a little impressed. She was pretty sure she hadn't had enough to drink for her accent to sneak out yet.

"Quite an astute ear," she said. "That's almost dead on. My dad's from Somerville, Winter Hill area. We moved when I was in junior high though, down to East Weymouth. You too, right?"

Saxon nodded as he sipped his drink, smiling right at her and staring into her eyes. Norris answered for him, since he seemed distracted.

"Grew up in Brookline. I live over in Newton now," he replied.

"Harvard man, our boy here," Norris added, slapping Saxon on the shoulder.

Diana raised her eyebrows and mouthed and comical "ooooh".

Saxon laughed.

"I know, I know. You were a little further down the Red Line than I was, but I wasn't chained to Harvard Square. I made it down to Southie a few times, took in a St. Patty's Day parade or two, maybe even a fight once or twice, now that I think of it. Some tough bars down there, back in my day."

"Still that way," she said.

He stretched his arm out and leaned on the table, boxing her in.

"So what brings such a pretty lady to one of these oh-so-boring seminars?" Saxon asked. Diana saw the ring on his finger, and he knew it. But he was flirting anyway. "What are you doing with a jerk like Norris, come to mention it?"

Norris stepped in, getting between them. She thanked him without saying a word, just a look.

"She used to be one of mine," he said.

Diana shot him a killer look.

Did you really just say what I think you said?

He continued without missing a beat.

"One of my agents, that is. She was the top profiler in the business, at one time. Diana literally wrote the book on the psychology of serial killers. Used to be one helluva field agent, but these days she's punching a clock over at Quantico."

Saxon cocked his head. Diana edged back from the table to a safe distance and answered the question she figured he was about to ask.

"Behavioral Sciences Department," she said. "Some analysis. A little research. But mostly teaching."

"Yeah, molding the minds of our impressionable new agents," Norris added. He elbowed Saxon in the ribs. "I'll tell you, I wish they had teachers that looked like you when I went there."

He winked at her, which he tended to do when he was giving a compliment. She ignored it. He did that all the time, especially after a few drinks. Another married guy who still liked to flirt. With Norris though, those little moments weren't quite unwelcome.

"Very true, very true," Saxon said. He extended his hand, with an eye toward making amends. Diana took it, but instead of a handshake, he lifted her hand to her mouth and kissed it.

"A pleasure to make your acquaintance," he said.

Oh please, she thought. Norris knew what she was thinking, but neither let on.

"How delightfully old fashioned, Mr. Saxon," she said, with one last attempt to deflect his attention.

He seemed to realize that she was no fan of feigned sincerity, even though she didn't realize she'd let on to that either. Maybe she had had one too many already.

"Well, I'm just an old soul," Saxon said. "But please, no formalities. This pomp and circumstance is more than enough. Any friend of Richard's is a friend of mine. Call me Roger."

Diana nodded, and looked over at Norris, who nodded back, a tacit acknowledgement of his little rescue. Even as they made a momentary eye contact, she thought about what Saxon said. She wasn't sure that she and Richard Norris *were friends*. They'd worked together for better than a decade, but he had always been her boss. Mentor maybe, school-girl crush for sure, but she had never thought of him as a friend.

Norris turned back to his old buddy.

"So, things still on track Roger?" he asked.

"Almost. You know how these things are, lawyers and paperwork. Lots of paperwork. Profit margins, debt burdens, salary structures.

Always more to do. I'm on the first flight out of Reagan tomorrow morning actually."

"Back up to Beantown?"

"Right, hopefully we'll have everything all sorted out at corporate H.Q. sometime tomorrow," he answered.

"Roger's company is in the middle of major acquisition talks," Norris explained.

"So I heard," Diana said.

"Reading the business pages now, are we?" Norris quipped.

She squinted at him, but only for an instant.

"Merging with Neutrino Industries," she said. "They made my phone. Good quality stuff. One of the emerging leaders in the next gen smartphone market, right?"

"They are," Saxon said, obviously impressed. "Their president is a friend of mine. An MIT gal, but I try not to hold that against her."

"How is Stephanie, it's been a while since I've seen her. Not since the last inaugural, I think," Norris said.

"Who's this?" she asked.

"Stephanie Bremmer, CEO of Neutrino Industries. Old friend of mine. One of the first female CEOs of a top tech firm," he answered. "Known her for ages, since she was tinkering with a TRS-80 in her garage back in the day."

"Jesus, do you know everybody?" Diana asked.

Norris smiled.

"Just a part of my job."

Diana finished her drink all at once.

"So how about we cut right to it?" she said. "Are you gonna be the next VP?"

Norris grimaced, and cleared his throat with a kind of low growl. Diana just snickered, enjoying the chance to make *him* uncomfortable.

"Oh, c'mon. You know there's no such thing as a secret in this town," she said, before turning back to Saxon. "Rumor is this merger is designed to let you cash out and divest yourself of day-to-day control."

Saxon grinned with a wicked smile that hid nothing—quite deliberately, she imagined.

"Is that what they're saying?" he replied.

"Of course there will be questions, with so many ties to the military-industrial complex—do they even still call it that? But once you're able to say there's no chance of a conflict of interest claim when the White House calls, Congressional approval should be easy enough," she continued. "At least, *that's what they say*."

Saxon's face turned dour, and Diana had to look to see if he was faking that as well.

"Such a terrible tragedy, what happened to Vice President Moore. I'm not sure the country is even over the shock of it yet," he said.

Norris stepped back in.

"Sudden brain hemorrhage, and on the golf course no less," he added. "You just never know, do you? You never see it coming."

Diana's smile only widened.

"Like I said, that's what they say," she replied.

Then she paid them both a good evening, and excused herself. Despite his deflections, she could feel Norris's eyes on her as she walked away. And that was enough.

DAY TWO

"I will take the divine tablet of destinies. Then I will control the decrees of all the gods."

— Manuscript fragment, circa 2000 BC, Royal Babylonian Library of Ashurbanipal, Nineveh

THREE

MUSEUM OF FINE ARTS
BOSTON, MA

Carter Shaw didn't like talking to people. Especially not in groups, and definitely not at work.

Giving guided tours was not a part of his job description. He reminded old lady Quinlan of that every time she tried to press him into service. She never listened. Aside from his rather surly disposition, there was no one at the MFA better qualified to the task. He'd been doing it for more than thirty years now, off and on. That had been how he'd gotten his start there, *she* always reminded *him*, as a college student in the eighties, a lanky, long-haired slob in sandals and tie-dyes who had hung around the museum on his summer breaks from BU so much that he knew more about the exhibits than the regular guides.

After a while, they started to pay him for being there.

In the years since, he didn't give tours much anymore. It wasn't from a lack of knowledge. Three degrees and a doctorate later, he now held the post of curator of Near Eastern Antiquities. It wasn't a fear of public speaking, either. Once he got going, he was as natural with a crowd as anyone. It was more the fact that Carter Shaw wasn't the sort of person the people who ran the MFA wanted as their public "face."

He still had the long hair, although now it was quite a bit thinner on top. He had long ago traded in the hippie wardrobe for oxford shirts and Jerry Garcia ties, but that wasn't a big deal. He was an academic, and a brilliant one at that. Some sartorial eccentricity was expected.

It was more the fact that, on the few occasions when Carter did speak to people, he had a tendency to be rather unpleasant.

When three guides all called out sick in one morning, Carter found himself once more drafted into duty. He gave Quinlan the usual earful. It was going to take him away from his regular duties, which meant he'd be there late tonight, and therefore she could expect to see him even later tomorrow.

She promised to buy him a coffee for his trouble.

«««—»»»

The tour group had already gathered by the time he got there. He introduced himself with a bad joke, about how his passion for Chalcolithic sculpture had contributed to his divorce. It met with a smattering of polite but uncomfortable laughter. The tourists didn't get it, and he didn't care. He was already counting the minutes until his time with *the great unwashed masses* was over.

The crowd was larger than usual. A group of senior citizens made up about half of them. He made no effort to disguise his groan. He'd probably have to repeat everything for their sake. The rest were college kids and a young couple with their toddler—no picnic there either. Aside from that, there was one unusual guest, a single, rather tall man in black who remained at the rear for the entire tour.

The man was clean shaven, including his head. His face was stoic. He wore a turtleneck sweater that looked military-issue, with a long pea-coat of the sort favored by sailors or dockworkers.

After shepherding them around the entire place for several hours, seeing just about everything that Carter could think to show them, and telling just about every story he could cram into the time frame, he brought them full circle. They gathered around right where they had begun.

"So this brings us to the end of our tour…finally," he said. "On behalf of the museum I'm supposed to thank you folks for coming out here today, and for putting up with me for…" he looked down at his watch—and sighed. "For almost three hours. So, any last questions?"

A few of the people smiled. Some chattered amongst themselves. Then someone took him up on his offer.

"What can you tell me about the Tablet of Destinies?"

The voice was deep, and spoken with an East-End London accent. It was strong enough to silence the crowd. Carter looked around, trying to identify the speaker. Most of the faces staring back at him looked bewildered. All but one. The man at the back.

"Excuse me?" Carter asked. "Did you say the Tablet of Destinies?"

"I did," the man in black answered.

Carter smiled a sarcastic grin.

"What can I tell you?" he began. "It's a myth. I'm a curator of actual antiquities, my friend, not imaginary ones."

"So you don't know about it?" the man asked.

Carter bristled. That sounded like a challenge. Of course he knew about it. He wasn't about to be shown up by some tourist.

"The piece you're referring to is the center of a legend that dates at least to the Babylonians, but probably goes back even further. In the story, the Tablet of Destinies was supposed to have been given by the gods to the hero Marduk, as the prize for defeating another god in combat. It was said to contain all the knowledge required to rule over humanity, and therefore whoever possessed it was destined to be king."

There were a fair amount of *oohs* and *aahs* from the crowd. But the man in the back didn't appear the least bit impressed. Carter figured that nothing he was going to say was likely to satisfy the guy, so ending the conversation seemed like the best idea.

"But it didn't exist, of course. It's just a story." He looked straight at the Englishman. "That's about all I can tell you. If you'd like to talk to someone in greater depth about legends or fables, I can send you over to Commonwealth Ave. Boston University has some excellent professors there who can tell you everything you want to know about mythological…"

"It isn't a myth," the Englishman answered. "You know better."

The crowd was beginning to grow anxious. The tone of the exchange was becoming tense.

"That's the official story," the Englishman continued. "But you can get that on Wikipedia. I want the real story. The one you don't tell the tourists. You know what I'm talking about."

Carter was losing his patience. This was the downside of giving tours, the occasional obnoxious tourist. Usually it was some armchair intellectual, the kind of guy who reads archaeology books on the weekends and subscribes to Scientific American, and who thinks he's going to impress his girlfriend by showing up the museum guide.

Much as he wanted to tell the guy to get lost, he knew better. In these situations, it was usually best to indulge the questioner, if for no other reason than to put the rest of the crowd at ease.

But asking the next question made him nervous.

"I'm not sure I do know what you're talking about. What *exactly* are you looking for?" he asked.

The Englishman looked him dead in the eyes.

"I want to hear about Azathoth."

Carter swore, under his breath, he hoped. The man in black was still staring at him. He wasn't getting out of this easily.

"You've done your homework, my friend," Carter spread his attention out to the rest of the crowd. "This gentleman is referring to what we might call an *alternate history* for the Tablet of Destinies. One that suggests it did, in fact, exist."

"What is that?" one of the tourists asked.

The man in the back was still glaring at him.

"Or what *was* it?" another said.

"The idea here, which its supporters call the Azathoth Theory, for reasons I'm not going to get into, is that a tablet matching the description of our mysterious artifact was supposed to have been mentioned as a source for some Arabic texts written in Baghdad during the eleventh and twelfth centuries. In those days, no one could read cuneiform script, so the content of this alleged text was open to speculation."

"So...what did *they* say it contained?" another tourist asked.

Carter frowned, and looked around like he didn't want to answer.

"Tell them," the man in the back said, almost as if issuing an order. "If you know."

Carter prefaced his reply with an expression of disdain.

"I'd rather not get into this, but if you insist," he said.

The crowd made it clear that they did.

"Okay, but I have to warn you, this isn't what archaeology is really about, these kinds of stories and things, but if you really want to know—here goes..."

The crowd was enrapt.

"If I recall correctly—it's been a while since I heard the whole sordid story—the Arabic texts claimed to be copies of much older tablets that dated from the Sassanian Persian period. Those, in turn, were supposed to have been transcribed from Akkadian tablets which had been stored at the library of Ashurbanipal in the seventh century B.C.," he said. "Those tablets were supposed to have themselves contained a record from the Sumerian Ziggurat at Uruk."

Carter looked back toward the gloomy man in the rear. He nodded in approval, but his face remained every bit as stern as it had been before.

"Now that goes back as far as history takes us, to the Sumerians. But if the Azathoth myth is to be believed, the Tablet of Destinies itself was actually a relic of an even older period," Carter continued.

"Older than the Sumerians?" a tourist asked.

"Right. The problem is that there *isn't anything* older than the Sumerians, nothing that qualifies as a literate civilization anyway—and by definition what we're talking about was essentially a piece of literature. That's why just about everyone working in this field considers it to be a myth. That, and the fact that the Library of Ashurbanipal was uncovered in 1853. I'll give you three guesses what they *didn't find* among the thousands of tablets there."

Several of the tourists muttered the words *Azathoth*, or something like it.

"Right," Carter said. "That makes perfect sense, given what this particular theory says it was supposed to have contained. Because not a single text that we possess, or any document that has ever been uncovered in Sumerian, makes a single reference to an older civilization."

"Except this one," the man in the back answered.

"So they say," Carter said.

"Well, what *did* it say?" a tourist questioned. The crowd was now hanging on his every word.

"No one really knows. When you're dealing with issues like this, it's ripe for someone to come along with a crackpot theory and confuse the hell out of people. That's what happened in this case."

"The Disciples of the Black Flame," the man in the back said.

Carter smiled.

"Maybe *you* should be giving this lecture," he said.

The man did not reply. He just shook his head and continued glaring at the antiquities curator.

"Black Flame, what's that?" someone asked. Carter grimaced as he gathered a breath to continue.

"The Black Flame was some sort of secret society around the end of the nineteenth century. I'm no expert on this, not my field, but I think they were supposed to have been some kind of a cult."

"Satanists?" someone asked.

Carter shrugged.

"Hard to say. There were quite a few of those Madame Blavatsky, black magic, neo-pagan types floating around in those days. They were pretty secretive and their ideas never gained much popularity, probably because of fixations like this Azathoth theory. Eventually they started to fade out, like all crackpots do. They ended up in the dustbin of history."

He left the crowd hanging after that. A pause settled over the museum halls.

"So what did the darn thing say?" an anxious tourist finally asked.

"As I said, no one knows. No one even knows for sure what these Black Flame folks *thought* it said. Since no one ever found it."

"Wow, I've never heard of this," one of the crowd said.

"Quite honestly, I'd prefer if you didn't repeat it," Carter said. "I'd hate for you to come away from today's tour with superstition and mysticism as your fondest memory. Best we can say is that, according to their hair-brained notions, they thought that it preserved some kind of lost knowledge handed down directly from the Great Old Ones to this imaginary pre-historic civilization of theirs."

"The Great Old Ones?" one of the listeners questioned. "Never heard of them."

"Well, again this is really pushing the boundaries of mythology more than archaeology," Carter said. "But since we're already this far along—the Great Old Ones and their masters, called the Outer Gods, were supposedly the first beings worshipped by man. Unlike the gods that came later, Zeus and Thor and Osiris and the types we're all familiar with, these things were not even remotely human. In fact, even in the best versions of these tales, they were supposed to be utterly monstrous. So as the story goes, they were vicious and cruel, and filled with rather unsavory appetites, demanding lots of human sacrifices, quenching their thirst with blood and so on.

"They were so awful apparently, that somehow or another they ended up banished from the Earth, either by the revolt of their subjects or by something else, no one claims to know. In any event, some kind of cataclysm involving them is supposed to have wiped out this original civilization, destroying it so completely that it was almost totally forgotten—except, of course, for these last few tablets they left behind, with the remnants of their rituals preserved even after they were long gone.

"The Sumerians and later the Babylonians, who inherited all of this stuff, didn't understand what it meant and over time corrupted the whole thing into the Tablet of Destinies legend that we have today.

"If I remember correctly, these cult folks spent a lot of time and money trying to find these things. Supposedly they figured that if they got their hands on the actual tablet, they would have had exactly what the Tablet of Destinies claimed to offer Marduk."

He left it there, partially for dramatic effect, and partially because he dreaded telling them the rest.

"Which was what, exactly?" one of the crowd finally asked.

"The power to summon the Old Ones, or even the Outer Gods themselves, and to bring back their reign over the Earth."

A few more *oohs* and *ahhs* whispered up from among the crowd.

"You see, very Spielberg, isn't it?" he said.

The crowd laughed. They seemed to be enjoying the story more than the tour.

"So no one has ever seen it?" someone asked.

"I doubt it," Carter answered. "If anyone had, I'm sure we'd know about it by now, especially if what the legends say about it was true."

"What's that?" someone else asked.

Carter smiled and sneered at the same time.

"Supposedly—let me make sure I get this right, it's been a while—this thing was inscribed on a ten foot tall, nine-sided slab of granite, with etchings that glowed blood red in the moonlight."

The suggestion brought out a collective gasp from the crowd, and Carter decided he'd had enough. Though the crowd seemed a little disappointed at the abrupt end of the tale, he paid them a few insincere compliments about how they were one of the best groups he'd ever had the pleasure to take around. He also encouraged all of them to come back again, and to visit the gift shop on their way out.

When he looked around one last time, the Englishman in the back was gone.

«««—»»»

Carter kept his head down as he made his way through the corridors behind the galleries, in the employees-only section of the museum. He had his wire-rimmed glasses sitting low on his nose, very much the academic. After negotiating the crates and boxes lining the hall, he found his way to his office. It was unlocked, just as he had left it.

He was startled however by the one thing in the office that hadn't been there before the tour. The obnoxious Englishman was waiting for him, standing behind his desk.

"You didn't tell them all of it," the man began. He neither acknowledged the intrusion, nor did he apologize for it.

Carter had had enough.

"What the hell do you think you're doing in here? I have to ask you to leave, sir," he said, emphasizing the last word as though it were a slur.

The man did not budge. For a moment, Carter considered leaving, turning his back and calling security, but he didn't do either.

Carter's office was cluttered. The dusty oak shelves were crammed with books, and every spare space was stuffed with papers in no apparent order. His desk was buried under files and stacks of paper. The man in black stood behind it as though he had every right to be there, and Carter had no way to make him move.

"Why didn't you tell them all of it?" he repeated.

Carter shrugged. His reply was hostile, but mannered nonetheless.

"By *all of it you* mean the tales of a medieval Arab who found the tablet and transcribed the text into a book full of so many horrors that it drove him mad?"

The man nodded.

"I get the feeling you knew all of that already," he answered.

The man continued to stare, but Carter sensed no threat.

"This is rude of me, I apologize. I should at least introduce myself. Xavier Martin Logan is my name. But you can simply call me Logan," the Englishman said.

"I'd say it was nice to meet you, Mr. Logan…"

"Just Logan."

Carter flashed a sarcastic grin.

"But it isn't. Nice to meet you, that is. I don't appreciate people badgering me with stupid questions, and I certainly don't appreciate people invading my privacy."

"I assure you, I haven't turned over a single piece of paper. I'm not interested in bothering you, Dr. Shaw…"

"Oh no, just Carter," he snapped back. "It's too late, by the way. You're already bothering me."

The man in black smiled.

"I have no desire to intrude. Our conversation earlier was no more than an introduction, an audition if you like. My employer entrusted me to learn if you were the kind of man he has been looking for. Perhaps I did not go about it in the most delicate way."

Carter took off his coat and set it on the hook behind his door. There were three tweed jackets already hanging there. Then he sat down behind his desk, and offered Logan the chair on the other side.

"Well then, *Logan*. What can I do for you, or your mysterious employer? If this cloak and dagger routine is any hint, I'm going to guess that you're keeping that information secret, for some unfathomable reason."

"For now," Logan said.

"I'm not sure how I can help you, I've already told you everything I know," he said.

"Not me. My employer."

"Who is that, again?"

"My employer is a wealthy man, and he finds himself very much in need of someone like you. Someone who knows the background on this material. Someone who can read cuneiform. Someone who is willing to travel," he said.

"Travel to where?"

"Nowhere outside of New England," Logan said.

"Okay, so not too far, I guess. When are we talking about?"

"Unfortunately this is a matter of some urgency," Logan answered. "Your presence would be required immediately. Within twenty-four hours, at most."

"How long would this job of yours last?"

"Impossible to say," Logan replied. "The work would be on a contractual basis, possibly open-ended, depending upon the needs of my employer."

Carter shook his head.

"Let me get this straight then," he said. "You want me to drop what I'm doing, here at the job…where I work…every day. You want me to head on out to some place…which you won't really specify… and you can't tell me who I'd be working for, what the job entails or how long I'd be there? Does that about sum it up?"

Logan did not even crack a smile.

"Your analysis is correct," he said.

Carter laughed.

"Oh, that's not analysis," he said. "Analysis would be saying that you haven't given this much thought, or that your offer is half-baked. All I did was re-state your nonsense in plain English."

Logan finally did grin, just a touch.

"I am quite familiar with the English language, thank you very much," he answered, in his London accent.

The irony was not lost on Carter.

"Touché," he said, throwing up his hands and gesturing to the cluttered office all around him. "Joking aside, I don't think I can help you. I have responsibilities, I can't just leave."

Logan produced a manila folder from his coat. He opened it across his lap and began to read from it.

"Underwater on your mortgage to the tune of some one hundred thousand dollars," he began. "Divorce decree awarding your ex-wife roughly half of your check every two weeks for spousal support, plus additional deductions for child support. Speaking of the child, it appears he attends a rather exclusive private school over in Brookline, also rather pricey isn't it?"

Carter edged as close to his desk as possible, balling his hands into fists on top of it.

"Then there are the credit cards, you've run those up in the last few years, haven't you? Seems you owe just over thirty thousand to various banks and lenders," Logan continued. "Oh, and this isn't good…you raided your retirement fund about six months ago, eh? Major penalties for early withdrawal must've taken a bite out of the bottom line there."

"What the hell is this?" Carter demanded. "Are you trying to extort me?"

"Extort you?" Logan replied. "No, it would seem that you are just about the last person anyone should hope to get money from."

"Then what are you doing here?"

"As I said, I come offering employment," Logan replied. "Hmmm, we never did touch on the remuneration did we?"

Carter leaned even further forward.

"So sorry," Logan continued. "You see, my employer is a very wealthy man, as I believe I indicated. He is obviously well aware of your…struggles. But since you appear to possess the qualifications he desires, he would be prepared to pay you more than enough to erase all of these problems. That and much more, as it turns out."

"How much more?" Carter asked.

"Seven figures," Logan replied.

Carter sat back and looked around his office one more time. His anger seemed to melt away, replaced with curiosity.

"Well since you put it that way—when can I start?" he asked.

FOUR

DANFIELD FEDERAL PENITENTIARY
NORTH COSHOCTON, OH

The sun had been down for hours, but no one in Danfield cared. It was always dark inside the labyrinth, under the tireless watch of fluorescent bulbs and men with angry eyes. There were no windows. Only walls. Solid, sound-proof, soul-crushing walls.

Corridors of unpainted concrete and old steel burrowed deep into the bowels of the Earth, drilled into the hard mid-western bedrock; a permanent human hive cut off from the world above. A world that, but for an hour a day, no longer existed outside those sterile, artificial halls. For the men sentenced to life in Danfield, there was no other world. And there never would be.

Sometimes, it felt that way to the men who worked there too.

It was already late as Deputy Chief Corrections Officer Wayne Earl started to make his rounds for the night. Bed-check was supposed to start at ten sharp. But Officer Earl wasn't a night person. He'd pulled his share of second and third shifts in his early years, before he'd earned enough seniority to land a permanent nine-to-six rotation. After that, he'd sworn them off for good, or so he thought. Over the last few weeks he'd been back on overnights by choice, trading all of his prized day shifts since he'd caught his wife in their double-wide with the bartender from R & J's.

He'd forgiven her. A good Christian did that, and she wasn't going to take that away from him too. But for now, for the time being, the less he saw of Debra Jo, the better.

Plus, on third shift he was in charge, with the warden and the other senior C.O.'s at home in their beds. There was no one there to supervise him, which meant that for a few hours in the dead of the night, *Wayne Earl got to be God.* Absolute power was his, complete control over the 204 broken men who lived inside his private domain.

He'd been at Danfield now for sixteen years, long enough for the other C.O.'s to respect him, for the lifers to fear his redneck temper and for the warden to trust him to run D-Block any way he wanted. Tonight, that meant starting the lights-out walk a few minutes behind schedule.

As usual, it went pretty smooth. He passed by every cell. There were no bars, just massive slab-like doors of solid steel that slid open and locked from the command station at the end of the unit. He checked every one in succession, peeking through the narrow Plexiglas window of each door just long enough to ascertain what was almost always a foregone conclusion. One cell. Two men. Both breathing.

Every so often there'd be minor excitement. Most of the time that meant tapping his nightstick against the door to break up an embrace of some sort, sometimes hostile, more often *amorous*. The thought still disgusted him, even after more than a decade and a half. It was a necessary, albeit unofficial evil. Strictly speaking, inmate relations were prohibited, but any C.O. would vouch for the fact that it kept the boys quiet. As happy as could be expected in close security lock-up.

More than anything, the hour-by-hour checks were a safety precaution, and that was where the lion's share of the drama came from. Inmates complained on a regular basis. Most of their moaning was for attention, and could be safely ignored. Some of it was legitimate though, health issues and injuries and such things. Those were the problems Earl had his eye out for as he walked the length of the block.

D-Block housed the worst men at the facility. Sexual predators. Gang bangers. Cold blooded killers. The fringe of society, and the fringe of the penal system. The inmates who couldn't function in other prisons, or even in Danfield's general population. The absolute bottom of the human barrel.

Most would just as soon slit his throat as speak to him. Nothing to lose. Few places in the world had ever had so many dangerous men in one place at one time. Just the thought of that had once been enough to make his heart race. Not anymore. Now it was routine.

It was amazing how much a person could get used to.

Despite that, Earl felt his feet moving just a bit slower as he neared the end of the inspection. D-Block was a long single hall with housing on three levels. Two-man cells occupied the length of the south side. They faced only a bare wall opposite. A high vaulted ceiling towered overhead. The whole unit stretched a full two-tenths of a mile from the command station to the last cell.

Earl made the rounds in a circuit, from the command station to the end of the first level, then up the back stairs to the second and back down the line, then up the front stairs to the third, and right down the path again.

It was when he got to the third level that he started to moderate his pace. He knew what was waiting for him at the end of the line. The dark corner. The last cell. He hated that spot. He dreaded it.

It was always colder at the end of the hall. The maintenance guys said it wasn't. Said their gauges registered normal. Said the vents and the ducts were in perfect working order. But Earl knew better. That last spot always gave him the chills.

He tapped on the glass of cell 333, the next-to-last one. He looked in. Morales and Jimenez both acknowledged him with a wave. They were already in bed.

He didn't want to go to the next one.

"Get your wetback asses to sleep!" he said.

Hopefully, the insult would embolden him just a little. Just enough to make it through the next minute and a half without wetting his pants.

He took small steps. He shuffled. But the door kept getting closer.

Finally it was in front of him. Cell 334. The numerals stared back at him in a gloss of black paint. He had nightmares about this one. Actual fucking nightmares. Best to get it over with as quickly as possible, as much as that never seemed to do any good.

Earl tried to do his job without looking in, with only a tap on the window and a gruff command.

The reply came in much the same disconcerting way as it always did.

"Okey-dokey."

The voice was Bobby-Lee Weaver. The Buckeye Butcher. Bobby-Lee was still breathing only because of his forty-eight IQ—enough to register as conscious, yet low enough to spare him the death penalty. More than adequate to manage to rape and murder seven women in five months however.

He'd been apprehended at a bus stop in Youngstown, waiting to get on a Greyhound for Detroit with a duffel bag and a copy of Penthouse. Security had stopped him because the bag had been leaking blood. They might never have realized, had he not flown into a rage that required five deputies to subdue him.

Afterwards, the bag was found to contain two left arms and a pair of severed feet, all female. Trophies from his final acts as a free man.

But Bobby Lee Weaver wasn't the reason Earl hated that last, cold cell. Of the two men who resided in that dead end of all dead ends, *the Butcher was the easy one*—the good one. It was the other one Earl hated…feared. The one whose empty stare could make a Paris Island-hardened jarhead tremble like a frightened schoolboy.

Earl waited. He could hear Bobby-Lee breathing. But nothing else. His cell mate didn't acknowledge.

Putting Bobby-Lee Weaver into this particular cell had been a joke—at first. The warden's idea of sending a message. It hadn't worked.

Earl still didn't look in. He wanted to avoid that at any cost. So he tapped again, louder. He tried his best to growl a bit as he demanded that Weaver's cell mate muster an answer. He blurted out the man's name.

"Vayne!"

Even saying the word gave him the chills. He could have sworn the air actually got colder whenever he said it.

There was no answer. He tried again.

"Luther Vayne! Head's up!"

Again, nothing.

Earl looked down. His hands were beginning to quiver. He clenched his nightstick with both fists. Beads of sweat were forming on his bald head. He still didn't want to look in. Not again.

"C'mon old man, just gimme a shout," he said.

Still there was no reply. That left him with no choice. Earl was going to have to check in person. Why the fuck should he be so goddamn afraid of a blind seventy-year-old?

Maybe this was finally it, after all. The night he and all of the C.O.'s on D-Block had been waiting for, *hoping for* all these years. Even though Luther Vayne had never shown even the slightest hint of an ailment in all the years Earl had worked there, not even a sneeze, older inmates were known to die without any warning whatsoever.

That was what he was praying for as he peeked his face into the cell. What he found scared him even more than he was prepared for.

"He's not here," Weaver said, by way of greeting.

Earl had never seen the man so lucid. He was just sitting there on the top bunk, as calm as a spring day. The bed beneath him was made up. It hadn't even been sat on, let alone slept in. There was no one else in the cell.

Earl felt his bones go weak. He compensated by raising his voice. It didn't stop him from shaking.

"Where the fuck is he? What the fuck happened to him? What the fuck is wrong with this picture?"

The more he repeated the f-word, the more he felt in control. He almost didn't care what he was saying.

Bobby-Lee Weaver, the maniacal hulk without a conscience, the man the psychiatrists said lacked any impulse control whatsoever, and whose only impulses were homicidal, replied with perfect poise.

"Wrong? Nothing's wrong. Everything is just right. Just as it should be. Just like he said it would be," Weaver answered.

Bobby-Lee had been assigned to Vayne's cell in the sincere hope that his psychotic rage would put an end to the creepiest inmate in the prison, the man everyone avoided, cons and C.O's alike. The blind man whose very stare gave Wayne Earl night sweats.

But it hadn't happened. Weaver had done nothing to harm Vayne. Moreover, the weird old man had somehow turned the tables, and appeared to control the three-hundred-pound giant like a human puppet. Now Weaver was even acting as the old man's mouthpiece, *in absentia*, no less.

Earl's anger finally overwhelmed his fear.

"What the fuck are you talking about? Where the hell's Vayne?"

Weaver smiled, almost as if he knew more than he was letting on, which Earl knew was impossible for an imbecile like him.

"I told you, he's not here anymore," Weaver continued. "He's not comin' back, neither. There's work to do, you know, and he's been waitin' for a long time to get to it. He says the time has come to finish it, once and for all."

Earl had his walkie-talkie in his sweaty hand. He signaled to the command station. The alert sounded. Lock-down commenced with a screeching whine and a loud buzz. Lights that had just been turned down flashed on all at once. One hundred and two cell doors clamped shut in unison.

Bobby-Lee didn't seem to mind.

"Don't feel bad, officer," he said. "You couldn't have done nothin'. Vayne stayed here by his own choice. He could have left any time he wanted."

Earl threw up his hands and double-checked the lock on the door of the cell. He didn't have any idea what the man was talking about. But he didn't have the time to figure it out. Impossibly, incredibly, he had an escape on his hands.

DAY THREE

"Such a notion offends our ego-centric view—in much the same way as the theories of Copernicus and Galileo once did. But scientific inquiry can never be subject to the dictates of popular belief. The evidence—philological, geological, archaeological—mandates but one conclusion: Humanity is neither the greatest, nor even the first intelligence to dominate this world."

"Before the Gods"
Professor Phillipe Gamaliel
Unofficial Translation from the
French Language Ed., 1989

FIVE

**RIVERSIDE PARK APARTMENTS
ALEXANDRIA, VA**

Green and white Celtics mug in hand, Diana Mancuso slouched down into her couch. She still had more than ninety minutes before she needed to be at work. The cable box was already set to Fox News. She slid an empty bottle of Alfasi out of the way on the table in front of the sofa and downed two Advil with her first sip of coffee.

Larger than life on her forty-eight inch flat-screen, a perfectly coiffed talking head read the latest headlines for two segments, bracketing commercials for baby diapers and school supplies and a bunch of other things that were not in her demographic. She was about to turn it off when something caught her attention.

"Finally, in the so-weird-it-has-to-be-true department this morning," the perky blonde anchor said. "Some of you may recall this man," she continued, with a head nod in the direction of the box over her shoulder that was only visible to the viewers at home. "Most of you probably won't."

Diana did. She put down her coffee.

The face staring back at her was unreal. Both eyes looked to have been torn out of their sockets. Every inch of skin was covered in odd symbols; an arcane series of brands and tattooed runes that were almost like ancient hieroglyphs.

"His name is Luther Vayne," the anchor continued. "This photo was taken at his sentencing hearing in 1975. In the days before Ted Bundy, Zodiac, BTK or Jeffrey Dahmer, before *serial killer* was even a household word, Luther Vayne was one of this country's most notorious mass murderers."

She sneered. *Mass murderer* and *serial killer* were two very different things.

"If you're old enough then, you might recall that Vayne was sentenced to life in prison back in 1975. Although largely forgotten now, eclipsed perhaps by the many well-documented killers who have come along since, in his day he managed to strike terror into a nation that was already in the grip of one of the most tumultuous times in its history. From the winter of 1973 until the autumn of 1974, Vayne was responsible for the abduction and ritualistic killing of thirteen women and their young children; all but one the wife of prominent American political figures, including a U.S. Senator and two Federal Judges.

"Perhaps most puzzling, though, is the fact that, after leaving a series of grisly crime scenes across eleven states, each one crammed with occult imagery, Luther Vayne abruptly turned himself in to law enforcement in October of '74. Although he made a detailed confession, no motive for the macabre slayings was ever revealed."

"So what's the news? Is he dead?" Diana asked out loud.

As if the television had heard her question, the Fox anchor announced just what she wanted to know.

"Amazingly today, reports are coming in from Ohio that Luther Vayne, after more than forty years in prison, escaped sometime last night."

Diana reached for the volume on her remote. She turned it way up.

"Federal Department of Corrections officials released a statement early this morning in conjunction with the Ohio State Police and the U.S. Marshal's Fugitive Task Force, indicating a massive manhunt is already underway. They're confident, as you might expect, that a blind, seventy-plus year-old fugitive with this distinctive face could not possibly get very far. Said Danfield Warden Harvey L. Garrand, and I quote: "*We'll get him. It's not a question of if—it's a question of when.*"

"Shit, that really is almost too-weird-to-be-true," she said to herself.

Then she turned off the TV and went to take her shower.

SIX

SAXON/LUX CORPORATE TOWER
BOSTON, MA

Saxon/Lux Inc. boasted offices in seventeen countries, but the largest of them was in downtown Boston. That was corporate H.Q., where the board met and the big decisions were made.

Never one to shy away from the pretentious, Roger Saxon had seen to it that the building reflected the size and stature of the world's leading micro-technology firm. One of the newest structures in the area, it was an architectural showpiece. Tour groups had already added it to their itineraries before construction was finished. Faced in mirrored glass and platinum-coated steel, on a sunny day it rose into the blue New England sky like a single beam of silver-white light.

Roger Saxon and Stephanie Bremmer did not speak to each other as they walked through the tower's oak-paneled halls, or even after they got into the elevator with brass buttons and railings. They both held their silence until they entered Roger Saxon's private suite, and he locked the double doors behind him.

On the top floor, in the office where Saxon spent most of his waking life, the view was magnificent. But neither one bothered to look outside.

"Are we secure in here?" Bremmer asked.

"Totally," Saxon replied. "Soundproofed and swept for bugs every day. Nothing we say leaves this room."

Bremmer nodded. She was a tall woman with a long ponytail. Although the CEO of a major tech firm herself, she dressed more like a latter-day hippie, in a loose fitting blouse and long skirt with simple sandals—quite a contrast to Saxon's two thousand dollar Italian suit and gleaming Bruno Magli shoes.

"So you heard about it?" she asked.

"Came through my newsfeed a little while ago," Saxon answered, holding up his smartphone. "Unbelievable. I'm still in shock."

"What are we going to do?" Bremmer asked.

"What *can* we do?" he replied.

"Have you contacted the others?" she asked.

"Not yet," Saxon said. "You're the first one I've seen, so you're the first one I'm talking to."

"We have to be careful," Bremmer answered. "Now more than ever."

"Agreed," Saxon said. "The rules are clear. No text messages. No emails. No phone calls except on secure lines."

"Can we afford to keep doing things the old fashioned way?" Bremmer asked. "Maybe it's time to break some of those old rules."

Saxon shook his head.

"We don't know what we're dealing with here yet," he answered. "The man's been gone for forty years. How much of a danger could he seriously pose now?"

Bremmer fretted.

"I know, I know," she said. "But right now? When we're so close to the Convergence? Don't tell me that's a coincidence."

"I don't disagree," Saxon answered. "I'm just saying we shouldn't panic."

"He knows everything," Bremmer said. "More than us, more than any of us. Except for Victor, maybe. Or the Reverend, obviously."

She got up from the table and finally wandered over to the window. Standing in front of the massive glass façade, she stared out across the Boston skyline. The buildings, the cars, the people.

"Do you ever wonder about them?" she asked.

"Wonder? About what?" Saxon replied.

Bremmer kept looking out on the urban vista.

"What life must be like for them," she said.

Saxon realized his associate wasn't just talking about the men in the conference room downstairs, working hard on the last details of their merger at that very moment.

"So limited. In so many ways. Trapped, almost by their very nature. Just aware enough—just conscious enough so that every so often the brightest of them grasps how little they know, how small they really are," she continued.

"I don't give it much thought, honestly," Saxon answered.

Bremmer turned her back to the polished glass.

"No," she said. "I know you don't. That's why you're perfect for this job you're about to get. That's nothing to take lightly either, with this madman on the loose."

She stepped away from the window, but kept her back turned toward Saxon.

"I need a drink," Saxon said. "You?"

"Got any Stoli?" Bremmer asked. She still hadn't turned around. She seemed mesmerized, either by the city, or by something else.

They spoke with the easy familiarity of friends who had known each other since childhood. It was impossible for either one to be rude to the other after so many years. Saxon looked over the bottles on his mini-bar. There was a tall, unopened bottle of vodka, but not the Stolichnaya Bremmer had asked for.

"How's Absolut?" he asked.

The bottle was already in his hands. He had started to open it before Bremmer answered.

"I'll take it straight," she said.

Bremmer turned around. Her eyes were narrowed. Her face was tight.

"To old friends," she said, with a sarcastic smile.

Saxon knew what she was talking about.

"I never thought it would come to this, honestly," he said, as he sat down behind his desk. Bremmer walked over to the other side of the room, took her glass from Saxon and swallowed the vodka in one gulp. She didn't sit down.

Saxon spun in his swivel chair. He sipped his gin and tonic.

"So what about the others?" Bremmer asked.

"Hayden's in D.C.," Saxon said.

"Is he coming up for your speech tonight?"

"He flies out later today. He has a prayer breakfast today at the White House. Lauren confirmed yesterday."

"He'll want to discuss this," Bremmer said.

"Probably," Saxon replied. "But I'm not changing a single thing until we hear from him. Through the usual channels."

"We need to be very careful. Having all of us in one place before the final night is a major risk," Bremmer said.

"We're almost ready," Saxon replied.

"Are we?" Bremmer asked.

Saxon stopped swiveling.

"You don't think so?"

"Like I said, the timing is no accident," Bremmer replied. "Now that we're so close. He knows. He's been watching us. All these years. Exactly as the Elders warned us."

"So let him come then," Saxon answered. "I'm tired of waiting."

Bremmer turned back to the cityscape below.

"You should cancel the press conference tonight, just to be safe. Release a joint statement saying the merger is finalized. We need to maintain a low profile, at least until we hear from the Reverend, or Victor."

Saxon put down his drink.

"Enough about them. This merger has taken months to put together. We're not just going to release a prepared statement. I'm not about to run and hide. Not because of that bastard. If you want to leave the spotlight to me, that's fine. But the press conference is happening. The Reverend has been a fine leader all these years, but in two days I'm going to be nominated for Vice President of the fucking United States, Stephanie."

Bremmer knew her old friend wasn't going to be persuaded.

"You're taking a big risk. He'll be watching."

Saxon shook his head.

"This was inevitable. It's what we've always known would happen. It's what we've been preparing for all of our lives. What they warned us about."

"I know," Bremmer answered. "That's exactly what has me so worried."

SEVEN

WHATELEY ESTATES
WILBURTON, MA

It was about time for a few days off. At least that was the message Carter had left on Old Lady Quinlan's voicemail at the MFA. She wouldn't be happy about it, but Carter didn't really care. She could fire him if she wanted.

There was a black Lincoln Town Car waiting for him outside his Back Bay brownstone at 10:00am. Logan was inside. He greeted the stoic Englishman, who grunted in reply. Once seated, his bag in the trunk, they departed. Still, Logan said nothing.

The two-hour ride out of Boston seemed to take twice as long. He didn't know where he was going, and Logan didn't seem inclined to explain further. The car exited Route 2 somewhere past Athol, and turned off the main roads as signs started appearing for Warwick State Forest. From there it was another hour along a secluded series of winding lanes that led up into the hill country, lined the entire way with dense stretches of winter-bare oaks and snow-capped pine groves.

As the monotony finally began to wear on him, threatening to lapse into a kind of half-slumber, Carter felt his phone buzz. He took it out of his pocket and saw that he'd missed a call, probably while passing through a dead zone with no tower coverage, he figured. There was a voicemail icon lit up on the screen.

For a moment, just for the instant that it took for him to press the PLAY on his iPhone, he entertained a glimmer of hope. Not real hope, nothing substantial, nothing based on any realistic expectation. He had no social life, no life at all beyond the musty walls of the museum, but every time he reached for the button, the hope came back.

It was his ex-wife. Back to reality.

"Carter?" Maura's voice shouted out of speaker. "Are you there? God damn it, why do you even have a cell number if you *never* answer for Christ's sake? This is ridiculous. You're not at the office and you're clearly ignoring all my texts."

She was right. He smiled.

"I thought you might like to know that while you were out, doing whatever the hell you do, Tyler broke his arm at basketball practice. We're taking him to the ER now, but he's on your insurance. Call me when you get this. We need to talk about the deductible, because I'm not paying for this."

That, at least, made Carter smile.

"Call me," she finished, with the tone of fake pleasantness that he had come to know so well during their marriage. "Talk to you soon."

Carter put the phone back into his jacket pocket. When he looked up, he saw Logan staring back at him.

"I don't know how we got along all these years without them," Carter said, putting his phone away.

"Recently divorced then?" the Englishman asked.

"We split up about nine years ago," Carter said.

"We've all been there, mate."

"Pretty much put an end to my sunny disposition. Well, that and the drinking."

This time Logan laughed.

"So that's why you're such a miserable bastard, eh?"

Carter had no choice but to smile, and agree.

«««—»»»

They stopped where the road ran up to an imposing double gate that centered a twelve-foot-high iron fence, topped with double rows of forbidding spikes. Crowning the gate was an ornate insignia, a piece of calligraphy wrought in dark metal, forming a "W" framed by eagle's wings wreathed in flame.

The driver only stopped to buzz in, waiting just long enough for the gates to swing inward so that the car could pass.

The house itself could barely be seen from there, secluded behind a bank of trees atop a knob of a hill. Only hints of it were visible, a tower and a cupola lording over the quiet grounds.

As they trundled up the cobblestone driveway, the stately Gilded Age relic began to reveal itself. Built to evoke the grandest of English manors, Whateley's main house was a massive Jacobean Revival. Each of the mansion's three levels boasted tall, cottage-pane style windows. Ivy crept up the sides of its weathered brick facades, under steep-gabled Tudor arches and high chimneys that linked a long balustrade above. Sculpted topiary and terraced landscaping hid the full expanse of the property behind it.

The driveway led right up to the front porch, which jutted out from the manor with blocks of aged white stone. Four Corinthian columns flanked the black oak door, beneath a carving of an Old World coat-of-arms.

Logan escorted him in. The main door opened into a spacious, antique-furnished foyer carpeted with the vibrant crimson of fine Turkish rugs. They were met by a beautiful redhead who appeared to be expecting their arrival. She acknowledged Logan. He winked back at her. It was the only overt display of emotion Carter had seen from the man all day.

"Welcome to Whateley Estates. My name is Janet, Mr. Gregorian's personal assistant," she said. "If you'll follow me, I know Mr. Gregorian is anxious to meet you."

Carter nodded at her. She did not reciprocate. He recognized the rather uncommon name. Gregorian. But he wasn't sure. He didn't have long to wait.

She led him down a long hall with a vaulted ceiling that was as much an old fashioned arcade as a simple corridor. Colorful Moroccan wall tapestries hung on every side, interspersed with massive neo-classical paintings in ornate frames. Faces from by-gone ages stared down at him from the sprawling artwork, aristocrats of various eras forever captured in stiff poses.

At the end of the gallery the hall opened into a solarium-like study. High arched windows drew in sunlight from every angle to a room that was like a small library. Shelves lined with volume after volume covered every wall. A wrought iron ladder on runners waited at the far end, so that the higher tomes could be reached. All the furnishings were antiques, from the century-old end tables topped with oiled-bronze lamps to the massive Indian floor vases that cradled manicured ferns. It smelled of wood polish and old cigars.

There was a large desk near the back, opposite a double set of floor-to-ceiling windows. Behind, a giant of a man was hunched over with his back turned, leaning on an elegant wooden walking staff. Next to him, a twenty-something blonde woman wearing nothing but red lingerie massaged his huge, slumping shoulders.

Janet announced their presence by tugging on a brass bell that hung near the entrance way. The figure began to turn at the signal, slowly to be sure. When he did finally come about-face however, Carter felt himself recoil involuntarily.

"Come in, come in," the man said. "My name is Victor Gregorian. Welcome to Whateley Estates."

Carter tried to disguise the lump in his throat, but it did not go unnoticed. Janet escorted him the rest of the way in, right up to the desk and its two, utterly un-self-conscious occupants.

"It's quite alright to stare," Gregorian continued. "I would not have invited you here if I'd wished to hide myself."

Carter nodded, as politely as he was able, but found that he had little to say in answer. He wasn't sure what to do.

Victor Gregorian was a strange and difficult man to gaze upon, even for those who knew him well. A wide midsection bulged from under his elegant robe, but his was no typical physique. Leaning heavily on his cane, his left side seemed to wilt under some invisible strain. His shoulder was compressed down into his torso, squeezing his abdomen such that a distended blob of flesh hung off of his middle like a saddlebag. His leg on that side was clearly crippled, and appeared to be no more than two-thirds the size of the right one.

While his left hand looked quite normal in proportion—the only part of that side of his body that seemed so, his right hand was grossly distorted. Twice the size of the other, it was almost claw-like with untrimmed yellow finger nails.

A silver-black beard conspired to hide some of the girth in his face, although his head was bald and deformed by several tumor-like growths. His baritone voice echoed with an odd, creaky lilt.

"Proteus Syndrome," Gregorian finally said.

"Excuse me?" Carter replied, his throat dry.

"That's what the doctors call my condition," he answered. "I assure you, it is not contagious."

The deformed giant smiled, and somehow that put Carter a little more at ease.

"I...I figured it wasn't..." Carter replied, for lack of much else to say.

"This is Katya, by the way," he continued, motioning to the pale, barely dressed blonde beside him. "You'll forgive her for not saying much herself, she speaks very little English."

"*Privyet*," she said softly, all the while still running her hands up and down Gregorian's huge back.

"Russian?" Carter asked.

"Ukrainian, actually," Gregorian replied. "Good ear, regardless."

"Thanks," Carter said. "So she is your...?"

Gregorian laughed at his discomfort.

"No need to be sheepish, my friend," he replied. "Katya is just as much an employee as any of the others you've met today. Her responsibilities however are obviously a little different."

Carter tried to remain polite, but feared his disdain might slip through no matter what. He was right.

"It's nothing to be ashamed of," Gregorian replied. "I have business concerns all over the world, you see. Many of these girls from Eastern Europe have no families, no prospects and no hope in the old country. I help them come here for a better life."

He waved at the girl, who Carter guessed to be not much older than twenty-five. She smiled a practiced grin.

"So if we might consider the introductions concluded, and at the risk of sounding pompous, I assume that you know a little about me," Gregorian continued.

Carter agreed that he did. He knew a lot about Victor Gregorian. Everyone did. The owner of a vast newspaper publishing empire, media mogul, real estate tycoon—and perhaps the most famous recluse in the world. Howard Hughes by way of Quasimodo.

"If you might allow me to return the compliment, I can say that I know a fair amount about you as well, Dr. Shaw," Gregorian added, groaning as he managed to re-seat himself in the massive, quilted leather chair behind his desk. Katya edged herself onto the arm beside him. "Bachelor's degree from Boston University, 1984, double major in Sanskrit and ancient Greek. Masters in '86."

"Mostly to piss off my parents," Carter said.

"I'm sure that would do so," Gregorian replied, pouring a glass of Ardbeg Corryvreckan that he offered to his guest. "I imagine your father wished for you to do something a little more, *traditional*, so to speak."

"He did, but after twelve years of snooty private schools, traditional wasn't on the menu anymore," Carter said, loosening his tie as he sipped the Scotch and took a seat across from the deformed billionaire. "Dead languages seemed like a nice, polite way of saying *fuck you*."

"Your parents didn't mind spending, what? Close to seventy-five thousand dollars for you to study languages no one speaks?"

"They minded, believe me. But they paid it anyway."

Gregorian smiled. He poured a second glass for himself.

"You followed that up with a Ph.D. from Columbia, no less. Very impressive. Then, for the last twenty-two years, you've been at the Museum of Fine Arts, the past nine as chief of Near-Eastern Antiquities. No small thing indeed."

"Thank you," Carter said. He still wasn't sure what the man wanted from him.

"Please, have a seat," Gregorian offered, pointing to the chair beside the desk.

He was still in the difficult process of taking a seat himself, groaning and wheezing as he did so. As he lowered himself, he put the black walking staff to the side. It was a fine piece of craftsmanship, with a polished silver head carved in a macabre fashion to resemble the horned skull of a goat. There were symbols etched along the length of the wood that Carter recognized as ancient Sumerian cuneiform.

While his host continued to get himself situated, Carter glanced around the room a little bit more. In addition to the seemingly endless rows of old books, there were several pieces of Greek and Roman statuary, some of which looked like originals, rather than replicas. Like the grand corridor outside, the walls held several larger-than-life portraits, oil paintings all done in a late colonial style. The largest and the most prominently displayed hung just to the right of Gregorian's desk—a stately woman posed in a black, lace-trimmed dress. Her eyes were as dark as her outfit, and sad somehow, Carter thought.

Gregorian noticed him staring at the picture.

"My mother," he said.

"It's lovely," Carter said, before scrambling to correct himself. "I mean, she's lovely. I mean the painting is…"

Gregorian laughed.

"Do not fear to give offense, my friend," he replied. "She had a hard life, it's true, and I believe the artist captured that very well."

"She's deceased?" Carter asked.

"Some time ago," Gregorian answered. "Quite a woman, I must say. She loved me regardless of…all this."

He gestured at his obvious deformity.

"Nothing quite like the love of a mother," Carter said.

"Oh, but Victoria Gregorian was not my natural mother, you see," the billionaire said. "She raised me as her own however, once my mother was…gone."

The memory appeared to bring the large man to a pause. Carter did nothing to interrupt him.

"Nostalgia aside, where were we?" Gregorian asked.

"You were reading my resume, I think," Carter joked.

"Ah yes. I must tell you, there is one thing in your background that I find particularly curious," Gregorian said.

Carter's face turned from a look of polite interest to a show of very real dread. He knew what was coming. It was the same damn question, every single time. Even after all these years, he still didn't have a good answer.

"You did not earn your Ph.D. until 1992. The six years between your masters and Columbia, though..."

"Miskatonic University," Carter interrupted. Because he knew where Gregorian was going.

The name seemed to put a stop to their conversation for a moment.

"So *that is* correct," Gregorian finally said, as though he was unsure until he heard the words from Carter's own lips. "Miskatonic University. That represents a bit of a *departure*, shall we say? Your field of study there would have been...?"

"The occult. Let's not beat around the bush, okay?" Carter answered. "I spent three years at Miskatonic University studying *theories*, if you want to call them that, which would have to be classified as occult."

"Under the tutelage of a Professor Phillipe Gamaliel," Gregorian said.

Mention of his old professor conjured a mental picture of the disheveled academic. Another momentary diversion.

"Gamaliel was a fine scholar, one of the greatest linguists I've ever known. A little eccentric sure, but a brilliant scholar," Carter said. "To a point, at least."

"So you don't respect his work?"

"I did, at one time. But I gave up on all that years ago."

"I see," Gregorian said.

"I think you may be wasting your time, if that's why your people were asking about Azathoth. Gamaliel spent years on that. All of it wasted."

"Does that include the time you spent as his research assistant on *Before the Gods*?"

Carter lowered his eyes.

"I'm impressed that you even know about that paper. It was rejected by the entire scientific establishment. We couldn't get it published anywhere in the English-speaking world. It ended up in a tiny French journal, and they printed an apology in their next issue."

"You didn't answer my question."

"Yes, I include my time on that as a waste. I don't believe in the Great Old Ones of ancient mythology. I don't believe in the summoning of demons or hidden messages in ancient texts. I also don't believe in the Loch Ness Monster, Bigfoot or the Yeti, while we're at it."

Gregorian sipped his drink. His eyes narrowed.

"But you did," he replied. "At one time, you did believe, or else you wouldn't have spent so much time working on these things."

Carter looked away for the second time.

"It's true, I did—once," he answered. "A long time ago. I was young."

"What changed?"

Carter smirked.

"I got older."

Gregorian kept his hands clasped together. He kept staring back at Carter, who knew the answer was not enough to satisfy. Eventually the silence got the better of him.

"Gamaliel was a good man," he said. "What he did was probably motivated by the best of intentions, but he got so wrapped up in all this, it ruined him. It pushed him to go somewhere I couldn't follow."

"Where was that?"

Carter didn't want to answer, but it was too late to stop.

"You have to understand, I loved the man. I wanted all of his theories to be true as much as he did."

"But you lost your faith," Gregorian said.

"Not sure I'd call it *faith*," Carter replied.

"You ceased to believe," Gregorian answered. "In the theories *and the man*, if I'm reading you correctly."

"After a while, the two became interchangeable," he said.

"How is that?"

Carter sighed, long and slow. He knew he was going to have to say it.

"Gamaliel was intensely private," he said. "Only let a few of us near his work. After a while, I found out why, and that's when I left."

"What was it that drove you away?"

"He betrayed us, and everything we were working on," Carter replied.

"Ah, now the plot thickens," Gregorian said.

"Gamaliel always kept a lot of his research material on lockdown, it was just his way. That wasn't unusual, either. A lot of this stuff, the old verses and writings we were translating, came from very old and very fragile clay tablets. Mostly we worked from notes, copies or transcriptions he'd made for us. He was a master at that. The old man could reproduce an entire tablet from memory. But it turned out, that wasn't what he was doing."

"How so?"

"After the publication, the journal got some complaints, as you can imagine. They asked us to follow up with some of our source material. Gamaliel was giving a lecture in Providence that day, so I had the keys to his office. I went looking for the documents. It turned out, they weren't there."

"What had he done with them?"

"Well that's just it, they were never there," Carter said. "No notes, no catalogue references to any actual clay pieces. Once I realized what he'd done, I went through all of his files. Everything was the same—he had no source material. All of the most important documents we were using, everything that supported his theories, they were all forgeries. He'd just written them up himself, without any original tablets at all."

"So you came to believe he was a fraud," Gregorian said. "I can see how that would alter your perception. Do you think that contributed to his eventual....demise?"

The conversation had already made Carter uncomfortable. Gregorian seemed to see that, but he didn't relent. Carter recognized that as a subtle test—although *of what*, he wasn't quite sure.

"I'm afraid I can't say. After we had our falling out, I left. We didn't speak for years after that. Eventually, I started to hear things through the grapevine."

Such as?"

"Nothing specific, just that he was having problems, complaints from students and that sort of thing. I drove out there one weekend, I guess this was maybe a year and a half ago. The administration was already on the verge of firing him."

"His fraud had finally come to light?"

"I don't think that was it. I never said anything, and I imagine he only became more secretive after I found him out. Honestly, I really can't say what happened to the man, I only know what other people told me."

"Which was…?"

"That he had become obsessed with Azathoth. There were all kinds of stories, Miskatonic University can be a creepy place anyway, so who knows what was true and what was *b.s.* Some people said he was going around trying to recruit his students into some kind of cult, others just said that he was sneaking off at night into the woods."

Gregorian smiled.

"What do *you* think?"

"I don't know about that stuff, but when I saw him that weekend, he wasn't the same man I studied under," Carter paused, as if to correct himself. "Well, that's not quite right. He was the same guy, but magnified ten times, if you follow me. He was always intense, and a deep thinker. When I knew him he was eccentric, but rational. The last time I saw him though he was almost crazed, unreasonable."

"You couldn't get through to him?"

"Not even close."

"That was the last time you saw him?" Gregorian asked.

Carter looked at the floor. At his shoes.

"Afraid so," he answered. "I got the news from an old friend, another former student. So sad. Hard to believe it's been over a year now since he died."

Gregorian waved his giant hand in the air and settled it down on top of his empty glass.

"My apologies," he said. "I did not bring you all the way out here to dredge up bad memories. I merely wished to make certain that you were indeed the man my people told me you were. That you possess the unique qualifications I'm looking for. It appears that you are, and that you do."

Carter still wasn't sure what to say. Gregorian poured him a second drink, though he had not yet finished the first.

"Again, not to be impolite," Carter said. "But I'm still a little confused. Qualifications for what, exactly?"

Gregorian brought his hands together, the small fist hidden entirely beneath the claw-like larger one. A kind of wise, disjointed smile came over his face.

"As I'm certain my associate Logan has already told you, I would like offer you a job, of sorts," he said.

"He mentioned that. He was a little vague though," Carter said. "What kind of job is this exactly?"

"Really more of an employment contract," Gregorian said. "A retainer, if you will. But I do pay very well."

"So I've been told," Carter said. "How well?"

"Five million dollars, plus expenses," Gregorian said.

Carter put down his drink.

"Excuse me?"

"I am a very wealthy man, there is no secret in that," Gregorian said. "When I want something, I am prepared to pay very well to get it."

"Okay, what exactly is it that you want me to do?" Carter asked.

Gregorian smiled.

"I would like you to read something to me."

EIGHT

**1600 PENNSYLVANIA AVE.
WASHINGTON, D.C.**

The Reverend Graham Thurmond Hayden had the ear of everyone in the room. All two-hundred and seventy-eight distinguished guests. Thirty-three congressmen and women. Sixteen senators. Five ambassadors. Four cabinet members, the Chairman of the Joint Chiefs and the President himself.

All of them hung on his every word.

"We all know the verse, don't we? Render unto Caesar that which is Caesar's," he said. Many of those in the audience nodded in silent agreement. Others were bold enough to mutter a gentle accord. "But how often do we ask *what exactly is Caesar's*?"

"Is that, after all nothing more than an endorsement of tax policy? Is that what the Lord was trying to tell us?"

The Reverend spoke with a twang that he made no attempt to conceal or moderate. An alumnus of Harvard Divinity, he could just as easily quote Virgil or Homer in their original languages as he could cherry-pick lines from the King James Version.

"Or is there a deeper message there? One that we miss in our normal reading of that frequently quoted passage?"

He paused. He let the words linger. It was an old country preacher's tactic. The Reverend knew very well after thirty-plus years on the pulpit—and the celebrity TV mega-church circuit—that the words themselves didn't always matter quite so much. The dividing line between the successful preacher and the average one, between the ones still rousing the faithful in schoolhouse churches in Mobile, Alabama and the ones regularly invited to prayer breakfasts at the White House, could be summed up in one word.

Charisma.

"I'm here to tell you that you are Caesar. You men and women in this room, and in that Capital Building out there on the hill."

He paused again. He lifted his hands from the podium as if calling on his flock to lift their attention to heaven. His audience was silent.

Revered Hayden looked over his crowd. He had a full, round face that communicated authority and gentility simultaneously. His hair was combed up in a deliberately old-fashioned gray pompadour. His pale blue eyes sparkled.

He was as much a celebrity as a reverend, as much Madison Avenue as man of the cloth. His weekly television ministry boasted upwards of twenty million viewers, making him one of the most widely seen, and widely followed evangelists in the nation. Those in attendance swooned at his sight, at his words, even just at the sound of his voice.

"You are Caesar. You have an obligation to see that your power is used responsibly. It is yours to…"

He stopped. At first, the audience, enrapt by his southern eloquence, assumed the pause was for dramatic effect.

It wasn't. Something else had snared his attention.

White House Chief of Staff Lauren Armstrong entered the back of the hall, tall and thin in a charcoal suit. She immediately drew the Reverend's attention, though she did little more than lift a finger and gesture in his direction. That was enough. The Reverend nodded.

"The power belongs to you. Power that even Caesar himself never dreamed of, and with the Lord as your guide, I'm sure that you will use it wisely," he said.

Then he excused himself from the podium, yielding to the Speaker of the House. He made his way to the rear of the chamber, where he went right to Armstrong.

The sharp-eyed brunette did not greet him. She merely waved him toward the door behind her.

Once the Reverend had cleared the polite gauntlet of handshakes and comments, he followed Armstrong out of the hall. They still did not speak. The two walked down a long hallway, up a flight of stairs past a pair of Marine guards in dress uniforms and into an empty office.

Armstrong opened the door in total silence. She walked in and Hayden followed. General Jack Krieger was waiting for them inside. It was a dark, windowless room. All the lights came on at once the moment the door closed, sealing them in a sound-proof chamber.

"He has made his first move," Armstrong finally said.

"When?" the Reverend asked.

"Last night. They just released it to the press this morning," Krieger replied. "Fucking zombie walked right out the goddamn place without anyone noticing."

Hayden grimaced.

"Are we sure?" he asked.

Armstrong nodded.

"There's no doubt," she said.

The Reverend pursed his lips. He took a long, deep breath.

"Then the moment truly is almost upon us," he said. "The day we've all been waiting for. No more games. Now we come to the final hour."

Armstrong did not appear quite as confident as her colleague.

"Has anyone spoken to Victor?" she asked. "He should be contacted right away."

Hayden sneered.

"Yes, by all means, our first priority should be contacting the crippled librarian," he complained.

"I only meant that he should be involved in any consultations," she answered.

"The man is as arrogant as he is weak and sickly, and personally I don't much care for him either," Krieger said. "But he is the guardian of the sacred texts. He has to be involved in the discussion."

"The Elders named him guardian because he couldn't do anything else," Hayden answered. "He's an afterthought. We are the strong. We will be the ones to face this horror."

Armstrong took a step back at the notion. Krieger grimaced.

"Still, we're all in this together," the general said. "That was the pact we made, the deal we all agreed to years ago. This is not the time to re-negotiate. This is the time to come together—for all of us."

"Well put," Armstrong said.

The Reverend clenched his fists.

"Fine," he said. "Contact the others and set up a meeting, through the usual channels."

"Already working on it," Armstrong said.

"Make no mistake, my friends," Reverend Hayden said. "The confrontation is coming. We must be ready. We must *all* be ready."

NINE

F.B.I. H.Q.
WASHINGTON, D.C.

The day was winding down as Diana Mancuso made a stop at Richard Norris's office. It had been a quiet one. There was always something going on, of course, but very little of what she did anymore ventured into the realm of active investigations. She was content to confine her time to her classes at Quantico. She signed a lot of documents and read a lot of reports. That was it. Her days on the street were a distant memory.

She hadn't seen Richard Norris all day, but that wasn't out of the ordinary either. He was an HBO, agent-speak for a High Bureau Official. There were only nine Assistant Directors, each answerable to the Director himself, and each in charge of supervising enormous operations. Norris's was the largest, the Criminal Investigation Division. That put him in charge of about eighty percent of the Bureau's field agents, working some seventy-thousand cases annually split over seven different sub-divisions.

He was a busy man.

Her own duties kept her a long way from the streets, as an instructor and part-time analyst at H.Q. and Quantico. Richard Norris, on the other hand, was the purest form of bureaucrat. HBO's spent most of their time in meetings, talking about policy, justifying expenditures and allocating resources. Even when he was at H.Q., he didn't get involved in actual day-to-day work, which was fine with her.

Dolores Reardon, Norris's private secretary, greeted her with a broad smile when she came up to the desk.

"Good timing," she said. "He's just about done for the day. Another five minutes and you would've missed him."

"Is he free then?" Diana asked.

Dolores rolled her eyes.

"He should be, but he's been on the phone all afternoon." She looked at the console on her desk. The main line was lit up, with two more blinking on hold.

"Any idea who he's on with?" Diana asked.

Dolores shrugged.

"Not sure. He's been taking calls all day though."

"No kidding?" Diana replied. "Any idea what's going on?"

Again, Dolores smiled politely as if to apologize for her lack of information.

Diana nodded.

"Can I go in? I need signatures on a couple of things before tomorrow morning," she said.

Dolores didn't seem to mind.

Diana picked up a Jolly Rancher from Dolores' candy dish.

She knocked and opened the door to Norris's office all at the same time. He never minded, so long as Dolores said it was okay. As soon as she got through the door though, she realized that for once, Dolores had been wrong.

Norris was agitated. His jacket was off, and slung carelessly over the back of his chair. His cufflinks sparkled on his desk, and his sleeves were rolled up.

Diana stopped when he looked up at her. He waved her in.

When she started to explain however, he put up his hand.

"I don't give a shit what they tell you," he said into the phone. "Do you hear me? You come to me with the bill. You got that? Me. I'm telling you, there is no question about the cost. Whatever they need."

Diana waved her hand, just enough to catch his attention. She pantomimed an exit. But he shook his head, and motioned for her to bring whatever she was holding over to him.

As he continued to listen to the voice on the other end of the phone, he did his own pantomime, arching his eyebrows and feigning a signature in the air. Diana nodded. She handed him the papers that required his name. He took them, gave each one a cursory glance and signed them all.

Norris handed them back to her without looking up. She waited.

And waited.

Norris rolled his eyes and told whoever was on the other end of the phone to hold for a moment. He looked up at her, right at her. He didn't say anything. His eyes spoke for him.

What do you want? I'm very busy.

Diana stepped back, almost by reflex. She didn't even realize she was back-peddling until her heel hit the floor.

"Dinner?" she whispered, even though they were alone. "Didn't we say…the other night…*this is* Monday, isn't it?"

Norris didn't even blink.

"Can't do it. Not tonight," he said. "Something's come up."

She closed her eyes.

"I see," she said.

"It isn't Julia, if that's what you're thinking."

"Right," Diana said.

He didn't say anything else. She waited. But nothing came.

"I'll see you later, then," she finally said.

She pivoted on her back heel, spun around and headed for the door. She wanted him to say something. She didn't walk fast, hoping he'd stop her; that he'd tell her to wait, that he'd take a minute to explain.

But he didn't.

«««—»»»

Ariadne Anastasakis smiled at her when the elevator doors opened.

"Going down?" she asked. Her Greek accent was only slight, but it colored everything she said with a unique cadence.

Diana stepped past her into the elevator.

"Guess so," Ariadne said. She'd worked with Diana Mancuso for several years, long enough to know that she never said any more than she needed to say. If a gesture or an action would suffice, then Diana had a tendency to say nothing at all. Most of the time, that left Ariadne to do most of the talking, which was just about exactly the way she liked it.

"Dinner plans?" Diana asked.

Ariadne looked at her cross-eyed. Her tan, delicate face sometimes looked lost under her long dark hair, especially when she shook her head for effect and it moved in and out of her brown eyes.

"You're asking me to dinner?" she asked.

Diana grumbled.

"Oh," she said. "Sorry, I just assumed you'd be busy. No plans with you and this mystery man of yours?"

Diana didn't answer. She also didn't look at Ariadne. She stared at the stainless steel elevator doors.

"Diana?"

"He's busy," she said. "Again."

Ariadne pursed her lips. Diana's delicate emphasis on the last word told her more than she intended.

"Hang on a second," she said. "Late night meetings, sneaking around all over the place. I can't believe I didn't put the pieces together before. Maybe I'm way off on this, and tell me if I am, by all means. But…?"

Diana stared her friend down. She guessed what was coming next.

"But what?"

Ariadne scowled a bit.

"By *busy*, do you mean as in, *with his wife*, maybe?"

Diana didn't answer. She didn't nod and she didn't even blink, and that was enough. Somehow that made the admission seem just a little less pathetic, a little more dignified that she didn't have to say it.

Ariadne slapped her friend on the arm.

"Were you ever planning on telling me?" she asked.

Her voice tended to rise and fall by whole octaves in a single sentence. With Ariadne, any mundane conversation could be elevated to the level of high drama. That was one of the reasons Diana loved her, there was no one she knew who could find such enthusiasm for the daily grind. But every so often, in the wrong mood, that kind of exuberance was just annoying. Today was that kind of a day.

"I just did," Diana said.

Ariadne switched from mock-annoyance to solace in as long as it took for her hand to turn from a fist to a comforting touch. She rubbed her fingers up and down Diana's arm.

"I'm sorry, honey. Do you want to talk about it?"

It plainly appeared she didn't. But a friend always asked. Especially her.

Diana shook her head.

"Did something happen?" Ariadne asked.

Diana turned her head with a sharp twist. Her eyes were narrow, almost predatory.

"What did I just say?"

Ariadne backed off.

"Sorry, force of habit."

Diana ignored the apology. They stood there as the lights on the elevator console flashed and chimed in conjunction with each floor they passed. Neither one spoke. For a minute.

"So did you have a fight…or?" Ariadne finally said.

The elevator opened. Diana walked out without answering.

Ariadne picked up her briefcase and jogged after her, no easy task in three-inch heels. She was generally considered among the most fashionable of anyone at F.B.I. H.Q., which was true, but wasn't much of an accomplishment—and it sometimes got in the way of her job. But it was a sacrifice she was more than willing to make.

"Okay, I get it. You *really* don't want to talk about it. Fine," she said as Diana approached the security desk. They each made their way toward the front doors, swiping their Bureau IDs as they left.

"So, dinner then?" Ariadne asked. "How about Hanoi Pho?"

Diana shook her head.

"Not again. I had Vietnamese already this week."

"McGuire's then?" Ariadne suggested.

Diana thought about it for a second. Dinner with Ariadne meant she was going to have to talk, and she really wasn't in the mood. But a beer in a pub was better than a beer on the couch, alone. Again.

"Okay, I could use a drink," she said.

Ariadne's face lit up. The glass doors closed as they exited, leaving the F.B.I. behind them, for at least a few hours.

TEN

WHATELEY ESTATES
WILBURTON, MA

Carter was sure he'd heard the man correctly, but he asked him to repeat himself all the same.

"I'm sorry, did you say you want me to read something to you?"

"Indeed, if you are willing, of course," Gregorian said.

Carter chuckled to himself just a bit.

"For five million dollars I'd read the damn phone book, naked in Alaska, in the middle of winter," he said.

"Very glad to hear it," Gregorian said. "I only hope you can maintain that level of exuberance as we go forward in this endeavor."

"So, what is it you want me to look at?" Carter asked.

"Logan tells me he discussed the Tablet of Destinies with you," Gregorian said.

Carter tried to conceal his disdain. Even the mention of that bothered him, but he now had quite a few new reasons to hold his tongue.

"He did, he seems to think you're interested in that old story."

"More than interested, in fact," Gregorian said, his peculiar eyes lighting up at the thought. "Some might say *obsessed*."

"Right," Carter answered. "Is that what this is about? No offense, but please tell me you're not one of those bored, super rich guys who wants me to go off and try to find the thing, are you?"

"No, no," Gregorian replied. "I have no intention of sending you away on some Indiana Jones quest, if that is your concern. As I said, all I require from you is your skill at reading."

"Respectfully then sir," Carter continued. "What *exactly* is it that you'd like me to read for you? As far as the Tablet stuff goes, you seem to know everything about it that I know, and if you're not interested in finding…"

"Oh, but it has been found," Gregorian said. "Back in the mid-nineteen-sixties, in fact."

Carter put down his drink. His mouth went dry again.

"Are you telling me that you know where it is?" Carter asked, his voice lapsed into a whisper. "You'll have to forgive my skepticism, but I've never read a single mention of it in any reputable journal."

Gregorian laughed.

"Respectable, your attitude. I would have had it no other way. But perhaps you should allow yourself to be a little more open-minded. We must always be open to new possibilities," he said.

Carter sat up in his chair.

Gregorian rolled back a few feet, and reached up to the mantle on the other side of his desk. There were a number of books stacked there. He took one and looked it over. Then he opened it to a marked page and handed it to Carter.

"Have you ever seen this man before?" he asked.

The page contained an old picture. The man in it was posed in a stiff, uncomfortable position, given his dour expression. He stood alone on a desert landscape, dressed in khakis. His face was thin, with a mustache that curved at the ends.

Carter shook his head.

"Never," he said.

Gregorian put aside his glass and lit a large cigar. He puffed on it several times and reclined back in his chair, somewhat awkwardly given his affliction.

"His name was Hiram Barker. A British archaeologist. Lived in Iraq before the Second World War."

"Never heard of him," Carter said. "But the British School of Archaeology in Iraq was founded at about that time, nineteen-thirty-two I believe. Was he affiliated with them?"

Gregorian shook his head.

"He wasn't what *you* would think of as an archaeologist," he replied. "More of a spirited amateur than a professional like yourself. We used to call them grave robbers."

"*We* still do," Carter answered.

Gregorian laughed. Smoke churned out of his mouth.

"He had his faults, to be sure. I've had my people track down everything written about him over the years, and by him as well. He was a fascinating character, veteran of the Somme, served the Empire in India for several years. Seems he saw himself as belonging to the same school as men like Sir Arthur Evans and Heinrich Schliemann. You must admit, for all we might criticize their methods, where would your discipline be without such men?"

"Where would we be without shameless self-promoters and relentless opportunists? Where would we be without treasure hunters who ran roughshod over precious antiquities? Without men who literally trampled irreplaceable artifacts to further their own reputations?"

The questions suggested their own answers.

"Point taken. Now I know I have the right man for the job," Gregorian said.

"Again…that would be…*what*?"

Gregorian got up from his desk, turning his back to his guest. He didn't appear interested in addressing Carter's concerns. Instead, he searched the shelves behind him, passing his outstretched finger over the spines of dozens of volumes, one after another, row after row, until he came to one in particular. He slipped it out of the tight sandwich of old tomes. It was leather-bound, a fine piece, but very old. Then he turned back to Carter, clutching the book close to him.

"Logan tells me you have heard of The Disciples of the Black Flame," Gregorian said.

"I have," he replied.

"But you don't know much about them, I take it," Gregorian said.

Carter shook his head.

"Does anyone?" he asked. "Some kind of a cult, right?"

Gregorian grinned. He handed the old book to the archaeologist.

"*Tolle et lege*, I believe you academics would say," he continued.

"Take it and read," Carter mouthed quietly as he grasped the volume.

The book's cover was emblazoned with a faded sigil, gold-stamped into the age-blackened leather. It was an uncommon marking, but one he had seen before. It sent a chill through his bones.

"The star of Azathoth," he whispered.

The ancient emblem was composed of a star within a star, thirteen points in all—the five points of the inner pentagram inverted and the outer eight points encircled by concentric black rings, dark sunbeams rendered into spiny tentacles.

Gregorian began to nod, and leaning heavily on his cane he stared up toward the windows of his study.

"Some did call them a cult, it's true, but that was quite an unfair characterization," he said, almost wistfully. "In any case, they're mostly forgotten today, consigned to barely a footnote in the history books, if at all. You hold in your hands the only chronicle of their existence. A shame really, they were men who saw far ahead of their time, although not quite far enough, in the end."

Carter had no idea what Gregorian was talking about, and his blank expression communicated that without a word. He opened the volume. It was dense with text, much of it in Latin and Greek, along with other, more ancient languages. Interspersed with the pages were prints of old ferrotypes, all of aristocratic men with late nineteenth century beards and stern eyes.

"In their day they were called futurists, men of education and philosophy who looked to a day when people would come to live in harmony with one another," Gregorian said, as though narrating what Carter was looking at, though the billionaire wasn't even looking at him.

"The dream of utopia," Carter said.

"They came together near the end of the Civil War, men of renown, captains of industry, even some of the more open-minded ministers of the day. You may have heard some of their names: General Sterling

Fisk Armstrong, Reverend J. Garfield Hayden, Senator Addison R. Baxter, and Jeremiah Francis Thorne, the railroad fortune heir, were some of their more prominent founding members."

"Sure, I've heard of a few of those guys."

"Bluebloods, every single one," Gregorian said. "Their money and their social standing permitted them entry into the highest levels of influence. Government, university, industry, the churches. They sought to change things for the better, from within. They were not alone."

"How so?"

"They were internationalists, their reach extended well into Victorian England; all manner of intellectuals and enlightened gentlemen of the day counted themselves among their number, including men like H.G. Wells and Jules Verne."

"So what happened to them?"

"As it always seems to happen to groups founded on big ideas, they didn't agree on how to reach the dream they shared. Some of them advocated the embrace of technology, as a salve to all of the nation's ills. Others looked to the advance of the spirit, to elevate mankind to a higher level of being. Still others maintained that utopia was not a dream of the future, but rather a lost relic of the past, one that mankind might reclaim, if they could re-learn the forgotten wisdom of their forefathers."

Carter began to smile, but he suppressed it, for fear of insulting his host. If nothing else, Gregorian appeared sincere. Carter guessed where it was all going. But he waited.

"Who won the argument?" Carter asked.

"The First World War settled the question," Gregorian answered. "Seeing that kind of wholesale slaughter, far worse even than the carnage they had seen at Antietam, or Cold Harbor or Gettysburg, The members grew to believe that more than fifty years of work had accomplished nothing. The world was further than ever from utopia.

"Most drifted away from that kind of idealism, from the idea of easy fixes. Some felt betrayed by the technology whose virtues they had advocated, other became convinced that the human spirit was unalterably cruel. Those who were left faded from public sight, to pursue their ideas more quietly."

"The *look back before we can look forward* crowd?" Carter asked.

"They were all that remained. By this time, around the nineteen-twenties, they were led by Thorne's granddaughter, a strong-willed young lady named Valeria. She continued to pursue the dream, only now in relative obscurity, some might say, secrecy."

"Well then," Carter said. "Your Mr. Barker in the photo there, he wouldn't by any chance have been…?"

Gregorian's face brightened into a broad smile.

"He was indeed one of them. A man who saw the promise of the future in the ruins of the past."

Carter laughed at the little joke—the first relaxed moment he'd had since his arrival.

"Barker was a close friend of Valeria Thorne. She grew up in the corridors of power, granddaughter of a tycoon, child of a prominent senator. At a time when women were largely consigned to the domestic sphere, she refused to march in lock-step. They say she was her grandfather's favorite, that he doted on her and gave her everything she desired. That he saw in her a quality that none of his male heirs possessed."

"What was that?"

"Vision. A vision of something greater. Using the money and connections inherited from her family, she traveled the world along with men like Barker, always seeking..."

"Seeking what?"

"Wisdom," Gregorian answered. "The lost wisdom of the past. You see, the more she studied and she traveled, the more Valeria came to believe that the purest knowledge to be found, the purest truth behind that which we think we know, was buried in the most ancient of texts."

Carter had heard these notions before.

"Azathoth," he whispered. "You'll forgive me, but this sounds a lot like what Gamaliel used to say—and all of that turned out to be… untrue."

"Patience," Gregorian replied. "Much like your old mentor, Valeria Thorne and those who came to follow her, believed that the path to the future lay in the study of the ancients, seeking answers in the pre-history of mankind. They sought to uncover, and to embrace the lost wisdom of the ancients, and they believed the Tablet of Destinies was the key."

"But they failed," Carter said.

"Why do you assume so?"

Carter grimaced.

"They must have, because *no one has ever heard of any of this*."

Gregorian smiled, and he nodded as if he'd expected exactly that reaction. Again, Carter's face reverted to a look of utter confusion.

Gregorian didn't answer. Instead, he reached back to the desk, cleared off some papers and picked up a small, leather-bound book. He tossed it over to Carter. The archaeologist caught it and opened it up. It was old. Inside were hundreds of pages, all yellowed from age and all jammed edge to edge with hand-printed material. None of it in English.

"Barker was a paranoid sort, you see. Didn't want *anyone* reading his notes," Gregorian said.

"This is it?" Carter said. "This is his actual journal?"

Gregorian nodded.

Carter read some of the lines. It was a modified version of cuneiform, adapted for use with a pencil and paper. It took a few minutes, but he quickly began to make sense of it.

"It's Akkadian," he said, thinking aloud. "These look like geographical notations, directions maybe."

Gregorian was beaming.

"Directions that pointed to the location of the tablet," he said.

"So he unearthed the thing?" Carter asked. "He found the actual Tablet of Destinies?"

"In a manner of speaking, I suppose," Gregorian replied. "He did locate the burial site, that is true. But sadly, he didn't live long enough to see his discovery taken from the ground. Seems he suffered a fatal heart attack shortly after his crew opened the chamber. Valeria Thorne was left to supervise the dig herself, and to bring the tablet back here."

"That's amazing," Carter said. "Truly amazing."

Gregorian sat back down behind his desk. Carter remained puzzled however.

"Respectfully sir," he continued. "I appreciate hearing all of this, but I still don't quite get why you're telling *me*. You've already had the tablet for years, and you must have hired someone else to translate everything already, which means you don't need me. Just exactly why am I here then?"

The question barely fazed the big man. He appeared to have expected it. He also seemed to be enjoying Carter's bewilderment. He leaned forward and folded his hands on his desk.

"As I said, I need you to read something for me," Gregorian said.

The notion slowly began to dawn on Carter. He looked at the notes again, and then back to the smiling billionaire.

"Wait a minute, are you saying you want me to...?" he began.

Gregorian began to get up from his seat, wheezing in the process. He gripped the gnarled black staff beside the desk to steady himself as he arose. Carter tried hard to conceal his own cringing as he watched the man move, quite obviously in pain with even that small exertion.

"Follow me please," he wheezed. "It will be better if I show you."

ELEVEN

MCGUIRE'S PUB
GEORGETOWN, D.C.

Dinner was already a hazy memory. The check was at least three pints ago. In the meantime, they'd retired to the bar, downed a couple of shots of Chivas and turned away two fresh-faced congressional staffers who'd offered to buy them another round.

After talking about almost everything else the two women could imagine, the conversation finally turned to the one thing they had come to a dim Irish pub to discuss.

But Diana wasn't ready to give in.

"I told you I don't want to talk about it," she said.

"I know, I know. It's just that…"

"What, Ari? It's just what?"

Ariadne wrinkled her brow and rubbed her eyes.

"Sometimes…in my experience…I've found that people in your position," she said.

Diana cut her off.

"My position? You have no idea what my position is," she said. A Boston accent crept into her vowels when she got annoyed, or drunk. She was already the first, and on her way to the second.

"Which is kind of my point, but seriously…sometimes people who say they don't want to talk about something really do, they just don't want to say they do," Ariadne continued.

Diana looked at her. She downed the rest of her pint.

"Have you ever known me to talk about my personal life?" she said. "Or my problems with men?"

"No, I got that, believe me," Ariadne said. A quizzical grin formed on her lips. "Of course, that more or less supposes that you have a personal life. So you could talk about it, but you choose not to."

Diana groaned.

"That'd put you at least one step ahead of me at this point," Ariadne said. "You know it'll make you feel better. Talking about it."

"Fuck you," Diana said.

"I'm serious," Ariadne replied.

"*It'll make you feel better*," Diana said. She lifted her voice, mocking Ariadne's. "You just want dirt."

Ariadne shrugged, as if to admit there was no point arguing.

"But you're not gonna stop asking, are you?" Diana said.

She threw up her hands and slammed them down on the brass bar railing. She waved to the bartender, showing two fingers to signal another round.

"Fuck it, you really want to know?"

Ariadne just looked at her.

Diana sighed, and looked up at the ceiling.

"Richard Norris," she said, as though confessing to a crime.

Ariadne's mouth fell open. She took the new glass right out of the bartender's hand and gulped half of it down.

"You've been dating the assistant director?"

"Dating?" Diana said. "Not quite."

Ariadne smiled.

"Right, not exactly *dating*, then. Isn't he happily…?"

"Married? Not so happily, I guess," Diana said. "He's got an anniversary coming up, on the thirteenth. Big party planned. I'm not invited."

Ariadne turned back to her drink.

"Well, I guess that makes sense," she said.

The comment almost seemed directed at her gin and tonic.

"It does?" Diana asked. "Having an affair with my married boss?"

"Yeah, not in the '*it's something you should be doing*' way, it doesn't make sense like that, but the other way..."

"Which is?"

"Why you didn't want to tell me who you were seeing, and why you haven't been dating anyone else for a while. I mean it makes sense that you wouldn't want people to know, that's all."

"I've been dating. I just don't talk about it much. Besides, there isn't much to talk about. Like Robert for instance."

"Please, not that again. I'm sorry, how many times do I have to say it? I'm sorry, I'm sorry, I'm sorry," Ariadne said.

"Once more," Diana replied.

Ariadne smiled even wider.

"I thought you two would hit it off. It looked good on paper," she said.

"He broke up with me after two weeks," Diana said. "We only went out three times—if you count the night you set us up in the first place."

"I know, I know. Total mistake," Ariadne said. "I've been there, trust me."

"You said you had no social life," Diana said.

"I did…I don't. Not anymore," she stammered. Ariadne lifted her left hand and wiggled the bare ring finger. "Divorced, remember? Coming up on three years in a couple of weeks."

"Sorry, I didn't mean to…"

"Don't be. Some marriages aren't meant to last. He's remarried, much happier. So am I, honestly."

They both chuckled.

"So, you gonna tell me about it?"

Diana shrugged.

"Not much to tell, really."

"More of physical thing, huh?"

"Right. Lots of sex. Not a lot of anything else. My fault, I guess. I let him get away with it," Diana said.

"Sounds like every guy's dream."

"I know. I thought maybe it would change, if we were together long enough, maybe he'd come around."

"But he never did," Ariadne said.

"Not yet, anyway," Diana looked down, toward the dirty, sticky floor. "Funny, when you really sit back and think about it. Sad, maybe."

"What's that?"

"Realizing at forty-three that the most significant relationship I've had in the last ten years was with me as the other woman."

"Home-wrecker," Ariadne joked.

"I can't blame him, though. I know it's so cliché, blaming her and not him. But I know how men think. His wife's gorgeous, she's young and her father owns a pharmaceutical company."

"Sounds like a babe," Ariadne said. "So how did you get into this in the first place?"

"Well, you know Richard. Every woman at the Bureau wants him, married or single. I'm no different. It kind of happened by accident, you know? It was a Monday afternoon; I remember that for some reason. December the second. He and Julia were having some problems. They'd separated in fact. As far as I knew the marriage was kind of on the rocks, you know? Anyway, I almost melted when he asked me to grab a drink with him after work."

"So he asked you out? The scumbag," she joked.

"I suppose. He was just looking for some company, and I happened to be there. I didn't give a shit at the time though."

"Just looking for a one-night stand, eh?"

"And you with no personal life," Diana said.

"I'm not kidding."

"No wonder."

"Anyway, you were saying…"

"Well, we went out, had a few drinks, talked a while. As we were sitting there, I realized that this might be my only chance. I mean, when was I gonna be out with Richard Norris again? Maybe never, right?"

"Right."

"So I threw myself at him."

"You did what?"

"Right there, at the bar. I jumped his bones. The beginning of a wonderful friendship. He didn't object, if you were wondering."

"I can imagine."

"He's no fool. He knew what he had with me, and as things smoothed over with her, he kept us a big secret. Like I said, I blame myself for that. I should have seen it coming."

"You were blinded by love, nothing wrong with that."

"Well, maybe not love."

"Ok, blinded by lust. Sounds like a romance novel. Or Cinemax After Dark," Ariadne said. "So how did you find out that you were…?"

"The other woman?"

"Yeah."

"By accident, from a mutual friend. Danielle, one of the computer analysts at Quantico."

"I don't think I know her."

"She dated Terrence Griffin for a while, he golfs with Richard, and they got sort of close. She didn't know about us, of course. I didn't tell her. But Danielle's one of those women who can't keep anything quiet.

"Anyway, a few months ago we were having lunch at a Thai place in D.C. You know how it is, women love to gossip about what other women are doing, and Danielle was all excited to tell me about how Richard was taking Julia to Cozumel for a week to reconcile. That's pretty much when I realized where I stood."

"Wow, what did you do?"

"I excused myself from the table, went to the ladies room and threw up," Diana said.

"That's understandable, sure. But I mean afterwards, with Richard."

"Oh, that," she said.

"Right, you did do something, didn't you?"

"Not really. Not unless you consider continuing to have sex with him for two more months getting even."

"Oh."

"Yeah. See what I mean?"

Ariadne called to the bartender.

"Looks like we're going to need another round over here," she said.

TWELVE

WHATELEY ESTATES
WILBURTON, MA

Gregorian hobbled past his desk, toward the center of the study. With Katya helping him on one side and the twisted wooden staff bracing him on the other, he limped a few feet forward, and then stopped. For a moment he rested, leaning heavily on his silver-topped cane. He did nothing else but aim his gaze at the floor. Carter simply watched for a long and rather uncomfortable moment, as the deformed man seemed to just stare at the ornate Oriental rug that decorated the middle of the room.

He was about to clear his throat, when something happened that made his prior, mild discomfort vanish entirely.

The rug moved on its own.

Each end lifted, spinning slowly as it shifted from its place, repositioned itself and proceeded to roll up without anyone touching it. Then it quite dutifully moved itself aside, exposing the lacquered oak planks that lay hidden beneath. Still Gregorian appeared focused on the floor with a kind of deliberate attention. Next, a latch clicked somewhere underneath. A trapdoor opened from within, lifting itself with as little human contact as the rug.

Carter tensed up as he saw what opened beneath the room—a staircase that led down into some kind of subterranean gloom.

He looked over to Gregorian, who extended a hand in the direction of the revealed chamber. Although Carter did not want to get up from his seat, he did anyway, and within a moment he found himself entering the hidden chamber.

"That will be all for now, Katya," Gregorian told his young companion. "I will call for you when we're finished."

She nodded and dutifully departed the room, leaving Gregorian to lead the way into the lower chambers—very slowly.

Carter followed him down the dusty stone steps into an underworld of complete shadow. Once they had descended, and the sitting room was left empty, the trapdoor closed itself back up. It re-latched from within. The chairs slid back into their original places. Then the carpet unrolled itself and shifted back into position, concealing all trace of where the men had gone.

«««—»»»

The concealed stairway opened into a black passage. Steep and treacherous, especially in near-blindness, the stone steps were not part of any normal construction, not set into place by masons with blocks and mortar. Instead, each dusty foothold had been cut from the natural rock. The entire tunnel had been carved out from under the mansion, piece by chipped and broken piece, chiseled by hands that were now lost to the anonymity of years.

Full descent required several minutes, which the men undertook in complete silence. The air was cooler near the bottom. It was damp, with a slight mustiness. The lights came on shortly afterward, when a series of white bulbs set into steel torch posts all flashed on at once.

Carter then saw that the hidden stairs terminated at the opening of a massive underground chamber. A planetarium-like artificial sky lorded overhead, an obsidian veil of perpetual night. The lower precincts were built on multiple concentric levels, in deliberate mimicry of the lost gardens of Babylon. The upper walls were lined with green marble between rough-hewn alcoves. Like the tunnel above, it too had been carved out of the rock beneath the mansion. The second, third and fourth levels, some ten to twenty feet down, were similarly adorned with polished marble, some in the same jade green as the upper level, others with finely-veined black and deep red. The final level could not be seen, terminating in the uncertain blackness of a pit every bit as impenetrable as the false heaven above.

Unlike the unadorned dim of the passageway, the chamber reveled in opulence. The circumference of the lair was decorated in priceless art. Fabulous carvings lined the upper levels with figures of myth and legend. Twin pillars of black diorite guarded the exit of the steps, their seven-foot faces chiseled with cuneiform. Each was an exact replica of the Code of Hammurabi. To the left, suspended by some invisible mechanism upon the stone wall, was a full-sized basalt statue of a winged Babylonian king, a long scepter in his hand and the head of his enemy at his feet. It was not a replica, but a piece of genuine Near Eastern antiquity.

On the other side a golden bull reared in frozen aggression. Its gleaming horns curved toward the ceiling and its plaited beard fell over its throat in delicate blue-black curls of lapis lazuli.

The Assyrian god Pazuzu dominated the far precinct, one arm raised and one arm lowered in the eternal demonic pose. Beside him stood a full-sized replica of the ancient emblem Gregorian had shown to him, the sigil of the Disciples of the Black Flame. The thirteen pointed star of Azathoth, wrought in shining obsidian and hundreds of blood-red rubies.

Carter was struck virtually speechless. The chamber was filled with more treasures than any private collection he had ever seen.

"I don't know what to say," he muttered. "This is amazing."

Gregorian laughed.

Carter looked over to him, taking his eyes from the wonders all around.

"That is kind of you to say," the billionaire recluse replied. "But at the risk of repeating myself, this is still not what I brought you here to see."

Carter was about to reply, but Gregorian motioned for him to follow him yet again. This time the pair descended further, tracing the spiral path that carried them down to each successive level. It took quite some time, with the hobbling recluse leading the way. When they finally came to the lowest level, Carter found himself awed one more time.

The circumference of the deep chamber was lined with ancient clay tablets, all inscribed with cuneiform. Carter looked them over, each was an original. He scanned some of the texts. Most were in Sumerian, and the rest were later writings, composed in the Akkadian language of the Babylonians.

One engraving in particular seemed to occupy a place of honor, set off on its own and framed by mirrored glass. Carter was drawn to the massive clay slab, given its rare display. It was in the finest condition of all the tablets.

"Ah, a keen eye indeed," Gregorian said, noting his interest in the rare specimen.

"Babylonian," Carter said, studying the first few lines. "Probably 10th century B.C. or so, not much later."

"Very good," Gregorian said. "Your reputation is well-deserved."

Carter continued reading it, and once he had seen enough he began to whisper the translation aloud.

"You shall count the passing of fifteen-thousand one-hundred and one journeys of Shamash. Then to the black sky you must look yet again, for when Sharru couples with Marduk above the White Kingdom of mighty Sin you will know that the way is open. Make your sacrifice then, place your offer of blood and flame upon the door in the heavens. The sacred word made flesh shall be the key. Then will the path to the Outer Gods be unlocked."

"You know the words," Gregorian said. "But do you understand the meaning, I wonder?"

Carter considered it for a moment, reading over a second time to make certain.

"I'd say it's an astronomical reference," he replied. "Shamash was the sun, so the first line marks just over fifteen thousand days."

"Correct, roughly forty-one and a half years," Gregorian said.

"Then the white kingdom of Sin would be a reference to the moon god, which means that Sharru, the word for king, probably refers to the king-star. In Babylonian astrology Marduk was associated with Jupiter. It's talking about an astronomical alignment of some kind."

Gregorian clapped his hands in a sort of exaggerated adulation, though his face remained sincere.

"Oh, you do know your subject, don't you?" he answered. "Absolutely correct on every score. A rare conjunction actually, seen once every forty-one odd years, when Jupiter rises in a perfect triangle with the full moon and the star the Babylonians knew as Sharru, which we now call Regulus."

"Which means what, exactly?" Carter asked.

Gregorian smiled.

"Again, patience," he replied.

He grew quiet once more, drawing his twisted hands close to his chest and lowering his eyes. This time, it was slightly less disconcerting to Carter when the floor began to shake.

Glows from the torch-posts stirred. Iridescent plumes arose out of the niches. Serpentine white coils curled over their heads. From the center of the deep chamber, the quaking ground broke. The darkness of the pit opened, and a gush of mist emerged. A dark spire arose amid the repetitive clanking of iron chains and an unseen mechanism of gears and pulleys. It pierced the shadows, sparkling with the borrowed light of the tapers overhead.

As it lifted higher, its full form came into the clear, and its true face was revealed. The greatest of all the antiquities in Gregorian's precious collection, the Tablet of Destinies itself, now lifted into their presence. It was a nine-sided slab of stone that could not have been lifted by any ordinary means. It was priceless. It was antediluvian. It was beautiful.

Carter studied the piece, dumbstruck. When the light fell on it from every side, row after row of a very strange script glowed blood-red across its multi-faceted surface. It was distinct, and unlike the other tablets it was not inscribed with cuneiform, or any other kind of familiar ancient writing. This piece was marked in a wholly different, almost unbelievable manner.

The entire obelisk was covered in peculiar, ancient runes—but for a damaged portion down near the bottom where the face of the stone had been scorched and a section of text had been sheared off by some long ago accident.

He staggered, almost unable to believe anything he had witnessed, or anything now confronting his eyes.

"You recognize the script, don't you?" Gregorian said.

Carter nodded.

"Gamaliel taught me to read it," he said, nearly breathless. "He called it the Elder Script. I've never seen it anywhere else. He claimed it was the true first writing, the precursor to cuneiform and hieroglyphics."

"A wise man indeed," Gregorian answered.

"He said it was given to man by the servants of Azathoth, the first source of all wisdom, all power," Carter said. "But he was lying. He made it all up. *There was no tablet.*"

"He was not lying," Gregorian answered. "Everything he told you was true."

Carter stammered, unable to process what he was seeing.

"I can't believe this," he said. "I can't believe this is real."

Gregorian was behind him however, and the strange man placed his deformed hand on Carter's shoulder.

"*Tolle, et lege*," he said.

THIRTEEN

3727 PICKWICK LANE
NEWTON, MA

Roger Saxon clicked the padlock button on his keychain fob. His BMW honked as the car alarm activated. Frozen grass crunched underfoot as he crossed from the driveway toward his front door. Snow coated the bushes and the lawn. The dusting of powder sparkled in the cloud-scattered moonlight.

Winter nights were quieter than other nights. Never more so than after a snowfall. No birds, no other sounds, except for the occasional whistle of the wind through the bare oak trees that circled his property.

Saxon's yard was large even for a posh suburb like Newton. In the spring it took his gardening service a half hour just to cut the front section. Landscaped on a slight incline, the lawn stretched out before his stone-faced Colonial style-home on the slope of a small hill. The space was as secluded as the suburbs allowed, bracketed by a white picket fence that framed the driveway on one side and pine hedges that lined the other, blocking off any hint of the neighbors.

It had been a long day. Eighteen solid hours without a break, a dozen interviews from media outlets all over the world, sandwiched between meetings and conference calls, followed by yet another press conference—this one dedicated to covering every imaginable facet of the now-finalized Neutrino Industries merger. He was exhausted.

As he got to his front steps, Saxon stopped for a moment. It was just a brief pause, to take a breath and to enjoy the silence. It was the first time he'd been able to do it all day.

His solitary moment done, and the chill of evening biting into his bare skin, he put his car keys in his pocket and fished around for his house key. It was almost midnight. His wife and his two sons would already be in bed. He didn't want to wake them. Once he found the key he fiddled with it for an instant before putting it to the lock.

Then he stopped again. He heard breathing, long and slow behind him. He smelled sulfur. He nodded to himself, put the key back into his pocket and let this hand settle at his side. He was no longer alone.

"I thought you might come," he said, before he even turned around. "But I have to admit, I'm surprised it was this fast."

He tried to muster up as much courage as he could, but when he did finally turn, he felt his knees go weak. Luther Vayne was standing only ten feet away. He was every bit the horror Saxon had imagined—and worse.

The killer barely moved. He didn't need to. His very presence was threat enough.

Vayne's face was a twisted ruin. Gaunt as a death camp inmate. Skull outlines protruded from under his pale skin, stretched taut over the bone. The ink and branding of inscrutable runes snaked across every inch of his flesh. The lines of ancient text left hardly a space untouched—save for two. The bare hollows where his eyes should have been.

His gaze was jarring, vacant and soulless as he stared out from those twin sockets, the skin around them gray and warped with gouging scars. His cheeks sank into the edges of his ragged beard. The hair had receded back from his crown, but was otherwise so long it trailed behind him like a frayed cloak; a mix of age-bleached streaks and dark tangles that fell past his naked shoulders to his waist. With every shift of the night wind, it flared and undulated like the hood of a cobra.

"A long way from Ohio," Saxon said, his mouth dry and his heart thumping.

"I go where I must," Vayne answered. "As I always have."

Even his voice was peculiar—frightening. He spoke in whispered tones, a slow hissing of sorts that stretched every syllable. The words seemed to echo, as though shouted from a great distance.

Saxon squared to face the intruder. He readied for a standoff, though he needed every ounce of strength just to hold himself together. He fought to control the trembling that nearly overcame his limbs, as sweat formed along his brow in the cold of a winter night.

Vayne was deathly still. He had shed most of his prison uniform, retaining only a pair of loose, ragged trousers and leaving the remainder of him exposed to the midnight frost. Runes not only covered his face, but the whole of his body. The blue-black symbols curled and danced over his chest, his hands and even his bare feet.

"I've heard so many stories. I had begun to wonder if I'd ever actually meet you. Now at least I can say I've had the pleasure," Saxon said, pushing his false bravado.

Vayne did not answer.

"The Elders warned us about you. They told us the history. They said you would be watching," Saxon continued.

"It is because of them that I am here," Vayne replied. "You should remember that in the moments to come."

"Why is that?"

Vayne smiled. His teeth were yellow and almost fang-like. His mouth was black with rot and decay.

"You will be tempted, I am quite certain, to blame me for the pain you are about to experience. But I would not be here if it were not for them. It is for their arrogance and their foolishness that I must visit great suffering upon you."

Saxon's throat seized. He could barely breathe. A chill ran through him that had nothing to do with the temperature.

"They're ready for you now, old man," Saxon said, as defiant and he could still manage to appear. "We all are."

"You are not. You will never be," Vayne replied.

Vayne's voice was somehow disconnected from him. At times his lips moved but made no sound, and yet when his mouth was still Saxon heard him speak. He began to move closer then, though Saxon could detect no hint of footsteps, nor any typical movement whatsoever. Even Vayne's bodily motion was wrong—*unreal*. He seemed to move forward and backward simultaneously, like a vintage film reel run in reverse, herky-jerky and missing frames as he bridged the cold space between them.

"I want to assure you, this need not take long," Vayne continued. "Your instinct will be to resist of course, I understand that. But the end can come as quickly as you choose."

Saxon stole himself for the confrontation, however hopeless he knew it to be. He tried to be brave, to stare back at the dark figure. To show no weakness. But it was a hopeless cause. As Vayne came closer the shadows around him began to move of their own accord, raising bat-like wings behind and writhing about his body with black tentacles.

"I won't tell you anything," Saxon said.

Vayne nodded.

"You misunderstand," he answered. "I have not come seeking information. I already know who you are. I am here for one reason only."

"Which is?" Saxon asked, defiant still.

"To destroy you," Vayne replied.

"You might get me, but you'll never get all of us," Saxon said. "We will endure."

"But I care nothing for the rest of you," Vayne said. "My work is nearly done now."

"What work?" Saxon said. "What do you want?"

"I seek the thirteenth," Vayne replied. "When the thirteenth is gone, all of her seed will have been erased from the Earth."

"Wait…her seed?" Saxon said.

"It has been brought to my attention that you may be the one I seek," Vayne said.

Saxon shook his head, trying to back away as the horrid specter closed the final gap between them. His time was running out.

"I'm not…I don't know what you're talking about," Saxon said.

"You will, of course, forgive me for not taking you at your word," Vayne answered. "In any case, I shall know soon enough."

Vayne closed the space between them in that moment. He clamped his cold, bony hand around Roger Saxon's throat, pulling him close as if to study the man.

"There is no need to lie, not anymore," Vayne said. "If you are indeed the leader of the Disciples, then you are the abomination. You must be destroyed."

"The leader…but you're wrong, I'm not the leader of anything," he said.

"Not the leader?" Vayne whispered, continuing to stare at him—*without eyes*—as he held him fast.

A long, quiet moment followed. Vayne studied Saxon, as if genuinely engaged in some sort of contemplation. Then, a different kind of glimmer appeared across the man's horrid face.

"Perhaps you *are* telling the truth," he continued. "If so, you must tell me everything you know of the Disciples of the Black Flame."

DAY FOUR

"Sleep eternal, Lord (of) Dreams, Ruler (of) Darkness (and) Fire (and) Sky."

— Vinca-Turdas Inscription, Banjica, Serbia
Phillipe Gamaliel translation 1983
(disputed by scholars)

He didn't need to see to understand his predicament.

His arms had been drawn out from his sides. He'd heard the shackles around them clamped and fastened to steel posts. He'd felt the fetters pulled and positioned and locked into place. The same for his ankles. They had secured him in a spread-eagle position facing up, his back against a large, cold slab of stone.

Then they left him. For hours. Long, silent, maddening hours.

Still there was no explanation. No reason for his sudden captivity.

Had he lost favor? Had he given insult without knowing? He couldn't imagine anything to justify it. He tried to backpedal in his mind, to catalogue the events of the past days, searching for any moment, any word, anything at all that might have unwittingly caused his fall from grace.

But there was nothing. His life was dedicated to single purpose. His was a picture of perfect service. If he'd had any fault, blind obedience to the Priestess was the only possible one. Yet that could not be to blame. There had to be an answer. There had to be a reason. The Priestess would not have abandoned him without one.

When the shuffle of footsteps signaled a return of his captors, he renewed his protestations, his demand for an answer. This time they replied with a blade.

Taking hold of his head, still blinded in the now-stinking hood, one woman held him fast while another penetrated the sack with the edge of sharp steel. Light and metal came to his eyes in one motion, the knife slicing through the burlap from his forehead down to his mouth. The rest was ripped free from him, finally allowing him to see again.

Before his eyes adjusted, he wished they hadn't.

They were faceless. Any sign of their eyes and human features were hidden behind black veils hung from tall red hoods. The cowls terminated around their necks. They wore little else, each one completely naked apart from the bizarre headgear. His vantage was limited, chained down and restricted in his movements, but he had little time to consider what he saw.

The knife came back into his view, and then a second and a third.

They all had them, standing over him with blades. No one spoke. Only a nod and motion from the one nearest his head was enough for them to return to work. They cut and they sawed and they tore, shredding every thread of his clothing. The remnants they discarded out of his sight, leaving him as exposed as they were.

He was cold and shivering. They did not appear to care.

Having finished baring his flesh, they immediately set to work on a further end. Tape rolls and ink wells appeared from what looked like a surgeon's table beside his dais. They seemed to be measuring him, stretching out lengths of rope and gauze over his body, while another used a pointed stylus to trace lines on his bare skin.

The process went on for hours. Their ministrations blocked his view, and his only inkling to their purpose had to be gleaned from the peculiar sensations of lines scrawled on his skin until his body had become a vast single page of living calligraphy.

Even then, he could see little of the handiwork. For the moment they concluded their strange task, they threw another hood over his head, blinding him before once more leaving him to ruminate on their purpose—again in darkness and solitude.

FOURTEEN

RIVERSIDE PARK APARTMENTS
ALEXANDRIA, VA

The phone woke Diana. Her cell *rang*, like an old-style telephone with a metal bell. She'd downloaded the ring-tone from the Neutrino Industries app store as a little bit of a nostalgic joke. At 5:13 in the morning though, it was just annoying.

She fought through the twisted web of sheets that ensnared her from half-a-night's worth of tossing and turning, and reached her hand out to her nightstand. She fiddled with the phone before hitting the "accept" icon on the screen.

She didn't need to say anything. It was Richard Norris on the other line.

"I need you down here," he said.

Diana sighed.

"What's up?" she asked.

"I'll explain when you get here," Norris answered.

"Not even a hint?"

As serious as their work could be, Diana knew that a little humor, even in the face of the most morose circumstances, was one of the only ways to maintain your sanity. She also knew that Norris understood that better than anybody. Not tonight.

"You haven't heard," he replied, deadpan. "Roger Saxon was murdered, right on his own front lawn, just a few hours ago. I want you on it."

"Shit, the goddamn Veep candidate was fucking assassinated?" she asked.

"We don't know it was an assassination yet."

"What the fuck else would you call it?"

She could still smell the alcohol on her own breath. The early stages of a massive headache were already throbbing.

"When you come in," he answered. "Too much to go over on the phone. You'll understand when you get here."

"Do you really need me *right this instant*?" she asked.

"It can't wait. Get over here now."

Diana grimaced.

"Fine. I'll be there in about a half-hour," she said.

Norris hung up without another word.

«««—»»»

The Huntington St. Metro stop was only a short walk from her complex, but the trains weren't going to start running again for a few hours. The drive downtown from Alexandria only took about ten minutes at that time of day anyway. There was no traffic, no sign of anyone. Driving the empty streets of D.C. in the early morning was a surreal experience. All the stately government buildings, the monuments and the arrogant, confident architecture of the Capital hibernated on the banks of the Potomac.

The streets, all so perfect and straight, felt bare. Evacuated. No one lived in the government district. There was no residential character to the area at all. Except for a scattering of lights from a few office windows and the overhead street lamps, there was nothing. There weren't even any cars parked along the street. In early February, even the trees were bare.

The District's overnight slumber rendered the J. Edgar Hoover Building an even more peculiar sight than usual, something she never failed to notice as she drove past along Pennsylvania Ave. It was only seven stories high on that side, considered the front of the building.

Because of some zoning law that she had never fully understood, F.B.I. H.Q. was eleven floors on the back side. The overhang that oddity produced would have been enough to mark it as a distinctive structure.

But the peculiarities neither began nor ended with the height of the building.

H.Q. was a massive cement honeycomb, a block-long urban fortress. The gray exterior felt as though it were designed for siege, with recessed windows at disciplined intervals and walls faced with concrete slabs that almost looked battle-scarred. It was authoritarian, controlled and deliberate.

The building itself was a statement.

The interior of H.Q. mirrored the severity of the outside. Even during a busy day, when the corridors were humming with people and brimming with the cacophony of telephones and urgent conversation, it was antiseptic. That too was a deliberate condition. The décor was stoic. No paintings interrupted the neutral walls. Every door was an identical shade of gray. There was nothing to distract the eye.

In the dead of night, the place was eerie.

Once she was up on the fifth floor she made her way to Norris's office.

He was at his desk. The door was open. But she didn't walk right in. For a moment, she stopped, just outside. He hadn't seen her yet.

She ran her hands over her hair, pulled back into a ponytail that suddenly felt too casual, even for this early in the morning. She looked down at herself, as if to critique her own wardrobe choices—made on the fly, half-asleep and in the dark. She immediately regretted her picks. No heels. Comfortable but shapeless slacks in a dull gray shade that did nothing for her hips. Bulky sweater that de-emphasized her chest and drew attention to her arms, which had always been a bit muscle-y and were generally not her best feature.

When she looked in and saw him with his tie lowered and his top button undone, his suit jacket off and his red suspenders stark against his crisp white shirt, she felt even more self-conscious. He was in every way the human embodiment of headquarters. Cold and unflappable beneath a concrete facade, Norris was the picture of power, restrained by nothing more than self-discipline.

In front of him, alone with him, that always made her feel a little weaker—and though she hated to admit it, that was also a big part of what made him so fucking attractive too.

He saw her there, and waved her in, apparently oblivious to how long she'd been lingering in the doorway, which she knew *felt* much longer than it really had been.

There was a blue file in front of him, opened to a series of green pages that were dense with text. Underneath were sheets in beige and yellow. She couldn't read any of them as she came in, or even as she took a seat on the other side of the desk.

She barely had the chance to cross her legs before he blurted out the most ridiculous thing she'd ever heard.

"It was Luther Vayne," Norris said.

She leered at him. Her face said it all.

You got me out of bed for this?

But he wasn't joking. He ignored her expression.

"You know the name, right?"

She nodded, but not enough to mask her disbelief.

"Of course I know him," she replied. "I wrote a paper on him as an undergrad, for an abnormal psych class."

"I need you to dust off your research then, do a brand new work-up on him. Full psych profile," Norris said. There wasn't even a hint of amusement in his voice.

Diana still didn't believe the meeting was anything other than a gag.

"Richard, c'mon. *Luther Vayne*? I love taking a walk down memory lane as much as the next girl, really I do..."

This time, Norris stopped her.

"Diana," he said, using her name as if it were a command. "This is not a joke. This is not funny, and this is not a request. I've already talked to Bill Thompson over at Quantico. Your classes will be taken over by him until further notice, and I'm suspending all of your other responsibilities, effective two minutes ago. This is the only thing I want you doing. Understood? You can have anyone you want. Put together your best team, literally anyone, but this is your only priority."

For the first time in a long time, Norris sounded like a boss. Not like a lover, or even a friend.

She moved forward in the big chair.

"Richard, cut the bullshit. We've got hundreds of agents for this sort of thing. You could put half the Behavioral Analysis Unit on this with one phone call. You don't need me. Even without my classes at Quantico, there's a mountain of paperwork on my desk."

He stared back at her. His cold blue eyes could not have been more serious. She stopped rambling.

"I need you on this," he said. "*You.* Not anyone else. Shit, you taught just about everyone we have over the BAU right now anyway. There isn't a damn thing those guys know that you didn't tell them first."

"You know I don't do field work anymore," she said. "And you know why."

He lowered his eyes, and for a moment diverted his sight to the papers on the desk. It was as much of an acknowledgement as she was likely to get from him, but she knew what it meant. *He understood, and he was asking in spite of that.*

"This isn't field work," he finally said. "It's strictly analysis, I promise. I've got plenty of field agents working the case already. But they're flying blind until we know what kind of sick shit is going on with this son of a bitch. What's in his head? What's driving him after all this time? Where's he gonna hit next? I need you to get back up on the horse for me kid, one last time. I need you to do what you do best."

"I appreciate that, but..."

"You'll have every resource of the Bureau at your disposal. I've got you on a plane for Boston this afternoon."

"A plane?" she replied. "Didn't you just say…?"

"I need you there, as close to this as possible," he replied. "I want you to dig up everything there is on this mother fucker, every old file, every report that's ever been out there. Hell, I want his fucking high school transcript pulled up out of mothballs if that's what it takes to get a complete picture of this psycho."

She nodded, and took a deep breath. Her head was still pounding.

"Look, you sold me, all right? I'll do whatever you want, you know that. You want me to fly up to Massachusetts, you got it. You need a profile on this guy, I'll drop what I'm doing and get to it. But you've got to help me out here. This just sounds…impossible. What makes you think a blind, escaped serial killer from the nineteen-seventies had something to do with the murder of a Veep candidate?"

Norris nodded.

"I know it sounds strange," he said.

"That's one way to put it," she replied. "Let's look at this rationally for a moment, all right? Luther Vayne would be somewhere in his seventies by now. He's been incarcerated for about forty years, give or take. Yeah, it's true he escaped from prison a day or two back, but that prison is in Ohio. That's got to be seven hundred miles away from Boston."

"Six hundred ninety-seven point four, door to door."

"You already did a *Mapquest* search, didn't you?"

"Six hundred-ninety-seven point four miles from the front gate of Danfield Prison to the driveway of Roger Saxon's fucking house."

"So isn't that your answer?" she said. "How in the world could a blind seventy year old fugitive get from there to here in what? A day? Day and a half maybe? It just isn't possible."

"It's possible," Norris replied.

"Hey, I know Roger was your friend, and you know I'd do anything to help catch whoever's responsible," she said. "You don't need to ask me twice. But shouldn't we be looking at actual suspects? I mean he was about to be nominated for Vice President, for Christ's sake. Who has a motive to de-rail that? Domestic terrorists maybe, or some…"

He turned over a photo that had been face down on the corner of his desk since she came in. He didn't pick it up. He just pushed it over toward her, as if even lifting it was too much for him to bear. It was

Roger Saxon, but the blood-splattered image depicted was so horrific it sent a chill even through her.

"Fuck…" she whispered. "Naked spread-eagle position. Impaled three different ways. Chest cavity torn open. Severed head. Vic laid out inside a circle of his own blood. Okay, you got my attention."

"I figured you'd recognize the signature."

"Pretty distinctive, even among serial murderers. There haven't been too many like him."

She put the photo aside, rubbed the last bit of sleep out of her eyes and thought for a moment.

"Could be a copycat though, someone trying to cover his work, or maybe looking to draw up some kind of tribute to the original," she said. "It's not perfect either, for one thing Vayne always killed two at a time. This is a solo vic."

"I already thought of that," Norris said, gritting his teeth and obviously annoyed.

"Fine, can we just concentrate on what we know for sure then?" she said. "This is pretty close to Vayne's kill pattern, sure. But that doesn't mean it definitely was him. I'm a bit rusty on this guy after all these years, but if I recall correctly, he targeted women and children—exclusively."

"And?"

"Guys like this, they have a zone they work in, a target range, like any predator. They have a specific prey in mind, and they rarely deviate."

"So maybe he changed his preferences after a few years on the shelf, who knows?"

She smiled a bit even as she shook off the suggestion.

"It's more than that," she said, picking up the photo again. "This whole set up, the posing and the torture and all that, it has a meaning. A very specific, definite meaning—I don't know exactly what that is, but I guarantee you, it means a lot to him—and the victim is a huge component of that. To him, at least. Changing the victim profile is extraordinarily rare."

"I hear you, believe me, I do," he said—although his unchanged expression suggested he still didn't seem at all convinced of her skepticism.

"I know the guy just escaped, and I get how it looks. Probably all the more reason someone would be inspired to use his signature just now, after so long. But until we have something else linking the real guy to this…"

This time it was Norris who shook his head.

"We do. Take a look at this," he said.

From the file on his desk, he fished out a single piece of paper. He handed it across the desk. It was a print-out from the lab. A fingerprint analysis.

"Saxon was killed just last night, only hours ago," she said. "How did you get this already?"

"It can be done, when necessary," he said, deadpan. "Prints were found all over the place. This set was lifted off of the lamp post where Roger was…impaled. The iron had been snapped in two like a twig."

Diana scanned it. A fifteen point match.

"Holy shit," she said. "That's fucking impossible."

"Obviously not," Norris answered.

She sat up in her chair.

"Give me the file," she said. "Let's get some coffee brewing in here, I've got a serious hangover going on and it looks like this is gonna be a long fucking day."

FIFTEEN

WHATELEY ESTATES
WILBURTON, MA

Carter was sweating, even though the underground chamber was quite chilly. The skin around his eyes was puffy and pink. The whites were burning red, every capillary swollen and tingling. His face was pale, as if all the blood had rushed to his eyes, leaving his cheeks nearly bone white.

It was morning, but he didn't know it. Deep in the bunker, cut off from the light and the air above, he had lost all track of time. There were only the words now. Ancient verses carved into stone. Words that shouted at him from across the gulf of ages, silent screams in a language that had been dead for eons—but still terrified him.

The grinding iron hinges of the trapdoor opening went unheeded. He heard it, along with the stuttering footsteps that followed; the sound of his new employer descending into his cold, private hell. But he ignored it all. He could not pull himself away from the text.

He continued to mouth the words in a hushed voice, as Victor Gregorian crept up behind him. One symbol at a time, each line a puzzle to be fitted together. Each solution even more incredible than the last.

He started talking when Gregorian got within a few feet of him, without even turning his head to face the strange billionaire.

"This is not just some inscription," he said, barely above a whisper.

Gregorian continued to approach.

"I am well aware of that."

"I'm not sure if you are," Carter said, finally turning away from the massive stone tablet, rubbing his eyes as he looked over to Gregorian. "This is different."

Gregorian paused, resting his weight on his cane.

"Tell me doctor, what did you learn in your evening of study?"

Carter glanced back over his shoulder, as if the obelisk itself was a part of the conversation—as if he dreaded speaking of it.

"Most pieces like this one, they tell a story," he began. "A record of a great battle or some rare event, maybe the achievement of a king preserved for posterity. Others are law codes or even inventories of goods and property. But this isn't any of those. Not even close."

"Go on," Gregorian said.

Carter wiped the perspiration from his face. His hands were shaking. He tried to settle them.

"I don't think you're listening," he said. "That thing outlines a ritual. Or most of one, at least. If I had to guess, I'd say that missing section down at the bottom probably contained the final incantation for the entire rite. Other than that though…"

"Yes, a very old ritual. One that has rarely been performed in all the history of mankind," Gregorian answered.

Carter was still trembling, unable to catch his breath. His eyes were frozen in a wide open position, as he turned from Gregorian and stared up at the darkness of the black ceiling. As if the thought had only then dawned on him, Carter turned back to Gregorian.

"You already know what this says, don't you?"

Gregorian nodded.

"The most famous transcription was made by in Baghdad, more than a thousand years ago. It is said the author drew from copied texts that were much older, writings likely made by the last human beings to gaze upon the face of this piece before it was interred."

"Al-Ahazred," Carter said. "The mad Arab."

"That is how he is remembered, yes," Gregorian said.

"The black text," Carter whispered. He looked back to the obelisk. "This is the *original*."

"What remains at least, as you pointed out," he answered, motioning toward the damaged section, where the face of the tablet was ruined. The text had been sheared off and the underlying stone was pitted and befouled with scorch marks. "The lower section was destroyed some years ago."

Carter could barely breathe, recounting the things he'd just read, the images conjured in his mind.

"You recognize this text, don't you?" Gregorian asked.

Carter nodded, still in disbelief.

"This is what Gamaliel showed me, all those years ago. I thought it was all a lie. A forgery. But this is it. This is real," he said. "Everything he said…everything he taught me…secrets and knowledge from distant reaches, the power behind the shadows of eternity… *it was all true*?"

Gregorian rested both hands upon his elegant cane.

"Your mentor was a learned man, indeed. One of the wisest I've ever known."

The suggestion caught Carter off guard, and for an instant he put aside the matters before him for the memory of his professor.

"Wait a minute. You knew Gamaliel?" he questioned. "You didn't mention that earlier."

A bit of a grin emerged across Gregorian's misshapen mouth,

"I knew him quite well, in fact. You'll forgive me, I trust, as I was obliged to remain rather guarded in our earlier conversations on these matters. But you have more than proven yourself to me, and since we are now officially engaged in a contractual relationship, I find myself able be more open with you."

"*How* did you know him?"

"You might call him an old friend of the family," Gregorian said, half joking.

"I don't understand."

"As I explained earlier, in her day Valeria Thorne scoured the ancient sites of the world, collecting the oldest tablets she could find, many of which were inscribed in this rather mysterious Elder script,"

Gregorian answered. "In those days, no one had ever been able to translate these writings, until the late nineteen-sixties, when Valeria found a brilliant young professor who could see what others could not."

"Gamaliel," Carter realized.

"His genius was unmatched, as was his knowledge of ancient writing systems. After years of tireless study, he finally did unlock the secrets of these texts, the secrets Valeria Thorne had long been seeking, secrets that had remained hidden for thousands of years. Secrets you are now privy to as well."

"The secrets of Azathoth," Carter said.

"Knowledge that mankind long ago deemed too dangerous for anyone to see," Gregorian answered. "They called it many things: black magic, demonic…evil. It was none of those."

"That's how he came to this," Carter said. "That's how he got started on all of those theories."

"Perhaps *too involved*," Gregorian replied. "It seems his exuberance made even Valeria uncomfortable. Once he had finished his translations and transliterations of her entire library, she was forced to send him away. She never permitted him access again."

"She fired him?"

"In so many words, yes," Gregorian replied. "She was very careful, you see. While Gamaliel was indeed brilliant, I believe he struck her as somewhat—unstable. Once she had what she needed from him, she ordered the original tablets locked away in these vaults. She kept the transcriptions under guard as well, which meant…"

"He had nothing else to rely on going forward," Carter said.

"But for his own recollections," Gregorian answered. "Though he did make excellent use of them in the years that followed."

"So that's why he was so obsessed with all this," Carter realized. "He saw these tablets as a young man and then couldn't prove to anyone that what he theorized was true. He spent the rest of his life trying to prove he was right, and no one—including me—believed him."

"Not everyone," Gregorian said. "Many years later, I sought him out again. Some years ago I was entrusted with this library of antiquities, the legacy of Valeria Thorne's life-long work. I inherited these originals, but many of the documents she had commissioned had not survived the intervening decades. I approached him and asked him to do the same for me that he had done for my predecessor."

"So what happened then?" Carter asked. "To him, I mean? What *really* happened? You know, don't you?"

Gregorian nodded, but he said nothing.

"Aren't you going to tell me? I think I deserve to know," Carter said.

"He saw," Gregorian said.

"Saw what?"

"What you have just now seen," he answered. "And much more besides. I'm afraid, after all those years it may have proven to be too much for him to handle, in the end."

"This is what pushed him over the edge," Carter said.

"Yes, unfortunately the experience does have that effect on many of those who delve so deep into such matters of the arcane. No matter how educated, or careful they may be. Your professor was supposed to provide me with a new text, a new transcription," Gregorian said. "But sadly, he fell victim to the same fate as the old Arab. He descended into madness before the task was finished. Of course, his most untimely death soon followed, leaving his work for me rather incomplete."

"So then you know how dangerous this is," Carter said.

"I do," Gregorian answered. "For that very reason I've kept that tablet here, locked away in this cold darkness for decades. But now the time has come to bring it out of the shadows, and that is why you are here. I require your services to assist me in this all-too rare endeavor. You understand what I'm asking of you, yes?"

"I'm not sure I really do, actually," Carter replied. "What is it you want, I mean *really want*?"

"To begin, I would ask that you complete the work your former mentor began, to transcribe what is engraved here so that these words may be carried with us."

"Carried with us?" Carter asked. "Where?"

"That will all be made clear to you, very soon," Gregorian answered. "When the time is right."

Carter looked up, and over at the tablets arrayed along the walls.

"Right for what…exactly?" he asked.

Gregorian smiled. He lifted his one good hand toward the ceiling.

"For the stars to align, of course," he answered.

Carter puzzled, then looked yet again at the Babylonian tablets.

"Once every fifteen thousand days, when the moon and the planet and the star align," he said.

Carter stammered, unsure of what to say.

"You seem like an intelligent person, and I don't want to insult you," he said, still treading lightly. "But you can't possibly believe all of this astrology stuff, right?"

"Astrology?" Gregorian replied. "Is that what you think we're talking about?"

"Isn't it?" Carter answered. "I mean, c'mon, isn't it a little…medieval to think that a certain planet rising at the same time as a particular star can really affect anything? You know that this stuff is bunk, right? Jupiter and the Moon only appear to be aligned, because of where the Earth happens to be, and throwing a star in the mix, well that's light years away. The three things have nothing to do with one another."

Gregorian tapped his fingers for a moment, as though impatient. But then he broke out in laughter, which only made Carter more uncomfortable.

"What's so funny?" he asked.

"This is my fault," Gregorian answered. "I'm afraid I was not clear in our earlier conversation."

"About what?" Carter asked.

"You are absolutely correct. The Convergence event we await is entirely an astronomical construct," Gregorian said. "It is merely a signal."

"Of what?"

"The positions of the stars do not *cause* the opening we seek to exploit, they merely tell us when it occurs," Gregorian said. "The motions of the sky are nothing but a calendar, a celestial time piece if you will, passed down to us from the ancients. No, what we await is not simply the alignment of some points in the sky. We merely look to that to alert us of the arrival of an event far more significant, one that cannot be seen so easily."

"What is that?" Carter asked.

Gregorian stepped back, lifting his head in the same way his old professor used to do.

"What did Gamaliel tell you of the nature of Azathoth?" he asked. "What did he believe it to be?"

Carter thought for a moment.

"That's not an easy question. He said it was many things, he wasn't entirely sure, I guess. The texts give hints, but nothing definitive," he said. "If I had to guess what Gamaliel believed, I'd say he thought Azathoth existed outside of normal time and space, somewhere else but accessible in some way."

"Very good," Gregorian replied. "The ancients who long ago summoned the Old Ones believed much the same thing. They recognized that the planes upon which Azathoth and the Outer Gods exist, the dimensions beyond our own, move to and fro, like ships upon a great cosmic sea. But like the tides that recede and then draw in close again, these other realms touch ours from time to time. When that happens, when their plane and ours coincide, a path can be opened between them—a bridge to the Other Side."

"Once every fifteen-thousand one-hundred and one days," Carter said. "This convergence, this is coming soon?"

"Within a matter of days, in fact," Gregorian replied.

He saw how Gregorian was looking at him, the clever, devious grin on his lips. He staggered across the room, over to the Babylonian tablet in the mirrored glass display. He read it again.

"Oh my god, that's what this is referring to, isn't it?" he said. "Make your sacrifice…open the door in the sky."

"Correct," Gregorian said.

"You want to actually do this? To open the way?" Carter said, before realizing he couldn't even bring himself to finish.

Gregorian moved closer, right up next to him, both of them gazing upon the ancient text.

"Imagine it," he said. "Everything you once believed, everything you once hoped. Knowledge…wisdom…every answer to every question man has ever asked."

"But at what cost?" Carter replied. "Madness?"

"Perhaps," Gregorian answered. "It has been so for some. With such great rewards there do come great risks. But for those who are willing to brave them…"

"The secrets of eternity await," Carter whispered, quoting his old professor.

Gregorian interrupted, his voice also fallen to a whisper.

"I offer you everything your mentor dreamt of, everything you once imagined, nothing less than the secrets of eternity," Gregorian replied. "What would you risk to know that? To have that power?"

"But what about the damage here?" Carter asked, pointing at the broken section. "This is the original, but we don't even have all of the text."

"That is true. Sadly this specimen has been compromised. However, Valeria did commission one perfect transcription, which I am in the process of obtaining as we speak."

"There's another one?" Carter asked. "Where is it?"

"Patience, my friend," Gregorian replied. "Let me deal with the logistics. I'm making all the necessary arrangements. First, study this. I want you to commit it to memory. Learn all that the tablet contains. Then, when the complete version comes to us, you will finally have what you have always wanted—the key to unlock *everything*."

Carter gazed upon the Elder Script, and the rows of ancient texts along the walls. He thought of his job, his marriage, his time with Gamaliel. He thought of his failures—his disappointments. Then he turned back to Gregorian.

"Count me in," he said.

SIXTEEN

F.B.I. FIELD OFFICE, ONE CENTER PLAZA
BOSTON, MA

Richard Norris was the last to arrive at the F.B.I. field office in Boston. His duties in D.C. had kept him busy until late in the morning, long after Diana had boarded a plane for Massachusetts. When he finally came in, late into the afternoon, things were already up and running at their makeshift command center.

On his orders they'd appropriated a huge section of the top floor, cleared out of all other personnel and dedicated entirely to their operation. Clocks set to all the major cities of the globe hung on three walls. A massive touch screen showing a digital map of the city covered most of the other wall. Computers and printers and telephones were humming. There were windows onto other rooms in the compound, but none that opened to the outside. It was a fortress within a fortress.

Diana was there, all the way in the back at a wide conference table stacked with papers and old folders. Ariadne was seated with her, clicking away at a laptop.

"Great timing, we're just starting to get somewhere," she began, before looking to Ariadne. "I think you know our assistant director, Richard Norris."

"Richard, you've met Ariadne once or twice before," she said.

The Asst. Director nodded. Ariadne did the same. It was all she could do to keep from looking over to Diana.

"Nice to see you again sir," she said, as polite as possible.

"No formalities," he said. "In here it's just Richard. We're going to be seeing a lot of each other in the next few days, maybe weeks. I don't want any titles or procedures getting in the way."

"Okay, *Richard*," Ariadne said.

"You're one of the computer hacks, right?" he asked.

Ariadne smiled.

"I think you mean hacker, and yes, I'm one of *those people*," she said.

Norris gave her a quick once-over. She was dressed to the nines, a sleek black blazer over a lavender silk blouse. With her hair spilling in delicate curls down her back she looked more like a designer at a New York fashion magazine than an F.B.I. computer analyst.

Then it was Norris's turn. He stepped aside to allow the African-American man on his right to step forward. He was more the typical special agent, blue suit, dark tie, white shirt; about thirty-five, square-jawed with close-cropped hair.

"This is S.A. Monroe Kendrick, flew up this morning from Atlanta," he said. "He'll be taking lead on the field investigation. I want you two to be in constant communication. If you turn up something on the research side, he needs to know ASAP."

Diana reached out to shake his hand. She spilled her coffee in the process.

"It's okay," she said. "That was almost empty."

"Old habits, eh?" he joked.

"You two know each other?" Richard asked.

"I taught him at Quantico," Diana continued. "Since then he's been assigned to the Newark Evidence Response Team, did some overseas work assisting with the embassy bombing investigation in Nairobi. He's one of the top forensics and crimes scene analysts on the East Coast."

"Didn't know you kept such close tabs on your old students," Norris said.

Diana smiled and put a hand on Kendrick's shoulder.

"Only the very good ones," she said. "Good to see you again, Monroe."

"Same here, looking forward to working with you," he answered.

"I've already briefed S.A. Kendrick," Norris said. "Where are we with the profile?"

"Still in the process of trying to gather and coordinate info," Diana answered. "It's taking a while because all of Vayne's files are so old. It's gonna take some time to get everything."

"How much time?" Norris asked.

"I've been on the phone and online all morning, putting in requests for every file on every murder investigation and prosecution for Vayne's first *outing*," Ariadne answered. "Some of this stuff has been archived and digitized. We've already got some electronic files back that we're starting to sort through. But some of this stuff, honestly—it might not even exist anymore."

"If it does, I want it," Norris said.

"Trust me, if it's out there—anywhere, I'll get it," she replied.

Kendrick stepped up to the table, and browsed through the papers laid out across it.

"As Director Norris...sorry—Richard, told you, he sent me the file on the Saxon murder, and briefed me over the phone. But I know Special Agent Mancuso well enough to know you've got more on this guy already. So fill me in, what's the scouting report on this S.O.B.?" he said.

"What do you know so far?" she asked.

"As far as I've read, our guy Vayne is some kind of leftover from the seventies, Charles Manson meets Alistair Crowley. Part political assassin, part crazed cultist. Am I on the right track?"

"That's the gist of what was reported at the time, yeah," Diana answered. "Over the course of several months in the early seventies, Vayne set out on a pretty ambitious killing spree. His murders were all over the map, quite literally, and other than the prominent societal role of his victims, there appear to have been no connection between any of them."

"Did I read that this guy is blind, too?" Kendrick asked, a little incredulous.

"He is now, although it's not clear how that happened," Diana said. "There was some conjecture back in the day that he gouged out his own eyes after he finished his personal crime wave. Couldn't even bear to look at what he'd done."

"Shit. He had a very specific victim profile as well, right? Killed women and children exclusively?" Kendrick asked.

"Exactly, he abducted and murdered the wives and young children of thirteen prominent citizens, among them two senators, a Rear Admiral, a state governor, a few judges and several wealthy industrialists."

"Except for the last one, right?" Ariadne interrupted. "I know I read something about that this morning."

"Yeah, that's right," Diana added, as the long suppressed information started to come back to her. "I forgot about that. The last murder, which was in Ohio, was the only one that didn't fit Luther Vayne's exact pattern. The mother wasn't married."

"She was rich though, according to what I read," Ariadne continued.

"I believe so," Diana said. "She was a single mother but she had recently come into some money via an inheritance from a distant relative. Still wealthy, but sort of *nouveau riche* and without the powerful spouse."

"So not all that much of a deviation, really," Kendrick said.

"Not really," Diana replied. "I do remember that he seems to have admitted in his confession that the last one was somehow a mistake on his part, though he never specified why he thought so. That could be it."

"Ok, what else?" Kendrick asked. "How about methodology—how did he kill?"

"There he never deviated one iota. In each case, the victims were taken despite high security, and killed in a very specific, very bizarre ritualistic fashion," Diana replied.

"How bizarre are we talking?" Norris asked.

"In each instance, Vayne snatched the victims by unknown means and took them to some deserted location relatively close to their place of abduction," Diana continued.

"Which suggests careful planning," Kendrick said.

"Right, I taught you well," she said. "Once there he killed his victims on site, always by impaling."

"I'm sorry," Ariadne interrupted again. "You said *impaling*, like Vlad fucking Dracula?"

"Afraid so," Diana said. "Post-mortem the bodies were posed in a very peculiar occult fashion: the child placed upside down on top of the mother, who was always decapitated. Both corpses were framed inside concentric circles drawn with a mixture of the victim's blood, kind of a twisted Vitruvian man pose. Both bodies were impaled three times, twice across the midsection and once from top to bottom."

"Jesus, that is some sick shit," Norris said.

"That's not quite all of it, I'm afraid," Diana continued. "The mother was decapitated, as I mentioned, but the child was not. Instead, the toddler's chest cavity was always torn out, and the mother's severed head was placed inside it."

"Holy mother of fucking God," Ariadne whispered.

"Right, but even *that's* not the end of the strangeness with this guy, if I recall," Kendrick added.

"True, the occult stuff is not terribly unusual for a killer of this type," Diana said. "Obsessed with every aspect of his ritual, keyed in on every single detail—the positioning of the victims, the method of inflicting the actual death blow, etc. But Vayne took the weirdness one step further. After the final murder, he simply walked into a police station and turned himself in."

"He confessed to everything with no prompting at all, right?" Kendrick asked.

"He did, and his confession was, predictably, as bizarre as his actions."

"What did he say?" Norris asked.

Diana furrowed her brow and took another sip of coffee.

"He claimed he was sent by talking shadows."

"Talking shadows?" Norris repeated, incredulous.

"I think that's the phrase," Diana said. "I've got a copy of it here somewhere, came through this morning from Ohio," she said, fishing around on the desk for a moment until she found it under a pile of old paperwork. "You can read it for yourself."

She handed it to him. The sheet was a copy of an old type-written form.

CLEVELAND POLICE DEPARTMENT
THIRD DISTRICT
2001 PAYNE AVENUE
OCTOBER 30, 1974
2:13 AM

Transcript of Voluntary Oral Statement

Interrogation conducted by: Detective Edward D. Sadowski
Badge No.: 366
Suspect Name: Luther Charles Vayne
DOB: 10/16/1944
Ht: 5'11"
Wt.: 185
Eyes: None
Distinguishing Marks: numerous tattoos and brandings, scars on face and hands

OFFICER: You have expressed your desire to waive the presence of counsel and to make a full confession. Is that correct?
VAYNE: It is.
OFFICER: This is regarding the murder of Anna Dressler and Eric Dressler?
VAYNE: Yes.
OFFICER: What is it you want me to know?
VAYNE: As I mentioned to your desk officer, I killed them both tonight.
OFFICER: What exactly did you do? Can you tell me that?
VAYNE: I have done only what I was sent here to do.

OFFICER: Sent? From where? By whom?

VAYNE: The shadows that speak to me are of no concern. All that matters for you is that I killed the woman and her child. That is enough, is it not? I have no wish to hide anything anymore.

OFFICER: Anymore? You've done this before?

VAYNE: *Yes, many times over the last year.*

OFFICER: You've been killing women and children for a year?

VAYNE: Patience, detective. As I told you, I have no wish to hide anything. The facts of this and every one of my deeds are yours to examine now.

OFFICER: You know who this boy and his mother were, don't you? Mrs. Dressler was an heiress. She had quite a large fortune. That's no accident is it? You targeted this kid, and his mother, didn't you?

VAYNE: I know who they were. And more importantly, who they were not. I know many things about them that you do not. Believe me detective, money was not involved, in this or any other of my recent acts. These were no mere children. At least until tonight, and for that I am very sorry.

OFFICER: Sorry? Ok, that's a start. Why don't you tell me what you did here?

VAYNE: I would have thought the act spoke for itself. If you'd like a narrative however, I am prepared to oblige. Simply stated, I cut the woman's head from her neck. I drove an iron rod through her body, then through the body of her child. Just before I cut out his heart. [Pause] *Would you like to hear about the others as well, detective? Or shall we take a break? You look like you might need some water.*

OFFICER: How many others are there?

VAYNE: *The boy and his mother tonight were the thirteenth.*

OFFICER: You're prepared to confess to thirteen murders? Thirteen double murders?

VAYNE: *I am. That is why I came here tonight, to confess to everything, to every killing I have committed. At your convenience, of course. This will have to be the end of it. For now.*

Norris put the sheet down.

"That is one crazy bastard," he said.

"Delusions like Vayne's can manifest with all sorts of highly unique specifics. The basic framework is often the same: a powerful motivating entity, usually hidden from view or at least from the view of the uninitiated, ordering the subject to perform these acts for some greater purpose," Diana explained.

"Son of Sam type stuff," Kendrick said, nodding.

"Exactly, but the devil's in the details, as they say," she continued. "That's what made Vayne so interesting…"

She saw the look in Richard's eye.

"From a clinical perspective, I mean," she self-corrected. "Vayne's was not the usual Satanic stuff, horns and tails and pitchforks. There doesn't appear to have been any psycho-sexual aspect to his profile either, which is also unusual. He killed women and children, but there were zero signs of any fetishistic or sexualized behaviors associated with the murders."

"So he didn't get off on it. What *was* he doing then?" Kendrick asked.

"Damned if I know, pardon the expression," Diana said. "I pulled out some of the notes from his psych interview earlier, I think they're around here somewhere too."

She sorted through the papers cluttering the table again, until she found a second document. She began to read from the page.

"This quote stuck with me," she said. "*It had many faces, each one more foul and monstrous than the last. To gaze upon any of them would condemn a good soul to the blackest depths, tortured by the madness of knowing what should not be known, of having seen what lies beyond. I stared upon it for ages, for eons perhaps, weeping at the dark, endless beauty, screaming at the unrelenting silence, drowning in the horror of its emptiness. Until the darkness looked back at me, and then I was truly lost.*"

"What the fuck?" Norris said.

"Yeah, that's pretty much what the response was back in seventy-four as well," Diana said.

"So he was seen by a shrink?" Kendrick asked.

"He was," Diana said. "Good one too, from the looks of it. In Federal Court."

"How'd that happen?" Kendrick asked.

"Two of Vayne's murders were back in D.C., and since he crossed state lines several times during his killings, he ended up in Federal Court," Diana answered. "Once his cases were disposed of there, the rest of the states where he'd confessed to crimes let the Feds keep him. After they got a look at his psych eval, that's no shock."

"Despite all that, he was declared both competent and sane?" Norris asked.

Diana nodded.

"Fucking quacks," Norris said.

"Well, not to be the pointy-headed asshole here," Kendrick said. "But I can see why that might have been the case. I worked as a D.A. before I applied to the Bureau. As we all know, legal insanity is not the same as clinical, medical insanity. If he could tell the docs that he knew right from wrong and he knew what he was doing, then crazy or not, he'd be legally sane."

"Yeah, that seems to be what happened," Diana said.

"Why wasn't this piece of shit executed?" Norris asked.

"In the early seventies the Supreme Court struck down the death penalty," Kendrick replied. "They brought it back by seventy-six, I think."

"By then Vayne had already been sentenced to life without parole," Diana said. "So that's why he's been rotting in prison for decades."

"Until now," Norris replied, almost angry.

Diana could see how personally he was taking his friend's death. She had never seen him show so much emotion, never seen him so vulnerable. She wanted to assure him, to convince him. To impress him.

"So here's the plan," she said. "Kendrick, you were planning to head out to the Saxon crime scene this afternoon, right?"

"Of course, I need to see what the local P.D.'s got. Maybe one of my team can spot something they missed."

She nodded.

"Good, I'm coming with you," she said.

Norris turned to look at her.

"I thought you didn't do field work anymore," he said.

She shook her head.

"I don't," she replied. "But you got me all the way up for a reason, right? I need to know as much as I can to fill in the profile, and we've got pretty fucking close to diddly-squat here right now. So I'm going out to Newton. Deal with it."

He nodded in agreement. She kept going.

"Ariadne, keep trying to get records for everything related to Vayne. *Everything*. I'm talking vaccination records, school transcripts, letters to him in prison, anything at all. Anything connected to him. I want all of it in this room A.S.A.P.," she continued. "Then we'll catalogue it by year, location, you name it. We're looking for patterns, things in common, anything that might tell us what he's likely to do next."

"Any ideas?" Ariadne asked.

"See if you can locate any surviving family members from the first round of victims, the kids. It's a long shot after all this time, but if you get any hits, I want to interview them. Might give us some kind of a clue that's not in the files," she answered. "Look at everyone connected to Vayne, prison officials, lawyers, etc. He's not doing this by himself. He's fucking blind and he's fucking old. Someone on the outside is helping this son of a bitch."

"I like it," Norris said. "I like it a lot. I want updates by the hour."

"Will do. But it'll have to wait until I get back in town."

"Back in town?" he asked. "You just got here. Don't you want to take a few hours, maybe see some family or friends? You grew up here, didn't you?"

"My parents moved down to Florida with my aunt a few years ago. My uncle died twelve years ago and all the friends I want to talk to I already keep in touch with. So…no, I'm good, thanks," she answered.

"I gotcha, all business. Fine by me," Norris replied.

"After we check out the Saxon scene, Kendrick and I are on a plane for Ohio, I've already got an appointment with the warden at Danfield," she said.

"More field work, huh?" Norris said.

Diana smiled, put her hand on his shoulder and squeezed just a little.

"Like I said, in this case, I'm making a few exceptions," she answered.

SEVENTEEN

3727 PICKWICK LANE
NEWTON, MA

A skeleton crew from the local police was still on scene when Diana got there. They were mostly uniformed cops, tasked with maintaining the integrity of the site; holding down the perimeter, keeping out reporters and the random curiosity seekers who always tried to get a close-up view of any public tragedy.

Special Agent Kendrick had arrived a few minutes ahead of her—mostly because she'd stopped for a double espresso on the way and he hadn't. It had already been that kind of day, a bit hung over and functioning on less than five hours sleep with no real break. She was looking forward to getting a little shut-eye on the late evening plane to Ohio—her second flight of the day.

Her former student was already at work when she parked at the edge of the crime scene tape that was blocking the driveway. She knew what he was doing, she'd taught him the procedure herself: taking his own measurements to check against the local PD file, running through a checklist of items in his head and studying the area for anything the detectives might have missed.

The sun was just setting, and the gloaming light of dusk had the entire place swimming in bluish shadows. She waited a moment before getting out of the car. The scene brought back a lot of memories, none of them good. An old, familiar feeling stirred in the pit of her stomach. Nausea, mixed with the kind of dread that made her limbs weak. She had to breathe in deep to try to get a handle on it.

This was for Richard, she kept telling herself. She had to put the past behind her, put the mistakes and the horrors behind her, put the images away for good. For him.

Even if he hadn't been her boss, she'd have gone back to pounding the pavement for him. She'd never seen him this way before. Saxon's death had broken something in him, opened a crack in his perfect confidence. She was determined to make that right—no matter what.

She had to flash her ID twice to skeptical local cops just to get past the entrance to the driveway. Maybe it was the drained expression on her face, maybe the wrinkled pantsuit or the increasingly obvious signs of sleep deprivation. She couldn't even fake the steely-eyed expression special agents always summoned up when dealing with regular police.

She walked up the driveway toward Kendrick, one of only two men in plain clothes in the entire yard. He was standing next to the other, a bit of a contrast to the well-dressed, clean shaven F.B.I. agent—a slouching, fiftyish man with a bushy mustache and an ill-fitting rain coat that barely covered a mismatched off-the-rack blazer and slacks.

"Find anything interesting?" she asked.

Kendrick nodded. She introduced herself to the other man, local homicide detective Emil Travers. He recognized her voice from the phone. He didn't look happy to see her. Local law enforcement rarely did.

"I want you to know, we're here to provide support, resources, whatever you guys need. I'm not here to step on anyone's toes," she said. "I'm sure you know that Mr. Saxon was a friend of Richard Norris. He's asked me to tell you that the Bureau is prepared to offer any assistance necessary."

The detective grinned. He didn't seem nearly as perturbed as she'd expected him to be.

"Under normal circumstances I'd tell you guys that we've got it all under control, and ask you to stay out of the way, but this time... this time I think maybe you Feds can have it all to himself. Looks like it might turn out to be an interstate deal anyway," the detective answered.

That suggestion brought a groan to Diana's throat. If an escaped Ohio inmate really was responsible for the murder, then the Bureau would not only have jurisdiction, they'd be in the best position to handle the case.

She nodded in agreement, then turned to Agent Kendrick.

"What have you got?" she asked.

"Well, the body was found there, for starters," he pointed to a marked-off area just before the front porch, where the railings had been ripped apart around the outline of a body. "You already know B.C.I. pulled prints off of the iron rods that were originally part of those steps, and that ended up *inside* our vic."

"Right, they're Vayne's," she said. "Richard showed me this morning. How the hell did he do that?"

"Beats me," Kendrick replied. "None of this makes any sense."

She studied the scene for a moment, taking in the new information and running through what she already knew.

"Okay, so we've got a similar methodology to the first round of kills and we're pretty sure this was in fact Luther Vayne, but we've also got some significant deviations from routine," she said.

"Right, solo vic here, double vics in the past," Kendrick said. "What else?"

Diana continued looking over every detail of the area.

"The old Vayne abducted his victims, transported them to a remote, pre-planned area and then performed his ritual," she continued. "This was all done here, on site."

"What does that tell us?" Kendrick asked.

"That he's in a hurry," she said. "He's rushing through his normal routine. Some kind of urgency that didn't exist before."

"But why?" Kendrick asked. "He's been out of circulation for forty years. What could have him in such a rush now?"

"No clue," she answered. "But that's not all. The scene is sloppy, for Vayne at least."

"How so?" Travers asked.

"As you pointed out a minute ago, there are prints all over the place," she said. "All of his first round of murders went unsolved until he confessed. He hardly left a shred of evidence. Now he's not only deviating from his routine, he's leaving obvious signs behind."

"It's almost like he doesn't care if we know it's him," Kendrick said.

"Our even worse, he wants us to know. That's bad news," she answered.

"Why?" Travers asked.

"If he's moving fast and he feels like he has nothing to lose, then there are going to be more of these. Count on it," Diana replied.

Kendrick cursed under his breath.

"I need to see everything. We have to take this thing apart piece by piece."

"We combed the place already," Travers said. "You guys know everything we do."

"No offense, detective," Diana replied. "But any little detail might be important, even if it doesn't look significant at first. Walk me through this."

He pointed her toward the lawn.

"Okay, right here we've got footprints in the snow. The temps have stayed below freezing since the murder, so nothing has melted."

She scanned them.

"Ok, but we both know footprints in snow aren't always great," she said. "What am I seeing?"

"Those are from Saxon," Kendrick said, pointing at the footprints leading away from the driveway across the ice-frosted lawn.

"Best as we can figure, he got out of his car and walked toward the door," detective Travers added, perhaps hoping to justify his presence.

The detective pointed to the BMW surrounded by orange cones and yellow police tape. It was right where Saxon had left it.

"He locked it and crossed over the bushes here," Kendrick continued, pointing out everything as he spoke. This time to the spot on the lawn where Saxon had first set foot. There still was an indentation in the frozen grass, marked by a red flag stuck into the ground.

"The he walked exactly twenty-six steps toward the front door. There he stopped, and turned around," Kendrick added.

"Sounds reasonable so far," Diana said.

"Well, that's just about the only thing that does make sense," Detective Travers said.

"What about Luther Vayne?" she asked.

"Well, that's for you guys to decide, isn't it?" he answered. "Judge for yourself. I'm stumped."

She looked at the second set of prints, marked by green flags where they'd been tagged.

"Just these?" she asked.

"Freaky, isn't it?" Kendrick replied.

"That can't be right," she said, looking all around for more footprints that were not there. "What did he do, drop out of the sky?"

"Sure looks that way, don't it?" the detective said.

Diana backed up, looking at the footprints in the snow one at a time, in person.

"Could he have jumped?" she asked.

"No sign of it," the detective answered. "He would have had to leap about twenty feet minimum and land without making any more of a dent than an ordinary step."

"Well he didn't just appear here, out of thin air," she said.

"Maybe not, but until we have some other explanation, that's looking like the most probable scenario," Kendrick answered.

"No way. There's an explanation. Something we're missing. Saxon's tracks line up perfectly, but this other guy's…"

"Vayne's?" Kendrick said.

She sneered.

"His start right here in the middle of the lawn. Nothing leading up to them, and except for a few steps in Saxon's direction, nothing leading away. How about blood spatter? I don't see any."

Travers turned his head.

"Detective?"

"They didn't brief you on this?" he answered.

"Just tell me," she said.

"Well…there isn't any."

"No blood spatter?" Diana questioned. "What about signs of a struggle? The tracks don't connect. This guy on the lawn, whoever he was, never got closer than about ten feet. You're saying there's no blood either?"

"I didn't say there was no blood," the detective answered. "Just no spatter."

He handed her another series of photos. They were shots of the body, some that she'd seen, others that she had not. She shivered when she saw the new ones.

A close up of Saxon's decapitated head showed his eyes were open, but rolled back. The whites were stained dark red, and streams of blood had been ejected from them like tears. His mouth was open as well, and it too was drenched in red, slathering his chin and neck in crimson. It looked as if he'd vomited blood before expiring. There were similar extrusions of bodily fluid emerging from his ears.

"So what caused all this? How did he get all of these injuries?" she asked.

This time the detective just shook his head. So did Kendrick.

"Will somebody please tell me what the hell is going on?"

"No idea ma'am. M.E.'s initial assessment is major internal hemorrhaging. Said he burst every blood vessel in his head at once," Travers said.

"OK, rules out blunt force," she replied. "Any ligature marks on the throat, any sign of pressure or strangulation?"

"Nope, far as we can tell, the neck was clean, except for the obvious…you know…where it was cut in two," Travers replied.

Diana looked through the rest of the photos of Saxon's corpse, splayed out across his front steps in a grotesque final pose. She looked over to that spot, and saw the outline where the body had been, then flipped back to the pictures. His suit and coat were nearly pristine. Other than the explosion of blood around his face, and the marks from the impaling, there was nothing.

"There's more. I looked at the coroner's report earlier," Kendrick continued. "The decapitation was post-mortem, so was the impaling."

Diana looked up.

"Excuse me?"

"That's what I said too," he replied. "None of that killed him. All of this ritual shit, the damage to the body and the posing, all of it was done after he was dead."

"Fuck," Diana said. "I didn't think this could actually get any weirder."

"Me neither. Saxon suffered some severe trauma before the decapitation. That's probably what killed him, but as for how that was inflicted…"

"How Vayne did it, you mean," she added.

He smirked in a way that perfectly matched her sarcastic grin.

"Right, other than what we can see here, there wasn't a single mark on him," Kendrick answered. "Coroner says the inside of Saxon's head—his brain that is—was essentially boiled from the inside. Said it looked like a computer that overloaded. All his circuits were fried."

"So, just to sum up," Diana said. "The evidence on scene shows us that Luther Vayne appeared out of thin air, melted Roger Saxon's brain inside his skull—from a distance, cut off his head, impaled and posed his body on the front lawn of his house without anyone noticing, then left without leaving any footprints."

Travers and Kendrick nodded in silence for a long, cold moment. Then the detective looked up, lit a cigarette and shook his head as he started to walk away.

"Yup, I'd say this one is all yours," he said.

DAY FIVE

"Let him not escape, let his strength become weakness...let his day turn to gloom."

— Purported Excerpt from the
"Tablet of Destinies"
Royal Babylonian Library
of Ashurbanipal, Ninevah

EIGHTEEN

DANFIELD FEDERAL PENITENTIARY
NORTH COSHOCTON, OH

An agent from the Columbus field office named Edward Porter was waiting for Diana and Kendrick at the airport. He said he was thirty-one, but he didn't look a day over twenty-five. He did the driving.

It was just after seven by the time they arrived at Danfield Prison.

The outside barriers were standard for a maximum security facility, a series of manned guard towers, an electrified fence that ringed the entire perimeter, endless coils of razor wire. The jagged edges sparkled in the early morning sun.

Inside the gates, they drove along a narrow causeway toward the visitors' parking lot. Beyond they could see the prison yard, an incongruous collection of picnic tables set up alongside green fields, where old men played chess while others tossed horseshoes in long pits. Some men were just wandering around. All of them were dressed in baggy jumpsuits in bright colors.

A few looked up when Diana and her escorts got out of the car, but most didn't.

The prison itself was not a single building, but a collection of several, spread out across the complex and divided by a maze of warrens, gates and fences. Agent Porter pointed her toward the main building.

Danfield Federal Prison was old, and it looked even older than she knew it could possibly be. The main building was long, and five stories tall, all built of gritty gray stone. It resembled nothing quite so much as a medieval castle, with square turrets that rose above the sloped roof at regular intervals and small windows framed with iron bars. Unlike the citadels of Europe however, it was a fortress devoted to keeping the barbarians in.

Inside, they checked their side-arms, registered and signed in with the desk clerk. He buzzed for the warden, who took nearly twenty minutes to appear in the lobby. He apologized, right after introducing himself. Diana had never heard a more insincere contrition in her life.

Warden Garrand was a fat man, with jowls that hung down from his jaw like an old bulldog, and a chin that had almost been swallowed by his inflated neck. To make matters worse, his nose was wide and flat, which lent him a swine-like appearance.

"I suppose we can skip the usual tour formalities," he joked in a folksy Southern Ohio accent.

Diana's tired expression answered for her.

"Right. So I guess you'll be wanting to get to it," he said.

He directed them toward the entrance gate, where the security guard buzzed them into an intermediary area, the prison equivalent of an air-lock.

"Well, follow me then, and let me tell you straight out, what I'm gonna show you is without a doubt some of the weirdest shit I've had the occasion to see in my thirty-two years in the corrections business. Consider yourselves warned."

«««—»»»

Notwithstanding his assurances to the contrary, Garrand spent the ten minutes it took to walk to D-Block regaling them about every notable piece of prison history he could think of along the way.

By the time they reached the control tower at D-Block, Diana didn't care what he had warned her about. She just wanted him to stop talking. After a brief run-down of the security measures for the specialized unit, he took them up the stairs.

Even then, Garrand couldn't seem to restrain himself.

"So…you folks in D.C. got any ideas about where our little old man might've gotten off to?" he asked.

Diana shook her head, not because she didn't have an answer, but because the warden should have known better than to ask.

"I can't really comment on the details; the investigation is in progress. You understand," she replied.

He did. But he didn't care.

"Hmm. All that fancy G.P.S. and C.O.D.I.S. and X-Y-Z, L-M-N-O-P." He pronounced every letter one at a time, an effect that was accentuated by his drawl. "And you ain't got any more of a clue than us country hicks out here, eh?"

This time she ignored him. They were in front of the cell. She looked at the numbers, 334 stenciled in black against the bare steel. There was yellow caution tape fastened in an "X" pattern across the entrance.

"Here we are, ma'am," Garrand said.

She inspected the outside of the cell, taking a quick look at the window, the sides of the door, the computer-controlled tracks on which it slid open and closed. Except for the tracks being in need of some lubricant, nothing appeared to be out of sorts.

Garrand stood there, hands on his hips as though he had something to be proud of.

"I figured the bastard was gonna die in there. Counted on it, even," he said.

Diana continued to wait. When it became clear that Garrand was not about to invite her in, she waved her hand in the direction of the window.

"We've come all this way, warden," she said. He nodded, but didn't seem to catch on. "Do you think you could open the door?" she asked, as politely as possible.

Garrand turned to look at her, and he stepped in between her and the cell. She stepped back.

"I can," he said.

She just stared at him, and let her expression answer for her.

"I will, if you really want me to," he said.

"That's why I'm here."

"I know. But I don't think it'd be fair to let you in there, if I didn't make sure you were really set on seeing it," he said.

"I'm just doing my job," she answered.

"Now see, that's what I mean. You best make sure you're up for it, because this ain't the usual shit," he said.

"Just open the cell," she said.

Warden Garrand smiled. It made his cheeks swell even more, which only accentuated the porcine resemblance.

He lifted his walkie-talkie, clicked on the side button and made the appropriate request. The radio buzzed with static. That was followed by some clicking and rolling from the wheels along the tracks connected to the cells.

"Welcome to Hotel Vayne," Garrand said as the cell door slid open. "One current vacancy."

Garrand stepped aside with an extended left hand, offering her the inside of the cell as though it were a table in a five-star restaurant. Fluorescent bulbs lit the interior from two recesses overhead. It painted the whole of the cell in flat white tones. Everything looked dull under that kind of institutional light, like an acrylic painting in three dimensions. It robbed the spirit from everything it touched, illuminating it and suffocating it at the same time.

Diana couldn't believe what she saw.

"How long has it been like this?" she asked.

Garrand was still standing outside. He hadn't followed her in. The concrete walls muffled her question. He had to ask her to repeat it. From outside.

"Don't know," Garrand said. His voice seemed like it was distant now, even though he was just beyond the door. Nothing penetrated the tiny cement room. The notion struck her as she stood in the middle of the cell. It was nothing more than a tomb for men who hadn't yet died.

"How could you not know that?" Kendrick replied. "This can't be normal."

"No...no it isn't."

"Don't you have regulations about this sort of thing?" Diana asked.

She scanned the whole of the tiny room. What she was seeing shouldn't have been there. She knew that. Yet there it was, staring back at her.

Graffiti. Every inch of the cell was covered in it. The walls, the floor, even the ceiling. The script varied. Some in block letters. Some words in elegant cursive. Some in slashes and twisted swirls. Not all of it was legible. She suspected that not all of it was even English. Some looked more like runes and hieroglyphics, but in a language she'd never seen. There were only two colors, red and black. The black looked like charcoal, or ash. The red had a purple tint.

"It's exactly what you think it is," Garrand said from outside.

"What's that?" she asked. She couldn't get past it. So much writing.

"Blood," Garrand said. "We had a swab taken. The red is blood. Vayne's cellmate's blood."

She put her fingers as close to the blocks as she could without touching them. Even with gloves on, she didn't want to disturb a thing.

"Pretty fucked up shit, ain't it?" Garrand said. He was now in the doorway, but he still hadn't entered the cell.

"It's unusual, that's for sure," she answered. "How is it that your men tolerated this?"

"That's the thing ma'am—they didn't," he said. "I've spoken to every one of my boys. Everybody who had access to this cell. They swear up and down—to a man—that this shit wasn't here until three days ago, until Vayne was gone."

"That's impossible," she said.

"You're welcome to talk to them," Garrand said. "But you should probably see the whole thing first."

"There's more?" she asked.

Garrand crossed the threshold.

"Over here, you've gotta move the bunk aside just a bit. But it's worth it, whatever the hell it is."

He grabbed the end of the bunk beds. They looked like they wouldn't have moved easily, but to her surprise they slid across the floor with very little trouble.

"Now you tell me, Miss Special Agent F-B-I," Garrand announced as he revealed the wall behind the bunk. "What the fuck is that?"

Sprawled across the cinderblocks was a macabre tableau. Stark against the gray stone was a symbol writ large in human blood. The lines were violent—jagged and angry brushstrokes. They formed unique symbol—a star within a star.

She studied the odd features, counting thirteen points in all. At the center of it was an inverted pentagram, the bottom point hugely elongated into a spire that stretched far under the entire glyph. Surrounding that was an eight pointed outer star cradled by a ring of blood, the outermost of three concentric red circles inside the figure.

Diana felt her stomach turn at the sight of it. She racked her brain trying to place it, and though it seemed somehow familiar, she couldn't figure out why.

She turned and looked at the words written on the walls all around it. In every case where the script was legible, they said the same thing. Three words, over and over. She finally read it out loud as they stood there, dumbfounded.

"Azathoth commands it."

NINETEEN

WHATELEY ESTATES
WILBURTON, MA

The Reverend Graham Thurmond Hayden slapped his hand on the mahogany table like it was a lectern in a church. Rising from his seat, the perfectly-coiffed televangelist lifted his arms and pointed in turn at each of the men and women sitting with him.

"We don't have much time, you all know this," he said. "We need to take action and we need to do it now."

Although they grumbled in silence, no one openly disagreed with the preacher's assessment. For the moment, those seated with him merely listened, just as he was accustomed to people doing whenever he spoke. Some looked out the iron-framed windows that towered from floor to ceiling, while others stared off at the shelves crammed with old books that lined the walls of the study. Even the bookcases themselves were a kind of art, carved with precision out of age-stained oak.

"I came here today under the impression that we were prepared to do just that. But I've yet to hear a serious suggestion. All we've done for the last hour is dance around the central point, making small talk and big drinks. If we're here to talk seriously then let's get to it," he continued.

Seated in a circle with him was a rare gathering of some of the most influential men and women in the nation—people not used to being addressed in such a tone. They had already begun to bristle at the cleric's attitude before he raised his voice. Now, as the tenor of his remarks rose to a crescendo, he rankled them all.

In the high-backed leather chair nearest the Reverend, White House Chief of Staff Lauren Armstrong sat cross-legged in a red skirt suit. She sat quietly, dangling her shoe from her foot as she sipped a glass of Glenlivet 18-year-old single malt, but her dark eyes left no question as to her mood. Anxious and worried.

General Jack Krieger was on Armstrong's left. Seated at attention, as always, he nevertheless looked uncomfortable. His medal-covered dress blue uniform was starched and ironed to perfection, but his face was frozen in a look of utter scorn.

Stephanie Bremmer occupied the chair next to him, directly opposite Armstrong. The Neutrino Industries CEO cut a figure that made her the complete opposite of the only other woman in the chamber, almost frumpy in an Earth Mother dress and Birkenstocks, but her expression was identical—practically snarling with anger as Hayden continued to lecture them.

"There are questions we need answers to," Hayden said. "How did he get free? How did he know about Roger? What did he learn from him before he died? These are matters of life and death, my friends!"

"I warned Roger," Bremmer said. "I told him it was too risky to make all these appearances with that madman on the loose. He just wouldn't listen. You know how stubborn he could be."

"He was only days away from the nomination," Armstrong said. "Our sources were indicating it was going to breeze through Congress. We had the votes."

"We were so close," Bremmer said. "Finally, we would have had one of our own a heartbeat away from the highest office in the land.

"That has to be why he chose now to re-appear, after all these years," Armstrong said.

Hayden scoffed.

"You're thinking too small, all of you," he said. "This isn't about nominations or political offices. Vayne was never concerned with that."

The Reverend paced back and forth before the vintage Oriental rug that lay between them all. It was woven in a peculiar design, with intricate Persian flourishes. The white swirls resembled skulls and bones.

"What are you saying?" Armstrong asked. "You don't mean…?"

"I do," he said, raising his hands as he began to harangue them. "Brothers and sisters, this is no mere criminal we face, no common lunatic. Remember your lessons, recall what the Elders taught us. The Convergence is nearly upon us again. This is what we have all been awaiting these many years. No, friends, this was no simple assassination, the death of our brother Roger Saxon means nothing less than the beginning of the end."

A tense silence fell over them with those words.

"We're not your congregation," Krieger finally said. "Why don't you take a seat, Rev? Have a drink and talk. It might relax you."

Hayden shrugged off his comrade's annoyance.

"Don't patronize me, Jack. This is no time for cocktails and chit chat, even for you."

He did not sit, nor did he tone down his rhetoric. Not even the level of his voice. Once the Reverend got worked up, there was no easy way to settle him down. He continued to pace across the hardwood floor.

Krieger sighed. Armstrong put her glass down with an impatient thud. Bremmer started to get up out of her chair to challenge the arrogant preacher directly, when a voice intruded from outside the study.

"Please Graham, we are all concerned by these recent tragic events, and all of our voices should be heard in discussing the response."

The large double doors behind them slid open as if moved by the words alone. But when they turned to look, there was no one standing there. For a moment the library fell eerily still. None of them dared to disturb the strange silence—not even the Reverend.

They all knew what was coming.

A shadow entered first, flooding the room with a dark shape that suggested something large. The black form swelled rapidly, though the midday lighting had not changed. It appeared to move in several directions at once, until it gathered itself into a single figure that loomed across the entire length of floor.

Behind it—inside it—a man hobbled toward them through the open doors, a malformed giant bracing his every faltering step with a silver-topped wooden staff. His body was shrouded in a voluminous velvet robe that dragged along the floor behind him. Katya flanked him, still dressed in little more than glorified underwear.

Carter followed in his wake, stepping lightly as though unsure that his presence was welcome, despite all assurances to the contrary.

"Victor," the Reverend said, his voice lowered at the appearance of the crippled recluse. "We're all grateful to you for hosting us here on such short notice. But these are matters that demand urgent attention."

"I do not disagree, Graham," he said, as he made his way slowly toward the front of the massive antique desk at the end of the library. Katya assisted him in sitting down as she took up her regular place at his side. "Introductions must first be made however. As you can see, we have among us a new initiate to our circle of friends."

He placed his "good" hand on Carter's shoulder.

"Ladies and gentlemen, this is the man I have been telling you all about, the finest scholar of the ancient texts since Gamaliel himself. I am pleased to report that he has agreed to assist us in our endeavors," he said, smiling at Carter. "To that end, I present to you the distinguished curator of Antiquities at the M.F.A. in Boston, and soon to be our newest brother, Dr. Carter Shaw."

Carter nodded to them before making the rounds, shaking hands with each and exchanging pleasantries. Then he took up a place beside Gregorian, remaining on his feet—and for the moment, out of the way.

"Now, you were making a point, Graham?" Gregorian continued.

Reverend Hayden bowed his head and lifted his hands in a kind of mild surrender as Gregorian stood before them all. Despite his grotesque appearance, he had a manner about him that suggested calm, a demeanor of authority that was gentler than either the stiff militarism of Krieger, or the naked hostility of Bremmer. His very presence demanded respect.

"I was just urging our brothers and sisters to action," Hayden replied.

Gregorian's twisted face settled into a serious glare. His wide eyes narrowed and his chin seemed to vanish into his beard and his distended throat.

"Yes, I was afraid that this day might come, as I know we all were," he said.

"We're so close to the Convergence," Hayden said. "There's no way the two aren't connected. He knows. He must know."

Gregorian nodded, but did not appear as concerned.

"I'm quite certain Luther Vayne knows exactly when the proper celestial alignment will occur," he said. "This is not a surprise. In his time there was no one closer to Valeria Thorne, no one who enjoyed her confidence more. We must therefore assume that anything known to the Priestess was known to him as well."

"I'm sorry," Carter interrupted. "I'm afraid I don't understand what we're talking about."

"Forgive him, brothers and sisters," Gregorian added. "Doctor Shaw is quite understandably still becoming acquainted with our situation, though I assure you all he has demonstrated his qualifications beyond dispute."

"What is that troubles you?" Hayden asked. "You may speak freely amongst us, have no fear."

"Is there someone else we have to be concerned about?" Carter asked.

Hayden looked to Gregorian

"He does not yet know of Vayne?" the Reverend asked.

"He has not yet been initiated," Gregorian replied.

Hayden nodded, looking over Carter with a curious eye.

"Then perhaps we need to correct that deficiency, before going any further," Hayden said.

Gregorian tapped his cane.

"Indeed, I agree. That is over-due already," he said. "Let us put aside these discussions briefly, shall we? So that we may do as the Elders taught us—purify ourselves in the old fashion, and welcome our new friend."

He looked to Reverend Hayden.

"High Priest, will you lead us in prayer again, as you have so many times before?" he asked the cleric.

Hayden nodded.

"Of course," he answered. "Let us retire to the sanctum, to bow our heads in the old way, and pay homage to our Elders and to the Old Ones. Then we will finish discussing what must be discussed."

The others agreed without a further word. Every one of them downed the last of their drinks and got up from their seats. As if on cue, the chairs slid backward across the floor, moving away from their former occupiers as though pushed by invisible hands. Gregorian stepped into the middle of the group, braced himself with one arm on his cane and waved his other hand. The Persian rug rolled up by itself, but none of the men and women present seemed to find anything unusual about the display.

The deformed tycoon next stared at the lacquered oak planks beneath, focusing on them with deliberate attention. Again, they answered him. A latch clicked somewhere under the floor. A trapdoor opened from within, revealing a staircase that led down into some subterranean gloom.

"Please, go on ahead my friends," he said. "As you know, I move slower and slower every day."

They followed Gregorian's instructions without a word, filing down the dusty stone steps into an underworld of shadow. Eventually, Gregorian too hobbled his way behind them, moving with caution as he shuffled into the dim. This time, he did not dismiss his young blonde companion, instead ushering her forward alongside him.

Once he had descended, and the sitting room was left empty, the trapdoor closed itself just as it had opened. It re-latched from within. The chairs slid back into their original places. Then the carpet unrolled itself and shifted back into position, concealing all trace of where they'd gone.

TWENTY

DANFIELD FEDERAL PENITENTIARY
NORTH COSHOCTON, OH

Diana sat alone in Garrand's office, staring at the wall. It was beige and it was blank—just as it should be. The warden came in through the open door, coffee in hand. He gave her a cup.

"Black, right?" he asked.

"Thanks."

There was a sill along the window behind Garrand's desk. He leaned against it as he sipped his coffee. He watched Diana for a moment, as she sat there with her hand on her chin, seemingly studying the empty wall.

"Your agent Kendrick's covering everything, just like you said he would. He's photographing every inch of the cell. Your boys from the Cleveland office just called ahead, they're about fifteen minutes out with the forensics team you called over for."

"Good," she said.

Garrand put his coffee down.

"You're having a hard time, ain't ya?" Garrand replied. "Well don't feel so bad. Vayne had a way of doing this to people. Everyone here's got a story about the guy. Creepy son of a bitch. I'll tell you, off the record, I'm almost happy he's gone."

She turned her head at the comment.

"Joking, of course," Garrand said. "But Vayne had a reputation."

"How do you mean?"

"Everyone's got a rep in a place like this. Among the other inmates, among the staff. Pretty much anyone who ever came in contact with him knew his. He was the guy you stayed away from."

Diana had expected to hear something like that. He had once been something of a celebrity defendant, and most of those guys had some kind of reputation follow them into the penitentiary.

"I imagine so, given his history," she said.

Garrand laughed. His belly bounced like a redneck Santa Claus.

"Something funny about that warden?"

"You have no idea," he said. He moved off of the sill and over to file cabinet behind his desk. He slid open the top drawer, fiddled between some papers for a moment, and then produced a file. He handed it to her.

Inside was a black and white photo of an African-American man with a rough beard and fierce eyes.

"That's Jefferson Johnson. Or at least, that *was* Jefferson Johnson," Garrand said.

"This man is dead?"

"He might as well be."

"Is he an inmate here?"

"Was, about five years ago. When that picture was taken he was considered one of the most violent inmates in the entire Federal prison system. Started out in the Heartless Felons gang as a juvenile, graduated to heroin trafficking, robbery, felonious assault and eventually murder. Killed a rival dealer with a chain saw.

"That's why he was sent here, to D-Block. Johnson was a monster. Six foot five, two-hundred-seventy-five pounds. He was impossible to control."

"How so?"

"He had nothing to lose, and he knew it. Killed a guard down in Mansfield, and bragged that he'd do it again. They couldn't house him on death row anywhere else, he was so violent. Not just against guards and other inmates. This son of a bitch tore a sink out of the wall once."

"How does he connect with Vayne?" she asked.

"Like I said, he was put on D-Block when he got here. Usually they're all under pretty strict supervision. A few weeks after this Johnson fella got here though, something happened. We think a guard might have screwed up, left a gate unlocked maybe, we never could find out for sure. Bottom line was, Jefferson Johnson got out of his area and took a run at Vayne."

"Why?"

"Sometimes it's for status, make a bigger name for yourself by killing a famous inmate. Other times it's just because of who a guy is. Child killers are the lowest of the low on the inside, no matter how old they are."

"So what happened?"

"Can't really say. We got cameras trained on all the yards, but the ones for this location decided to go on the fritz that day, wouldn't you know it?"

She smiled.

"End result was that Jefferson Johnson got transferred out of Danfield the very next day."

"To where?"

"Northcoast Mental Hospital, it's a secure facility for the clinically insane."

"I don't understand," she said.

"Neither do we, but that's sort of the point, isn't it?"

"I'm not following."

"The guards discovered the mistake, the open gate, after a little while. They realized the situation right away, and called for back-up. But it wasn't necessary. When they got into the walking area, Vayne was fine. It was Johnson who was in trouble."

"What happened to him?"

"No one knows. He was crying when the guards got to him."

"Crying?"

"Like a little girl, so they tell me. Poor bastard was curled up in a ball in the corner of the yard, weeping. Shaking like a leaf. As far as I know, he's still like that today. The shrink said he suffered massive brain damage, like someone reached into his skull and squeezed all his gray matter. He has to be sedated every night. Suffers from constant nightmares, and when he's awake he hallucinates. Says the shadows are talking to him. The man's a wreck."

The last part caught Diana's attention.

"What did you say?"

Garrand puzzled.

"He's a wreck."

"No, before that—talking shadows?"

Garrand looked a little sheepish.

"I know, I know," he answered. "It's crazy shit. You can't make sense of it."

Diana whispered it to herself one more time.

"So we're sure Luther Vayne did…*something* to him?"

"No, but I don't know who else to blame. All's I can say is, he wasn't like that before. Five minutes in the yard with Vayne and he's wetting his pants? You figure it out. Guys pretty much stayed out of his way after that, except for Bobby Lee."

"Who's that?"

"Bobby Lee Weaver. Vayne's cell mate, until a few days ago."

"Shit," she said.

"Uh, that's not quite everything though. There is one more thing you should see," he said, almost as an apology.

She looked over to him, and did recall something else they'd discussed before she arrived.

"Right, they told me there was a letter. Do you have it?"

He nodded.

"Got a copy right here. Original was sealed up in an evidence bag and turned over to your team when they first got here," he said. "But they told me you profile people would want to see it too."

From his desk he handed her a photocopy of a single sheet and an envelope.

"Was mailed from somewhere in Boston, but that's all we know. No return address, just a postmark," he said.

She looked it over. It was a clipping of a news story from three days before, about Roger Saxon's potential VP nomination. The story featured a file photo of Saxon's headshot, probably a publicity still sent out by his PR people. Scrawled in the margin next to his image was the same symbol she'd just seen in Vayne's cell—a thirteen-pointed star.

"Jesus fucking Christ," she whispered. "Somebody on the outside tipped him off. How did your people miss this? Did this just magically appear after he escaped as well?"

"We do open all the inmate mail, but at the time I think the screeners just thought this was some kind of doodle," he said. "Besides, the man was blind as a bat. What harm could come from giving him a photo, it's not like he could see it himself, right?"

"Son of a bitch," she said.

"What's that?"

"His cell mate?" she replied. "Bobby Lee…*whatever*. Could he have seen the letter?"

Garrand pondered, as if the thought had not even occurred to him before.

"Well I suppose he just might have," he said. "I guess you'd be wanting to talk to him too, in that case?"

"You better believe it," she said.

Garrand nodded, but folded his hands in front of him before continuing.

"I feel I gotta warn you though, special agent," he began. "You see, Weaver kinda went the other way, compared to Johnson, if you catch my drift."

"Not sure that I do."

"Let's put it this way," Garrand said. "Weaver was pretty close to insane to begin with, but after bunking up with Vayne for a while… well, just talk to him yourself. Draw your own conclusions."

«««—»»»

Bobby-Lee Weaver had been transferred to an isolation cell in C-Block indefinitely. Even though the solitary guys weren't supposed to have visitors, or even leave their cells except for one hour of walking time per day, but Garrand made an exception for Weaver.

Diana met with him in the interview room. A hard-nosed guard with a thin mustache and Marine-style crew-cut brought Vayne's ex-roommate in from his cell. Weaver was dressed in the yellow jumpsuit of his special unit, shackled at the ankles and the wrists, with a chain that ran between his legs. He shuffled along in his prison-issued slippers.

"You got a visitor Butch," the guard said. "Be nice huh? Don't scare the lady. You act up and you ain't gonna see the sun for a month, got it?"

"Butch?" Diana asked as the guard retreated for the seclusion of the corner, and his rolled-up copy of *Motor Trend.*

"Short for Butcher," he said.

She looked at Bobby Lee from across the table. Agent Kendrick joined her, nodding as he sat down next to her. Even though she knew she was in no real danger, the maniacal giant still gave her the chills.

"Mr. Weaver? My name is Special Agent Mancuso. This is Special Agent Kendrick. We're with the F.B.I. Would you mind if I asked you a few questions?" she said, presenting her ID. Bobby Lee didn't bother to look at either one.

He remained seated, staring into space. His arms were all bandaged up, covered in what appeared to be dozens of self-inflicted cuts. That explained the blood on the walls, at least.

"What about?" he asked.

"Luther Vayne," she said.

Weaver turned toward her. Immediately his eyes lit up.

"He said you'd come. He said you'd want to know things."

"Who did?" she asked.

"He did," Weaver said. He edged up as close to the table as he could, with his mobility hampered by the shackles. Even sitting down, he towered over her. Unexpectedly, he craned his neck to crouch down to her eye level. His gaze was gentle, like a child's. His voice was calm.

"Vayne?" Diana asked. "He told you I'd be coming?"

The Butcher looked her over once again, then shook his head.

"He didn't say who exactly. Just said that someone would be coming, and that it was okay to tell you things, if you asked me."

"What did he say you could tell me?"

"Just what I said, that I could tell you things, if you asked me," he answered.

"What things?" Kendrick attempted.

"Whatever you ask me," Weaver answered.

Diana looked at Kendrick, and his expression told her he was thinking the same thing she was—they weren't likely to get much out of the man. According to Garrand, even in the best of times he suffered from severe mental handicaps. If he did know anything, he probably wouldn't be much help anyway.

"Thank you Mr. Weaver, I didn't mean to bother you," she said, getting up.

Bobby Lee stopped her. He had more to say.

"He showed me something," he said.

She turned just slightly as she was getting up for the door.

"What's that?' she asked, expecting very little. "Did he show you the letter?"

"No, much more than that."

"What did he show you, Bobby Lee?"

He stared right back at her.

"He showed me Azathoth."

Diana stopped. She remembered the writing in the cell, and the eerie words of Vayne's long-ago confession. She sat back down.

"Tell me," she asked. "What is that? What is Azathoth?"

Bobby Lee just kept staring at her. He smiled.

"Is it a place? Is that where he went?" Kendrick said, more demanding this time.

Bobby Lee looked off to the ceiling. His voice drifted with his wandering gaze.

"He let me see it, a little of it, anyway," Weaver continued.

Kendrick was becoming visibly annoyed.

"Listen kid, we don't have time to waste on…"

Diana stopped him.

"Let him finish," she said. Then she turned back to Weaver, urging him on gently. "Please, go on."

He required no more prompting.

"There is no light there. Not like what we call light, anyway. There never has been," he began. "It's cold. It's always cold."

Diana studied the man's face. He was an ogre, ugly and huge and slow. But he was looking right at her. He seemed so sincere. She just listened.

"There is no laughter, either. Never. It's never warmed by the sun. Never brightened by the smile of a child. Nothing but shadows. The shadows of madness, always whispering their foul verses. He cannot escape them. They are always with him. Commanding him. He must obey."

"To do what?" she asked. "What are the voices telling him to do? What does Azathoth command?"

He looked back at her as if she had asked the most obvious question in the world, and in that moment she realized *he seemed to feel pity for her*.

"To destroy them, of course. All of them, finally."

"Destroy who?" she asked.

"You truly know so little," Weaver answered. "He said you would be this way, like children."

"Please, I need to know," she said. "You're right, I want to understand. I want to learn. Can you tell me?"

He smiled.

"Of course," he replied. "I told you, he said I was allowed to tell you, if you asked."

"Who does he want to destroy?"

Weaver shook his head.

"Oh, he does not wish to. No, he certainly does not. But he is commanded, and he must obey," he continued.

Kendrick got up next to her, whispering in her ear.

"You're feeding into the delusion," he warned. "You taught me not to do that, remember?"

She waved him off.

"I know what I'm doing," she answered. "It's not *his* delusion I'm interested in—it's Vayne's."

She looked back to Weaver.

"Can you tell me," she asked. "What is he commanded to do?"

"He must undo what has been done. He must destroy that which should never have been," he continued. "He cannot rest until all that was done by the whore of Sothoth has been undone. Until all thirteen have been destroyed."

"All thirteen?" she replied. "All thirteen what?"

"There were thirteen murders, right?" Kendrick asked.

She nodded.

"Thirteen killings?" she asked. "Is that what he was commanded to do?"

"The abomination must be destroyed. The work of the whore of Sothoth must be destroyed," he answered.

"Sothoth? Do you mean Azathoth? What the hell are you saying? Why is he still killing?" Kendrick demanded, slamming his hands down on the table, his patience gone.

Weaver seemed to not even notice. He just kept on talking, reciting almost. His diction had changed. He was somehow eloquent, articulate.

"It's haunted, that lonely place. But not by ghosts or demons. Not by any superstitions or phantasms. Things far stranger. Far harder to dismiss by naming them, that's what Luther said. His companions. His master and his oldest friend. It is the only thing he fears. The thing he hates the most."

Bobby Lee smiled at her. She recoiled. Kendrick stepped back in frustration.

"Can you show any of this to me?" she said. "Can we see it?"

Bobby Lee shook his head.

"No," he said. "Not Azathoth. You can't see that. Not yet. Maybe not ever. That's the end of the journey. But *you can* help him get there."

"Why would we want to help him?" Kendrick interrupted.

Bobby Lee ignored the other agent. He kept his eyes on Diana. But he didn't seem as though he had anything else to offer. After a long, silent pause, she started to get up.

"Officer," she said, motioning to the guard in the corner. "I want to thank you Mr. Weaver, you've been a great help to us," she said.

He looked up from the table. The Buckeye Butcher smiled.

"He's watching us, you know. Right now. He can see you," Weaver said. "Very soon, he'll speak to you himself."

TWENTY-ONE

WHATELEY ESTATES
WILBURTON, MA

The Reverend Hayden led the way. The others began to hum as they walked, lifting a soft chorus in the underground. They all seemed to know the tune, a rhythmic chant of deep vibrations and whispered refrains.

With his head lowered, Hayden walked ahead of them along the winding path that led down each concentric level of the deep chamber. When they all reached the lowest level, where the great tablet stood alone in the dim, he turned as the others gathered in a circle around the obelisk.

He clasped his hands and said a prayer that the others echoed. Finally, his eyes still gazing downward, he removed his jacket and let it fall to the floor behind him. Gregorian's assistant Janet appeared behind him, along with Katya. Working in tandem, they proceeded to remove his tie and unbutton his shirt, taking his clothes and putting them aside. Like a king attended by minions, he allowed them take his undershirt, belt and pants as well, until he was standing in only his boxers and socks. These the ladies soon removed as well, leaving him naked in front of the gathered.

Carter tried to look around without attracting any attention, hoping to gauge the reactions of the others to the odd display. But none of them seemed to find it strange. They merely continued to hum, and to whisper in the same eerie way.

A moment later, Logan entered the chamber as well. He gathered up the Reverend's discarded clothing and deposited it in a chest along the wall. Then he took an unlit brazier from a post just above it. He approached the Reverend, who kept his head lowered but outstretched his arms, palms uplifted. Logan scattered the cinders and ash contained within the cold brazier, coating Hayden's naked skin with the soot.

When it was finished and the dust was spread across his entire naked frame, Janet returned to him. She held a black hood and a crimson cowl, both of which she placed over Hayden's head. The hood was opaque, forming a complete cover that hid his face. The cowl fit over it, tied off with twin ribbons around the neck that she fastened and let hang behind his back.

"Join with me now, brothers and sisters," the naked, faceless Hayden announced, the occlusion of the mask rendering his voice somehow more sinister. "Purify yourselves in the ashes of fires gone cold as we make ready for our supplications."

Carter watched in silence as they all followed the same ritual—Katya and Janet undressing them and handing their clothing to Logan to put away. For each of them Logan followed suit as he had with the Reverend, only now he doused the remainder of them together in a mass baptism of black soot. Once they were all naked and covered in ash, Janet gave each of them the same face-obscuring hood she'd handed Hayden. They secured them each and followed with black cowls, plain of decoration and unlike the silk-lined head-covering Hayden wore.

Only Gregorian remained dressed. Covered in his voluminous silken robe he was spared from the naked ritual, perhaps in concession to his peculiar affliction, Carter imagined.

They continued to hum their maddening tune as Logan and Janet donned black robes that hid every inch of their bodies. They then took a pair of ritual drums, one from each side of the chamber and seated themselves on their knees, the ancient instruments nestled before them. The drums looked tribal, strung with beads and adorned with rows of age-yellowed fangs or tusks. With only their hands, they began to tap the stretched leather skins, following the rhythm of the group hum.

The barrel-shaped drums sounded with a peculiar resonance, and each beat echoed in the confines of the subterranean chamber. Two beats became four. Four became eight. The longer they tapped the surfaces of the ritual instruments, the more the room seemed to fill with the haunting sound, as if an army of distant drummers joined them from somewhere in the shadows.

Then Katya came to Carter. Standing in front of him, she removed what little clothing she had on, before setting to work on him. Taking his cues from the others, he stood passive as the nude young woman removed each piece of his clothing, until he too was naked in the underground.

Unlike with the others however, Logan did not douse him with soot. Instead, Katya took his hand and led him toward a door on the far side of the deep chamber. In the darkness he had not noticed it earlier. But even on this lowest level of the inner sanctum there seemed to be yet one more portal to enter. She walked him toward it and the others followed behind, entering a cold, black room. With only the spill-over light from outside, Carter could see just a few feet ahead of him, and could discern no detail from the chamber itself.

"Cross this threshold, and you will become one of us," Hayden said. "Enter the darkness, my friend, and walk with us behind the shadows."

TWENTY-TWO

DANFIELD FEDERAL PENITENTIARY
NORTH COSHOCTON, OH

Diana had never been so relieved to exit a building as she was when she finally passed through the gates of Danfield Prison, twelve very long hours after she'd entered it. Kendrick noticed the change in her demeanor as they left. In all the years he'd known her, she'd never looked the way she did when they walked out of that bleak concrete fortress.

He sat next to her in the backseat as Agent Porter drove them to their motel.

"Flight's at seven tomorrow morning," she said. She ignored the fact that he was leaving the front passenger seat vacant to be next to her. "I want to review everything again at the motel. Then we're on the road to the airport at five a.m. sharp."

Kendrick acknowledged her plan with nod. She kept staring straight ahead.

"You okay?" he asked.

She didn't respond.

"Hey," he said. "You're going zombie on me? What's wrong?"

Diana rolled her eyes.

"None of this shit makes any sense. Seventy-something year-old con walks out of a high security facility? Leaves his cellmate to mark up the walls, in blood for the most part. Then his prints show up hundreds of miles away at the oddest crime scene ever documented, all in the space of a day?"

"I know, this is one for the books," Kendrick said.

"It's not just that. We were talking about this yesterday. Luther Vayne was a predator who targeted women and children exclusively. All of his victims fit exactly the same profile. Now, he's killing middle-aged men? Doesn't add up, serial killers are highly routine-oriented. They change their patterns like a tiger changes its stripes."

"There's a pattern here, there's always a pattern—you taught me that. Just gotta find it. Gotta get in his head, right?" Kendrick said. "Figure out this Sothoth and Azathoth shit."

"I know. But this one, he's…"

"What?"

"What the hell did he do to that Weaver kid?"

Her phone rang before Kendrick could answer. It was Ariadne.

Diana bypassed the greeting, and Ariadne didn't mind.

"You got anything?"

"I just got some more files this morning, N.Y.P.D. this time," Ariadne answered. "The Whitfield murders."

"Oh right, the father was a Circuit Court Judge?" Diana said. "If I remember he was a guy they were talking about as a possible Supreme Court nominee back in the day."

"That's him," Ariadne replied. "Quit the bench not long after the murders though, went into seclusion."

"Anything interesting jump out at you?"

"Well," Ariadne said. "There is one thing."

Ariadne paused. Diana's patience was rubbed thin already, and she snapped.

"C'mon, spit it out, will you?"

Ariadne sighed but complied.

"He's still alive," she said.

"The dad?" Diana asked.

"Yup, and I did some checking. He lives in a retirement community in Rockland County, New York, just outside of the city. Place called Shady Meadows," she answered. "I called ahead. They're expecting you the day after tomorrow."

"Great," Diana whispered. "More field work, right Richard?"

"What's that?" Ariadne replied. "I think you dropped out for a second. Were you asking about Richard?"

"No, but since you mention it, have you heard anything from him? I can't get him on his cell," Diana asked.

"No, he's not here," Ariadne said. "He left a few hours ago, I think. You got something you need to run by him?"

"Nothing that can't wait until tomorrow."

"What did you get out there?"

Diana motioned to Kendrick. He already had his tablet on.

"You got a signal?" she asked him.

He nodded and plugged in a thumb drive to one of his USB ports.

"Send the photos now if you can, we'll see what she can make of them," Diana said. Then she got back on with Ariadne.

"Kendrick's emailing you a bunch of pics from Luther Vayne's cell. There are some words in them…names maybe, we're not sure. I need you to check them out. I don't think it's anything you can just google though. You might have to get creative," she said.

Diana leaned over to look at Kendrick's screen. She scrolled through the images until she came to the one that still haunted her. Ariadne was opening the file on her computer on the other end. She let Diana know when it was downloaded.

"Take a look at the thirty-sixth photo, it's a close-up on a wall," she said.

Ariadne found it.

"What the hell is that?" she said.

"Vayne's cellmate painted it onto the cinderblocks behind his bunk—in his own blood. Ever seen it before?"

"What does that say? *Azathoth*?" Ariadne said, working through the pronunciation slowly. "No, never."

"Get me everything you can find on it," Diana said. "And another odd word to go with that…Sothoth."

"Are these names, or…?"

"I have no idea. It's…"

She stopped. Weaver's weird voice whispered in her ear.

"You still there?" Ariadne asked.

Diana snapped back.

"We're on our way to the motel right now. Kendrick will send you everything we have. Let me know what turns up on your end," she said.

"Of course," Ariadne said. "There's one more thing, I suppose it can wait…"

"What is it?"

"Not much, but while I have you, the report came back on the envelope from Vayne's inmate mail," she said. "The forensics guys scoured it, inside and out."

"They came up with something?"

"Not exactly," Ariadne replied. "Nothing huge, at least."

"I'll take anything right now."

"Well, it says here there's no DNA, no fingerprints and no fibers for analysis."

"So what *did* they find?"

"Just one interesting thing. Evidently the envelope itself is unusual."

"How so?"

"There's a serial number on the bottom. Came back to a paper supply company in Boston. It's a special order item, made for a single company—Dunwich Properties Inc."

"What's that?"

"Well here's the interesting thing," she continued. "That's a holding company for a number of subsidiaries, the most well-known of which is the Gregorian Media Group, who owns the Boston Tribune, among other things."

"As in Victor Gregorian?" Diana asked.

"Exactly, and guess which newspaper the clipping inside the envelope is from?"

"The Tribune."

"Right," Ariadne said. "I've already checked with several company outlets, but they're all giving me the run-around. No one's talking."

"How about Gregorian himself?"

"He has a bit of a reputation for being *unavailable*."

"Do you know where to find him?"

"Address is listed as right here in Massachusetts, a place called Whateley Estates, way out in the boonies, from the looks of things."

"Send me the info, we'll pay him a visit on our way back from the airport," Diana said.

"You don't seriously think Victor Gregorian has anything to do with this, do you?"

"Maybe not, but he's the big dog, right?" Diana said. "If no one else is talking, let's put the pressure on top and see if it flushes anything out."

TWENTY-THREE

WHATELEY ESTATES
WILBURTON, MA

Standing beside him in the darkness, Hayden raised his arms and his covered face.

"All honor and praise do we give to thee, O Lord."

The group filed in and gathered shoulder-to-shoulder behind them. They answered with a practiced refrain.

"Beyond the shadows, beyond the stars, beyond the edge of the cosmic sea. Lord of all that is, was and ever will be."

"Before your majesty we bare ourselves, humbled and exposed to you," Hayden continued. "Drenched in the ash of the sacred flames, burned in your holy name, we lay ourselves open to you."

Again came the joint response.

"Beyond the shadows, beyond the stars, beyond the edge of the cosmic sea. Lord of all that is, was and ever will be."

"In you we become one," Hayden said. "Thus do we cover our faces, for in your glorious shadow there are no individuals. We are all joined in you, mighty Azathoth."

"Lord of all that is, was and ever will be."

Gregorian stepped forward then, his features distinct even with his face obscured. He pointed to the heart of the chamber. All the others bowed their heads. Gregorian snapped his fingers and a series of candles ignited on their own across the edges of the chamber's vaulted ceiling. The pale light that spilled over them revealed that they had made their way into a room that resembled nothing so much as a tomb, a place that made Carter shiver merely on sight.

A three-tiered black pyramid stood against the far wall. By the macabre décor alone, he knew it was some kind of altar. The lowest level was inscribed with runes that Carter recognized as Elder Script. Like the inscriptions on the great tablet, they gleamed with a faint, blood-red hue in the wan light.

The second level was built around a tabernacle of sorts, an oblong stone box that resembled a coffin, bare of markings and polished smooth. Atop the triple dais there stood a single figure, its uncommon girth rising above a pile of skulls and femurs and ribs as though seated upon a throne of human bones.

"Let the newcomer step forward," Hayden announced.

Carter knew that he had no choice. When he stepped forward the group converged on him, dumping the soot over him until his naked flesh was covered in the cinder and ash.

"New initiate. Go to the holy of holies. Prostrate yourself before it and beg the favor of the Lord of Shadows."

Again, Carter knew there was no option but obedience. He began to step slowly toward the horrific display, urged on by the steady, echoing drums and the constant tide of humming behind.

As he neared, he began to detect a vibration in the floor and with it came a series of odd noises. First was the dry grind of stone-on-stone. A peculiar hissing accompanied it though, followed by a low, weak moan. Pressing forward despite that, he discerned that the noises were centered on the tabernacle. He focused his attentions more directly upon it. Although a massive piece of black granite, he was stunned to see that the stone box moved ever so slightly with each hint of sound from within—as if something inside was just then roused from slumber, or threatening to break out.

When he came to the foot of the altar, he was made to kneel. Katya once again accompanied him, lowering herself beside him as the drums and the low moan of the worshippers filled the chamber with a pulsating echo.

"Now, let that which is offered to the Lord of Darkness come forth," Hayden bellowed from somewhere behind.

Carter moved to lift himself from the floor, but Katya put her hand on his arm and stopped him. He looked back at her. She shook her head once, locking her sad blue eyes with his for a moment.

"Keep your head down," she said, apparently able to muster some English after all. "Do not look up until you are told. Understand?"

He nodded.

She took him by the chin.

"Understand?" she repeated, with a peculiar blend of warning and demanding.

"I understand," he replied.

"No matter what," she said.

He nodded.

Just for good measure, she helped him return to his pose of absolute prostration, kneeling and head lowered, buried in his arms before him. Behind him, he could hear the others shuffling closer, the tide of their moaning and the beat of the drums intensifying with every moment.

Carter did as he was ordered. He kept his face buried in his arms and his eyes squeezed shut. But he could still hear, and what met his ears in those moments made him tremble.

The stone-on-stone grind he'd detected earlier grew up again, much louder this time and without a doubt coming from the altar in front of him, from the sarcophagus-like tabernacle. With it came a putrid reek, as though a tight seal had just then been broken, dumping out a long-festering bilge of fetid odor. The stench of rotting flesh that fell over him soon made it hard for him to breathe. In moments he found himself nearly choking on the miasma. He wanted to lift his head, to gasp for air. But what he heard next kept his face rooted to the floor.

A growling began to rise up over the moan and the beat of the drums, and with it the hard scrape of something sharp cutting against stone. Snarls of a kind he had never heard soon followed, predatory and almost reptilian in their slithering intensity. What sounded like the flittering of a serpent's tongue and the wet gnashing of fangs slobbering with drool came next.

Then there was a scream.

It was a female voice, from dead ahead. Not a cry of fear, but even worse, Carter knew it to be a squeal of pain. More followed. Each whistle of whipping claws slicing through flesh brought a new wail of agony. Thrashing came next, the horrible sound of a body dragged and lifted and slammed from side to side, of bone shattering and flesh tearing, each new violation mixed with yelps and cries.

Still Carter kept his eyes averted, even as the smells and the echoes of torture made his gut roil, and the dry heaving in his throat threw warm bile into his mouth.

The torment did not relent. It only changed as the horrible, slow moments slid one in the next. Screaming faded into gurgling, and then the sound of ripping muscle and the squish of teeth biting into raw meat. Ravenous howls so unlike any beast or animal came with them.

Carter jumped when the first rivulets of blood touched his arms and his folded hands. The warm red fluid soon pooled before him, congealing and collecting as the horrific sounds finally began to die down.

Even then, as he once more heard the grind of stone-on-stone and the cries of torment and evil hunger faded away, he kept his face to the floor. Until a hand touched his shoulder.

"You may rise, initiate," Hayden said.

Carter forced himself up. He was shaking. His heart was racing and his stomach convulsed. His legs barely held him, quivering as he tried to come to his feet. What he saw before him did nothing to ameliorate his trauma.

The altar was slathered in crimson. Blood dripped from everything, as if sprayed by a hose. Pieces of human flesh, body parts that were barely recognizable littered the steps—a toe or a finger or a leg bone shorn of all muscle and sinew, broken across the middle. They were all that remained of Katya now.

On each side of the tabernacle, two of the naked, faceless minions struggled to secure the heavy stone lid. A green-black tentacle slithered out from the partially open top. Its spiny end was a mouth of sorts, dripping in blood and still chewing what appeared to be a hunk of human leg. The supplicants wrangled the kraken-claw and forced it back into the tabernacle, promptly sealing back inside the rest of whatever had just then emerged—and from the sounds coming out of the coffin, it did not wish to return to that isolation.

Once they were finished, and Carter managed to steady himself on his feet, Gregorian came to his other side. Flanked by the two men, he stared at the steaming, dripping altar in stunned silence.

"You must now beg the favor of Azathoth," Hayden said. "Place yourself upon the altar, climb to the crest and swear fealty."

Certain now that he faced no choice, Carter did as ordered. He slogged through the blood in his bare feel, once again kneeling upon the altar itself. Fully upon the platform now, it was the highest of the three levels that began to draw his attention. Above him, a gruesome countenance slowly came into view. Dripping in blood like everything else, the ghastly features revealed themselves one by one as he slowly climbed to the top, illuminated only by the pale glow of thin, flickering candles.

The head was of a conical shape, vaguely cephalopod in character. Unlike any squid or octopus however, the cone was warped and uneven; the edges appeared to be fringed by rows of serrated teeth.

Huge bulging eyes wrapped themselves around the sides of it like a pair of bloated parasites, glassy and black and betraying no hint of any other color or feature. Empty and soulless but somehow alive, glaring back at him with a sense of consciousness—or intelligence. There was nothing beneath them that could be regarded as a face, rather more a cascade of horrid flesh. A swarm of fat tentacles seemed to writhe and twist like a nest of worms, stretching down the entire length of the beast and brushing against the hairy knuckles of its massive claw-like feet.

Behind the squatted creature and growing out from its carapace were two webbed, bat-like wings; spiny and bony and covered by fine bristles of fur that shimmered in the candle light.

Carter's eyes burned the more he gazed upon it, an involuntary response to the unease the figure stirred in his gut. Little by little his movement grew stunted, until his progress was reduced to the barest shuffling. He was suddenly self-conscious even of that, sweat mixing with Katya's blood dripping from his brow.

When he finally closed the gap enough to come face-to-face with the beast, he was once again shocked, but for an altogether different reason. The figure which, from a distance had seemed constantly shifting its pose in long, languorous movements now appeared, upon closer inspection, to be merely a statue. Though it was not at all clear from what variety of stone the carving was hewn, it was undoubtedly something uncommon given the sheen of reflected light that almost suggested a liquid consistency to the piece.

"This is Azathoth?" he stammered.

Hayden laughed from behind him, as though amused by the ignorance of a child.

"Hardly," he answered. "Though the power this being represents far eclipses anything contemplated by the caricatures held up for worship by the ignorant masses of our world."

As if to echo the sentiment, the tabernacle rattled and shook itself yet again, and the minions behind once more took up their chant.

"This is what we wish to summon?" Carter asked.

Hayden shook his head.

"No, this is but a messenger," he answered. "This is a herald of the One Who Will Come, the keeper of the way, the guardian of the gate between the worlds."

Carter recognized the phrase, from verses he had once heard his old professor whispering, half-mad, over ancient texts.

"Sothoth," Carter said. "You speak of Yog Sothoth."

"Gamaliel was wise teacher indeed," Gregorian said. "It is true, Yog Sothoth is the way, the gate-keeper to the Other Side. Which is why we must prepare, for you to recite the rites you have transcribed and for us to join together in the ritual to open the gate."

"This really is all true. *Every word of what Gamaliel taught me was true,*" he said, still astonished.

"Exactly as you were instructed," Gregorian replied. "But that is merely the beginning. For even he that we summon, as powerful and incomprehensible to our minds as can be imagined, he too is but a servant, a loyal follower of the true High Lord.

"Sothoth opens the way," Carter echoed.

"He that we seek spans the gulf between all time and all space. He in whom all is one, beyond all that can be seen and known, the fulcrum of primal chaos that is the fountain of all things," Gregorian said.

"Azathoth," Carter whispered.

"Of him there can be no depictions, no statues or poor representations in stone or bronze, for to gaze upon Azathoth is to lose yourself to eternity."

"Like Gamaliel," Carter whispered.

"Now you understand, and now I trust you may be cautioned to avoid the fate he suffered," Gregorian said. "For if I may paraphrase the philosopher of which I am most fond, *take care that you should stare too long into the abyss, else it will soon begin to stare back at you.*"

Carter shivered. He ran his hands through his blood-soaked hair, down to the back of his neck, now drenched in cold sweat.

"I don't think Nietzsche meant it literally," he said, barely above a whisper.

Gregorian laughed.

"Behind the darkness out there lies the source of all wisdom, all power. All the answers are there, waiting for us to find them," Carter said.

"Beyond anything mankind has ever imagined," Gregorian answered.

Carter looked back at Gregorian, and at the altar. What had once looked horrific seemed now somehow transcendent, almost magical. He lowered his head, kissed the blood-soaked statue and whispered the prayer of fealty chanted by the others.

"Beyond the shadows, beyond the stars, beyond the edge of the cosmic sea. Lord of all that is, was and ever will be."

TWENTY-FOUR

BUDGET INN MOTEL
COSHOCTON, OH

She had tossed and turned for hours. Diana Mancuso had never been able to sleep well in motel rooms.

Fatigue wasn't the issue. She was dead tired. It was something about the environment, the strangeness of the room. The lingering smell of cleaning products in the bathroom, the stale odor of *something organic* baked into the wallpaper and the carpet and the sheets. Bed should be a sanctuary, a refuge. No rented room ever seemed to fit the bill.

Checking the clock radio on the bureau every fifteen minutes didn't help. Neither did looking at her phone each time, just to check if the two clocks agreed. They always did. The pale red glow of the digital numbers ridiculed her, ticking off the minutes in a mindless, cruel succession.

It was maddening. Trapped in some groggy limbo, too exhausted to get up and too uncomfortable to fall asleep.

Hours passed. The stream of headlights from cars passing outside her window weakened. There was always a crack in the curtains, no matter how she tried to close them. But as one day passed into the next, midnight coming and going without anything more than a glance, the cars stopped passing. Then there was just the moon.

After a while, fatigue finally overcame anxiety. Troubled thoughts blurred. Worries faded. Until she drifted away.

«««—»»»

Her arm snapped toward the nightstand. She knocked the glass of water off the table. It spilled and shattered. Her hand found the butt end of her forty caliber Smith & Wesson on the nightstand. She whipped it out of the shoulder holster. It met her other hand in a practiced grip, pointed at the intruder.

"You have been ordered to find me," he said, every word both hissing and echoing within the cold room. "I will save you the trouble. You need not look any further."

Her breath condensed as she breathed. She had fallen asleep in a warm motel room. She had awakened in a meat-locker.

"Fuck you," she said. "Let me see those fucking hands!"

Adrenaline kept her from shivering. This couldn't be happening. It couldn't be real. Luther Vayne could not be in her room.

But there he stood.

She couldn't see well in the dim. But what she could discern from the shadows challenged her to deny it.

He was standing next to the television just beyond the foot of her bed, only a few feet away. The door was shut tight. The chain lock and lever were still in place. The break in the curtains, so annoying only a short while earlier, was now an asset. Light from outside sliced a triangle of illumination through the dim. The glow lit Vayne's horrific face and the top of his shoulders.

"I said hands!" she repeated.

"Of course," Vayne said, raising a pair of tattooed palms outward. His hands were uncommonly long. The fingers were thin and skeletal. Tipped with pointed yellow nails, they flexed like spider's legs, each one moving to its own purpose. "You may see any part of me you wish."

"Keep your mouth shut! Not another fucking word," she spat back.

Diana was up on her knees now. She kept the forty caliber pointed as she shifted herself off of the bed. She had to sidestep the broken glass and the water that was already crystallizing into ice on the carpet. Her feet were bare.

It was so cold.

Her attention was focused straight ahead, but her senses had kicked into overdrive. She was immediately aware of every detail of her surroundings—and they terrified her.

The heater under the window was encrusted with frost. Icicles dripped in frozen stalactites from the ceiling. She heard teeth chattering somewhere in the distance. She heard someone laughing. Whispering her name and whispering something else.

Azathoth commands it.

Then something touched her. From behind. Cold fingers caressed her spine. Her muscles seized. She could not turn. The touch slithered further down her back.

"No need for foul language, young lady. I have not been impolite to you," Vayne said. "The obvious intrusion notwithstanding."

"You're in my fucking room!"

She was standing opposite from him now. The cadaverous, invisible hand reached the small of her back. Tears began to form in her eyes, obscuring her view.

"I realize it is late. I am sure you understand, given my current situation I am not in a position to call during regular hours," he answered.

"What did I say?" she said. "Just shut the fuck up and keep your hands where I can see them, old man."

She could still command her voice, and she had no intention of relinquishing that power. It was all she had. The icy, unseen fingers rolled over her shoulder, and brushed across her cheek. They wiped a tear away. She almost broke down. She was on the verge of hyperventilating. Her skin was burning from the cold. It was starting to go numb.

He did not comply with her order, lowering his hands until they vanished in the darkness.

"I said keep those fucking hands…"

She didn't finish. She couldn't.

"I understand what you are doing, but it is both unnecessary and unwise," he said. "To that end, I have come to warn you."

Luther Vayne stepped closer to her, somehow staring at her without any eyes. Every movement he made seemed somehow backwards, disjointed and erratic. His presence was almost holographic, there and yet not there; solid and yet ghostly.

"Hold it right there," she ordered. "Not another step."

He paused.

"As you wish," he answered.

"What do you want from me?" she demanded.

"I want nothing from you. As I said, I have come to warn you."

"About what?"

"You cannot stop me," he continued. "My work is very nearly done. This will all be at an end soon."

"What will? What do you mean?"

"I must fulfill the commands of Azathoth," he said.

"That means nothing to me," she replied.

"So it should remain," he answered.

"You can't scare me off, if that's what you're trying to do. That goes for all of us," she said. "We're not going to stop hunting you—ever."

He smiled.

"I understand the dictates of your masters. I too must obey the powers that compel me. That is not the purpose of my warning to you. Your efforts are of no concern to me. You can do nothing to impede my work."

"Then what do you want?"

"Your task is not merely futile," he answered. "To continue down the path you are now following is to court madness, and horrors the likes of which you cannot imagine. Go no further."

"Fuck you," she said, ignoring his words entirely. "You really are insane if you think we'd ever just give up, and let you get away with all this, I swear to fucking God."

Vayne seemed to snicker just a little. He edged closer to her again.

"Now, now Diana," he hissed. "We both know you do not believe in God."

He stepped even closer. He reached his hand out close to touch the end of the pistol.

Diana fired.

The muzzle flash erupted in the dark room. Hot smoke churned in the frozen air. The gun recoiled. The percussion effect deafened her for a moment. She steadied her hand, and fired again. Another ear-splitting report concussed her head. Another muzzle flash blinded her.

Then she did it again. And again.

She opened her eyes.

There was nothing,

No smoke. No blood, no carnage. No Luther Vayne.

She was in bed. The room was warm. Sunlight peeked through the curtains. The clock radio was flashing 7:00 am, and with each flash the alarm blared. She shivered as a chill crept along her back. *It was only a nightmare*, she told herself.

Then she felt the trail of a half-dried tear lingering on her cheek.

DAY SIX

"By the dawn of what scholars now call 'civilization' there were already thousands of much older, well-developed traditions in existence, most of which were subsequently lost or corrupted by those who came after. Our efforts have sought to unravel those later changes, to see through the mythology and to peel back the layers of time. What we found was nothing short of startling. Without exception, every one of these ancient devotions can be traced back to a common root—a founding element that all of them assert was not of this Earth."

"Before the Gods"
Professor Phillipe Gamaliel
Unofficial Translation from the
French Language Ed., 1989

Still their purpose was opaque.

It had been days upon days now that he'd lay there. He had no idea how long. No release, no respite. Some water poured on his face was his only daily sustenance, forcing him to catch as much as he could in his dry mouth. His bodily functions had betrayed him already, his bowels and his bladder releasing involuntarily until he could no longer even pretend they were his own.

His belly was empty. It had growled mercilessly for the first few days, until settling into a kind of passive surrender that no longer even craved food. In fact, after a while the very thought of it sickened him.

Even that soon paled by comparison, as a new round of torment began, and his very conception of pain was replaced forever. Cut and sliced and burned away.

Now when they removed his hood, he said nothing. He was beyond argument, beyond anger. Even if that had not been the case however, the moment his vision cleared from a hazy, dim blur, he'd have had no more use for words. Only terror.

Looking down across his naked frame, he finally saw the fruits of all that labor. It was much as he'd suspected, judging by his other senses. But to see it, laid out and vibrant across his own skin, was another matter altogether.

Beside the altar stood a massive obelisk. Across its nine-sided face lay line after line of ancient, inscrutable text. Now those symbols were etched onto his own skin. The acolytes had stenciled line upon line of text upon him, copying out the bizarre inscriptions directly from the old tablet. Each row was perfectly ordered and filled with hundreds upon hundreds of figures that he did not recognize. They were shapes, symbols of some type, he imagined. Triangles, slashes and combinations of the two made up most of them, along with ovals and a few more complex designs.

Still he had no idea why. Why had they inscribed his flesh with markings of that ancient script?

He did not have long to wait before an answer did finally come. A horrible, brutal reply to a question he had not even dared to ask.

The woman nearest to him no longer held a large blade or a thin stylus. Instead, she now moved toward him with an item that was something of a cross between the two, a scalpel of sorts that would not have been out of place in hospital. But this was no place of healing, he very well knew, and the use to which it was now put brought a scream to his throat.

She cut into him with the cold blade. The slice opened his flesh. That spurred an unrestrained peel of agony from his lips and brought tears to his eyes. She did more than simply cut however. Under her guidance, the scalpel sliced in a careful pattern, moving in one direction and then another, each time sawing another tiny, vicious wound into his skin and the soft muscle below.

His head jerked and yanked side-to-side, howling between gasps for breath. When he finally managed to find the strength to lift his neck, he peered down at the cruel surgery. His mind reeled at the sight.

The acolyte was tracing the outlines of the ink, cutting into his skin at every angle and marking. That was when he finally realized, the massive task of writing upon him was no end in itself. It was merely a prelude to a far more horrific task. They had taken days merely outlining, preparing the way for the path of the knife—for ten thousand tiny cuts to come, on every surface of his naked frame.

Still that was not enough.

With each symbol carved into his broken flesh, another attendant soaked up the blood. Yet a third brought forth an even worse implement, an iron poker, the end glowing orange-red and the tip burning white-hot.

The smoldering point seared the cuts in his skin, sending wave after wave of unspeakable agony through his bones, and calling up screams from his deepest gut that thundered until he shouted himself hoarse. Then he merely mouthed the agony all the same.

The work of cutting and branding however, went on unabated. He was a large man, and there was a great deal of him that needed to be marked for the Priestess of Azathoth.

TWENTY-FIVE

WHATELEY ESTATES
WILBURTON, MA

It was morning by the time they emerged from the depths of the sanctum. Cleaned and dressed following the black rite—purified in blood, as Hayden had promised, the Disciples of the Black Flame once more returned to the elegant sitting room. For all but one, it seemed as normal a morning as any other.

"Shall we conclude our discussions then?" Reverend Hayden asked. "It's time we got back to the central issue of this gathering."

The Disciples once again settled into their seats around the fireplace. As the wealthy recluse's servants stoked the flames within the hearth, his fellows quickly turned their attentions back to the matter at hand. Carter, for his part, took a place in a chair off to the side, admitted to the circle but reluctant to enter the conversation.

"We've had our purification," Gregorian began. "As you say, Graham, we cannot wait any longer to deal with this problem."

"Isn't the answer clear?" Hayden answered. "We must face him, and we must destroy him."

"Agreed," Armstrong said. "Just as he destroyed our brethren."

"Merciless and cruel," Hayden continued. "That is all he deserves, and it is long overdue."

Some nervous chatter followed. It was clear that the mood of the room was split. Some rallied to his call, raising a fist or a glass in solidarity. Others remained nervous or unconvinced, shifting in their seats and looking to Gregorian rather than the Reverend.

"None of us here lament those losses, those terrible crimes, more than I do," Gregorian replied. "The question is not how to exact our long-awaited retribution upon the beast Vayne. It is how best to do so."

"How else do you deal with a rabid dog?" Hayden answered, lapsing into his trademarked southern drawl. "Brothers and sisters I tell you now—you put that foaming hound-dog down. It's that simple."

"It is most assuredly *not* that simple," Gregorian said. "That it appears so to you only demonstrates that you fail to grasp the situation."

Hayden stepped back, perhaps feigning greater indignation than he genuinely felt, but communicating it effectively enough for the others.

"Failure?" he said. "You accuse me of failing to understand?"

Armstrong put her hand on his arm, as if to try to rein him in. It did not work.

"Is this the right time, Reverend?" she asked. "Shouldn't we wait until…?"

"Wait?" he replied, stepping forward with renewed purpose. "No, I dare say we've all waited quite long enough, Lauren. Have any of us considered the possibility that the real failure we should be dealing with is yours, Victor?"

Krieger appeared to take exception, and he rose to Gregorian's defense.

"What are you talking about, Rev?" he said. "This man here has never wavered. Never steered us wrong in all the years any of us have known him, not when we were children all learning from the Elders and not since the last of them died. He is the very definition of leadership, if you ask me. I should know!"

Hayden smirked.

"Well, quite frankly, no one did ask you, Jack," he replied.

Krieger got up from his seat the second the insult hit him, knocking over the end table and lunging toward the preacher on the other side of the room. Armstrong leaped to stop him just in time, blocking his path. The general yielded to her, but kept his eyes trained on Hayden.

"Petty violence solves nothing," Hayden said, scolding the man. "A lesson I see you never learned."

Krieger looked to Gregorian, who advised him to sit back down.

"I do agree with you on one score," Gregorian said, his calm demeanor intact even as he looked back to the Reverend. "Fighting amongst ourselves accomplishes nothing. We must face this threat."

"How do you suggest we do that?" Bremmer asked.

"The Convergence is nearly upon us," Gregorian answered. "That is too rare an occurrence and I have prepared for far too long to let that moment go to waste. He must not be allowed to interfere. You should all remain here for now. With our newest member of the circle ready and willing to assist us, the sacred texts are not only protected, the rites they outline can be performed perfectly. I will see to it that all of our plans proceed accordingly. When the day arrives, I will open the pathway once more. Then I will have the power to deal with Luther Vayne."

Some nods of agreement followed.

The Reverend still appeared unconvinced however. He paced back and forth, most likely for dramatic effect, scratching his chin and tapping his foot at each turn.

"Is that what this is about, Victor?" he asked. "*I will see to it. I will have the power*. Is this all about you? Need I remind you, I am the High Priest of the Disciples. Unless you wish to choose this moment to contest my leadership?"

Gregorian threw up his hands, as if disputing such an accusation were beneath him—even though he knew it was true.

"You are correct, of course," Bremmer said. "You are our leader, and you have always been a good one. We will follow you, as ever. But for just as long now Victor has been the keeper of our lore. We all trust his counsel."

"Yes, we've trusted Victor to make the proper arrangements and to prepare the way for the *big day*. We've all waited patiently since we first heard the stories, haven't we? Told to us by our mothers and fathers, loyal Disciples of the Black Flame themselves, since they pointed our eyes to the night sky, since they told us the old tales."

The others nodded in agreement, recalling their own childhood memories.

"Look to the stars, they told us," Hayden continued, in his sermon-like manner. "For one day, many years from now, the heavens will be in perfect order. Then the path across the darkness can be opened. Then Yog Sothoth can return to open the way."

The gathered bowed their heads, in reverence for the tale that was, for them, the most sacred of the canon. All but Gregorian. He merely stared back at Hayden, his eyes boiling but his calm demeanor holding steady.

"I have done just as I was tasked to do, when the last of the Elders passed away and entrusted me with the sacred texts, I have prepared everything, and I will continue to do so," Gregorian said. "But we must do it together, and it must be done right."

"By waiting?" Hayden replied.

"By going into hiding—for now," Gregorian answered.

Once more, some grumbling arose among them.

"Run away?" Hayden mocked. "Cowardice is no solution."

"It is not cowardice," Gregorian continued. "It is the only viable option."

Hayden raised a finger.

"What do you mean, the only *viable* option?" he asked.

Gregorian shook his head, looking down and away from the others.

"A figure of speech, nothing more," he said, still keeping his eyes averted.

"No, there's more to it, isn't there?" Hayden said. "I've known you for over forty years, Victor. You always choose your words carefully. What aren't you telling us?"

Gregorian looked up, but his eyes were heavy.

"There is another way, but I'm loathe to even discuss it," he said. "I dare say I'm afraid to consider it."

"Tell us," Hayden said.

"If I do, you must agree to consider my words rationally, and with all due deliberation," Gregorian said. "This is not the time for hasty decisions."

"I will do what is best for all of us,' Hayden replied. "That is all I can promise."

"Very well. We talked about the old rites and the sacred texts a moment ago," Gregorian said. "We all learned to read them as children, did we not? Only to forget what we'd been taught as we got older. So many decades later I'd bet very few of us really could read those books now."

"Except for you, Victor—and me," Hayden replied. "And of course, our newest initiate."

"What are you getting at, Victor?" Bremmer asked.

"Luther Vayne was condemned to the abyss, was he not?" Gregorian said.

"So we are told," Armstrong answered.

"Yet he returned," Gregorian continued. "He came back from the flames and the darkness of that damnation. While we do not know how or why, we do know that he came forth just as any demon does—he emerged from the gateway of Azathoth."

"We all know this. But how does it help?" Bremmer asked.

Hayden already seemed to know however, the spark of realization brightened his fat, red face. He got up from his chair.

"How many of you remember Book Seven, Verse Nine of the Sacred Texts of Fha Nha'thoom?" Gregorian asked.

"Of course, the Rites of Domination and Control," Hayden said.

There was some nodding and low chatter.

"The text that outlines the way to harness whatever entity you have summoned from the Other Side," Hayden added.

"What Valeria Thorne used to bend Sothoth to her will?" Armstrong asked.

"Yes, but any of us could wield that power, if we had the proper transliteration of the sacred text before us," Hayden said.

"To what end?" Krieger asked.

Armstrong was ahead of the others.

"Vayne came back from the Other Side," she said. "If he passed through the gates of Azathoth, you could use it to control *him*, just as the Priestess used it to corral Yog Sothoth."

Hayden beamed.

"Exactly, good sister Lauren," he said.

Hayden turned to Gregorian.

"I must say, Victor, I find it curious that you failed to mention this before now," he said. "As we all know, these texts were long ago entrusted to you, as keeper of our lore. What reason could you have had to withhold this most interesting piece of information—until now? Until it was almost too late?"

Gregorian nodded, but his face made it clear that he suffered little concern for the ire of the others, nor for any agreements between them.

"It is true, in my stewardship I have largely chosen to keep such matters confined to the shadows," Gregorian answered. "But for only the best of reasons, my friends. It was too much of a risk to permit such knowledge to escape my control."

The men and women looked around at one another; anger and frustration giving way to nervous gestures.

"We're not talking about anything escaping your control, Victor," Hayden said. "We're talking about using every weapon we possess to fight this monster. We're talking about self-defense."

"I feared you would say precisely this," Gregorian answered. "I do not recommend this path. We must remain dedicated to the course upon which we have long been set. The Convergence is only days away. We must be prepared."

"Yes, but you yourself have assured us that that proper arrangements have already been made. You merely need to hold on long enough to employ the rites, is that not correct?" Hayden asked.

"That is true," Gregorian said.

"So if one of us were to take these texts, alone perhaps, but armed against the threat," Hayden said. "That man could face the beast Vayne. Either to defeat him, or to simply hold him off long enough to insure that the Convergence Rite is not interrupted."

The others finally seemed to understand. They began to bristle at the notion.

"That man would be you?' Gregorian asked.

"If need be," Hayden answered.

"You are our chosen leader, if you wish to possess the sacred text you need say nothing more," Gregorian replied.

He placed both hands on his cane, making them wait even longer as he hobbled over to the bookcase nearest his desk. He first pulled out one of the oldest-looking volumes from the stacks, but that was not what he sought. Instead, it was soon revealed to be a clever mechanism, triggering the opening of an old fashioned hidden shelf behind the one presented for common view.

Lining the inner shelf was a collection of old volumes that looked to have been untouched for years, the leather bindings all coated in a thin layer of dust. Gregorian fiddled with them before producing one of them and drawing it forth. As the Reverend had mentioned, it was marked with Roman numerals as the Seventh Book in a series.

Set on a mantle directly above the volumes, put in place and evidently left there for many years, just as the books had been, were two elegant daggers. The hilts were carved out of ivory in the shape of a sea serpent with a curved and spiky tail. The blades were long and forged in the *kris* fashion, with seven distinct waves over the length of the steel.

"I believe this is what you seek," he said, freely handing the tome to Reverend Hayden.

The book was ancient. Its spine was bound with brass hinges and rusted iron rivets. The cover was a peculiar kind of leather, a deep burgundy with veins of darker red struck through it. Green verdigris had crept out from the binding. Black splotches and stains blackened every side. Elder Script runes were stamped across the facing.

Hayden received the book as if it were a newborn child, taking it in his arms and opening it gently. The pages were thick vellum, yellow-brown and tattered along the edges. They stank like spoiled eggs and mold. He leafed carefully through the crisp old pages, drinking in the musty odor as well as the ancient words printed on its sheets.

"And the knives?" Armstrong asked.

"The Daggers of Dagon," Gregorian answered, cradling them next in his hands with just as much care as he had employed with the text. "Blessed by the Priestess and consecrated with the blood of Vayne himself. To enact the rite, you must bind the entity to some earthly object. These daggers are among the only such weapons that can be used for that purpose."

Armstrong took them, looking them over in awe.

"So you see, I conceal nothing," Gregorian said. "We are all Disciples of the True Lord, and we should remain united now more than ever."

"I will take this," Hayden said. "These will be our weapons."

Gregorian prickled.

"Do you have a problem with that, Victor?" Hayden said.

The billionaire sighed.

"These volumes are our greatest treasures, passed down to us by the Elders and to them by their Elders. Here rests the gathered lore of the generations who worshipped the Old Ones and the Outer Gods. They are, quite simply, priceless," he said.

"What are you saying, that you refuse to let me have this?" Hayden said. "What game are you playing, Victor? This is the only weapon we have against the beast and you're trying to keep me from taking it?"

Gregorian raised his one good hand as if in defense.

"I did not say that," he replied. "I merely suggest that this volume itself is irreplaceable. There is, however, another way. If you will allow."

Hayden put down the text.

"What is that?" he asked.

"I expected that this might one day become an issue. To that end, many years back I commissioned our old friend Gamaliel to produce new transliterations from the original texts. Happily, it was one of the tasks he did manage to complete before his tragic demise."

"So there is a copy?" Hayden replied.

"There is, and it is both a copy of the text and a transliteration for ease of use," Gregorian said. "If you are to take a volume from me, to confront the beast, I beg of you, take that instead."

Hayden considered for a moment.

"Let me see it," he finally said.

Gregorian waved at Carter, who scanned the second shelf of the internal bookcase. There he looked over several newer texts all inscribed with Gamaliel's familiar handwriting. He read the bindings until he found the one Gregorian referenced. He took it out, and with the billionaire's permission, handed it to Hayden.

"This text is a perfect copy," Gregorian said. "If you must do this, please use it instead, for if something…if anything were to happen…"

Hayden didn't seem to be paying attention to him anymore, enrapt with the newer book in his hands.

"But my offer stands," Gregorian said. "You should all remain here with me. Here we will be safe until the appointed hour arrives. In the meantime, we may take the time remaining to prepare ourselves for the awakening of Lord Azathoth, and for the long-delayed return of his servant."

Still Hayden did not reply. When he finally looked up, his face had turned confident, and his eyes were gleaming.

"I'm not staying," he said. "With this text, with these weapons, I can face Luther Vayne—and I will. No more running away. No more hiding and no more cowering."

"What are you saying?" Bremmer asked. "You're breaking the Circle?"

"You need not come with me. Stay with Victor if you wish. I am facing the demon head-on. Those who wish to follow me are welcome to join me—in fighting for what we believe in."

He began to walk toward the door.

"Who is with me?" he asked.

After a moment of quiet consideration, Lauren Armstrong walked to his side, daggers in hand. The Reverend put his arm around her.

"You're not going to try to stop them?" Krieger complained.

Gregorian nodded.

"We all must walk our own path to Azathoth," he said, before turning to Hayden and Armstrong. "You are life-long brothers and sisters of the Black Flame. Should you choose to remain you are welcome, if not I wish you good fortune in your endeavors."

Hayden merely shook his head. With Armstrong in tow they both walked out, leaving the rest of the Disciples behind.

The remainder began to take their seats once again. As he went to sit however, Carter felt a hand grab his shoulder. It was Victor Gregorian.

"The time has come for you to depart as well—for now," the billionaire told him.

Carter stammered.

"But I thought…"

"That you were inducted into our circle?" Gregorian replied. "And so you have been. But your role to play in the events to come is a special one, as we have already discussed. That is why you have been brought into the fold."

Carter looked around. The others were all looking back at him, some even glared at him as though he had already over-stayed his welcome.

Gregorian faced him, turning him so that he looked right at the deformed man's rather unsightly face.

"I want you to return home. To your job and to your life," Gregorian said. "I want you to return as if nothing has changed—although you know very well that *everything* has changed."

"I do," he said.

"You will be called upon when your services are next required," Gregorian said. "In the meantime, take this text with you."

He handed Carter the old tome, bound in brass and aged leather. The book he had declined to give to Hayden only moments earlier.

"You'll need a new transcription now, I take it?" Carter asked.

"No, you are to commit this to memory," Gregorian replied.

"You want me to memorize this? What for?" Carter asked.

The billionaire leaned in closer to him, whispering in his ear for a long moment before they both separated. When he turned to bid a brief farewell to his new comrades, all the color had gone out of Carter Shaw's face.

TWENTY-SIX

COOLIDGE CORNER NEIGHBORHOOD
BROOKLINE, MA

After having been released by Victor Gregorian, Carter quickly found himself escorted out of the mansion. Logan, of course, did the honors. The big Brit had been waiting for him right outside of the library, apparently having been informed of his exit ahead of time.

Ushered away with even more deference and courtesy than he had been shown on the way in, Carter followed along without question. After what he had seen in the last twenty four hours—*and what he hadn't seen*—he couldn't think of much to say.

The familiar black Lincoln was waiting in the driveway, already running with the driver at the ready. Logan said nothing on the way out. Carter didn't care. Not only did he not mind the VIP treatment, small talk now seemed both unnecessary and irrelevant.

He simply opened the rear passenger side door, allowed Carter to enter and then closed it behind him. A tap on the roof was all the signal he gave to the driver, who started off without a word.

Carter instructed the driver to return him home directly, and within moments he was back on the road, taking in the scenery as the Town Car wound its way through the tree-lined roads of central Massachusetts. He sat in silence for the rest of the car ride, replaying everything from the strangest day of his life over and over in his head.

Once the driver left him at his doorstep, again without so much as a word, he stood on the stoop for a long while before going inside. Again, he just stared—at the door, at the window, at the knotted old maple tree next to the street lamp. Everything was the same as it was the day before.

And nothing was the same. He'd seen through blood and fire and shadow; now he knew that nothing would ever be the same again.

«‹‹—››»

He only stayed in his apartment for a few minutes. Long enough to walk around the place once, still half-dazed, before he remembered. Maura. His son. The basketball accident.

He pulled his phone out of his pocket, scrolled down through his contacts and dialed. It rang and rang. No one picked up. When it went to voicemail he hit "end" and then tried a second time.

Same result. He grabbed his keys. He hustled down to the garage, got in his beat-up old hatchback and drove off. The twenty minutes it took for him to get down Commonwealth Avenue through all the student foot traffic at BU seemed more like an hour. Once he was by Kenmore Square heading out of the city the congestion let up, but the endless series of stoplights on Beacon Street that led over towards Brookline slowed him down again. He cursed the Green Line every time a train cut him off on the surface tracks.

He turned off the main road at Coolidge Corner and by the time he pulled up at Maura's, a restored Victorian tucked away on a tree-lined road just off Harvard St., he was desperate. He'd tried to call three more times—and each one had gone unanswered.

Carter couldn't find a spot so he parked illegally, right in front of a hydrant a few houses down. He jogged up the steps to the front porch and banged on the door. A moment later, his ex-wife Maura finally answered.

"Carter?" she began. "What the hell are you doing here?"

"You didn't answer your phone," he said, almost as an accusation.

"Well *hello* to you too," she replied.

"Why didn't you answer? I've been calling all morning."

She shrugged and threw up her hands.

"Must have left my phone in my purse, you know how I am with that thing. What's so important anyway?"

"*You* called me," he replied.

"Yeah, yesterday," she said.

"Are you going to let me in, Maura?"

She stepped aside and allowed him to enter.

"Tyler's fine, if that's what this is all about. I might have been exaggerating on the message a little bit, okay? Turns out his arm's not broken. We spent four hours at the E.R. last night to find that out, but what can you do? I was gonna call you later."

"I'll pay for all of it," he said. "Anything you need."

"Are you sure you can…" she asked, a little sheepish.

"I said *anything*," he replied, with an air of confidence he had rarely used in their time together. "How's he doing?"

"He's in back, playing with Bobby from next door."

Carter came in just far enough to see through the large French doors at the back of the living room. He could see his son running around with the neighbor boy, perfectly fine just as he hoped.

"Are you okay? You look a little pale," Maura said.

"Thanks, nice to see you too," he answered.

"You know what I mean," she replied. "I'm just surprised to see you. You don't have him until the weekend."

"I know," he said, just watching the boys play in the yard. "Truth is—I've never been better."

He just kept looking out the back window, watching his son run around with his friend. She waited a long moment before pressing him.

"Carter, is something wrong?" she asked. "This isn't like you—dropping in, saying you're fine. *You're never fine*."

He didn't reply. He just kept watching his son.

"Hey, c'mon, snap out of it," she said. "You're starting to worry me here."

Finally he turned away, back toward her. He breathed deep and long and then put his hand on hers.

"Nothing's wrong," he said. "Nothing at all is wrong."

He looked back toward his son yet again.

"I just wanted to see," he said.

"See what?"

"Tyler. You," he said.

"There you go again," she said.

"I want to tell you, from here on out, if you need anything—I mean anything at all, you just call. Understand?"

She nodded, obviously puzzled. Carter didn't care. He'd expected that reaction.

"This should cover the E.R. visit, plus a little extra just for you two," he said, handing her a check from his shirt pocket. It was already filled out. She gasped when she read it.

"Ten thousand?" she muttered. "Are you sure you can…?"

He nodded.

"I gotta go," he said.

"Don't you want to see Tyler?"

He took one more gaze into the backyard.

"I just did," he said. "Let him play. He's gonna be fine. From now on, we're all going to be fine."

"I'll tell him you came by," she said.

"Thanks."

Just as he was about to leave, Carter stopped. He turned, and kissed his ex-wife on the forehead.

"What was that for?" she asked.

"For everything," he said, as he made his way back toward the front door.

"See you later, Carter," she said.

He looked back over his shoulder as he walked out.

"Goodbye, Maura," he said, before walking out the door.

TWENTY-SEVEN

WHATELEY ESTATES
WILBURTON, MA

Whateley Estates was not an easy place to find.

Even the Bureau car's G.P.S. got lost, sending Diana and Kendrick off in the wrong direction three times before she finally stopped at a roadside Citgo station to ask for directions. To make matters worse, the man in the Red Sox cap and grimy overalls that worked there pretended to have never heard of the mansion. It was only after pulling out her Bureau ID that he scrunched up his hat in his hands, acted like he hadn't really heard her the first time and gave in.

They needed another half hour after that to pull up to the outer edge of the property, the main entrance blocked by the massive stone towers and iron gates. Although the house itself was set way back, perched on the hill and surrounded by a small forest, the trees were all winter-bare. She could see tall gables and a snow-swept roof in the distance.

The initial response from the call box indicated that further clearance would be necessary before granting them admittance, and that was followed by a second voice who merely told them to wait longer. Diana was just about to lose her patience when a phalanx of armed guards appeared from the direction of the mansion. Logan was at their lead. They fanned out at his direction around the perimeter of the gate as the Brit stepped up to examine the F.B.I. credentials of both agents. Even after that, they had to wait for yet another round of clearance before being buzzed in and escorted up to the house.

It didn't end there.

Rather than being ushered into the front door, they were instead directed toward a side entrance off to the far right of the driveway. There they were shown a door that looked like a servant's entrance. As the guards remained behind them, Janet opened it from the inside, offered a brief welcome and showed them in. There was only a sparsely furnished foyer waiting for them, old wood paneling and two simple chairs.

Janet insisted on being briefed about the purpose of their visit. Although Kendrick at first refused, Diana overruled him, and in the interest of comity, gave Janet a quick and somewhat abbreviated explanation of what Ariadne had told her.

They were asked to wait as she departed. It was another ten minutes before they were greeted again.

When the inner door opened next, it was Victor Gregorian himself who hobbled in to meet them. Dressed as usual in his silk robe, he winced with every step. But his distorted face was beaming with a broad smile.

Too broad, in Diana's opinion.

"Apologies, apologies," he began. "I wish you had called ahead, this has been a particularly busy day. Terribly sorry to keep you both waiting."

Diana and Kendrick smiled politely.

"Janet tells me you are from the F.B.I., Special Agents Mancuso and Kendrick, and that this is in regard to some kind of a letter, do I have that correct?"

"You do, sir," Diana replied.

"Well then, what is it that I can help you with?" Gregorian asked. "As you are probably aware, I head several very large corporations, with literally thousands of employees. I do try to keep abreast of what goes on in my name, but I must confess that I cannot be aware of everything."

"With all due respect, sir," Diana said. "We don't need to ask you about everything, just one very specific thing."

Gregorian's beaming, faux-smiled melted into a truer, sly grin. He gave Diana a wink.

"Of course," he answered. "So this letter, I'm to understand that it was received by an inmate at a Federal Prison?"

"An inmate who escaped right after he got it," Kendrick said, betraying less patience than his colleague.

"You're wondering if my people had anything to do with that?"

"Your people…or you," Kendrick said, in a sharp tone.

Gregorian answered with a chuckle. Even if he had something to hide, Diana realized, he was too good of a liar to give anything away.

"I've agreed to take time out of my schedule to meet with you both as a courtesy, but if you're only here to level baseless accusations, then I will simply refer you to my legal team," he replied.

Diana stepped in.

"No need for that sir," she said. "We're really just hoping you could shed some light on this situation."

"Unfortunately, I'm not certain that I can," he replied.

"All due respect. You have no idea why someone in your organization would send one of your envelopes, with a news clipping from one of your papers, to one of the most dangerous inmates in the Federal system?" she asked.

Gregorian nodded slowly, clasping both hands on the silver head of his cane.

"I think I know what's happening here," he said.

Diana smiled.

"What is that, sir?" she answered.

"You've been sent on something of a wild goose chase," Gregorian replied.

"How is that?"

"This envelope that's causing you so much consternation, this was one that my office uses, manufactured to our specifications, and it contained a clipping from a newspaper owned by one of my companies, yes?"

"That's right," Diana said.

"Well don't you see what this is?" he asked. "Clearly someone has gone to great lengths to make it *appear* that I have some involvement here."

"A frame up?" Kendrick replied, making no effort to disguise his disbelief.

"You don't reach the position that I occupy without making enemies," Gregorian answered. "Trust me, there are many people who would celebrate my ruin. Don't you think this would be a fine way to go about just that?"

"So you are saying this is a set up?" Diana replied.

He tapped his cane and smiled, almost as if he felt sorry for them.

"Far be it for me to tell you how to do your job, Special Agent Mancuso, but please give this some thought, would you?" he said. "Don't you think that if I did want to do the kind of thing you're talking about, cluing in some murderer to his next victim, that I would use my own newspaper and my own company's envelope to do so?"

Diana sighed and looked back to Kendrick. She was as frustrated as he was, but did a better job of hiding it.

"This is an attempt to cast aspersions upon me and my company, nothing more," Gregorian continued.

Diana was about to press him further, but he never gave her the chance.

"Now, if you'll forgive me, as I believe I noted earlier, this has been a very busy day. I've been away from my business for as long as I can allow," Gregorian said. "Please understand, I have every desire to assist your investigation in any way that I might be able. If you'd be so kind as to leave your contact information with Janet, I assure you that I will have my people look into this, and the moment we uncover anything useful to you, I will be sure to have it forwarded on to the F.B.I. without delay."

Before either Diana or Kendrick had a chance to so much as respond, Victor Gregorian turned and exited the way he'd come. Janet came in after him, ready to show them out.

«««—»»»

They walked back down the long, winding driveway slower than they needed to, Diana taking note of the small fleet of luxury sedans parked in front of the house.

"He's lying," Kendrick said.

"Of course he is," she replied.

"That doesn't bother you?"

She looked over the vehicles one last time as they made their way down the hill.

"See all those cars?" she said. "There's obviously some kind of a meeting going on in there. Some kind of business. He wasn't lying about that."

"But he was lying to us."

"Even so, he gave us what we needed, didn't he?"

"Which is?"

"We know he's involved," she said. "That's enough for right now."

"Wait, how's that?"

"We never told him who the inmate was or what the envelope made Vayne do," she said. "But he knew that already."

It dawned on Kendrick just then.

"*Cluing in some murderer about his next victim*," he said. "Now what?"

"We keep our eye on him, and we see where it leads," she said.

TWENTY-EIGHT

F.B.I. FIELD OFFICE, ONE CENTER PLAZA
BOSTON, MA

Richard Norris had to negotiate a maze of boxes, papers and files to find Diana. She was in the middle of reading something. In the chaos of the massive conference room, she didn't seem to notice him.

"Sorry I didn't see you this morning," he began.

"No problem, I ran a little errand on the way back from the airport, didn't get back here until around noon anyway. Ariadne said you called in that you were running late too," she said.

He remained stone-faced.

"I was tied up," he replied.

Diana didn't look up. She was buried in old files.

"With what?" she asked.

He groaned, and put his hands on the desk.

"Paperwork. Emails. A shit storm of media requests. Nothing worth discussing," he said. "What have you got here, any developments?"

He watched her, kept his eyes fixed as she sifted through piles of documents spread across the table.

"Not really, I've been buried in this stuff since I got back, but so far—nothing," she said.

She felt him staring at her. She tried to ignore him. He wouldn't let her.

"How was Ohio?" he asked.

She thought for a moment.

"Strange."

He seemed to know that she didn't want to talk. Nevertheless, he kept standing there. He kept talking anyway.

"How so?"

She didn't answer. Norris waited. He kept staring. But there was no way she was going to tell him.

"I'd rather not get into it," she said.

She tossed her reading glasses off of her face. They fell to the table. She rubbed her fingertips against her temples. She squinted and winced.

"Sorry, didn't sleep well," she said. "Bad dreams…I think."

Norris wasn't surprised.

"Headache?"

He was on the other side of the table when she lifted her eyes, holding a plastic bottle. She noticed the washed-out expression across his face. If she hadn't known better, she would've thought he looked worried. But that was impossible.

"Aspirin?" he offered.

"You always know when I can use a couple of those, don't you," she said.

She took the bottle and spilled a pair of white tablets into her hand. There was a half-empty Diet Coke hiding behind a stack of files that she used to drown the pills.

"Can't blame you," he said. "This kind of thing can keep you up at night. I know what you're doing for me, and I really do thank you for it."

"I hate motel rooms. And early flights. And…"

"And what?" he asked.

She frowned, breathed deep and broke eye contact.

"Nothing," she said. "Like you said, this is a crazy case."

Norris picked up a couple of papers and read the flap on a nearby box.

"You're looking through the old files?" he asked.

"They came in this morning, just after I got here. I don't think these things have been touched in forty years," she said. Her headache began to fade.

He looked over the mess of age-worn typing paper spread out across the desk and the floor and the shelves. Dusty manila envelopes lay in stacks. Binders stained with water or coffee or mold lay piled in the corners, by cardboard columns of ancient-looking boxes.

"We're not getting any closer are we?" he asked.

This time it was her turn to offer some comfort. She put her hand on his arm.

"I'm working on it," she said. "Trust me."

The moment she reached out, the instant she put her hand on his body, she second-guessed herself. Another moment and she would have held her hand back. But she didn't, and he welcomed the contact.

His mouth showed a hint of a smile. She rubbed her hand against his forearm. She wanted to say something to him, something other than procedural details and facts from old files. But she didn't.

For a moment, they just sat there. Staring at each other.

"We haven't really talked about the other day, back in D.C.," he said.

She knew what he meant.

"No, but this hasn't been a normal week," she said. "You'd just found out about your friend, I understand that. I should be the one apologizing to you."

"How's that?"

"I jumped to conclusions," she answered. "I figured the worst—for me anyway. Here you are dealing with the loss of a friend, and I'm pissed that you and your wife might have patched things up."

He put his hand on hers.

"We haven't," he said. "Julia and I, that is. We haven't patched anything up."

Her heart beat a little harder when she heard that. She hated herself for it, but at the moment, she didn't care. She looked at Norris. He looked back at her, put his other hand on her chin.

"We can't," she whispered. "Not here. We're in the middle of a fucking F.B.I. building for Christ's sake."

He kissed her anyway.

She held him off, just enough to keep his lips away from hers, but not a bit harder than that.

"If we get caught..." she whispered.

Norris looked right into her eyes.

"Isn't that thrill of it?" he asked.

She grabbed him.

"But if we did..." she said.

"We won't."

It was almost a declaration. Total confidence.

She kissed him back.

TWENTY-NINE

F.B.I. FIELD OFFICE, ONE CENTER PLAZA
BOSTON, MA

Ariadne and Kendrick came in together as Diana was buttoning her blouse. Norris was already dressed. He stood on the other side of the table, offering a moment of cover as she finished straightening herself up.

"Who the hell changed the access code?" Ariadne asked.

"What's that?" Norris replied, doing a very good job of feigning ignorance.

She was carrying more boxes with old files and did not appear to notice anything unusual. Kendrick had apparently taken up half of her bundle in his own arms and both of them were still over-loaded with reams of yellowed paper in brown cardboard.

"The access code for the outer door," she said. "It's only changed once a day. I tried to get in five minutes ago, but neither of our cards worked. Had to call Tech. They said the code was changed a little while ago. Couldn't say how."

Norris looked back at Diana, who managed to keep her smile in check.

"New policy," Norris said. "Codes will be changed every twelve hours for the duration of this investigation."

Ariadne shrugged it off. She found an empty space on a nearby folding table where she could set down the boxes. Kendrick did the same.

"So," Diana said, anxious to change the subject. "You got anything based on what we sent from Ohio?"

"I do, but it's gonna take me a second to open up and log in on the laptop," she answered. "While I'm doing that though, you might want to look at some of this old stuff in hardcopy. Came through late last night, it was sitting in storage all these years."

"What have you got?"

"Mostly background info, but you said to leave no stone unturned. Some of it's pretty interesting actually," Ariadne replied.

"Like what?" Norris asked, picking through the papers himself.

Ariadne passed a box over to him.

"His war record, for one," she said.

"Vayne was a soldier?" Kendrick asked.

Diana nodded as she poured herself a new cup of coffee.

"Yeah, a paratrooper actually, if I remember correctly," she added.

"Right," Ariadne said. "101st Airborne, served in Vietnam from sixty-seven to sixty-nine."

"Screaming Eagles," Kendrick added.

"Pretty brave guy too, from the looks of things. Won two purple hearts," Diana said.

"Okay. So he's a vet. Strong sense of duty," Kendrick said. "That could certainly play into his motivation."

"Probably saw a lot of shit over there. Maybe P.T.S.D.?" Norris asked.

Diana tilted her head.

"Maybe. Post-traumatic stress disorder manifests in lots of different ways, but they weren't as good at identifying the signs back then."

She sorted through the mess of paperwork.

"I looked at his DD-214 this morning. The information that came along with discharge papers does note some issues, but honestly there was nothing in there you'd call terribly unusual for a combat vet."

Ariadne sifted through some papers until she found another file.

"Speaking of that," she said. "We were talking yesterday about Vayne being seen by a shrink, right?"

"Yeah, he was evaluated by the court clinic for his sentencing in seventy-five."

"The full report just came through by email while I was toasting a bagel earlier."

She clicked on her laptop, and opened a file.

"You gotta see this," she said, handing the computer to Diana.

It was a scan of a much older paper, and it still bore the hallmarks of its mid-seventies origin. The old manual type-face, the blurred ink and the little imperfections scattered across it, where folds and creases in the original had left their permanent mark on all subsequent generations.

Diana read over it, clicking through to the end.

"*Evidence of fixed delusional beliefs. Probable psychotic disorder, unspecified type,*" she said, quoting the doctor's findings.

"So was he crazy or not?" Norris asked.

"Maybe just evil," Ariadne added.

"Okay, so we know he's a psychopath and we know he was a soldier," Norris said. "What about in between, after the war but before the murders? Do we know anything about that?"

Ariadne shook her head.

"Seems Vayne drifted for a while after his discharge in sixty-nine. Social security records have him spending the next few years bouncing around New England, working odd jobs, nothing substantial. Dishwasher at a greasy spoon in Hartford, did some security work after that."

"What kind of security?" Diana asked.

Ariadne frowned as she sorted through the documents.

"Nothing serious. Bouncer at a bar in Providence then some private work, *personal security* this says. Looks like maybe low level body guard type stuff, watching some rich guy's money, I guess."

"Then what?"

"Then, one day he just…drops off the map."

"What do you mean?" Norris said.

"Just what I said," she replied. "Around 1973 it's like he went into a cave and hibernated. No more tax records. No license, no rentals, no leases. Nada."

"That's not possible. There has to be something," Norris said.

Diana threw the yellowed papers down on the table.

"I'm telling you, there's jack squat. So far as we can tell, Vayne's paper trail just stops," Ariadne said. "After that he dropped off the face of the Earth."

"Until he turned himself in," Norris said.

"Yeah, but that wasn't until the autumn of 1974. We literally have no other record of him until then," Ariadne answered.

"The murders started in late seventy-three, right?" Norris said. "So we at least know where he was when those were committed."

"Sure, we can infer his movements, roughly," she said, flicking her mouse-pad and pointing them toward the larger screen against the far wall. A giant display of a U.S. map flashed across it.

"These are the locations of his murders," she continued, clicking again so that a series of glowing red dots popped up all across the face of the virtual map. "Besides Cleveland we've got Omaha, Rochester, Massachusetts, New York City, two in the District and then one each down in Texas, Florida and Louisiana, and also out in San Diego and up the coast in San Jose and San Fran."

They all marveled for a moment at the wide scope of Vayne's kill zone.

"But for the rest of the time, we have no clue," Ariadne continued. "Like I said, no driver's license or tax returns. No bank accounts. No apartment rentals, no home ownerships. Not even a car. The man was a ghost. He floated around for almost a year," Ariadne said.

"For all that time he was killing at will and leaving no traces. Then he walks into a police station and turns himself in? It doesn't make any sense," Kendrick said.

"He had psych issues at the end of the war, and he wasn't doing anything more substantial than dishwasher and leg breaker type work," Diana said. "How could he pull off that kind of disappearing act?"

"You're the profiler," Norris replied. "You're supposed to tell us that."

She threw up her hands, then turned to Ariadne.

"You said you had something based on the prison photos, right?"

"In fact I do," Ariadne answered. "But I'm gonna warn you, it's crazy weird stuff."

"How 'bout we just start at the top?" Diana said.

"Ok, but you asked for it," Ariadne said.

Diana wasn't in the mood for repartee. She stared right at her friend, and her squinting eyes left no doubt about her mood.

"Ariadne, just tell me, for Christ's sake," she answered.

"Fine, fine. But I don't know if this is going to help."

Diana inhaled as though she was about to snap at her friend. Norris pre-empted her. Despite the past few minutes, her lack of sleep had left her in a rotten mood.

"What exactly did you find?" he asked, in a much gentler tone than Diana would have used.

"The first thing I did was run the name on the wall, the one written in blood," Ariadne began. "You were right, by the way. The usual search engines weren't much help. I had to go a little deeper for this one."

"And you got?" Norris asked, obviously impatient.

"The short answer is: Azathoth is—*or was*—the name of a very old Near Eastern deity," she answered.

"So a god, then, in plain English?" Norris said.

"I've never heard of him…it…whatever," Diana said.

"Neither had I," Ariadne replied. "Like I said, Azathoth isn't well known. In fact the name barely appears in any texts that survive. Only two or three references exist in original cuneiform tablets. Those are *very old*, from the early Uruk period in Sumeria. After that the name hardly pops up at all."

"Great work Ariadne," Norris said, with a hint of sarcasm.

Ariadne ignored her boss. Diana stepped in.

"What about the other one…Sothoth, I think it was?"

"I had even less luck with that one, even tried all kinds of a variant spellings, you name it," she said. "There has only been one paper published in the last fifty odd years that mentions both of the names Azathoth and Sothoth. Nothing in the mainstream of linguistics or archaeology. Most of what I turned up, when it mentions Azathoth at all, says it was a fiction, or mistranslation, like early references to the Egyptian god Thoth, for example."

"That narrows things down a bit. What did this one paper say?" Diana asked.

"It was out of an obscure journal published in the eighties. The paper wasn't in English. I had to have it translated. Written by a guy named Phillipe Gamaliel."

"Never heard of him," Norris said.

"No one has. He was a linguist, specialized in ancient Near Eastern languages, and he was an accomplished archaeologist too. But his theories got him pretty much laughed out of the scientific community by the time the paper was published. He does mention Azathoth quite a bit though, Sothoth too. Apparently he believed that was some kind of lesser god, a messenger or herald if I recall correctly."

"Ok, so what does *he* say?" Diana asked.

"According to this paper of his, Gamaliel translated some Sumerian texts, and compared them with some Egyptian sources that supposedly pre-dated the Old Kingdom. Then he cross-referenced those with some un-translated symbols found at late Neolithic sites like Catal-Huyuk. He even matched those up with much, much older inscriptions from Dolni Vestonice. We're talking twenty-five thousand years old."

"Un-translated?" Norris interrupted. "How do you cross-reference an un-translated symbol?"

Diana had an idea.

"As in, a double star with thirteen points?" she asked.

Ariadne smiled.

"Bing! Bing! Bing!" she said. "Give that agent a prize."

"To just about everyone else these symbols remain un-translated. But Gamaliel seems to have seen a pattern in all of it. The thirteen-pointed star, for example. He found evidence of that in multiple, unrelated cultures."

"Which means what?" Diana asked.

"Damned if I know," Ariadne said. "But Gamaliel fancied himself something of a rogue, kind of an outside-of-the-box thinker. He proposed that the similarities between unknown symbols and characters in known ancient languages proved a connection between several ancient cultures, which in turn proved his theory that all of them dated back to a much earlier, undiscovered mother civilization."

Diana was intrigued, but confused.

"Fine, but how do the names of little-known near-eastern gods end up on the wall of a prison cell in Ohio?" Kendrick asked.

"No clue," Ariadne answered. "Gamaliel thought that Azathoth was some sort of a proto-deity worshipped a long time ago by his proto-civilization. Kind of a parent god to the sky gods and Earth goddesses we know from ancient literature."

"I'm still not following," Diana said.

"It seems the etymology of the name doesn't fit with any known language, so he theorized that it was a relic from this forgotten civilization that survived into historical times. He claimed Azathoth formed the basis for several ancient Near Eastern deities. For example, the Sumerian Tiamat, the Hittite Illuyanka, and the Canaanite Lotan. They all share a basic character, and a similar story. Gamaliel took that as evidence that they were all remnants of an older story that got filtered through subsequent generations."

"So which was he, a god or a goddess?" Diana asked.

"Both. Neither. Gamaliel argued that Azathoth represented the original consciousness. Neither male nor female. God nor goddess. The first power from which all knowledge flowed."

"The prime mover," Norris said.

"Gamaliel claimed it was this primary figure, lost in the shadows of a distant past, that left traces in all the cultures we know about," Ariadne said. "The source of all wisdom. The lost god of a lost civilization."

"So this is what got him black-balled?"

Ariadne smiled.

"Well, that's the rest of the story. Old Gamaliel took things a step further, you see. Strayed a bit too far off the reservation, as one of my old law school professors used to say."

"How's that?" Norris asked.

"The crux of his theory, this paper I was talking about called *Before the Gods*, was that all of our conceptions of god or the supernatural derived from Azathoth. But he didn't think they were just concepts. Gamaliel proposed that they had a basis in actual fact. That Azathoth wasn't just a theoretical myth. *He thought Azathoth was real.*"

"Excuse me?" Norris said.

"That's right. Gamaliel didn't just propose that Azathoth was some kind of archetype, or that he was the remnant of a forgotten proto-society," Ariadne continued. "He claimed that Azathoth *actually existed.* And that he was, let's say…not of this world."

"It doesn't surprise me that they laughed him out of the business, if he started to believe his own fairy tales," Diana said.

"Well, that's not quite it," Ariadne continued. "If you read his paper, it's actually very interesting. Gamaliel proposed the existence of a powerful intellect from somewhere out there. A being so far beyond human intelligence, perhaps billions of years beyond us, that it was capable not only of interstellar travel, but *inter-dimensional travel.* Something beyond time and space, so to speak."

"Okay, that is pretty out-there, I guess," Diana answered.

"If this info was floating around in the ether, it's possible that Vayne got wind of it somewhere along the line, right?" Kendrick said. "Maybe got himself fixated on this ancient god mumbo jumbo and twisted it to fit his delusions."

"Not only that, someone on the outside sent Vayne a letter targeting Roger Saxon, and marked it with that star symbol," Diana added.

"You think it was this guy?" Kendrick asked.

"Well, as long as Victor Gregorian and his people aren't talking, I'd say that'd have to be our best theory so far," Diana said. Then she turned back to Ariadne. "We need to talk to this guy, this Gamaliel."

Ariadne shook her head.

"No can do, I'm afraid," she said.

She flipped through the rest of her papers until she found a magazine with an article folded out and marked. She handed it to Diana. Kendrick read it over her shoulder.

"Fuck," he mouthed as they looked it over.

The piece wasn't a full article, but a notice posted in an academic journal from Miskatonic University. It stated that Phillipe Gamaliel was no longer employed by the institution as a professor, and that his tenure had been revoked. It went on to deny "recent claims of irregular activities."

"Any idea what kind of irregular stuff they're talking about?" Diana asked.

"I do, as a matter of fact," Ariadne said. "Seems he started to disappear for long periods on end, ignoring his classes. There were rumors. Then there was the scandal."

"Scandal?" Norris asked.

"According to some students he started to lose it about eighteen months ago. The school finally got wind of it and fired him, but before he could even clean out his office, he put a gun in his mouth and blew his brains out. This was sometime early last year."

"So if the only guy who knows all about this Azathoth shit died over a year ago, who the hell sent the letter to Vayne?" Kendrick asked.

Diana scanned the whole paper as she listened. When she got to the end, she took a look at the names under the byline.

"Hang on," she cautioned. "Who is this guy?"

Ariadne looked at the bottom of the page. There were two names listed as authors.

"Hmm, second guy was a grad student research assistant, from the look of it," she said.

"What are you thinking?" Norris asked.

"Our Gamaliel guy may be dead and buried," she replied. "But this other guy might still be around—I want to know everything we can find on him. If he knew what Gamaliel knew, and Luther Vayne knows all of that too—then he might be our missing link."

Ariadne had already started typing.

"I'm on it," she said. "You might as well call it a night. Early morning ahead for you."

"Why is that?" Diana asked.

"You've got an appointment at Shady Meadows down in New York, remember?" she answered. "I-95 traffic is always awful."

"Shit, that's right," she said.

"You want me to go instead?" Kendrick offered.

"No, I need to check on this myself," she replied.

"Don't worry," Ariadne said. "Give me a few hours and you'll have everything there is on this guy. By the time you get back tomorrow we'll have a lead—promise."

"Great," Diana said. "Call as soon as you get anything."

"Believe me," Ariadne said. "I'll hit you back the moment I dig up anything on Doctor Carter Shaw."

THIRTY

NEW BETHLEHEM EPISCOPAL CATHEDRAL
BOSTON, MA

Reverend Hayden and Lauren Armstrong had left nothing to chance. They made their way out of Whateley Estates under heavy guard from his private security team, who drove them non-stop back to Boston via an armored car that had been waiting to take them to New Bethlehem.

The Gothic Revival cathedral was impressive from the outside. One of the tallest structures in downtown Boston, it resembled a French medieval church, built in a cruciform pattern with massive façades and ornate flying buttresses topped with carvings of gargoyles and wreathed faces.

Inside the bronze double doors and the huge gate it was even more spectacular. A long gallery stretched toward the altar under a seven-vaulted nave, supported by fourteen fluted Corinthian columns, everything faced in white travertine. The high arched windows were filled with stained glass depictions of the Stages of the Cross, done in brilliant reds and purples and shades of yellow.

Polished cherry-wood pews filled the hall as far as the transepts, where the red marble floor opened to accommodate a wide choir box in advance of the dais and the pulpit. The chancel itself was housed in the lower sections of a high tower at the far end, presided over by a gleaming oak cross draped in purple and white vestments.

Once they were inside the cavernous and quite empty church, Hayden dismissed his security team. That made Armstrong gasp in protest.

"What are you doing?" she demanded.

He seemed distracted, gazing around at the interior of the cathedral as if seeing it for the first time.

"We don't need them anymore," he replied. "They can't help us against the enemy we face."

"What do you know about him? I get the feeling there are things you haven't told me," she said.

He turned. He began to pace back and forth, as was his habit when pondering. His eyes grew serious, as though he hated even speaking what he was now required to say.

"You're young. You newer initiates never had the benefit of learning from the Elders, those who knew Vayne before, and some who encountered him after. They warned us. They told us things even some of the Disciples, like yourself, do not know."

"What do you mean?"

"Our adversary is not human, not anymore. He has been to the other side, the black abyss where the Outer Gods reside."

"How did he come back?"

"That is something that no one has ever known, not even the Elders," Hayden replied. "But make no mistake, the very fact that he did so is testament to his power. What we face is a thing that somehow rebelled against the forces beyond, like some rebel angel of Lucifer's host, and fought his way back. That is no small feat. Luther Vayne may once have been a man, but he has now been twisted by the darkness of Azathoth, a cosmic storm we cannot fathom. No one truly knows what powers that corruption bestowed upon him.

"He can kill with a word. He commands the obedience of the shadows and all that lurks within them," Hayden said. "And he wants to destroy us."

Armstrong's face went pale.

"Is this really the best place for us to be right now?" she asked. "He's hunting us. He hunted Saxon and he'll track us just the same."

The Reverend looked bemused by her concern, which only exacerbated her worry.

"I do my nationally televised service from here every Sunday," he answered, rather off-handedly.

"My point exactly," she replied. "Isn't this kind of like putting out a bull's eye on ourselves? Vayne will find us here in no time."

"That's exactly what I'm hoping," he answered.

She began to follow.

"You *want* him to find us?"

"Are we not armed against him now?" Hayden replied, brandishing the *kris* daggers from his coat and handing them to her. "The Convergence is coming. In two night's time the alignment will be in place, and the path will once again be open. Vayne knows this. He wants to destroy us. He has to strike before then. Before we are too powerful even for him."

"You're choosing your own ground for the battle," she said, nodding as his premise became clear to her. "But why here?"

"This is the perfect location for our needs," he said.

"How so?" she asked. "This place is over a hundred years old."

"Call me paranoid, but I've never been one to leave things to chance," Hayden answered. "Or to Victor, for that matter. When I took over this cathedral some years ago, around the time I began doing my television mass, I had the entire place retro-fitted with top-of-the-line security measures," he said.

"For Vayne?"

"Not specifically," he said. "As you might imagine, televangelists can sometimes be just as hated as we are loved. So I had my security team install a full, state-of-the-art system. This hundred year old cathedral is now fitted with laser sensors around the entire perimeter. When they're activated nothing gets in or out without me knowing. I have motion detectors outside every window and every door, plus two dozen closed-circuit cameras all connected to a master control in the basement safe-room."

"So what do we do, just stay down there until Vayne shows up?"

"Not at all," he answered. "The entire system is linked to my cell, so I have instant access and control of every security measure in real time. Trust me, when Luther Vayne shows his face—and he will—we will know it. We control this entire area. This time, we will be ready."

THIRTY-ONE

MUSEUM OF FINE ARTS
BOSTON, MA

Diana had just made it to her car when her phone rang. It was Ariadne.

"Damn, that was fast," she answered.

"Figured I'd catch you before you got back to the hotel," the analyst said. "I already got a hit on our guy, and it's close. Really close."

"How close?"

"Like right in our backyard," she replied.

"What are you talking about?" Diana asked.

"Doctor Carter Shaw works here in Boston. He's no slouch either, twenty-plus years at the Museum of Fine Arts, of all places. I just talked to his boss."

"Seems he's been out of the office the last few days, unexpectedly and with no explanation," Ariadne said.

"Hmm, that's interesting."

"I thought so too, but as luck would have it, he just got back—today," Ariadne replied. "His supervisor said he has nothing on his schedule, so you can meet with him any time."

"Fantastic," Diana said. "Text me the info. I'll be over there in five."

«««—»»»

Museum Director Dr. Eunice Quinlan had offered to take her to Carter's office. She was a short, chubby lady who wore her steel gray hair tied back in a big, old-fashioned bun. Diana thought she dressed like the nuns she knew in Catholic school, the ones who had given up wearing a habit but still managed to find a way to look like the most uptight librarians imaginable.

With Quinlan as the guide, they made their way into the main hall, then down a side corridor and through a back door to where the private offices were located. The old lady made polite small talk as she led her through the dim, musty inner halls to a quiet corner of the museum, well outside of the public view. Diana could tell she was uncomfortable though. Finally, she tried to address the proverbial elephant in the room.

"You've known Dr. Shaw for a while?" Diana asked as they continued to walk.

"Over twenty years," Quinlan replied, appearing almost relieved to be reaching the main point of the visit.

"What can you tell me about him?"

"Well, I can't imagine what all of this is about, for one thing," the museum director answered.

"I'm just here to ask him a few questions ma'am," Diana said. "Anything you can tell me before I go on in would certainly be appreciated."

The answer did not seem to satisfy the old woman, but Diana guessed she was too intimidated by the F.B.I. aura to press the issue.

"Like I told your people on the phone, Carter Shaw was never all-that-pleasant of a person," Quinlan said. "But the F.B.I.? I can tell you this...he's no criminal. I'm sure of that."

That piqued Diana's interest.

"How do you mean, not-that-pleasant?" she asked. "Is this guy gonna give me trouble?"

Quinlan laughed, almost sarcastically as she shook her head.

"Look, do you want to know what I really think?" she said, fretting over her words like she was about to confess to some kind of sin herself.

"I wouldn't have asked if I didn't," Diana replied.

Quinlan lowered her voice, speaking in a stage whisper and slowing her pace a bit even as they continued walking.

"Carter is one of the smartest people I've ever met, hell maybe *the* smartest," she said. "That is exactly what makes him such an intolerable asshole, if you'll excuse my French."

"I don't understand," Diana said.

"He's brilliant, there's no two ways around that. The thing is—he knows it too. He knows that any time he walks into a room, he's automatically the smartest guy in there. Sometimes that makes him impossible to talk to."

"I see."

"I admit, that's part of what drew me to him in the first place. Why I hired him. He's confident—at least he was back then."

"How do you mean?"

"Well, this is the thing you have to know about him. He's just about the best person in the world at what he does, but what he does is something that almost no one else in the world cares much about."

"Old languages, right?"

"Really old," Quinlan replied. "He knows about a dozen of them. He can read almost any kind of ancient writing you put in front of him like it was *See Spot Run*."

"Seems pretty talented to me. What's the issue then?"

"The problem is, no one notices. No one *has ever* noticed. He's been published several times, he's got a resume you wouldn't believe, but it's literally done nothing for him. He hasn't made any real money—ever. He's been here at the MFA for years and he barely gets by. He's written books and they don't sell, he's tried to get teaching positions but they pay worse than what he makes here."

"So he's pissed?"

"I'd say he feels like the world owes him something, sure," Quinlan answered.

"I see. Seems like what you're telling me is that this guy thinks he's smarter than everyone else but he's mad that no one else agrees," Diana said.

"He definitely feels like he's never received the credit he deserves," Quinlan answered. "So I'd say you're mostly right about that, yes."

"*Mostly* right?" Diana replied. "What did I miss?"

Quinlan leaned in a little closer, with a hint of a smile on her gray lips.

"You said *he thinks* he's smarter than everyone else," she replied.

"Right...so?"

Quinlan smirked as she put her hand on Diana's arm, pointing her ahead. Carter's office door was right there. It was closed but the light was on inside.

"Carter is arrogant, annoying and he can be a real son of a bitch, but there's one thing I'm sure of—he *really is* smarter than almost everyone else," she said.

"Thanks for your help," Diana replied.

"This is his office," Quinlan said. "I'll be back at my desk if you need anything."

She turned and walked back down the musty hall, leaving Diana standing alone outside his door. Diana didn't go right in though. For a moment, she just stood there.

A pane of frosted glass was all that stood between her and the best lead they had so far. Possibly even a suspect, which was why she decided to forego knocking. The element of surprise might put him off guard. If he was involved, having an F.B.I. agent burst right in on him was sure to rattle him. She'd met plenty of academics over her years as an instructor. None of them were cool enough under pressure to keep their composure if you pushed hard enough.

As it turned out, she didn't need to push at all. She opened the door without a sound and came in with her standard line, delivered with as much melodramatic force as she could summon.

"Dr. Shaw...Special Agent Diana Mancuso, F.B.I.!"

He was across the room, sitting at his desk with his back to the door. The screen of his laptop was visible from there. Her eyes went to it right away. Word bubbles filled with text in two colors alternating the whole length of the screen.

He was logged in to a chat site.

The intrusion jolted him, as she'd expected. He shuddered and swung around in his swivel chair. It took him a second to catch his breath, but rather than protest her entrance, he scrambled to reach back to his keyboard.

"Hey, keep off!" Diana shouted back. "Hands where I can see them."

He complied, lifting his arms all the way up in the unabashed manner that suspects in movie scenes always did—and not the half-assed, slow lifting of a real con.

She approached, and took a closer look at his computer.

"BigDaddeeCS," she said, reading the first name on the exchange. "That's you?"

He nodded.

She looked at the header on the page. It said *Sugar Daddies R Us*.

"NastiChick919?" she asked.

His face was already flushed.

"She's over eighteen," he said. "It's not illegal."

Diana smirked.

"Don't worry, doc. I couldn't care less who you want to ..." she started to read from the last line on the chat screen, "*Ride like an angry bucking Texas bronco*."

He didn't seem convinced.

"It's just that...you know..." he stammered.

Diana took the initiative to click a few keys herself, reading what she was writing as he typed.

"*Gotta run babe. Talk 2 u later. Smooches*."

Then she signed off and closed the window.

Carter leaned back in his chair, relieved but crestfallen.

"*Smooches*?" he said. "Thanks. I'll never hear from her again."

"Lots of fish in the sea, doc," she replied.

He tried to settle himself, wiping the sweat from his forehead. His face was flushed, but whether it was from nerves or just embarrassment was impossible to tell.

"Again, you're not..."

Diana scoffed.

"Look doc, I wasn't kidding," she replied. "Your private life is just that—private. Trust me, I've got nothing to brag about in that category myself. That's not why I'm here."

Although he had turned to face her fully, it seemed to take him a moment to even see her, as if he was looking past her somehow. Immediately that gave her a very strange feeling, almost as though *he* was studying *her*.

"Okay then, what is it that you need, Special Agent…Mancuso was it?" he asked.

She decided to go right for it. Keep up the pressure. Try to get him off balance.

"Have you heard of a man named Luther Vayne?" she asked.

Carter scratched his scruffy chin. He paused for a long while, as though pondering. Finally he just shook his head.

"Can't say that I have," he replied.

"He got a fair amount of press in the early seventies," she said. "Not much since, until recently anyway."

"I'm sorry, did you say the early seventies?" he asked.

She nodded. She edged a little closer, in case he was about to say or do something one of them might regret. But his response was underwhelming.

"I was in grade school back in those days," he said.

"Sure, of course," she said, looking him over once more. "Maybe you heard that he escaped recently, from a prison in Ohio?"

Again, he shook his head.

"I've been a bit…busy lately," he said. "Can I ask what exactly this is about, Agent Mancuso?"

Diana realized that was going to require a more skillful line of inquiry. Either he was hiding everything, or he really had no idea about anything. Despite his odd reaction to her entrance, she still wasn't completely sure.

"You studied with a man named Phillipe Gamaliel, about twenty five years ago, is that right?"

He clasped his hands. They were trembling, she thought, but she couldn't be sure once he clenched them together.

"Yeah, that's right, I did. Not really proud of it, but I'm guilty as charged, officer," he replied. "What does that have to do with your guy Mister Luther?"

"Mr. Vayne," she corrected. "And that's what I'm here to find out."

Carter nodded, shifting in his seat and swallowing hard as he tried to breathe. Despite that, he managed to extend his hand to the open chair.

"Why don't you have a seat, agent? This sounds like it might be serious," he said.

Again she looked him up and down, even as she accepted his invitation. His face was red and he was still perspiring a little, but he seemed to be pulling himself together.

"You worked on a paper called *Before the Gods*, right?" she asked.

"I did, for a few semesters back in the eighties, yes."

"So you're familiar with the name Azathoth?"

He sat up in his chair.

"Okay, you have my attention. What is it you're looking for, exactly?"

She elected to take a more direct shot.

"Can you explain to me why a convicted murderer would paint, or more accurately have painted, the name Azathoth all over his prison cell walls, in human blood?"

Carter cleared his throat and squirmed a bit in his seat again.

"Umm, no. No, I don't think I can explain that."

"Azathoth is an ancient god, correct?"

He leaned back a ways and tilted his head, as if he was unsure of the answer.

"In a way, I suppose."

"Is he or isn't he?"

"It's not that simple," he said. "It's not even a he or a she. Gamaliel's work—since you asked about the old professor, and he was the real expert, not me—he called Azathoth the...nuclear chaos"

"Nuclear?"

"Not nuclear as in hydrogen bombs or atomic reactors, but as in, the heart of *everything*. The nucleus of existence."

She grimaced.

"Okay, so let's say *god* and move on, all right?"

"Not a believer, eh?" he asked.

"Agnostic," she answered. "Also irrelevant."

"Fair enough."

"As you may know, it's not at all uncommon for serial killers, especially ones with occult leanings to fixate on some kind of bizarre mythology or fringe religion," she said. "It looks like that's what Luther Vayne was doing, but there isn't a lot of information about this Azathoth thing. You happen to be one of the only people we know of who can tell us something about it."

He shifted in his seat once more, as if the realization finally dawned on him.

"I'm sorry, am I a suspect or something?" he asked.

"That depends," she said.

"On?"

"Whether you did anything to help Luther Vayne," she said.

"I already told you, I don't even know who this guy is," he protested.

She looked at him again, slowly. She still couldn't get a read on him.

"Why don't we start with this, I need to know what Luther Vayne thinks Azathoth is, and what he thinks it's making him do. Can you can help me get a better handle on that?"

"Maybe," he said. "But knowing anything about Azathoth on its own, I doubt that would be of much help. Maybe if I had an idea of what this Vayne guy did, I could help give you some ideas."

"It might be easier to show you," she said.

She passed him a manila folder with some blown up eight by tens from several of the original murders. He opened it, began to leaf through them and immediately reacted—badly.

"Holy mother of God," he gasped. "These are from the 1970s? I've never seen any of these," he said.

She kept her eyes on him as he looked them over. The way the color left his face when he saw the pictures, the way his hands trembled as he held them, and the sweat that was beading on his forehead—if *she* hadn't make him nervous, somehow these photos did.

"Very few of the original crime scene photos were ever released to the public," she said. "All of the victims were high profile, wealthy folks. Their families had the power and the influence to keep the grisly stuff out of the papers."

"Later?" he asked. "This guy was convicted, right?"

"He was, but the odd thing is, he confessed to everything all at once," she replied. "All thirteen murders were essentially solved in one fell swoop, so there was never any real follow up. No further investigation."

"Guess they had their guy," he said.

"Exactly," she replied. "Until now. These were taken a few days ago."

She handed him a second folder, this one containing the Saxon photos. Unlike the aged, faded first set, these were in full, lifelike color. The scarlet of the blood stark and clear against the bright white snow.

"Jesus Christ, he's doing it to them again," Carter whispered.

"Excuse me?" she said, stopping herself.

She looked over at him. He was clearly enrapt by the pictures, studying every detail.

"What did you just say?" she asked.

He was a long time in answering. Eventually, he lowered his reading glasses from the end of his nose and took a long, deep breath.

"I think I might be able to help you, after all," he said.

But he did not continue. He just sat there, staring back at the photos on his desk.

"Don't hold back, this isn't the time to be shy," she encouraged.

He didn't even look up.

"Oh, I'm not. Trust me," he said. "What you have here is not just any murder."

"Yeah, we know that," she replied.

"Do you?" he asked, finally making eye contact again. "Do you really know what you're dealing with?"

"I don't understand."

"You're right about the occult practices. These signatures, these details—they're not random and they're not anything you can get on the internet, or even a book in your local library. This is an old ritual, *a very old ritual.*"

"I'm not sure what you're saying. You know you're not the first person to see these, right? These pictures may not be out in the public domain, but these crimes *have* been studied. No one has ever mentioned what you're telling me," she said.

"I'm not surprised," he replied. "Because very few people would know what they're seeing here. Hell, I wouldn't have either, until just a few years ago."

"A few years ago?" she asked. "What are you talking about? These are almost forty years old."

"I know, and that's what's so strange about it," he said.

"Explain."

"I'm trying to," he answered. "But it doesn't make much sense."

"Trust me, you're not alone there," she replied.

He held up one of the pictures, and he gestured to the positions of the bodies.

"You see this, the child on top of the mother? The way they're both splayed out, spread eagle almost?"

"Yeah, it's one of the things that's unique to Vayne's crime scenes, his distinct signature," she answered.

"No, it isn't," he replied. "Unique, that is."

"I'm not following, are you saying you've seen this exact display before?"

"That's precisely what I'm saying," he replied.

"Where?" she asked.

"Actually, a better question would probably be *when.*"

"When?"

He leaned forward to his computer and began typing at a quick clip. In less than thirty seconds, he sat back, then turned the screen toward her on the other side of his desk. Diana felt her blood run cold the instant she saw it.

The image was startling. There were two bodies excavated from a dirt pit, nothing more than skeletons. But their positioning was precise. A perfect match—one on top of the other, the younger, smaller body inverted and the skull of the older figure placed at the center. Iron rods impaled both victims from either side and one long spike ran through them top-to-bottom.

"What is this?"

"You're looking at a burial discovered in Iraq in the late 1980s, from the lowest region of a ziggurat at Uruk."

"Iraq?"

"Right. It was found completely intact, sealed in a crypt well below ground level. Based on what we know about the ziggurat itself, these bodies were put there no later than 3500 B.C."

"Over five thousand years ago," she whispered.

"They've found a few more since, always the same positioning, always very old."

"How old?"

"Put it this way, this is *the most recent one*," he said.

"Finally, some progress," she said. "So Vayne's re-enacting an old Sumerian ritual. I need to know everything you can tell me about that."

"Well, that's gonna be a problem," Carter said.

"Pardon?"

"It is old, and it is Sumerian," he said. "But what I just told you was true. These burials weren't found until the late eighties. Before then, no one had ever seen one of these before. At least not for five millennia."

"So how would Vayne have known in 1974?"

"Beats me. What you've got here is someone in the early 1970s employing a ritual mainstream archaeology didn't even know about until maybe fifteen to twenty years after that. A practice that was already old when the pyramids were built, something literally buried and forgotten for ages."

"So once again, nothing adds up," she said. "Why would he do that?"

"I can't tell you that, but what I can tell you is why *they* did it."

"The Sumerians?" she asked. "How do you know?"

"As I mentioned, this is very odd type of burial, but it was evidently so specific that they always left a cuneiform inscription along with the bodies. There isn't much to go on. But I can tell you this: it's exactly the same in every documented case."

"Which is?"

"This rite was designed for a very specific purpose," he said. "It wasn't to torture or to inflict pain. The tablets found with these bodies all say the same thing. Every inscription tells us that there was only ever one reason to do this."

"What's that?"

"To annihilate the souls of the victims," he said.

The words hung in the air between them for a long moment before he continued.

"Total spiritual destruction. The texts are very clear. To be killed in this way was to negate any chance of an afterlife, any survival of the spirit at all. This was not just death, this was meant to utterly and completely destroy."

"Why?"

"According to the tablets, this rite was employed only for those whose souls had been polluted."

"By what?"

"Black magic."

"That doesn't help me," she said.

"Didn't think it would," he said. "As far as we can tell, the victims of those ancient burial sacrifices had transgressed in some way."

"They were criminals?"

"In a manner of speaking," he answered. "The translation is controversial. Some say they consorted with the dark forces, or attempted to summon the shadows. You see the positioning, the arms spread out, the legs and the bronze spikes?"

She looked again, as he counted out the points—thirteen of them, an inner set and an outer set. It hit her all of a sudden.

"The star of Azathoth," she said. "The victims form the star."

"Right. The one I showed you, in particular, says the victims were actually the bride and the offspring of a demon."

"The bride?" she asked.

"Well, not really. That's the polite version. The translation is a bit inexact. The true word would be something closer to consort or even *whore* I guess."

Diana stopped. She put down the papers in her hand.

"What demon?"

"I'm sorry?"

"What was the name of the demon?"

"It's a little known figure, nothing you would have heard of," he said.

She reached across the desk.

"Tell me, doc," she demanded.

"Okay, fine, just a sec," he said, as he scanned the ancient writing. "It was called Yog…Soth…oth. Yog…"

"Sothoth," she said.

He nodded, as she leaned back.

"Fuck," she muttered.

"Excuse me?"

"The whore of Sothoth," she said.

"I suppose that would be correct, yes," he said.

"So these people, these victims, they supposedly tried to mate with this demon Sothoth?" she asked.

"That's a reasonable inference, but as I said, the text is limited," he replied. "It's hard to say for sure. Does that mean something to you?"

"It might," she whispered. "It just might."

«««—»»»

Carter waited a long while after Diana Mancuso left his office. He sat behind his desk, barely moving, until he was sure she was really gone. Then he checked the lock on his door, sat back down and took his phone out of his pocket. There was a new number at the top of his contacts list. He hit it and waited for someone to pick up.

It was Logan on the other end.

"Tell Mr. Gregorian we may have a problem," he said.

THIRTY-TWO

NORTH END
BOSTON, MA

Diana's head was aching again by the time she left the M.F.A. The only thing she wanted was to make it back to her hotel. After so many days on the move, she couldn't wait to hit the pillow.

The Bureau had them staying at a place near Faneuil Hall, a short walk from the F.B.I. field office. When she came up to State Street though, a re-paving crew was blocking her way. The maze of orange barrels and detour signs forced her to go halfway around the North End to get back to her hotel.

Driving up Salem Street to try to cut across to the harbor she was further delayed when a large group of pedestrians crossed like a slow-moving herd right into the street. Tourists, in all likelihood. When she saw a woman leading them by the light of a fake lantern, dressed in Revolutionary-era costume, she was sure. The group was crossing the street toward the Old North Church.

She used the pause as an opportunity to take her glasses off, to rub the fatigue out of her eyes. It didn't help. Everything was still blurry. She needed a good night's sleep—desperately.

She was about to let her foot off of the brake, as the last few stragglers caught up to the tour, when something caught her eye. Standing on the far side of the street, under a tree on the brick sidewalk.

It was him.

Everything came back to her in an instant. The dream in the motel room. The cold fingers on her back. The gunshots that never were.

Luther Vayne. Only this time she was awake. This time it was real.

He was standing alone, an old man cloaked in the evening shadows.

She pulled over along the iron fence beside the church courtyard. She checked her sidearm, as much good as it had done her the last time. Diana kept her eyes fixed on him. She got out of the car.

Vayne didn't move. He remained still as she crossed the street, as she moved toward him with her gun pointed at his head. Though he was plainly blind, he seemed to see her nonetheless.

"You should know better by now," he said.

She kept the gun trained on him.

"I'm not afraid of you," she said.

He smiled.

"Of course you are," he replied.

He was right.

Even from a distance his voice made her shiver. It was suddenly very cold again. His presence somehow stole any warmth from her blood. The temperature dropped ten degrees in the moment it took her to cross the street.

He owned the night. Every gesture, every hint of his posture asserted his dominance. He stared at her. With his horrid, mangled, empty face.

Her stomach revolted. Acid bubbled into her throat. She suppressed it. Clenched her jaw against the vomit reflex. But the rest of her body betrayed her. Her arms quivered. Her legs buckled. Just standing up required effort.

Vayne spoke with the same hoarse whisper that haunted her sleep. His tone was no longer beseeching. He spoke with an air of authority.

"You have not heeded my warning," he said.

Diana tensed. She contracted every muscle she could control. She let a deep breath ease out of her lungs. She knew she had to keep her cool.

After a long pause, she managed a reply.

"You're my job. That's all. Fuck you and all of your fucking mind games. Whatever you think you're doing. You're coming in with me," she said. "You're under arrest, for the murder of Roger Saxon."

The gun quivered in her hand. She cursed herself for not being able to hold it steady. Somehow, even she didn't believe her own words.

"You are a stubborn one indeed," he said. "Very well. If you insist on walking this path, you must be free to do so with your eyes open. You will not make any progress as long as you let your fear control you."

"Like I said, I'm not afraid of you," she repeated, a necessary lie she tried hard to believe. *He terrified her*. She kept talking. South Boston crept into her syllables. It helped. "You need to be put down like a fucking dog. I don't fear people like you. Pity maybe, but never fear. You're a sad old man. A monster."

The F.B.I. façade faded. Standing there in the freezing night, facing the horror, she reverted. She was the girl in her brother's hand-me-down Cam Neely road jersey, ready to drop her gloves with anyone in the neighborhood.

"*Yer a fahkin' mawn-stuh.*"

Vayne shook his head. The shifting tangles of hair alternated shadows and light across his ruined face. Her subtle metamorphosis appeared to amuse him.

"That is no way to talk to me, Ms. Mancuso," he said. "I have not done anything to warrant such insults."

She almost laughed.

"You're a goddamn child-killer," she spat back.

"Really, Ms. Mancuso, you disappoint me," he continued. His words fell to a whisper, more like a feline hiss than a human voice. "After all that you now have learned, I expected better from someone of your caliber, someone with so inquisitive a mind. You more than anyone should recognize the value of learning all of the facts before you pass judgment."

"I don't know what you think we're talking about," she began.

He silenced her with a gesture. The breath evaporated from her lungs.

"You require further convincing," he said. "Unless you choose to turn away, as I advised. This will be your final chance to do so."

"You're offering help?" she said. "You're gonna help me? Not likely."

"In a manner of speaking," he said.

He seemed to ignore her disdain. He extended a hand.

Diana kept her gun pointed at him, but breathed a sigh of relief. Her momentary reversion had done the trick, kept her in the game long enough to get past her fear, and to get him talking. He *wanted* to tell her things, demented fantasies and paranoid delusions probably. But it was what she needed. Her training could take over. She needed him to keep talking.

"Okay…enlighten me," she said.

"You need not humor me," he answered.

She had crossed a line. Establishing boundaries was important. She needed him to believe that she saw the situation as he did. She needed to understand him.

"Perhaps you might be better served by listening," he continued. "You are a woman of intellect. I will ask no more of you than to rely on that which you trust—your own mind. If need be, I can do more than tell you, but you must be ready for that."

She nodded. Diana understood. He was not going to harm her. He was trying to recruit her.

"You'll need to convince me. F.B.I. agents don't switch allegiances lightly."

She was lying again. She had no intention of allowing him to persuade her. But she needed him to think that she was at least open to the possibility.

"I do not come bearing the hand of treason," he replied.

"Then what are you offering?"

She looked right at him. She let herself stare back at his tortured face.

"Answers."

It was at that moment that she realized why his expression was so disconcerting. His lips weren't moving. She heard his words. But Vayne hadn't opened his mouth. He hadn't done so since their conversation had begun.

The epiphany shattered her careful demeanor. Dizziness flooded her. She staggered, and fell to one knee.

He was there beside her.

"I was afraid it might come to this," he whispered. "I must show you."

"Show me?"

"I know what you need to believe. What you tell yourself in the dark corners of your mind. But none of that is necessary. I can see your fear, as plain as you can see me standing here," he said.

Diana scoffed at his peculiar answer.

"You can see fear?" she asked. "Fine, show me."

"You would rather I did not," he said.

She persisted.

"You want me to believe you—show me."

An instant later, everything went black.

They stood together in the darkness for a long while, before the shadows began to fade. As soon as they did, she wished they wouldn't.

"Stairs," he said. "Old wooden stairs."

"What?"

"The fear is yours, not mine."

"I'm afraid of wooden stairs?"

Vayne narrated as his words became images. Everything he voiced came to life, and Diana felt herself begin to quiver.

They stood on the top of a stairwell, leading down into a cellar. There was only the light from a single incandescent bulb to illuminate the whole of the basement. A door closed on rusty hinges behind them.

She recognized the place. Somehow Vayne was walking her through her own memory, a living nightmare that she wanted to forget.

Most of the place was obscured in shadow, far too large for the tiny light to reach every corner. The stairs were hand-made, but they hadn't been mended in ages. Corroded nails creaked inside the lumber.

She knew what was coming next.

The reek of human odors. Stale sweat. Excrement.

There were six cages in the basement. Tools and other implements rested in niches on the west wall, pliers, pitchforks and ice-picks. Most were dirty, caked in purple, dried blood.

Only three of the pens were occupied, one woman in each. The girls were crammed into tiny quarters, on floors lined with straw that was stained with urine. Their heads had been shaved and their wrists were bound. Blindfolds were wrapped over their eyes and leather gags muffled their mouths.

"Puyallup, Washington. June 22nd, 2003," Diana said. "I'll never forget it. Lenny Andrew Edgars. He killed seventeen women in this basement."

"The last one less than twelve hours before you got there," he said.

Diana's face went pale. She shivered.

"Melinda Chambers. She was only nineteen, pre-med at U-Dub," she said.

She shook her head, as if she could shake the memory away. But it was right there in front of her.

"I had his name," she stammered. "I had a witness, a neighbor who'd seen some suspicious behavior, but I didn't apply for the warrant right away. I thought we needed more evidence. By the time we got there, she was already dead. He dissected her. He numbed her extremities and kept her conscious the whole time. He cut her into little pieces while she was still alive. While I was doing paperwork."

"Your last day of field work," Vayne said.

Tears blinded her.

"I couldn't do it anymore. I couldn't see it anymore. It made me sick. I hated him, hated myself, hated all of it. Hated everything. It made me question…"

She stopped. The dreamscape faded.

"Question what?" Vayne asked, far softer than she could ever have imagined such a beast to be. She wasn't sure she could continue.

"Everything," she answered.

Vayne remained beside her as the images died. The blackness returned to shroud them in perfect shadow. Her face was flushed. Her eyes swelled with tears. He put his hand on her shoulder, and she felt the same cadaverous, icy touch from the night in the motel room.

"Now you may begin," he said.

«««—»»»

Diana woke up, jolted from a restless sleep. She was in her hotel—but she had no idea how she'd gotten there. Her head still throbbed. Her pillow was wet. She was shaking.

The wind blew through the trees outside her window and she heard a familiar voice whispering through the winter gale. All she could tell was that it kept saying the same damn thing—*Azathoth commands it.*

Although she had never been more exhausted, she couldn't get back to sleep at all that night.

DAY SEVEN

"In summary, these many manuscripts that we have been able to study, though they hail from varied cultures and are separated by thousands of miles and many thousands of years, yet retain a common core. They all point to a single figure. It is this god or god-like being who was undoubtedly the source from which all the later deities we know can be traced."

"Before the Gods"
Professor Phillipe Gamaliel
Unofficial Translation from the
French Language Ed., 1989

THIRTY-THREE

SHADY MEADOWS RETIREMENT VILLAGE
PEARL RIVER, NY

Even though she got an early start—she wasn't sleeping anyway—the two hundred and fifty mile trek down to New York took Diana over five hours, most of it spent crawling along in heavy traffic down the I-95 corridor.

The moment she pulled into the parking lot however, she realized that it was exactly the kind of place where she did not want to end up. The well-manicured shrubbery out front, the white-washed concrete of the steps and the archways, the immaculate beige siding, all of it was designed to reassure visitors and family that the *Shady Meadows Senior Living Community and Retirement Village* was anything but the sort of place that it actually was. A place where people came to die.

Once inside she felt a cold sting in the air. Fluorescent bulbs buzzed over pale walls and tiled floors and a staff in pastel scrubs. Fake flowers decorated the reception desk. Merciless, institutional sterility.

Her phone rang just as she was getting to reception. It was Ariadne, of course.

"I've got some more info on this Shaw guy," she began.

"I spoke to him yesterday, still not sure what to make of him," Diana replied.

"Richard sent out agents from the Boston office to do some background on him, check out his apartment, his ex-wife's place and his job."

"Great, anything yet?"

"They spoke to his ex-wife."

"What's she say?"

"That he's a jerk, mostly," she joked. "Also he came by unannounced yesterday, acting a little strange."

"How so?"

"She didn't really specify."

"I'd say this guy is starting to look very promising, right about now," Diana said.

"Agreed. What do you want me to do?" Ariadne asked.

Diana thought on it for a second.

"Have them keep his place under surveillance, and his job too. Round the clock.

"You want me to tell the F.B.I. Office here in Boston to set up a stakeout?" Ariadne asked. "Commit six or seven special agents to twenty-four-seven spy detail, for a guy who may or may not have done anything?"

"Right."

"They're not gonna like that."

"I don't give a shit," Diana said. "I got a feeling about this guy. Tell them it's coming directly from Richard."

"Gotcha," Ariadne said.

Then she hung up.

«««—»»»

A thin, middle-aged nurse named Prentice met Diana at the front desk, and led her down a long, bare corridor to what she described as an activity room. It was full of people, but not a single one of them seemed the least bit *active*.

There was a 32-inch flat screen playing *Wheel of Fortune* at the far end, with a group of elderly folks gathered around it, some in wheelchairs. A few men were playing cards at a table behind them, and a scattering of couches and chairs were filled with women knitting and doing crossword puzzles.

The nurse pointed at a wiry, hunched figure near the back corner, seated with a home-made blanket over his lap next to the window.

"Excuse me, your honor," Diana began.

The man did not appear to hear her. He simply continued staring out the window, at nothing in particular. She tried again, this time just a little louder.

"Judge Whitfield, sir? Sorry for the interruption. My name is Special Agent Diana Mancuso. With the F.B.I.," she began.

The elderly man still didn't acknowledge her, until she finally placed a hand on his shoulder. It was bony, a living skeleton in a cable-knit sweater.

"Well you're a pretty one, such nice eyes. What's your name dear?" the man asked.

She repeated the introduction.

"F.B.I.?" Mr. Whitfield said. "Is this about the taxes again, because I settled everything with the I.R.S. years ago."

Even his voice was frail. His lungs strained with every breath.

"I'm not here about your taxes, your honor," Diana said. "I'd like to ask you a few questions about your son."

"No, I don't drink regular, not anymore, but a cup of decaf would be just fine, thank you," he replied.

Diana realized that the man was at least partially deaf, and got along by reading lips. She stepped back and got Nurse Prentice's attention.

"You have to look at him when you talk," she said. "He refuses to wear a hearing aid. I should have mentioned that."

"Would you be able to get us some coffee?" Diana asked. "One decaf and one regular?"

Prentice nodded.

"Certainly," she replied, before turning to the old man with a smile that was at least a little forced. "I'll be back shortly judge. You take care of everything while I'm gone, ok?"

Whitfield nodded and managed a half-hearted salute that turned into a weak wave as she headed toward the adjacent kitchenette. Diana looked back to him as the nurse vanished from sight though, just in time to see the old man's expression sour and his wave turn into a middle finger.

"Condescending bitch," he whispered.

Diana laughed as she pulled up a chair and sat across from the widower.

"Judge Whitfield, your honor," she began.

"Please, call me Tom," he answered, now apparently quite lucid. "Or Mr. Whitfield, if you prefer. I haven't been a judge in thirty years. Besides, no one here listens to me anyway."

She smiled.

"I need to ask you a few questions about…"

"Peter, yes I heard you before," he answered. "I just don't want *her* to hear," he continued, pointing toward the kitchenette.

"Got it," Diana said, noting that the man was probably at least a little senile after all.

"You don't understand," he added, lowering his voice even more. "They see everything. They hear everything. We have to be very careful."

"Understood," she replied, now rather convinced he was losing it.

The old widower nodded. He closed the untouched Sudoku puzzle book in his hands and laid it down on his lap. He looked toward the ceiling, and over at the other retirees sitting like zombies in front of the television.

"You asked about Peter. But what you really want to know is all about *him*, isn't it?" he whispered.

Diana looked at the old judge with a bit of confusion.

"Wait…who are we talking about?" Diana asked.

She noticed the widower was starting to tremble. She picked up an afghan from the nearby couch and draped it over his shoulders, even though she guessed it wasn't really the temperature that was to blame.

Whitfield looked Diana square in the eye.

"Vayne," the man whispered.

Diana stammered.

"How did you know…?"

The old man looked around again, seemingly checking that the nurse was still out of the room before continuing.

"I saw him on the news yesterday. Soon as I saw it I knew someone would come, sooner or later. I knew it."

"I don't understand," she said. "Someone would come for what?"

The old man seemed to drift off again, as though the memory occupying his attention was more substantial than the world around him.

"Please, Mr. Whitfield," Diana said, extending her hand again, to both comfort the widower, and to draw him back to the present. "I know this must be hard, but I have to know as much as you can remember. Anything might help."

The widower clenched her hand tight. He turned and looked her dead in the eye.

"Young lady, I remember every single detail," he said. "*I wish I could forget.*"

"Every detail of what?"

"I saw them taken," he said.

Diana paused.

"Your wife and son?" she asked. "Are you saying you witnessed their abduction?"

"It was late, close to midnight. I was in my office, downstairs. A judge sometimes has to be on call at all hours, you see, and many of us keep an office at home," he said. "Something crashed. I heard glass breaking, then two screams."

"This is…I never heard…" Diana said.

The old man kept going, as if he needed to say it.

"I ran upstairs, into the nursery. As soon as I got there all I wanted was to run away. But I couldn't move. Every bone in my body froze. I've never been so afraid, before or since," he was trembling again. Diana could feel the widower's hand shaking. "I couldn't even close my eyes. But I knew. In that moment, I knew it had finally come to an end."

"What was ending?" Diana asked.

"The nightmare," he said. "Then all hell broke loose, if you'll forgive the expression."

Diana pressed the widower.

"What does that mean, judge?"

"He was calm. The rest of the room wasn't. Everything was crazy. The curtains were shaking like there was hurricane blowing them, but there was no wind. The windows opened and closed on their own. I remember them latching and unlatching. But nobody was near them. Chairs and toys and papers were everywhere, flying all around in the air. The bed was lifting itself off of the floor. My wife was on her knees in front of him, screaming, holding the child."

"Sounds like the fucking Exorcist," she said, under her breath.

Whitfield ignored her. His face was lost in a blank stare. He was seeing it all over again, no less terrified after almost half a century.

"He knew I was there. He looked right at me. I will never forget that face, covered in tattoos with both eyes missing. I can see it now as if it were as close to me as you are. I knew in that moment why he was there. I knew that he had come for them."

"What happened next?"

"He did just as I imagined," he said. "He took them."

He stopped then, rubbing his hands together in his lap. He didn't look like he was going to continue. Diana got up and clasped hands with him. His fingers were ice cold.

"I'm so sorry," she said.

Unexpectedly, he began to smile—and that made her even more uneasy.

"You don't understand, do you?" he asked. "I have never been so relieved in my life as I was in that moment."

She stepped back.

"What?" Diana said, because she couldn't think of anything else.

"The authorities were alerted by the alarm, and they arrived shortly afterwards," Whitfield continued. "The police were never able to figure out where he went, or how. There were no tracks, no trail and no clues. They were just gone."

"You never told any of this to the police?" she said.

"Of course not," he replied. "I never wanted that monster in my house, but there was nothing I could do."

Diana put her hand on the widower's arm, still not sure she did understand what she was being told.

"Believe me, sir. I know it's been a long, long time. But I'm here to make sure Luther Vayne never hurts anyone again," she said.

Yet again, Whitfield looked up, turning back to face Diana.

"Oh my dear, I'm afraid I haven't explained this well at all. You *still* don't understand, do you?" he said. "The monster I'm talking about was the child."

"Your son?"

"That thing wasn't my son," he answered. "I was happy to see it gone."

"Wait…what are you saying?" she replied. "If Peter wasn't your son, then whose son…"

Just then the nurse re-entered the room, two cups of coffee in ceramic mugs and saucers balanced on a cafeteria tray. The moment he saw her, Whitfield recoiled, clammed up and returned to the near-catatonic state she'd found him in moments earlier.

"Mr. Whitfield, sir?" Diana tried, gently nudging him.

Nurse Prentice arrived and put down the tray on the coffee table.

"Still not talking much, I see," she said. "I thought you'd have trouble getting anything out of this one."

She handed one of the saucers to Diana. Then she turned her attention to the widower.

"Not feeling very talkative today, are we, your honor?" she asked.

"Actually he was just talking quite a bit," Diana said. "I'm not sure why he stopped."

The nurse fretted.

"Now that doesn't sound like him," she said. "Maybe a little sip of joe would perk him up."

She took the cup and saucer and held it out in front of him. Without a hint of warning, Whitfield's arm jerked, reaching up like a reflex action and knocking the coffee out of Prentice's hand. The mug and saucer fell to the tile floor, shattering on the hard surface.

The nurse gasped, startled by the sudden shock. Upon seeing that Whitfield returned to his prior state of near catatonia the very next moment, she settled her nerves quickly.

"Are you okay?" Diana asked.

"Oh, I'm fine. Occupational hazard," the nurse answered. "Sometimes these folks do that, especially when they're beginning to slip away. Very sad, really. I'll go clean it up."

She got up and made her way over to a broom and dustpan set against the far wall, only a few feet away. Diana watched her, but caught something out of the corner of her eye—again, the very moment the nurse's back was turned.

Once more liberated from his frozen state, Whitfield moved with unlikely speed. He reached down to the floor and snatched up the largest fragment of jagged ceramic from the ruins of the mug and saucer.

The jolt caught Nurse Prentice's attention as well. She turned with a look of shock on her face.

Whitfield held the sharp piece like a prize. He looked right at Diana again.

"I've already told you too much. They know. They'll come for me too now," he said.

Diana reached out both hands, but not quite far enough to touch him.

"You want an answer to your question," he said.

Nurse Prentice was across the room in a heartbeat. Whitfield's eyes darted between the two women, and he raised the jagged fragment to his neck as the nurse approached.

"Which question?" Diana asked.

"The child," Whitfield said, his voice panicky now. "You asked me who his real father was."

Diana moved closer, but just then the nurse reached him and put her hands on the old man, trying to steady him. It didn't work. The instant she got to him, Whitfield responded with the same speed as before, and this time he jammed the sharp edge of the fragment deep into his own throat.

Nurse Prentice screamed as the first warm spurt of blood from his jugular sprayed red into her face. Seemingly not content with even that deep of a wound however, Whitfield continued stabbing at his own neck several more times, repeatedly chopping his soft flesh until blood was spilling out all over him.

Diana leaped from her seat, though she knew it was already too late. As the nurse fell to one knee, horrified and wiping red fluid from her eyes, Diana clasped hands with the old man. She shuddered when she realized that he was smiling.

"Sothoth," he managed to whisper, as the breath faded from his lips.

She got as close as she could, blood drenching her hands as she held him to his last breath. As his eyes closed, he managed to whisper it one last time.

"The answer is…Yog Sothoth."

THIRTY-FOUR

MUSEUM OF FINE ARTS
BOSTON, MA

Logan was waiting for him at his office when he came in, late as usual.

"I was told we had a problem," the Englishman said, by way of greeting.

Carter ignored the intrusion, but he didn't answer right away. Instead, he took off his coat, put it on the rack and placed his coffee on his desk as he sat down. All of it was a deliberate display, making the big man wait. He wanted it very clear that he was no longer treating Logan as an authority figure. On the contrary, he now he spoke to him more like an employee.

"If you consider the F.B.I. barging in on me, asking all kinds of questions about Azathoth and Luther Vayne a problem—then yeah, we have a *slight* problem," he said.

"Mr. Gregorian is aware of the F.B.I.'s involvement. He expected there might be a complication like this," Logan said. "I am here to address it."

"Fine," Carter replied. "That's all I ask."

"What did you tell her, this Agent Mancuso who keeps nosing around?"

Carter smiled, pleased with himself for leading her on without giving himself away.

"Nothing she couldn't have found out herself," he replied.

"If she returns?"

"I can string her along for a while, feed her enough information to keep her occupied. But there's only so much I can do. Eventually, I'm going to run out of things to say. That's bad for me, bad for you and bad for our boss."

"That's what this is for," Logan answered.

He reached into his coat and pulled out a pistol. It was sleek and black, with a brown grip-handle and a squared barrel, affixed to a rounded extension. He placed it on the desk.

"It's a Browning H.P., thirteen round clip of nine millimeter ammo," Logan said. "Only weighs about a kilo. Easy to use, very little recoil and devastating at close range. The silencer on the end will suppress most of the muzzle noise, very quiet indeed."

Carter stammered, taken off-guard again.

"Are you telling me to kill an F.B.I. agent?"

"*I* am not telling you to do anything," Logan replied.

"Gregorian," Carter whispered.

"You know his orders. Nothing can be permitted to interfere with our plans."

"Then get me out of here," Carter said. "The others are protected, hiding out until the Convergence."

Logan shook his head.

"You know that's not possible, *and you know why*," he answered. "You have a special role to play, and you will be summoned when the time is right, just as Mr. Gregorian said."

"If I do run out of things to tell her before then?"

Logan pushed the pistol across the desk toward him.

"You should be ready, in that case."

"To do what?"

"Whatever is bloody well necessary to protect the Black Flame," Logan replied. "You know what's at stake here, and you know what all of us have to gain—including you."

Carter reclined in his desk chair, leaving Logan standing, stoic as ever.

"I wonder about that," he said. "What do you have to gain here, exactly?"

Logan's expression did not change.

"I do as I am told," he replied. "That is all…"

Carter didn't let him finish.

"That's all you care about," he interrupted. "You're a foot soldier, aren't you? A drone. You don't really even understand what we're doing, do you?"

The Englishman looked perturbed.

"I did not come here to…"

A second time, Carter stopped him in mid-sentence.

"Spare me the duty and honor bullshit," he said. "You really have no idea what this all about. You're loyal and you get paid, and that's enough for you."

"I know as much as I need to know," Logan answered.

Carter handled the gun, picking it up and pointing it at various items around the office, squinting as he studied the sightline. Then he put it down and looked back at Logan.

"You know nothing," he said. "You have no idea what you're a part of, no idea at all."

Logan simply stared back at him.

"Imagine if you could open a door to every dream mankind has ever had, to the knowledge of eternity itself," Carter said. "The answer to every question. To pierce the veil of every mystery, to know the true nature of the universe, of all the secrets behind the darkness. Do you know what that would give you?"

Logan shook his head very slightly.

"No, you really don't know, do you?" Carter replied.

Again, Logan seemed unable to answer.

Carter's last response became more like a command than an answer.

"You can go tell Mr. Gregorian, from me," Carter said, looking back at the weapon and then at Logan. "I won't allow anything to interfere with what we're doing."

THIRTY-FIVE

F.B.I. FIELD OFFICE, ONE CENTER PLAZA
BOSTON, MA

Diana drove the whole way back up to Boston in stunned silence. She didn't even turn the radio on. She just sat there, staring at the road and at her hands—gripping the wheel tight to keep them from trembling.

Instead of answers, she had nothing but questions. Maddening… insane…impossible questions.

It was already dark, well past seven o'clock, by the time she got back. Ariadne was waiting for her when she came into the command center, but Diana didn't say anything when she entered the room. She just stood there, stone-faced and dead quiet.

"Hey, there you are," the analyst said, barely looking up with her eyes glued to her laptop. "I've been calling you for the last few hours. You never picked up."

Still Diana said nothing. Finally, Ariadne looked up from her screen and got a look at her friend. Diana's face was pale. Her eyes were bloodshot. She still hadn't even sat down. She was just standing there, in front of the table.

"Are you okay?" Ariadne asked.

She got up and came around the table to help.

"Here, sit," Ariadne said, easing her into the chair. "You look awful. What the hell happened down there?"

She opened a bottle of water and put it in front of Diana.

"I don't know," Diana said, still not looking at her. "Honestly, I really don't know."

"Did you meet with the dad, the judge?"

"I did," Diana replied, her face blank.

"So...what did he say?"

Diana look straight ahead.

"He's dead."

Ariadne sat back down.

"What? You just said you met with him," she replied. "What's going on Diana, you're kind of scaring me right now."

"He was talking to me and then...he was gone," she answered, fully aware that she wasn't coming close to conveying the horror she'd witnessed, but also totally unable to repeat it.

"Hmm, I'm sorry, that's awful," Ariadne said. "What did he say before he passed? Anything helpful?"

Diana continued staring ahead. Ariadne waited a beat, then repeated her query.

"Hey, did he say anything?" she asked.

"Umm, he says he wasn't the father," Diana answered.

Ariadne puzzled for a minute, then went back to her laptop.

"Well, he may be right about that," she said.

That got Diana's attention.

"Excuse me?" she asked.

"If I remember right, there was a note in the file for that case, said the child was actually not theirs," she replied, clicking through some sub-menus before she found the pdf she was looking for. "Yeah, here it is, he was right. Peter Whitfield was actually adopted, about a year before he was killed."

Diana nodded.

"You think that has anything to do with the murder?"

Diana bent over and put her hands to her face.

"I have no fucking idea," she said.

"You need some sleep," Ariadne said. "Go home. We really didn't get anywhere today. Kendrick already called it quits. Richard too. I was about to throw in the towel myself. Hardly left this room all goddamn day and we've got nothing to show for it."

Diana looked up finally, but just kept staring, blank and straight ahead. Ariadne noticed and reached across the table, shaking her by the shoulder. Even that didn't work. Ariadne put her hands on Diana's.

"You've done enough for one day. Go home. If something pops we'll know as soon as it happens."

Diana finally took a deep breath, and looked at her friend for the first time since entering the room.

"Maybe you're right," she said. "This whole thing is just getting to me, that's all."

"You're dedicated, always have been. Nothing wrong with that," Ariadne replied. "But you're not going to do anyone any good unless you get some rest. Now go, get out of here. I'll see you in the morning."

DAY EIGHT

"His names are as numerous as the places and cultures that once worshipped him: blind idiot god, daemon sultan, the chaos beyond, the madness of the void. They must all be considered little more than hints, fleeting glimpses of that which cannot be seen, which cannot ever be known—and entity that human consciousness cannot understand, and should not try to perceive—this is Azathoth."

"Before the Gods"
Professor Phillipe Gamaliel
Unofficial Translation from the
French Language Ed., 1989

THIRTY-SIX

F.B.I. FIELD OFFICE, ONE CENTER PLAZA
BOSTON, MA

She wasn't sleeping. She was just lying there in her bed, staring at the ceiling.

The clanging, simulated electronic bells of her phone jolted Diana Mancuso back to reality. The flashing display lit up the dim of her hotel room. She saw Ariadne's smiling face on the screen.

"You're not gonna believe this," Ariadne began.

Diana squinted, her eyes sore from lack of sleep. The past few day's events—if that was what they were—had her going around in circles in her head, trying to make sense of a situation that was now beginning to seem utterly senseless.

"Try me," Diana finally said.

"They're *all* adopted," Ariadne replied. "All the victims."

Diana got up. She was already on her way out of bed when she answered.

"I'll be right there," she said.

«««—»»»

Diana rushed through the sliding door to the inner confines of the command center with a renewed burst of energy.

"So, what's the deal?" she asked. "You got something on the kids?"

Ariadne was at the main table, behind the always-expanding cardboard fort. Her face lit up when Diana came in.

"What's the deal with *you*?" Ariadne replied.

"What are you talking about?"

Ariadne motioned toward Diana with a flick of the fingers.

"You're wearing a skirt. You never wear a skirt."

Diana grumbled.

"Long story," she replied.

"Wait, is this because of..." Ariadne lowered her voice to a whisper, "*Richard?*"

Diana's face morphed from annoyed to angry.

"I'm out of fucking pants, okay! I didn't pack much for this trip and I haven't exactly had time to do laundry. This is all I've got right now."

Ariadne smiled.

"Gotcha, sorry."

"Can we get to actual business, or would you like to talk about my shoes too?"

Ariadne looked at her pumps for an instant, then right back to her laptop.

"Not the pair I would've picked with that outfit, but fine," she said. "Let's get to it. You might want to sit down for this—especially in those heels."

Diana was too fired up. She refused.

"Fine, have it your way. What you said last night got me thinking, so before I went home I played a hunch. I ran some of the other names," she said. "You'll never, ever guess what I found."

Diana just peered at her over her giant coffee.

"All the kids were adopted?" Diana said. "You told me that on the phone."

"Sure, but that's not the big news," Ariadne replied. "The big is news is *where they were adopted from*."

"I don't understand."

"Every single child victim came from the exact same place," she said. "An agency called *Hope of Tomorrow*."

"Now we're getting somewhere. Great work, Ari, that's the closest thing to a pattern in Vayne's behavior that I've seen so far," she said.

"Maybe he had some kind of connection with this place. Not so strange for a child predator to insinuate himself into a position where he'd have access to kids. In those days, it might have gone unnoticed."

"Well, I thought the same thing," Ariadne said. "So I dug deeper. Looked for anything I could get on this *Hope of Tomorrow* place."

"And?" Diana asked.

"Patience, patience," Ariadne replied. "We'll get there. Trust me, you want to hear this."

"Okay, get to it then."

"I'm just wondering how nobody ever picked up on this before," Ariadne said.

"I can see it," Diana said. "These murders were spread out over multiple jurisdictions. No one was cross-referencing info, and once Vayne confessed, everyone closed the book. No further investigation needed."

"Makes sense, I guess."

"So, what else did you get? You said you had more?"

"Here's the thing. There isn't much to go on with this place, and what little I could find was strange," Ariadne said.

"Everything on this case is strange," Diana replied.

"Right, but this is *really* strange," Ariadne continued.

Diana smiled. *You have no idea what strange is*, she thought.

"I dug up the certificate of incorporation," Ariadne continued. "They were registered up in Massachusetts, but the agency only operated for one month, back in seventy-three."

"You're right, that is odd," Diana replied. "The business only existed for a month?"

"Yup. I ran a search for all the records last night. Things like adoption certificates are usually buried pretty deep, but if you know what you're doing it's just a matter of getting to them."

"Aren't those confidential?" Diana asked.

"Supposed to be," Ariadne answered with a sly grin. "Like I said, you've gotta know what you're doing. I have a trick or two that you probably shouldn't know about, boss. Not strictly *legal*, if you know what I mean."

"Gotcha, so what did you dig up?"

"Get a load of this: they only adopted out fourteen children. Then they closed down forever."

"Fourteen, one more than the murders back then," Diana said. "So there *was always another one*. Vayne talked about unfinished business, I didn't know what he meant. So let me guess—Saxon is the fourteenth?"

Ariadne shook her head.

"Nope, that was what I thought too, but his name never pops up. I double checked, Roger Saxon's birth certificate is on file in Maryland, he was definitely not one of them," she replied.

"Damn, so what's left?" Diana asked. "Who were these kids? Where did they come from?"

"No clue," Ariadne replied. "There wasn't much to go on. No records exist anywhere else and there's no mention of them in any other sources. If I had to guess, it looks like a front, a place set up to make things look legal in case anyone gave it a glance, but nothing more."

"Illegal adoptions?" Diana said. "There's no way that's what all this is about."

"Well, here's where the rubber really meets the road. I did a Lexis-Nexis search on the founder of the agency, a woman named Valeria Thorne," Ariadne said. "Ever heard of her?"

"Sounds vaguely familiar, why?"

"Interesting character, from what I've seen."

"How so?"

"She was a philanthropist, for one. Super wealthy, granddaughter of one of those nineteenth century railroad barons."

"Okay, that's where I know the name," Diana said. "History Channel did a series on those guys last summer. Vanderbilts, Rockefellers, J.P. Morgan. That kind of money, right?"

"Exactly. Anyway, she had an interesting life. Traveled around a lot when she was young, then appears to have dedicated herself to various charity projects in her later years, finding ways to spend her family's fortune, I guess."

"So nothing out of the ordinary."

"At least until she gets older, and that's where it gets interesting. Really fucking interesting."

"How so?"

Ariadne pulled up a news article. It was dated August 1968. She'd already read it, so she summarized even as Diana looked on.

"Apparently she had a bit of a falling out with the rest of her family," she said. "Says here they thought she was losing it, there were even accusations she had fallen in with some kind of a cult."

"A cult? What kind?" Diana asked.

"Doesn't say, could be anything, this was the late sixties, looks like she had some counter culture leanings back then. Could have been just the way her WASPy blue-blood family saw things. Anyway, seems that the last straw took place in the early seventies. Says here she went and dropped a ton of money on acres and acres of worthless land way the hell out in western Massachusetts."

"There's not much out there," Diana said.

"Right, just hill country, according to this," Ariadne said, continuing to scroll through the documents she'd saved to her folder earlier that morning, until she came to one that piqued her interest. "Ah, this is interesting."

"What's that?"

"Supposedly the property was some kind of sacred Indian burial ground or something," she answered.

"Indian ground? Here in Massachusetts?"

"Yeah, ever heard of Mystery Hill?" Ariadne asked.

"Sure, up in New Hampshire. I saw it once on a field trip in high school, why?'

"There's a few of these spots up here, out in the New England boonies. Old stone monuments, no one really knows how they got there or who built them, kind of America's answer to Stonehenge."

"She bought one of them?" Diana asked.

"Yeah, a huge plot of land that contained a hill with a bunch of old burial grounds and great big standing stones. The locals call the place Ghost Moon Hill," she said.

"Kind of a spooky name."

"For good reason, evidently. Says here the stones erected around the top are a rare form of granite. Had a tendency to sparkle in the moonlight."

"No kidding?" Diana replied.

"They say that on nights when the moon is full the whole top of the hill glows like a second one."

"Hence the name."

"Exactly."

"So why the hell did she buy this place?"

"Well, no one ever really figured that out. Speculation was that she was setting up some kind of a commune, given the cult rumors, mysterious old Indian burial grounds and all. Anyway, I guess the family cut her off at that point."

"So what happened to her?"

"Apparently she disappeared up there, went out one day into the woods and was literally never heard from again," Ariadne answered.

"Shit…"

"Oh, you ain't seen nothing yet," Ariadne said. "This says some family members went up to look for her a few months after she tuned in and dropped out, so to speak. Looks like they found the Indian burial stones, but that's all. What was weird though, was that they reported that the entire area looked to have been burned by a recent fire. No trees were standing for a half mile in any direction, and the grounds were totally scorched."

"Let me see that."

Diana studied the black and white photo on the screen.

"Her body was never found," Ariadne said. "She just vanished."

Diana sat back.

"When was this?" she asked.

"Looks like they went up to look for her around January of seventy-four," Ariadne said.

"When were the adoptions?"

"Back in…October of seventy-three."

"That can't be a coincidence."

"My thoughts exactly," she said.

Diana turned around. For a long moment she stared at the wall, puzzling over the deluge of new information, running through combinations and permutations in her head like a chess player.

"What are you thinking?" Ariadne finally asked.

Diana turned. Her eyes were wide open.

"Remember the other day, when you said that Luther Vayne's employment records were sketchy?" she asked.

"Yeah, dishwasher in Hartford, bouncer in Providence, bodyguard somewhere, right?"

"Do you have those?"

Ariadne flipped through some pages, and clicked through some files on her laptop.

"Got his W2s," she said. "Why?"

"Pull them up," Diana said.

Ariadne did, opening several windows on her screen at once, all of them pdf scans of old tax documents.

"What are you looking for?" she asked.

Diana scrolled through them.

"We weren't checking the names of his employers before," she said.

A moment later she stopped scrolling. She highlighted a section of old type-faced text and muttered under her breath.

"Mother–fucker."

Ariadne saw it an instant later.

"He worked as a body guard for none other than …" she began.

"Valeria Thorne," Diana said. "How's that for a goddamn connection?"

"Unbelievable."

"Vayne drops off the map when?" Diana followed up.

Ariadne leafed through some documents.

"Last record of him is September of seventy-three," she said. "Right before the kids were adopted."

Diana turned around again. She paced across the floor for a moment before continuing.

"Let's put this all together: Vayne's cellmate said he was ordered to undo the work of the whore of Sothoth," she said.

"Right, because *Azathoth commands it*...supposedly," Ariadne replied.

"His kill ritual is based on a five thousand year old Sumerian rite."

"And Azathoth is a god-figure worshiped by Sumerians five thousand years ago," Ariadne added. "I'm with you so far."

"A rite designed to destroy the souls of the victims," Diana continued. "The souls of those who consorted with the demon."

"A demon like...Sothoth?" Ariadne said.

"It's gotta be," Diana said.

"Where does that lead us?"

Diana shook her head. Finally, she sat down, and she breathed deep. Then she put her head in her hands before looking up again.

"I didn't tell you everything yesterday," she said.

"About what?"

"Whitfield."

"You said he died," Ariadne replied. "What could be worse than that?"

"He killed himself," she answered. "Right in front of me. Because of me. Because of what he had to tell me. He was afraid."

"Of what?"

"I wish I knew," Diana said.

Ariadne got up, she pulled a chair up directly across from Diana. She put her hands on her knees.

"What exactly did this guy tell you out there at Shady Meadows?" Ariadne asked.

Diana didn't reply directly, but she did keep on going, thinking out loud or maybe just trying to get it all of it out of her system.

"He knew. I thought maybe he was senile...*but he knew. He knew about Sothoth.*"

"Sothoth? Wait a second, what do you mean, he knew?" Ariadne asked.

"It's not just that the kids, the victims, were adopted," Diana continued.

"Diana! What the hell did he say?" Ariadne demanded.

Diana finally looked her in the eyes,

"He said that Sothoth was the father of his child. *Yog Sothoth*. That was the real father," she said.

"Son of a bitch."

"The child of Sothoth...the whore of Sothoth...Azathoth commands it...they must be destroyed...total spiritual annihilation..." Diana continued.

"Vayne believes the children he killed were the spawn of a demon?" Ariadne asked.

"Exactly," Diana replied. "Valeria Thorne's family thought she'd gotten involved with some kind of a cult, right?"

"Supposedly."

"A cult of Yog Sothoth, maybe?"

"Could be," Ariadne replied.

She looked harder at Diana. Her eyes were focused, determined. Serious.

"Umm, just to be clear here, and don't take this the wrong way," Ariadne added. "But, you don't actually....you know...believe any of this...right?"

Diana shot her back an icy stare.

"I don't know," she answered. "I honestly don't know what to believe anymore."

"So then, what do we do?"

"We follow the evidence," Diane replied. "Wherever it goes."

Ariadne nodded and opened her hands as if to surrender the point.

"Okay, so these kids, and this phony adoption agency. They had something to do with all this, agreed? We know Vayne was there. *We know that*. Somehow he got wrapped up in this cult with Thorne and by the end of it all, he believed that these kids were demon children."

"Okay, fine. But the numbers don't add up," Ariadne said. "Vayne's cellmate told you there were only thirteen, right?"

"Yeah, and we know there were fourteen kids adopted," Diana replied.

"That's a problem."

"Hang on," Diana said. "What if Vayne screwed up?"

"What do you mean screwed up?"

"I can't believe I didn't see this before. Where's that statement, the one from Cleveland? The Dressler murders."

Ariadne searched around until she found it. She handed it to Diana, who scanned it until she found the passage she remembered from the other day. She read it out loud.

"Believe me detective, money was not involved, in this or any other of my recent deeds. These were no mere children. At least until tonight, and for that I am very sorry."

"*They were no mere children*," Ariadne echoed.

"*Until tonight*," Diana said.

"Holy shit…he killed the wrong kid?" Ariadne realized.

"And he's been looking to fix that ever since," Diana said. "He has one more left to kill. But he doesn't know who it is."

"Why now, all of a sudden, after so long?"

Diana puzzled.

"The letter," she said.

"Someone on the outside tipped him off. Directed him to Roger Saxon," Ariadne said.

"Not just someone," Diana replied. "Victor Gregorian or somebody close to him had a hand in that. I'm sure of it, I just don't know why and I can't fucking prove it. Not yet, anyway."

Diana tapped her fingers on the table.

"Let's take another look at Saxon," she said. "See if he ties into Gregorian in any way. He's the missing link in all this. There's got to be something."

"We know Saxon wasn't adopted, he wasn't one of the fourteen," Ariadne replied.

Diana was back up on her feet and already heading for the door.

"Right, but there has to be some connection," she said, on her way out. "Keep checking, dig into his history. Family, associates, school. It's there. If Gregorian tipped Vayne off to Saxon there's got to be a reason. If Saxon wasn't the final target, then he was a lead, a clue—to something…someone. We need to know who that is."

"Where are you going?"

"Demon hunting," she said.

THIRTY-SEVEN

GHOST MOON HILL
WEST LAVINIA, MA

A slow caravan of vehicles emerged from the woodlands. The only road in sight, a rocky unpaved course that was little more than a trail, snaked up the edge of the forested hill before ending near the crest, where a wide clearing opened. There were two Lincolns, two Mercedes SUVs and a black Rolls Royce at the center. They stopped where the road stopped, running up to an empty, eerie complex that stood out against the murky wilderness.

Barren forest encircled the site, forming a kind of natural palisade that only made it seem more secluded. Stout trunks of oak and hemlock mingled among ragged-edged shagbark hickory. Slumbering through the depths of winter, their skeletal fingers reached up from the lower branches into a dense canopy. Even bare of foliage, the tangled brush still cast most of the undergrowth in permanent shadow. The harsh green of conifer needles made for the only hints of color across the field.

Though the summit of the hill had long ago been cleared, the passage of intervening decades had seen the forest creep ever closer to reclaiming the entire site. Saplings protruded from the spaces between standing stones, slowly pushing the ancient monuments aside. A frozen carpet of last autumn's leaves lay scattered over the grounds, cradling pristine swathes of snow.

The inner-most precincts remained free of significant growth, leaving the largest of the megaliths to stand bare beneath the cloudy New England skies.

The doors opened all at once, and a cadre of men and women stepped out into the cold highland air. They waited for Victor Gregorian to step out of his Rolls last, and they lined up behind him as he led the way into the site.

Slate dominated the field. A series of cairns, some half-buried or crumbling into ruin dotted the open area. In between them, set in no apparent order, were menhirs of varying heights. Some were surrounded by circles of smaller stones or connected by trails of rocks, arranged in patterns that were broken by the intrusion of weeds or fallen, decaying timbers.

All the structures formed a frame around the largest monument, at the center of the complex. There a barrow rose some fifteen feet higher than any other spot on the hill, forming a secondary crest. Atop it was a granite circle of thirteen standing stones, all hewn from the same quarry, but now varying in height after centuries of exposure. Some were broken down to little more than stubs, others retained nearly the full measure of their original glory, though their faces were pitted and worn.

This shattered crown was itself an adornment, guarding a central tower that lorded over the entire field. Rising from a squat, diamond-shaped foundation, the tower narrowed as it climbed to a flat pinnacle, no more than ten feet across. Links of rusted chain lay discarded atop it, where the stone had been stained black with soot and dried blood.

"My friends, here will we right the wrongs of those who have gone before us," Gregorian began. "Here will be the final act of this long play of horrors."

They all bowed their heads.

"The first act of a new age."

They moaned and chanted in unison. But among all of them, James Krieger was unsettled. He kept lifting his head, checking around him as if he worried they were not alone. Gregorian noticed, and he wasted no time calling out his old friend.

"You need not fear any intrusions," Gregorian assured him.

"I know you say that, but is this wise?" Krieger replied. "The Convergence is still more than twenty-four hours away, is it not?"

"It is," Gregorian answered.

"Then shouldn't we stay out of sight until then?' Krieger asked. "It seems like an unnecessary risk to come out here now, to expose ourselves like this."

"Always thinking like a general," Gregorian said. "I understand your concern, but you need not worry."

"How can you be so certain?" Krieger asked. "Vayne has tracked us at every turn, how do you know he won't find us here?"

"You misunderstand, James," Gregorian answered. "Vayne is indeed coming here, and that is just as I desire."

The others grumbled, nearly thrown into panic by that single comment.

"Coming here?" Bremmer asked. "I thought we were careful, we took every precaution!"

Gregorian nodded.

"Vayne *must* come here," Gregorian said. "Just as we must. That has always been inevitable. I chose to control the events, to guide him. But make no mistake, he is coming. We will welcome him when he does."

The others chattered amongst themselves, protesting and arguing. Gregorian suffered none of it.

"Enough," he replied. "My plans will become clear to you when I choose to reveal them. Until then, we must make ready. There is work to be done before Vayne arrives, and before the door can be opened once more."

THIRTY-EIGHT

MUSEUM OF FINE ARTS
BOSTON, MA

This time, Diana knocked.

The voice on the other side of the door hesitated a moment before answering. She heard the shuffling of some papers and a chair sliding across the floor in the interim. She had a pretty good idea what that meant—and she didn't care a bit.

Dr. Shaw eventually opened the door for her, stand-offish as ever, but welcoming nonetheless.

"Ah, Agent Mancuso," he greeted her, much more confident than he'd been the day before. "Back so soon?"

She didn't even bother with politeness.

"What you told me yesterday, about...mating with a demon, mating with Sothoth," she began. "Has anyone ever tried to do that?"

"Excuse me?" he replied, stopping as he got to his desk. He turned back to look at her very slowly. "What did you just say?"

"What I mean is: what if someone did believe in all that?" she stammered. "What would they think? Has anyone ever tried to do that?"

"I thought you were an agnostic," he answered.

"I am, but I'm also following the evidence," she said. "Now please, indulge me for a second, okay? What would someone do if...this was what they wanted to do...?"

"Honestly, I'm not sure I can help you with this," he replied. "I mean, now we're getting into pure folklore."

"I don't care," she said. "I need to know."

"Okay, if you really want to hear about this, there is one story I remember," he continued. "It's just an urban legend, so take it for what it's worth."

"What is it?"

He offered a seat, as he too got back behind his desk. Although Diana was edgy and buzzing from caffeine, she took him up on it. She didn't even notice him reaching under his desk, and she couldn't see the Browning sitting in the half-open drawer next to his hand.

"They tell this story up at Miskatonic, where I studied with Gamaliel. Maybe just to scare freshman," Carter said. "Anyway, supposedly someone did try to do what you're talking about, a long time ago. As you can imagine, it didn't turn out well."

"I want to hear it," she replied.

Her tone left no doubt as to her seriousness. Even then however, though he nodded and sat back as if to take one last deep, peaceful breath before launching into the telling, he seemed intent to delay as long as possible. He fiddled with a handkerchief from his pocket, before fidgeting around in his chair.

"You have to imagine, this was maybe a hundred years ago, maybe more even. Out in the hill country somewhere," he began.

"Hill country?" she interrupted. "As in, out in western Massachusetts?"

"Yeah, exactly," he answered.

"Fuck," she whispered. He paused, until she looked back to him. "I'm sorry, please, go on."

"This recluse—I forget his name—he had a run-down old place in the sticks, not really near any town. God knows how true any of this is, but the story goes that he was one of the last of a very long and very old tradition of witchcraft."

"Like the Salem witches?" Diana asked.

"Not exactly," he answered. "You have to understand, what we're talking about isn't *double bubble toil and trouble*, or *black cauldrons and eye of newt*. This is really esoteric, really rare stuff."

"I understand."

"I'm not sure that you do," he said. "When I say *witchcraft*, when people out in those little towns in the forests in western New England say *witchcraft*, they're not talking about it the way the rest of us do. It's not just folklore to them. They mean it. They're talking about witchcraft in the oldest sense of the word, the summoning and harnessing of things from beyond this world."

"Demons?"

"Call them whatever you want," he said. "No name we could give them would really describe the horrors recounted in these tales."

"*Things far stranger. Far harder to dismiss by naming them,*" she said, too low for him to make out.

"What's that?" he asked.

She shook her head.

"Nothing, please go on," she replied.

"Right, well this old guy is supposed to have had the means to summon the gate-keeper," he continued.

"Yog Sothoth."

"Correct. That in-and-of-itself is no small thing," he said. "Even Gamaliel had no clue how to do something like that, and I doubt he'd have even attempted it if he did."

"Why?"

He looked at her sideways. His face got deadly serious.

"Let's just say that's not a door you'd want to open," he replied.

She nodded.

"The story goes that he went through great trouble to get the ritual just right, every little detail just perfect, and when he finally did, he didn't waste the chance."

"What did he do?" she asked. "Whatever it was, I'd have to guess he didn't succeed right? Otherwise everyone would know this story."

"Oh, he succeeded, that wasn't the issue. In fact, the problem turned out to be that he did exactly what he wanted to do. He summoned the entity, and for a little while anyway, he did bend it to his will, so to speak."

"Then how come I've never heard of this?"

"Stay with me, Agent Mancuso," he cautioned. "You see, this guy had a daughter, and the story goes that once he summoned the beast he managed to…shall we say…play matchmaker."

Diana's face went pale.

"He did what?"

"Yup, exactly," Carter answered. "They say Yog Sothoth had some kind of intercourse with her, and he was able to impregnate the daughter."

"The whore of Sothoth," she said.

"Right."

"So what happened to the child?"

"Children—plural," he corrected. "Supposedly she had twins. As for how they ended up, well, that's a whole 'nother story. Like I said though, it didn't end well—for any of them."

"The fucking whore of Sothoth," she muttered again.

"I suppose you could call her that," he said.

She shook her head.

"No, sorry, I was just thinking out loud," she replied. "This woman, this daughter, she didn't survive, I take it?"

"In the story you mean?" he asked. "Because you're almost looking like you might believe this stuff."

"I'm serious," she said.

"I know, and that's what worries me," he said.

Her expression was total no nonsense, and she didn't need to say another word.

"Okay, okay. Like I was saying, this was over a hundred years ago. They'd all be dead by now anyway, of course. But the story goes that the act of mating with the beast was somewhat…hazardous to her health. The half breed children were pretty monstrous too, apparently."

"No one's tried to do this since?"

"Summon Yog Sothoth?"

"And mate with him, right."

He paused, and slowly leaned closer in his chair; a worried, almost pained expression now coming over his craggy face.

"It's just a story. Like I said, they tell it up in Miskatonic to scare the freshmen."

"But what if someone did do it, did try it?" she asked.

Carter puzzled, but eventually did answer.

"If the stories were true, you mean?"

"Exactly."

"Well, according to the myths, if someone ever did do this, open a doorway for Yog Sothoth, it would usher forth unimaginable things into our world."

"How so?"

"We're talking about dark forces too terrible to fathom, eldritch powers beyond human contemplation," he answered. "For those unprepared to contend with such things, it would cause certain madness."

He stared off to the ceiling as he spoke the words, enrapt by his own telling. Diana didn't even notice.

"So it would have to be destroyed," she said.

He looked down, then back to her with a hint of a smile, as if she had missed the whole point.

"Of course, I suppose it would."

"Utterly and totally destroyed. Absolute annihilation," she said, recalling the photos of the ancient sacrificial victims, impaled and splayed out in so grisly a fashion.

"Right."

She dropped her voice to a whisper.

"Azathoth commands it," she said.

"Excuse me?" he asked.

"Thank you, professor," she said, reaching out to shake his hand as she got up from the chair. "You've been very helpful."

He smiled.

"Of course," he replied. "Anything I can do for you, agent."

She turned and left. The moment she was gone, he pulled open the lower drawer of his desk, and ran his hand over the pistol.

"Anything at all," he said.

THIRTY-NINE

F.B.I. FIELD OFFICE, ONE CENTER PLAZA
BOSTON, MA

As Richard Norris's private secretary, Dolores Reardon had accompanied the Assistant Director from Washington up to the Boston field office. Dutiful as ever, she continued to tend to his every administrative need during the duration of their stay there.

She was packing up her things for the night when Diana and Ariadne came rushing in to her temporary office.

"We need to see the boss," Diana said.

"He's taking a call from D.C., someone on the appropriations committee," Dolores said. "I was told to let no one in."

Diana looked at the secretary, loyal and honest as ever.

"Dolores, you've known me a while now, right?"

The woman agreed.

"I'm going in to see Richard," she continued. "Get out of here now and I'll say I never saw you. You were already gone when we got here."

"If I don't?" Dolores said.

Diana got closer to her, invaded her personal space.

"Like I said, you've known me a while. Do you really want to know the answer to that?" she said.

Dolores took her purse and walked out.

They were in Richard's office a moment later. As promised, he was on a call. When he saw them both barging in, he motioned for them to sit and he cut off the man on the other end of the phone.

"Hope that wasn't important," Diana said.

"No, just a Senator," he replied, with more than a hint of sarcasm. He let it drop an instant later. "What's going on? You have something?"

"More than that," Diana said. "We got a major break."

"How so?" he asked.

"A connection between all the vics," Diana replied. "I know what Vayne is doing."

"It's super freaky," Ariadne said, opening up her laptop as she placed it down on his desk. "Check this out."

He looked at the rows and rows of tabbed and saved documents on her screen. There were dozens, maybe hundreds. Plus, Diana came in holding reams of paper, and they were tabbed in a rainbow jumble of paper and plastic. Everything landed right on his desk.

"Okay, you got my attention," Norris said.

"We went back through everyone's history; I'm talking way back. Parents and grandparents type stuff," Diana said, her voice racing from caffeine overload and lack of sleep.

"I found an article in a legal journal from 1966 that talks about Roger Saxon's father's law firm. His dad, William Saxon was law partners with a guy Diana just met," Ariadne said.

"Just met…who is that?" Norris asked.

"Before he became a judge, Thomas Whitfield was a named partner with Armstrong, Saxon and Whitfield," Diana replied.

Norris shifted in his chair.

"Okay, that is odd, I grant you," he said. "What does that mean in the here and now though?"

"Just wait. That other guy, Lawrence Armstrong—well his daughter Lauren is the current White House Chief of Staff," Ariadne said.

The blank expression on the director's face left no doubt that he was unimpressed, and more than a little confused.

"They all know each other," Diana said. "Saxon's family and the Whitfields. That's why Vayne targeted Roger."

"Wait a second, slow down. I thought he was contacted, by someone on the outside," Norris said. "Wasn't there a letter you got from the prison?"

"Right, Saxon's face with the Star of Azathoth drawn next to it," she replied. "But I think that was just a lead. Vayne already knew that Saxon was in on it. That he was connected. I think he tracked down Roger not to kill him, but to get information."

Norris pondered. He reclined back in his chair, clasping his hands together, as if the insinuation of his friend's involvement was too difficult to process.

"But *he did* kill him," he said, through gritted teeth.

"I think that was to send a message," she answered.

"To who?"

"To the rest of them. To the real target. The thirteenth child of the demon," she said.

Norris sat up. He cocked his head in a self-conscious double-take, looking at Diana sideways. His eyes read anger and shock at once, but she didn't see it. She just kept right on going.

"There's more," she continued, oblivious to his growing concern.

Norris glanced over to Ariadne, who shrank a bit under his harsh, increasingly agitated stare.

"Armstrong, Saxon and Whitfield were heavy hitters on the D.C. legal circuit back in the day, and one of their biggest clients was a charity called the Thorne Foundation," she said.

"As in Valeria Thorne?" Norris asked.

"Founder and C.E.O.," Diana added. "Wait 'til you hear who was on their board. There were three directors who ran the thing, one was the Reverend Charles Leland Hayden, father to *America's Pastor*, Graham Thurman Hayden."

Norris nodded.

"The other directors were department store magnate James Krieger, whose son you know as the Chairman of the Joint Chiefs and Senator Samuel F. Walker, father of Joshua and husband of Emily."

"Vayne double murder number three," Ariadne added.

"It goes deep. Once we got the ball rolling, it just kept going," Diana said. "Among the major contributors to the Thorne Foundation, as listed in their non-profit disclosure statement from 1973: Archibald Bremmer, whose daughter runs Neutrino Industries today, Congressman William J. Fisk, husband and father of Jennifer and Arthur Fisk, murder number eight."

"It goes on and on," Ariadne said.

"I'm telling you, Richard. This is it. Every single one of the victims was associated with this. The ones who didn't adopt a kid are the only ones who survived, and every one of those kids grew up to take on a major role in government or industry."

Norris placed his hands on his desk. His eyes were seething.

"Just exactly how wide of net are we casting here, ladies?" he asked, obviously uncomfortable.

"*Ladies*?" Diana replied, eyeing him with a snarl. "Don't you get it? All the vics were connected, except for one."

"Who's that?" he asked.

"Erica Dressler," Diana said.

"The Ohio murder. The last one," he said.

"Right, she wasn't married and she wasn't a member of the Thorne Foundation. In fact, she wasn't even wealthy, at least until after the adoption. So we did some more digging. Before she inherited her money, tax records indicate she worked as a maid," Diana said.

"A maid?" he asked.

"A maid and then a personal assistant—for Valeria Thorne," Ariadne said.

"So at exactly the same time Thorne vanishes, she comes into a ton of money, and an adopted son," Diana said. "Hell of a severance package."

Norris nodded, shifting back and forth in his chair.

"We know all of these folks were connected, and we know it all has to do with their relationship to Valeria Thorne. The problem is, that still leaves us with one missing kid," Diana said.

"Right, *Hope of Tomorrow* adopted out fourteen kids," Ariadne replied. "But we still only have thirteen victims, plus Saxon. We know *he wasn't* adopted."

"You see, he's looking for the last one, one more. The last demon child," Diana said.

"The last *kid*, you mean?" Norris asked.

"One more, yeah," Diana said, ignoring his attempt at a correction. "This Thorne woman, she had all these rich big wigs throwing money at her, and she does what with it all?"

Norris shook his head.

"She buys Indian burial ground out in the middle of nowhere," Diana continued. "On some kind of mission to start a cult. She founds an adoption agency for only fourteen kids—who all go to donors of hers, and she vanishes under mysterious circumstances right after the kids show up.

"Then Vayne, her former bodyguard who dropped off the map at the same time she did, goes off on a killing spree, tracking down all of these kids and killing them along with their mothers," she said.

"I'm still not sure what this all adds up to," Norris said.

Diana threw up her hands. She got up from her chair and banged her fist on the end of the desk.

"Damn it, don't you see?" she said, raising her voice. Her hands were trembling in a rush of adrenaline and exasperation. "Valeria Thorne was running her fucking cult out there, a cult of Azathoth or Sothoth—maybe both. Hell, she might have even been the fucking whore of Sothoth herself, for all I know."

Norris looked to Ariadne once more, now almost fuming. Diana still didn't notice. She just kept going.

"Whatever happened up there, Vayne came away believing the same thing that Judge Whitfield believed—that these kids were demonic. The spawn of Sothoth. They all had to be destroyed. My bet is he killed her and then he worked his way through all of the kids. But when he got to the last one…or what he must have thought was the last one…somehow he knew that there was still one more."

Norris shook his head, clearly dumbfounded.

"Now he's trying to find the one he missed, forty-some years later, all grown up," Diana said. "The last demon child of Sothoth."

Finally Norris lost his patience. He slammed his fists down on his desk, so hard he cracked the finish. Diana turned. The flash of anger caught her completely off-guard.

"Damn it, Diana, that's enough!" he shouted.

She stepped back.

"What are you talking about?" she asked.

"I put you on this file to do what you do best, to work up a profile, to give the field team some leads," he said.

"And?" she replied.

He leaned forward.

"Are you even listening to yourself?" he asked. "The demon child of Sothoth? You sound like you really believe all of this!"

She stared him down, her eyes like daggers.

"Don't you dare pull that on me," she replied. "I told you, damn it, I fucking told you when this whole thing started."

"Told me what?"

"If you want to do this job you can't go halfway," Diana said. "You have to go all in. You gotta get inside the heads of these bastards. You gotta see what they see. You gotta understand how they see the world—and why. That's what I do. That's what I'm doing now. I'm in Vayne's head."

"You sure he's not in yours?" Norris asked.

She looked down. The suggestion hit closer to home than he could ever know, but she wasn't about to let on.

"What do you think?" she finally answered, apparently settled down a bit, but still eyeing him with a fierce glare. "Do you think I'm crazy, is that what you're saying? That I've gone off the deep end, or something? If that's what you think, then fucking say it. Say it to my face, don't dance around it."

Norris sat back, rocking in his chair for a moment. He lowered his voice, trying to calm down her Irish temper with a softer tone.

"You're right, Diana. This is my fault," he said. "Look, you said it yourself when we got started on this. You're not field personnel. Your job is to build a profile. I let you go out there. Hell, I sent you out there. Now look at you."

"I'm trying to tell you what's really going on!" she snapped back.

"What's really going on?" he answered. "How much sleep have you gotten in the last week?"

She sneered at him.

"I'm serious," he said. "You look terrible, and honestly, this isn't you. You're barging in here, dumping old papers and half-baked dime novel theories on me, and what I need is a genuine psych profile to nail this prick."

Now it was Diana's turn to seethe.

"Fuck you," she said.

"Hey, goddamn it, I'm your fucking boss!" he shot back.

"Don't you do that, not now," she answered. "You can't be the boss when you want and…something else the rest of the time."

Norris looked over at Ariadne.

"Forget it, she knows," Diana said.

"Great, just fucking great Diana," he said. "Did you post it on Facebook too?"

She laughed a little. Then she walked slowly toward his desk. She lingered for a moment and then went around it, over to his side, invading his space. He didn't protest. He didn't seem to know what to do.

Diana leaned down. She grabbed him by the jacket lapels, so rough that she nearly tore the stitching. Then pulled him close and locked lips with him—hard and long.

By the time she pulled back, he was breathless. She kept her grip on his coat and she whispered to him.

"Go to hell…boss."

Then she turned and walked out of his office.

FORTY

GHOST MOON HILL
WEST LAVINIA, MA

Dusk came early at mid-winter, and as the gloaming sky darkened over the forest, Gregorian's people hurried to finish unpacking everything from their caravan. They carried no artificial lights, and thus worked quickly, hammering stakes and pitching tents right up until the sun sank below the horizon.

By the last of the light they had succeeded in setting up an elaborate campsite; a small complex of fencing and temporary shelters that sprawled across the hilltop.

Everything was centered around the main dais, the highest point on the crest of Ghost Moon Hill. It was there that Victor Gregorian had set himself down upon their arrival, and where he remained whilst his comrades put themselves to the task at hand. Seated in his wooden folding chair like some traveling sultan, idle as his servants labored all around, he had buried himself for hours in one final contemplation of the old manuscripts, taking every last moment of natural light to scan the yellowed pages yet again.

As night finally closed in, dropping the temperature well below freezing, Janet and Logan both approached him. They had bundled themselves up in parkas and mittens and woolen hats. Gregorian however, seemed untroubled by the chill, and remained dressed in his robe, as though engaged in nothing more than a leisurely afternoon in his study.

"Nearly everything is set up, only a few more nips and tucks and we'll be snug as a bug. But we've lost the light," Logan said. "I know you ordered us to leave the torches in the cars, but unless…"

"The tents will wait," Gregorian answered. "We have more immediate concerns now."

"Do you mean?" Logan asked, his voice betraying a rare hint of unease.

"It's time," Gregorian replied. "The moon will rise within the hour, and our next task must be completed before then."

Logan's face went blank at the suggestion.

"But tonight?" he asked. "I thought we were still a day away from…"

Gregorian's head turned with a sharp glare. His eyes had grown wide, as though nearly enraged by the very hint of a question. Rather than reply, he banged his goat-headed cane on the rocks, seizing the attention of all the gathered. Then he reached down and untied the belt of his robe. When it fell open, the Disciples gasped in unison. What lay beneath was not what they expected.

His naked form, distended by what he had long claimed to be a rare genetic affliction, was now revealed to be anything but that. The lower reaches of his body were utterly inhuman. His stunted legs were covered with long, thick fur. They were more like the haunches of a goat than a man.

Where his belly should have been, what looked from the outside as little more than a bloated lump of flesh, was actually something horrific and unreal. His midsection was dominated by a series of coiled tentacles, which reached out as they unspooled from their apparent slumber. Each one was a mottled green-black, dripping in slime along rows of rigid scales and suckers. All of the strange arms ended with a separate maw, hissing and yammering with a half dozen fang-lined mouths.

He shed his silken robe entirely then, revealing that his upper arms and torso were covered in hard ridges of scales that resembled crocodile skin. From behind him, a fat, hairy tail curled around his body, undulating as it shivered in the cold.

His followers were dumbstruck, in awe of his true self laid bare, a monstrosity from which they could not look away and every one of them knew they had little choice but to obey.

"Now you see why we have come," Gregorian finally said. "Do any dare question me?"

He was met with utter silence.

"Everything must be done precisely according to plan," he continued. "I will permit no errors. You will all do exactly as I say, when I say it. Understood?"

Logan lowered his head, chastened and obedient. He stepped back, waving to Krieger beside him.

"It's time," the Englishman said.

"Fucking hell," Krieger answered.

«««—»»»

The two men returned a short time later, each one holding up the end of a long, steel storage-container removed from the rear of the SUV. Just the short distance between the cars and the center of the camp put them to great strain. Both men were sweating despite the sub-zero weather by the time they managed to haul it before Gregorian himself.

In near total darkness, with only the scattered sparkling of a handful of stars to guide them, they laid it down at his feet. In so doing, the two men were careful to place it on the ground as gently as possible, treating the contents as one might a sheet of glass or a fragile antique.

Gregorian shooed them all away once it was in front of him. None of them needed to be warned off any harder than that. They seemed anxious to step away. Gregorian, on the other hand, gazed upon the box with an almost solemn eye. He stepped closer, fighting through the discomfort of every step, wheezing and hobbling as his bovid legs trembled beneath his enormous girth. But he did not remain on his feet for long. Nearly staggering across the short length of ground toward the steel box, he came to his knees upon reaching it. He ran his hands along the beveled edge the way a collector might handle a long-lost heirloom.

The others held their silence, tense and unsteady, but muted in their discomfort and safely at a distance.

Unlike the ancient stone tabernacle of his subterranean temple, this sleek sarcophagus was high-tech. A control panel on the side nearest to Gregorian lit up when he touched the face, revealing a keypad and a liquid crystal display. The readout showed the temperature within the container, as well as humidity levels and air pressure.

He studied the numbers for a moment, then entered a numerical code. The controls chirped at the command. That brought an involuntary gasp from one of the gathered. Gregorian ignored it. He fixed his attention on the top of the container. A moment later, the code panel chirped a second time and the lid shifted.

A short burst of air rushed in when the seal broke, sending a puff of steam up from inside. The panel only slid open partially, providing a space no wider than a few feet. That was exactly as Gregorian had intended.

Once the container was open, he placed his hand on the edge of the lid, lowering his face as near to it as possible. A low groan answered from somewhere within, followed by a second rush of air, this time putrid with a stink like rotten eggs.

Gregorian inhaled the fumes, relishing them as one might a sweet perfume.

Something was moving inside. Noises began to stir within the darkness. A slurping and then a sloshing sounded, followed by the sucker-tip of a tentacle reaching up. At first it paused, as though stunted by the chill of the New England winter. But urged on by the whispers of Gregorian, the whole of it soon slithered up into view.

It was a fat arm, lined across the bottom with hundreds of tiny sucker-mouths dripping slime. A fringe of cilia shivered along the edges, and the top was scaly and rough as Gregorian's own warped skin. It seemed to feel around blind, like an antenna, before it met the waiting hand of Victor Gregorian. He cradled it, taking it in his palm and petting it with as much care as one would give a housecat.

"There we are," he said, in a soothing, almost paternal voice. "Not long now, I promise. How long have we waited, both you and I? So patient, for so many years."

The tentacle jerked in answer to his words, and a deeper moaning echoed from inside the container.

"I know, I know," Gregorian counseled. "Almost there. Just hold on a little more."

The moaning turned to grumbling, and then a second arm poked up through the narrow opening. There was barely room for the two, but it wormed its way out, fighting past the first tentacle for space. This one however was quite unlike the first. Although twisted and reptilian, the end was not a single point. Instead there seemed to be five distinct endings; shriveled and stunted though they were, it looked to be the remnants of a hand that now reached up to Gregorian. When the tentacle flexed, it became even more obvious, releasing the five protrusions so that they almost looked like fingers.

Gregorian reached toward them with both of his hands, clasping the slimy, distorted fingers with all the force he could muster. Then he brought his lips to it, and kissed the back of the tentacle.

"You know I love you. I always have," he whispered.

From the inside of the container, the groans subsided. A trilling kind of a purr replaced them, as Gregorian slowly stroked the end of the hand-like tentacle, like a mother caring for a sickly child.

The others continued to watch from several paces back, but in the dim they could barely see, even from that short distance. Gregorian did not leave them much time to wonder after his affections however. He braced himself on the steel capsule, and he called for them to join him.

"It's time, my children," he said. "We must consecrate the altar, tonight on the eve of the Convergence."

Prepared well in advance, Krieger and Logan duly stepped up. They once again took their positions at either end of the container, lifting it and carrying it up the treacherous final few steps to the highest point on the hill—the stone dais above Gregorian's perch.

Janet and Stephanie Bremmer joined Gregorian in watching the men bring the massive item up. Once they were done, they returned to the trio at the base of the dais.

"I trust you are all prepared for what we must now do," Gregorian said.

"We are," they answered, all but one.

Standing amongst the gathered, Janet alone looked confused.

"I apologize, sir," she said. "But I'm afraid you may have neglected to brief me on this. I'm not clear on what you need from me here."

Gregorian turned to her.

"I have not neglected anything," he replied.

Then he nodded to Logan. He and Krieger once again moved as one, this time directing their actions toward Janet. They were on either side of her before she could react, each man seizing hold of her arms and holding her fast.

"I merely refrained from informing you of your part to play, as I anticipated that you would not be an entirely willing participant," Gregorian continued.

Janet struggled, frantic as the sudden horror of her situation became clear.

"What? Why? I've been nothing but loyal!" she protested. "I've done everything you asked of me! Everything!"

Gregorian nodded.

"I could not agree more," he said. "You have been in every respect an excellent employee. But today is where our relationship comes to an end, for I must now demand one final act of loyalty. You may take solace in the fact that it is perhaps the most important thing you have ever done for me."

Her panicked attempts to break free from Krieger and Logan made it very clear that she did not see things the same way.

"The texts are very specific, you see," Gregorian said. "The altar must be consecrated on the eve of the summoning. They call for only one satisfactory method—it must be done with the blood of a loyal servant."

Janet screamed. She fought hard to tear free, but the two men held her far too tight for any hope of release. They lifted her, which only made her flailing and kicking legs seem all the more pathetic as they carried her, wailing and weeping, to the top of the dais.

Once upon the platform, they put her down upon the still-partially opened steel container, holding her against it as she kept fighting in a desperate last bid to save herself. It did no good. A moment after they pushed her down against the lid, a spiny tentacle reached out, coiled itself around her throat and pulled her toward the darkness within.

FORTY-ONE

GOVERNMENT CENTER DISTRICT
BOSTON, MA

Even as she got into the car, and pulled out on the road, Diana Mancuso had no idea where she was going. She just started driving.

That was hours ago.

Her head was spinning. Her eyes were heavy. They burned from lack of sleep. Images repeated in her mind: crime scene photos, prison cell walls, musty old documents. They all led to something, *they had to*, but the answers were worse than the questions. She replayed everything, every inference and supposition. She tried to focus, to make sense out of the mess. Only it didn't make sense. The harder she tried, the longer she kept at it, the less it all fit together.

Maybe Richard was right. Maybe she'd gone too far. And he didn't even know the half of it—*Vayne really was in her head.*

But if that were true, if she wasn't just unhinged, if those dreams—those fucking nightmares—really weren't just her imagination, then what?

She knew the answer, but it was almost impossible to say it out loud, let alone believe it. If she wasn't losing her grip, if everything she'd seen and heard and found was real—then *nothing added up*. None of the evidence made sense. There was no way to explain any of it.

The ancient death rites. Valeria Thorne's cult. Judge Whitfield. The suspicious adoptions. The mysterious envelope. The connection with Saxon. The nightmares that were more than nightmares.

If all of it were true, if she allowed herself to believe it—then that left her with one incredible, inevitable conclusion: Luther Vayne wasn't the true threat.

He was hunting it.

She wanted to find him. She *needed* to find him. But where? Maybe he was hiding out somewhere. There had to be a clue. There had to be something.

"Where the fuck are you?" she said.

The last thing she expected was a reply. But she got one. Whispered in her ear like the cold hiss of a snake.

"*Right beside you*."

She slammed on the brakes, right in the middle of an intersection. At that hour, there were no other cars in sight. She knew that voice. Even just three words were enough to trigger it. Everything came back to her. She shivered.

She closed her eyes, shut them hard and held them tight. She didn't want to listen, to see. The sounds of the pre-dawn morning fell away. Utter silence. Even the sound of her engine, idling in the middle of the street, faded out. But something smelled. It was stifling. It was the odor of sulfur.

Inside her car.

Then she heard it. Breathing. Next to her.

She froze. Paralyzed. She wanted to look. Almost as much as she wanted it all to go away. In a fit of courage, she turned her head. She opened her eyes.

Vayne was sitting next to her. She passed out before she could scream.

«««—»»»

The first thing she heard was weeping. Then screams. They were faint, like whispers in the distance, wailing somewhere beyond sight.

"What is that?" she asked, groggy and just coming around.

Luther Vayne answered.

"Voices of suffering," he said.

"Suffering?" she replied, as the fog in her eyes began to lift. "But who is…"

Her voice trailed off as her eyes cleared. She looked out in disbelief, straining to see and to understand. Words were little use as she realized that she was not where she should have been. *Or anywhere she could have been.*

A storm-tossed sea rolled overhead. The water was impenetrable and black. Moon beams from somewhere under their feet shattered on the surface. The sky was a pure shade of emptiness. Color ran from her eyes in vanishing, ephemeral waves. The horizon shivered, shimmering into focus, then fading back into featureless smog.

The ground beneath their feet did much the same, flashing into perfect order, then losing coherence as if nothing more than a mirage. The disconcerting effect made her head throb.

Diana rubbed her eyes, swamped with the worst sense of vertigo she had ever known.

"Your vision is fine," Vayne said. "Believe me, I should know."

She could not argue.

"You asked about suffering," he continued. "You now walk beside me. You hear what I hear. You see what I see."

"What *you see*?" she asked.

"Do you doubt that my sight extends beyond what human eyes can show you?" asked.

She knew he was right.

"Okay, but all of this," she replied. "What is it?"

"Eternal torment. Mindless, endless misery. So ancient and so deep that the pain of the nothingness has become a kind of pleasure," Vayne answered. "The only comfort in the cold reaches of forever is the agony itself, the consoling certainty, the emptiness of the abyss."

Diana shuddered.

"Why are you doing this?" she asked. "Toying with me?"

"I do no such thing," he answered. "Look around you. Do you consider this merely toying?"

"Bullshit, whatever this is, you're fucking with me and we both know it. I don't know how, and maybe I don't want to know, but let's quit screwing around here."

He nodded like a professor giving a lecture.

"Yes, there it is," he said.

"There *what* is?"

"Exactly what I find so appealing about you," he answered.

"What the fuck are you talking about?"

"Your persistence. Your drive. Although I warned you away, you pressed onward even harder. You continue to do so even now. That is intriguing to me."

"Let me get this straight…I intrigue you?"

"Believe me, Miss Mancuso, when one has existed for as long as I have, there is very little left to rouse curiosity. But you possess something unique, something truly interesting."

"Yeah? What's that?"

"Your spirit."

"My what?"

"Your soul is troubled. So very sad. Defeated and yet somehow still determined. I find that uncommonly interesting. And I find very little interesting anymore."

"Thanks…*I think.*"

"It has been a very long time since any member of your kind piqued my interest."

"My kind?" she asked.

"Humanity," he replied, without a hint of irony.

"But aren't you…?"

"I was, once. That is a distant memory, one I find it ever harder to recall as the time passes."

"Forty years on ice is a long time," she replied.

Much to her surprise, he smiled and then, even stranger—he began to laugh.

"Something funny about that?" she asked.

"Young lady, those years you speak of were but the blink of an eye. The time I refer to would be unimaginable to you. Eons uncounted."

She looked around again, lost in a dreamscape of horrors, a nightmare come alive.

"I don't understand."

"You will, very soon," he replied. "But you must first come along the way. You must see how this began, and then you may see how it will end—and why."

He extended his bony, tattooed hand. She looked at it for a long time, hesitant and trying hard to conceal her trembling.

"The history that brings us together is no secret to you now," he said. "You have followed the path this far. The only question that remains is whether you are prepared to go where it leads."

"I suppose there's no point in denying that," she replied.

Vayne looked back at her—looked through her with that icy, empty stare.

"You believe what you can see," he said. "You have seen much already. It is time you saw the rest."

She knew what he meant. She remembered all too well the trauma of being forced to walk through her own memories, to relive them. The intrusion, the shattering of her conscious self. *The raiding of her thoughts by another. She couldn't bear it. To feel that again—to feel everything again*. The pain. The horror. The suffering.

"I don't need that," she said. "I don't want it. Not again."

Vayne smirked. That sent a shudder through her.

"But you misunderstand," he answered. "This time it is not your mind that we must scour. It is mine. You walk now within my realm."

Somehow, that frightened her even more.

"You know how I began this journey," he said.

"I know you were a drifter after Vietnam, a veteran with no family and no future," she said. "I know you ended up working for Valeria Thorne. But not much more than that, not for sure, at least."

He nodded, extending his hands before him. As she had now come to expect, mist and shadow answered him, bending to his will, conjuring images from nothingness.

"She found me when I was at my lowest. It was accidental, almost fateful perhaps. That was what she used to say. I was drinking myself to death, trying to drown out the screams and push away the nightmares of what I had seen in the jungle. Working security at a dive bar in Providence only made that slow suicide easier. That was where our paths crossed, and everything changed."

She began to see it. Out of the mist, shapes were taking form in front of her. Walls, buildings, people. A barely recognizable man took shape, ghostly translucent and staggering toward them, yet very much distant. Separated by years as much as by inches and feet, a Kodachrome image from a bygone time brought to life one more time.

He was dressed in ratty olive drab fatigue pants and a torn Harley Davidson t-shirt. He was looking at something. She followed the line of his eyesight. It was a woman, just as phantom-like as his own apparition, another vintage Polaroid somehow made real. She was elegant, dressed to the nines in a mink coat, spiky heels and diamond earrings. Although well past middle age, her face was flawless and her narrow eyes were sharp.

"Valeria wandered into one of the worst bars in one of the worst parts of town," he continued. "Dock workers, unemployed vets and petty criminals looking for a mark. Drunk and angry, all the time. She was out of her element. Her car was broken down outside. She was lost and just looking to call a taxi."

Diana saw what happened next.

The ghostly projections moved like frames of super 8 film—halting and choppy, flickering in utter silence.

Valeria tried to make her way through a crowd of roughnecks, stymied and blocked at every turn by leering men, pawed at by a gauntlet of grimy hands. She pushed and she persisted, stubborn but outnumbered, until the human tide forced her to a corner table, and a crowd congregated around her.

Silent jeers erupted from the mouths of the phantoms, their hoots and hollers muted but evident from their furious gestures. They were closing in on her. One of them stroked her hair. Another smacked her rear. She put her hands up, ready to hold her own, as desperate as that fight would have been.

A moment later the scene changed. That familiar figure, lightly bearded under a bushy head of hair, pushed his way through the crowd.

It was Vayne, a shaggy, unscarred twenty-something with thick arms and serious eyes.

He swatted one of the goons away. He belted a second across the jaw, and then a third square in the nose.

Half of the crowd backed away. Someone took a swing at him with a pool cue. On contact with Vayne's forearm the stick snapped in two. He snatched the end away and plunged it into the neck of his attacker. The profusion of blood turned back the rest.

"I rescued her in that moment," Vayne continued. "But she was the one who really saved me—both from the police on that day, and from the hole I was falling into. She brought me out of it, and ushered me into a whole new world."

They watched as a new series of ghostly events played out before them, one after another in no apparent order. Scenes of black tie galas, back room deals and excursions to exotic locales—in every one Vayne was there, beside his benefactor; liege and loyal vassal to a modern day queen.

"By her side, I soon learned that she was more than the wealthy philanthropist the public saw. Behind closed doors, in the silence of the night, she showed me the truth behind all of her good works. The end to which she strived. She showed me…"

"Azathoth," Diana said.

"I was hesitant, of course," Vayne continued. "Only a lunatic would be otherwise. But I needed something. Something that only she offered me."

"What was that?"

"She promised peace, she promised wisdom and she promised perfection. She told us that Azathoth was the source, the true center of all things. That his path was the path to enlightenment."

"She promised everything," Diana said.

"Nothing short of it, indeed. But I wasn't the only one seduced by her," he said. "Valeria surrounded herself with a cabal of adherents. Chief among them were the twelve other priestesses, a mirror shadow of the twelve apostles, if you will—all women and all secretive. In keeping with her philosophy, each one exerted influence behind the scenes: wives and mothers of some of the most influential men in the country. The power behind the powerful.

"In every instance, the women indoctrinated the men in their lives, inducting them into the cult once they had attained full status. Much as she did with me."

Diana remembered Judge Whitfield, and his haunting recollections.

"In time I became her most loyal, her most zealous follower. Ready to obey her orders to the letter, engaging in brutality at her command, against those perceived to be heretics or merely anyone who ran afoul of her notorious temper."

"But how did you…?" Diana asked.

"My worthiness ultimately proved to be my own undoing," he replied.

"What do you mean?"

"Patience," he answered. "That is enough. For now."

The images began to fade, and with them, the figure of Luther Vayne himself.

"I still don't understand. Why are you showing me all of this?" she asked.

Vayne met her sight with his twisted visage.

"As I told you, I find your spirit worthy of interest," he said.

"No, there's more to this, isn't there?"

"You sought answers, did you not?" he replied. "You sought to know why I did such heinous things, such awful crimes. Now perhaps, you can begin to see."

"You're trying to clear your conscience, is that what this is?"

"I have no conscience to clear," he said.

"But you still haven't told me *why*," she said.

"Because you must see for yourself."

"See what?"

"Valeria Thorne believed that Azathoth was the source of all wisdom, the fountain from which all knowledge is borne. But I have been to the other side. There is as much madness as there is wisdom to be found in the eternal dreaming."

She couldn't answer. She just stared at him, as everything around her began to dissolve—including Vayne. He grew transparent as she watched.

"There are some who still believe her black gospel. The last of her spawn seeks to rectify her failure, to awaken Azathoth and to bring him into this world," he said. "I must stop them."

"Why are you showing me all of this?" she asked.

"Because you are a part of this battle," he replied. "Now, you must choose your side."

Then he vanished, subsumed into the mist from which it seemed he had come. As the fog cleared and her eyes once more adjusted to the light, she found herself right where she had been before—sitting in her car on a deserted street in Boston.

She breathed deep. She squeezed the steering wheel, anything to settle herself down. But it was a long while before she stopped shaking.

FORTY-TWO

NEW BETHLEHEM EPISCOPAL CATHEDRAL
BOSTON, MA

The Reverend Graham Thurmond Hayden Jr. lifted his head when everything fell still.

There hadn't been much noise to start. The cathedral was empty. He'd just closed it down for the night, leaving behind a quiet gloom; a silence rendered more solemn by the reverent décor. But this was different. He squinted as he looked behind him, from the pulpit and down the long aisle of pews toward the offertory in the foyer.

There was no movement. There was no wind. No traffic outside. No sound penetrated at all. It was utterly still. Even the flickering candles near the front double doors had somehow frozen, the fire halted like a photograph.

He checked his smartphone. None of his security measures had been tripped. But he knew. He fired off a quick text to Armstrong.

They were not alone. The moment had come.

A voice confirmed his suspicion. It spoke from nowhere, just as Luther Vayne stepped into the light—right out of the vestibule shadows.

"It is time, Reverend."

The sibilant words echoed in the empty church, repeating the whisper like a taunt, over and over until they faded away.

When Hayden looked again he was faced with the macabre figure. A half-naked old man scarred with tattoos across a body twisted by the years.

"Time for what?" Hayden replied, trying to hold his composure.

Vayne smiled, at ease despite the looming confrontation.

"Come now. Do we really need to keep up this façade? After so many years I would have thought we could at least be honest with one another," Vayne said.

Hayden recoiled.

"Honesty? You betrayed everything that you swore to protect," he answered. Reverend Hayden walked toward the center of the altar, his eyes focused on the ragged intruder as he tried to muster every ounce of courage in his bones. "You were a fool then, and you are a fool now."

Vayne acknowledged the comment. The insult seemed to amuse him.

"I have no shortage of regrets. I was a fool indeed. I am not proud of my actions. But you owe your life to my foolishness. I would have thought you, out of all of the demon's children, would recognize the value of forgiveness," he said.

Hayden sneered at the affront, feigned though his vocation might have been.

"They used you and cast you aside. If only they had finished the job, we would already have ascended to our rightful place," the Reverend replied. "If you'd like, *you can thank us* for putting you out of your misery."

Ever so subtly, he gave a wink and nod in Vayne's direction. But his gesture was not meant for the blind intruder.

A scream broke the still just then, echoing in the cavernous cathedral halls. From behind Luther Vayne, the figure of Lauren Armstrong leaped out of the darkness. She carried one of the daggers of Dagon, raised overhead. Carried through the air from her perch in the balcony above, she fell upon Vayne with the blade bared.

But it never touched him.

Vayne raised his hand. That alone was enough to halt Armstrong in her downward momentum. She stopped in mid-air, frozen in time as well as space. For a long, painful moment Vayne let her hang there, before lowering his arm slowly. As his hand came down, so too did she, brought to the floor in a kind of living slow motion until she stood only a few feet away from him.

He looked her over briefly, the blade still pointed at him. She was paralyzed somehow, with only her face free to move as she wished. Her eyes spoke for her. There was hatred in them, and then, as he neared—fear.

"One of the foolish newcomers to this old fight," he said. "You should know that your endeavors would not have ended well, whether you had prevailed against me or not. That must be your only comfort now."

Vayne waved his fingers toward her. Her limbs possessed by the force of a mind not her own, her hands turned the dagger from him and back upon herself. The fear in her eyes turned to terror. She began to shake, to quiver in horror as she could do nothing but watch her own hands draw the steel closer to her throat.

In a moment it was over. Her rebellious hands put the blade to her neck and then drove it deep into her flesh. She made no sound as she fell, only the soft trickle of blood drooling out of her punctured throat and the thud of her corpse hitting the floor.

Vayne turned back to face Hayden. He shook his head. The salt and pepper mop writhed across his shoulders, exposing rune-stenciled flesh and vacant eye sockets. He exhaled a long breath.

"Now, back to your very tempting offer," he said. Hayden recoiled in disgust, which seemed not to bother Vayne in the least. "You will never know how tempting it is, in fact. All that I know, all that I can remember, is a nightmare from which I cannot wake. There is only one thing that will put me to rest."

Hayden knew what that was.

"So I must decline your generous suggestion," Vayne continued. "You are the last, and now you must join your brothers who have gone before you. The time has come for you to be put down, Reverend. I doubt you have any prayers to offer, despite the pretense of your collar."

"You'll learn nothing from me," Hayden said. "I won't give you a thing."

Behind him, the railings alongside the altar ripped themselves out of the floor. The broken iron rose up like wisps of smoke, lifting into the air on either side of the Reverend, a dozen twisted spears ready to strike. The cross above came tumbling down, landing and fracturing on the altar.

"Unfortunately for you, I already know everything that I need to know," Vayne replied. "Your brother Saxon gave you away. I know that you are the leader. You are the final son of Sothoth, and tonight you will join the others."

He stepped closer. The shadows of the columns and the pews came alive in his wake.

Black figures arose, spawned from nothing more than candle smoke and darkness, twisting themselves into demonic horrors—creatures called forth from the deepest nightmares. At first merely phantasms, shimmering in the dim, they quickly coalesced into something more substantial, something almost like flesh.

They hissed and they groaned in the throes of their bastard genesis, tangled coils of multi-headed serpents slithering forward beside tottering ruins with segmented bodies and spiky carapaces. Above them a rage of dark angels arose, lofted on ragged wings of mist and flame, clamoring for blood.

Brimstone fumes churned around them in a rancid fog. Black slime oozed from the fangs gnashing within their wide, yammering maws.

The candle flames at the offertory erupted in a sudden rage, an inferno that framed the figure of Vayne and his cadre of frightful minions. In moments he stood at the center of a hell-storm of shadows and fire, brought to life by his unspoken command, as though he stepped forth from the black gates of Perdition.

Despite all that he had imagined, and all that he had prepared, the sight petrified the Reverend. Trembling turned to outright quivering. Urine spilled out onto his pants as his bodily functions betrayed him. He did everything he could to muster some last ounce of courage.

"I don't know what unspeakable things you did to Saxon to get him to reveal our secrets to you, but I promise you, I won't go down easily. No matter what happens here tonight, the rest of us will continue to fight you. We will never give in to your madness," Hayden said.

As if to punctuate his point, the Reverend raised his arms in defiance, the second dagger in his hand even as the iron poniards menaced him in mid-air only a few feet away.

Vayne answered with a wave of his hand. The stained glass in every one of the cathedral windows shattered with the gesture. His minions swarmed, sweeping over every inch of the walls and the floor. In moments Hayden was surrounded. No longer standing within his own domain, he was now at the center of a maelstrom.

"You speak of honesty, and with your next breath you deny the very core of your being," Vayne said, as he stepped forward amid the chaos. "I care nothing for the others you lead, the pathetic worshippers who choose to follow the bastard spawn of Sothoth."

Hayden sneered.

"Spawn of Sothoth?" he said. "My God, *you are* a mad man. The demon children are all dead—killed by your own hand. Forty years ago."

"More lies," Vayne answered. "The ruse is over. *You are the last.* Valeria was clever, indeed. I still do not know how she hid you away from me, but the deception has ended. I must destroy you, as I destroyed all the others."

Hayden stammered. He tried to edge backward, but had nowhere to step. Sweat poured off of him as he feverishly struggled to recall the verses he'd only recently memorized—the verses that were said to control such creatures from the abyss.

"You're insane," he said.

"Any man who has seen what I have seen would be," Vayne answered. "But that is of no consequence here."

"I'm ready for you."

"We will soon see," Vayne answered.

He stepped closer. Hayden edged further backward.

Hayden let his thoughts settle. He kept his eyes locked on Vayne. He tried to bring the words to his lips despite the pounding of his heart and the adrenaline pulsing through his veins.

"*Ya hi'ya. Ya hi'ya fylaah rytha,*" he began.

Vayne stopped. The army of horrors around him halted as well. He simply stared as Hayden continued the incantation.

"*Cha'yath shaa. F'thaam thathaam ry'leathaa.*"

Vayne didn't move, as if the words had indeed paralyzed him. The black runes carved in his skin began to glow, pulsing with a faint bluish hue. He stood there watching, looking back at Hayden as he recited the entire routine, gesticulating and waving the curved dagger at him as though giving the greatest sermon of his life.

When he was finished, and the entire rite had been issued, Hayden paused. Vayne still had not moved. For a moment, he allowed himself to believe the impossible. He allowed himself to believe that he had won.

But the illusion of triumph lasted only an instant. The color faded from the runes of Elder Script in Vayne's flesh. Then he moved again.

Although apparently unaffected by the incantation, Vayne nevertheless proceeded in a manner wholly different from even a moment before.

He stepped forward slowly, leaving the creatures of shadow and flame to recede behind him. Hayden staggered, falling backward in a clumsy attempt to retreat. Vayne did not relent however, and while unnatural forces remained mustered to his call, he approached Hayden man-to-man.

When he got the Reverend backed up against the wall, directly beneath the empty space where the giant cross had hung above the altar, he grabbed the cleric. He lifted him by his collar, staring into his eyes with his bare, empty sockets.

Hayden made one last, valiant effort.

"I command you, by the sacred texts of Fha Nha'thoom," he said, though he could barely breathe.

"Yes, I know," Vayne answered, still holding him against the back wall.

"I don't understand," Hayden replied, letting the now-useless dagger fall from his hand. "This should have worked. All of it. The daggers. The incantation."

Vayne smiled.

"If you speak of the blades borne by you and your fallen minion, they were nothing but antiques. If you were led to believe they held any special power, then you were terribly deceived," he said. "As for your rite, I do know the text you speak. Or perhaps I should say, the text you were trying to speak."

"What do you mean?"

"Your words were not incorrect," Vayne said. "That was truly a text from the Book of Fha Nha'thoom. You gave a near perfect rendition of the Rites of Domination, in fact. But for the final verse, and that was your undoing."

Hayden clenched his fists, recalling the *new* transliteration he had been given.

"Gregorian, you fucking snake," he whispered.

"You did not know that, did you?" Vayne said.

Hayden's frightened and defeated face answered for him.

"Those daggers and that rite—those were given to you by someone?" Vayne continued. "Given to you by someone who knew the true ritual. Someone who wished to mislead you—and me."

Hayden nodded.

Vayne held out his hand, keeping Hayden pinned against the wall with his other. He drew his long fingernail across Hayden's bare cheek, slicing into the flesh.

Hayden yelped.

Vayne raised the bloodied end to his mouth, tasting it. Then he let Hayden loose. The preacher fell in a heap.

"You are not the child of Sothoth," Vayne said.

Hayden tried to catch his breath from the floor.

"No, I'm not."

"But you know the one I seek," Vayne continued. "The one who led you down this path. The one who gave you the flawed incantation. The one who betrayed your comrade Saxon to me."

"What do you mean?"

"You truly do not know?" Vayne said. "I was sent to him, your brother Saxon. Led to him under the pretense that he was the true son of Sothoth,

I suspect by the same deceitful fiend who dispatched you to face me—knowing that Saxon was only a follower and that he would, in turn, point me to you. On pain of death he told me *you* were their leader."

"I was," Hayden replied, still wheezing. "Or, at least I thought I was. That fucking bastard was manipulating me too, all along."

"Who?" Vayne asked.

"Victor Gregorian." Hayden said. "The man you're looking for is Victor Gregorian."

"Where is he?"

"I don't know," Hayden said.

Vayne glared at him.

"I swear," he said. "He and the others went into hiding. I don't know where. He never told me. No one else…"

Hayden stopped.

"Finish," Vayne commanded.

"I don't know where he has gone, honestly," he continued. "But I know who might. Our newest initiate—Carter Shaw."

Vayne turned his back on the defeated, whimpering man.

"You have been more helpful than you realize, Reverend," he said.

He began to walk away, leaving Hayden crumpled on the floor. As he watched the rune-covered man depart, the Reverend looked out on his ruined church; windows shattered, pews ravaged, blood spilled all over the marble floor. He saw the broken corpse of Lauren Armstrong, his old friend and most loyal aide, discarded like trash.

He even gazed at himself. His pants were soaked from pissing himself in terror. His fat body was bruised and he lay in tatters, sprawled out like a sack of trash.

Anger and humiliation welled up within him, along with an image of Victor Gregorian's awful face. Everything he had, everything he'd worked for had all gone away in a moment.

It was too much to bear.

Scanning the ground around him, he snatched up a fragment of the cross, smashed and shattered beside him. He took it up in both hands, wielding it like a holy lance.

He did not expect to succeed. Nor did he expect to survive. But he screamed nonetheless, raising the jagged stake in the air and leaping up with the last of his strength. He charged down the steps of the altar, plunging himself toward the figure who had just taken everything from him.

Like Armstrong before him, he never made it.

From each side of Luther Vayne, the demonic shadows once again arose. In an instant they twisted themselves into fat, spiny tentacles and spectral claws. The living darkness seized Hayden, ripping through his flesh and constricting about him like a nest of serpents. He couldn't even bring a last curse to his lips, with his throat squeezed shut.

For a long, horrible moment he hung there, suspended above his church by forces he could not comprehend, the life wringing out of him. Just as he was about to expire however, as the tingling overcame his extremities and shadows fell over his bulging eyes, the black hands released him. As suddenly as they had appeared, they vanished, leaving Hayden suspended in mid-air.

He had only an instant to contemplate his fate.

The railings that had been ripped from the altar lifted once again. Moved by hands unseen, they pivoted, aimed and thrust themselves in perfect unison, striking the Reverend Graham Thurmond Hayden in a half dozen places at once. Not content with even that butchery, the iron spikes pushed on, driving the man's body against the back wall of his church, impaling him against the same spot where the great holy cross had once presided.

"So sad," Vayne said, as he walked away. "I almost let you live."

DAY NINE

"Let your terrifying cry overcome him, let him experience darkness, let his sight change for the worse."

Purported Excerpt from the "Tablet of Destinies" circa 2000 B.C., Royal Babylonian Library of Ashurbanipal, Ninevah

He had grown to love the chains.

The rusted iron links clanked when he moved—never by much and never on purpose. A slow, laborious rattle followed every twitch of his muscles, every involuntary spasm. Those were hopeful sounds, he now knew. Every jerk of his tormented flesh reminded him, stirring another rustle from the fetters. They were his friends, his constant companions, and they were going to carry him all the way. All the way to that desperate, desired end.

Each slink of metal against stone brought him closer, signaling the passing of moments as no timepiece could. Every instant passed away, as he must soon pass away. And with him, the agony.

There was no forgetting. No hope of escape. No hope but one, that final release he craved, the end he'd so long been denied.

Numbness had lately crept into his extremities, a most wonderful stroke of fortune. The barbed steel hooks piercing the tendons of his ankles were nearly impossible to feel anymore. He only sensed them when he allowed himself the momentary horror of looking down across his body, splayed out now upon a different slab. All the way at the end, so very far it seemed. The sharpened steel punctured his skin, drawing it out and holding it taut—posts for a tent of living flesh.

Winched into place by some rusty crank and wheel mechanism below, the wicked silvery curls rooted his legs to the foot of the dais just as their twins held his arms at the other end.

Stretched to each side, the cruelty inflicted upon those limbs was elevated yet another degree. There the massive, ersatz fish hooks penetrated him twice in each arm, sewn through muscle and bone; woven in a tapestry of warm, wet meat. The steel entered through the underside of the wrists. He recalled how the servants of the Priestess had carried him there, high upon the crest of that lonely hill. How they'd laid him out upon that altar of stone, how they'd held his arms out, palms facing up. They were now frozen in that position, locked in permanent supplication to a darkness as-yet-unseen.

Threaded between the radius and the ulna, the steel emerged on the other side, but its work was not yet done. In a comedy of horrors, they had pulled the metal through his flesh, drawing it down and behind until they were ready for the second insult to his already tortured form. The end of the barbed hooks had been forced up from beneath, emerging through the soft skin inches in front of his elbow joints. There they remained, maroon-stained with blood dried so long now the hardened paste was beginning to flake and chip away.

This was his reality. Whatever had been before—whoever he had been—he could barely recall. Hints and half-remembered visions were all that remained, drowned in a fog of suffering. His entire world was now upon this altar, this carnival of broken flesh and pain.

They'd left him there. Left him to contemplate the only possessions he now had—burning, straining and the relentless aching, the emptiness that loomed above and the worst horror of all—the unknown that awaited him.

He knew those faceless women would return; eventually—inevitably.

Only now he no longer dreaded it. Now he hoped it would be soon.

FORTY-THREE

NEW BETHLEHEM EPISCOPAL CATHEDRAL
BOSTON, MA

Kendrick was at the crime scene ahead of her—again. Diana had stopped for a double espresso on the way. That was going to have to substitute for missing yet another night of sleep, which was fast becoming a distant memory.

The call had come in only a half hour ago. Six in the morning. There were more bodies—plural this time. Two more prominent victims.

She crossed the line of police tape and used her bureau credentials to ease her way through the gauntlet of reporters gathering around the church like horseflies. Kendrick was standing outside, doing his best to keep the throng of reporters at bay.

"You look like hell," he said, by way of greeting.

"Thanks. That seems to be the consensus lately," she said.

"Trouble sleeping?"

"Jesus Christ, can we please leave my sleeping habits alone?"

Kendrick shrank under her angry words. She realized it, and apologized.

"Sorry kid, you're right, I have been having trouble sleeping, but that's my problem. Let's concentrate on what we've got here, okay?"

"You don't need to be here, you know," he said. "I'd be happy to give you the full report back at H.Q.. You've done a ton of field work on this one already, more than you bargained for, I know."

"I appreciate the concern," she said, in a tone that suggested exactly the opposite. "I'm here. Why don't you just walk me through it, okay?"

"Fine, in that case, let's go on inside," Kendrick answered.

As she got to the giant bronze doors, she paused for a moment.

"Something wrong?" he asked.

Diana shook her head.

"I know you gave up this kind of thing a while ago," he said. "And I know why. But there's nothing in there you haven't seen before. I mean…well, you know what I mean."

She shrugged her shoulders, eyeing the verdigris-washed doors with their bas-relief scripture scenes.

"It's not that," she finally said. "I still hate these places."

"Crime scenes?" he said. "You ever think you might be in the wrong business?"

She smiled.

"No, not that. Churches," she said. "Can't stand them. Never could. I haven't been inside one in years."

"This is a crime scene. That's all," Kendrick said.

She wasn't hearing him.

"Fucking perfect though, isn't it?" she said.

"What's that?"

"The bodies are inside, right?"

Kendrick nodded.

"Reverend Hayden, America's favorite television preacher, murdered in his own church. Ironic, isn't it?" she said.

"I don't understand."

"They act like they know, but they really don't. No more than the rest of us."

Kendrick was confused, and he didn't mind saying so. Diana traced the outline of the door, careful not to touch anything with her bare fingers.

"I asked them. Every chance I got. How did they explain it? There must be some explanation, right? There must be some plan. At least some kind of an idea about how all of this nasty shit happens."

"Still not following," Kendrick said.

"Haven't you ever wondered?" she said. "All the crap you've seen at the Bureau. The cases we deal with, I mean the really fucked up ones. The child rapists, the sadists, the things you can't tell your family about."

"Part of the job, right?"

"Yeah, but *why*? That's what they could never answer, those little men in black. They never had any answers. Faith in a higher purpose. That's the best they could do."

"Not good enough for you?"

"I stopped asking," she said. "There is no answer. It's just us. Just who we are. This is a sick world. It always will be."

"A little harsh," Kendrick said.

"Don't let the guys in places like this tell you any different," she said. "They don't know a damn thing."

Then she slipped on a glove, pushed the doors open and walked into the church.

The body of the famous preacher was the first thing that she saw, even though it was on the exact opposite side of the church. It was impossible to miss. The empty shell of Graham Thurmond Hayden towered over the altar, dominating the pulpit in death with an authority even he had never quite managed to achieve by mortal means.

His blood painted the back wall purple-red. Dry streaks and the outlines of half-evaporated tributaries ran down the whole of the facade, as if sprung from a fountain. Diana pointed at the vault that overhung the altar. It was pure white, untouched by even a spatter of red.

"He was killed *up there*?" Diana whispered, not even believing her own question.

Kendrick shrugged.

"Looks like it," he replied. "Armstrong's body is just over there."

He pointed her toward the corpse of Lauren Armstrong. Her head was barely connected to her body, daggers in hand where she'd fallen.

"Fucking White House Chief of Staff," Kendrick continued. "What a nightmare."

Diana looked at the body. A woman whose family was intimately connected to the Thorne Foundation—to Luther Vayne.

"You have no idea," she answered.

Before Kendrick could question her further she pushed ahead, fighting through the jumble of agents, local P.D. and crime scene investigators toward the front of the church. The polished wooden cross that had once owned the place of honor above the offertory now rested on the floor, broken and thrown against the back wall. Blood from above had pooled beneath it, and drawn red smears across its splintered halves.

Hayden himself had replaced it above the altar.

A mockery of all that he had claimed to represent, Hayden's ruined form hung in reverse-crucifixion, shoulders below and feet above. The iron rods that had been torn away from the railings on either side of the altar acted as nails. Driven through his wrists and his gathered feet, the twisted black metal impaled his flesh, securing the weight of his body against the wall, fifteen feet above the floor. The force of their impact had dented the plaster. Cracks rippled out from the epicenters. His face was the only part of him unscathed. His blue eyes remained open, staring out in a final, frozen instant of horror.

"This was Vayne," Diana said. "No doubt."

"I suppose that's as good an explanation as any," Kendrick said. "No fingerprints. Nothing at all, except for the obvious."

"We know everything we need to know," she answered.

"Maybe *you think* you know everything, but we deal in hard evidence, not kooky theories," Richard Norris said, stepping forward from the mass of gathered investigators in the rear of the church.

"I told you," Diana said. "I fucking warned you about this. Armstrong's father and Hayden's father were connected to Valeria Thorne. You thought I was crazy."

"I never said crazy," Norris replied.

"But that's what you meant," she answered.

"Don't put words into my mouth, Diana," he said, "I was worried about you, hell I still am. This is a murder investigation. We need hard evidence and a solid profile. You came to me with a forty-year-old family tree. How was I supposed to take that?"

"You were supposed to take it seriously," she snapped.

Norris nodded. He looked over the scene and then back to Diana.

"Look, I admit, you might be on to something here," Norris answered. "You say all these victims are connected by way of some old family ties, right?"

"Exactly, Valeria Thorne's Foundation which was…"

He cut her off.

"Whoa, hang on," he said. "If this is legit, we'll follow up on it, trust me. But not here, not this way."

"What do you want then? I'm telling you how it is," she said.

"What I want is for you to do the job you agreed to do," he replied. "Lay it all out for me, in order, in detail—on paper. Put it all down so that we can get this sorted, and get it out to the people who are actually supposed to be doing the fieldwork."

"You want me to go back to the office. Be a loyal foot solider," she said. "Aye-aye, captain."

"That's the Navy, not the Army," he replied, with a flash of that movie star grin she both loved and hated.

Norris edged closer to her, as close as he could get in public without arousing suspicion.

"Hey, you want me to say it? I'm sorry I didn't listen to you," he said, his voice lower and softer. "But you have to take care of yourself."

He looked her up and down. Her hair was matted and tied back in a loose ponytail with stray locks hanging out all over. Her clothes were the same ones she'd been wearing the day before. They looked like she'd slept in them.

"This?" he continued. "This isn't you."

"I know," she said. "It's been…a rough week."

"Get back to headquarters. Get with Ariadne and get this whole thing outlined for me," he said. "I have a ton of bullshit to wade through here. This is a fucking P.R. nightmare. I've got media requests coming out of my ass and all sorts of inter-agency cooperation headaches to deal with. I'll be back later today. Then we'll sit down—and we'll talk."

She put her hand on his hand. That was as much as they could do. It only lasted a moment. Then someone from the gaggle of reporters called out for him from the other side of the church.

"Duty calls," he said, as he walked away.

Diana found her way back to Kendrick, who was just concluding his own examination of the Hayden body.

"Have you sent any pictures to Ariadne yet?" she asked him.

"C.S.U. just finished covering the whole scene when we got her. I'll have them do it now," Kendrick answered.

"Let me try her," she said, already scrolling through her contacts list.

The phone only rang once. Ariadne picked up and started talking without even so much as a "hello."

"I was just about to call you," she began. "You're not gonna believe this."

Diana looked over the scene in front of her one more time. She didn't mind her friend's abruptness.

"Don't be so sure," she answered.

"Remember our girl Valeria Thorne? Well after her disappearance, her family had her declared legally dead. This was in the spring of 1974."

"Awfully quick."

"Rich folks, they had the juice," Ariadne replied. "So I managed to get a look at the probate court records from back then. Thorne left a will."

"Nothing unusual there."

"Most of it is pretty standard stuff, but there is one clause that was very interesting," Ariadne continued. "She bequeathed a large portion of her estate, including a mansion out in Wilburton, Massachusetts to another former employee."

"This woman was pretty damn generous to her staff."

"According to the probate filing, she was already living in the residence, a place called Whateley Estates."

The name struck a chord.

"Wait, as in…"

"Exactly," Ariadne replied. "Upon Thorne's death the property and everything associated with it passed to her, to be held in trust until her son reached twenty-five."

"Son of a bitch," Diana whispered.

"The woman's name was Victoria Gregorian," Ariadne said.

"Victor Gregorian's mother."

"The very same," Ariadne answered. "Census records indicate she lived there until she died sometime in the late eighties, along with her son Victor. *Her adopted son*."

"God damn it, I knew it," Diana said. "It's him. Victor Gregorian is the thirteenth."

"My thoughts exactly," Ariadne said.

"I'll be right there," Diana replied.

FORTY-FOUR

F.B.I. FIELD OFFICE, ONE CENTER PLAZA
BOSTON, MA

Diana limped into the command center a disheveled mess. Dark circles cradled her blood-shot eyes. Greasy hair hung over her face. She had been in the same clothes for two days. Her blouse was untucked, yellow pit stains were beginning to creep out from under her arms. She was pale.

Ariadne rushed over to her. She got some water from the cooler, helped Diana to a chair and put it to her lips.

"Where'd you get off to last night?" Ariadne said. "You didn't answer your cell. I left you like five voicemails. What happened?"

Diana took the cup of water from Ariadne. She sipped it. She hadn't realized how parched her throat was until the water hit her lips.

"I can't explain, not right now," she said.

Ariadne stomped her feet. Anger mixed with concern in her brown eyes.

"You run off and disappear for hours and you can't explain it?" she said.

"*I can explain*, just not right now," Diana replied.

Ariadne eased up. She had a plastic bag on the table and she handed it to Diana.

"Here, I brought you a change of clothes," she said.

Diana opened it up. Her charcoal gray pantsuit was inside, along with her favorite pair of black, low heeled boots.

"I sent someone over to the hotel, had them take your laundry out to get done. I figured you weren't getting around to it anytime soon," Ariadne continued.

Diana ran her hands through her unwashed hair.

"Thanks," she said.

"We'll find him," Ariadne replied. She put her hand on Diana's shoulder, rubbed it back and forth gently. "*We will* find him."

Diana whispered her answer.

"I know," she said. "That's not what worries me."

A ping came from Ariadne's laptop just then. She glanced at the screen.

"Hang on, this might be something," she said.

"What's that?"

"Bay State Bank," Ariadne replied.

She opened the email, scanned it and then clicked on the attachment. That in turn opened a *pdf* which she proceeded to scroll through—until she came to something that made her grin. She pushed back the computer and looked at Diana.

"You're gonna love this," Ariadne said.

"What are you talking about?" she asked.

She took a glance at the screen. It was just a spreadsheet with columns of numbers.

"If you remember the other day, we had an agent talk to your friend Carter Shaw's ex-wife," Ariadne said.

"Vaguely."

"She said he recently came into some money, but she didn't know how," Ariadne said. "So I ran a check on his financial statements. Nothing unusual until just a few days ago and then…bingo."

"What?"

"Check it out," Ariadne replied, pointing at one column on the screen.

Diana studied it. There was a recent deposit for half a million dollars.

"Where the hell did all that money come from?"

"That's the part you're gonna love," Ariadne said. "The deposit is from an account belonging to Dunwich Properties."

"Hang on. I've heard that name before."

"You were just at their headquarters—Whateley Estates," Ariadne answered.

"Victor Gregorian again," Diana said.

Ariadne nodded.

"Carter Shaw is on Gregorian's payroll, and for a lot of money."

"Those sons of bitches have been lying to me from the beginning," Diana said, getting up from her seat. She was already on her way to the exit. "That ends now."

Ariadne grabbed her coat.

"Hold up," she said. "First of all, you're getting changed. Second, I'm coming with you."

Diana turned. She put her hand up to block Ariadne.

"You're not a field agent," she said.

Ariadne smirked.

"Technically, neither are you," she replied. "I'm not letting you out of my sight again so soon, not after last night."

Diana put her arm down.

"Okay, but if this gets rough—" she said.

"Trust me, I won't get in the way," Ariadne answered.

FORTY-FIVE

MUSEUM OF FINE ARTS
BOSTON, MA

They wound their way through the labyrinthine inner hallways of the M.F.A. The dim, musty route was all too familiar to Diana by now.

"How are you planning to go at this guy?" Ariadne asked.

"Not sure," she replied.

"You haven't given this any thought?" Ariadne said. "He's our only lead, isn't he? Shouldn't we figure out a game plan before we go all gangbusters on him?"

Diana's face was like stone when they came to Carter's door. She was focused and betraying nothing.

"I let you come with me, but that's it," she said. "Wait outside."

"You can't just wing it, can you?" Ariadne protested.

Diana looked back at her with a sharp glare.

"I have to do this alone," she said.

"Okay, okay," Ariadne said. "But I'm not going anywhere. I'll be right outside if things go bad."

Diana nodded as she put her hand on the door.

"It's already gone bad," she said. "From here it only gets worse."

Diana turned the knob and pushed the door open, without ever taking her eyes off the nameplate.

Ariadne looked bit puzzled, but nodded and remained on the other side of the door as Diana walked into the office. Carter was sitting behind his desk, tilted back in his chair and angled toward the bookshelf along his wall. He turned when she came in.

"Agent Mancuso," he said—almost as if he'd been expecting her. "This is becoming something of a regular visit. What can I help you with today?"

"You could start with the truth," she replied, closing the door behind her. "For a change, that is."

Carter frowned, clearly feigning disappointment.

"Now, you're not calling me a liar, are you?" he replied. "That's just insulting. Here I thought we were becoming friends."

She laughed a little as she walked across the room, shaking her head. At the edge of his cluttered desk she leaned down and put her hands on the top of it. She was only a few feet away from him, close enough to look right in his eyes.

"I'm just about out of patience," she said.

Diana's voice was raw. She was almost hoarse.

Carter didn't flinch. He looked right back at her.

"Patience?" he said. "This is the third time you've barged in on me like this. If anyone should be losing patience, it's me."

His voice was flat. She noticed that only one of his hands was visible above the table, but she didn't think much of it.

"Let's put away the bullshit once and for all, shall we?" she answered. "You might as well come clean. I already know what you've been up to. Your best bet right now is to cooperate. If you give me something I can use, I'll do my best to try and help you out."

Carter's face didn't change. He took off his spectacles and nodded.

"Is that so?" he said. "What is it that you think you know, I wonder?"

He wasn't giving anything away.

"I know you've been on leave. And I know you lied to your wife about it."

He smirked.

"Ex-wife," he said.

"Either way, you lied to her about where you've been recently," she repeated.

She waited. It was a typical move. Throw out a little information to see if it produced a response; to see if the subject gave anything away. Carter didn't. He just looked back at her, staring her in the eyes.

"If you're here to arrest me for lying to my ex-wife, then you're going to end up putting half the country in jail."

"That's not why I'm here, and you know it," she answered. "But right now, you are my prime suspect."

"Suspect?" he answered. "For what, may I ask?"

"I think you know that too," she said. "Why don't we start with the five hundred thousand Victor Gregorian deposited in your account two days ago."

Carter's expression finally changed.

"I see," he said. "I was afraid it might come to this."

For the first time, he blinked, and he looked away. She could tell she'd hit a nerve. He leaned back and he tapped his desk with his folded glasses, his other hand still under the desk.

For a moment, she eased up, lifting her hands from the desk and edging back a step as she let herself take a breath. She even closed her eyes for a moment, a second longer than she meant to, which only reminded her how dead tired she was.

When she looked back though, a jolt went right through her. Carter's Browning pistol was staring her in the face.

"I didn't want it to go this way," Carter said, rising from his seat as he kept the pistol aimed at her forehead.

Diana cursed herself for letting him keep his hand under the desk, for underestimating him so badly. Adrenaline was surging through her. She was shaking. It took every ounce of concentration to hold her composure.

"You're pointing a gun at a federal agent," she said. "Do you have any idea where this is gonna land you?"

"You carry handcuffs, right?" he asked.

"Let's take this down a notch, okay?" she replied, her hands raised.

"I asked you a question," he said, more stern than she had ever heard him.

"Yeah, on my belt," she answered, pointing at them with her left hand.

"Taken them out, please," he said. "I'm going to need you to put them on."

Keeping her right hand up, she carefully lowered her left, settling it on the cuffs.

"Look, I know you're wrapped up in something, something much bigger than just you. I know it's probably more than you bargained for," she said. "But this is no solution."

"Trust me, Agent Mancuso, you don't know anything," he said.

"I know more than you think," she said, lifting the cuffs and holding them up for him to see.

Carter looked back at Diana with a stare she had rarely seen in someone like him, someone cultured, educated—privileged. He looked right into her eyes. Then past them. It put her off guard. He answered with confidence, and his eyes confirmed it.

"If you'd seen what I've seen, you wouldn't say that."

Diana stared back at him. She recognized something in his eyes—something she hadn't seen before. Something haunted him, just like it did her.

"You'd be surprised," she said.

"Oh yeah, what have you seen?" he asked.

She waited a moment before answering. She thought about what Vayne had shown her; of the nightmares and strange visions that words could barely capture.

"What lies behind the shadows," she finally said.

He stammered, just for a moment. Just as she hoped.

"What…what did you say?" he replied, taken off guard.

"The darkness beyond. The darkness within," she continued, replaying every oddity in her mind. "Secrets too horrible, too frightening to consider—calling out to you, whispering and shouting with…"

She let her voice trail off, leaving the thought unfinished,

"With what?" he questioned.

She waited another moment, struggling to put what she'd seen into words.

"The madness of eternity," she answered.

Carter froze. He stared right at her. Into her eyes yet again. But this time it was different.

"Azathoth," he whispered.

"You know *exactly* what I mean, don't you?" she continued.

"I do," he answered. "I can't believe it. *You know*. You really do know, don't you?"

Diana moved closer to him.

"Like I said, I know just enough to know that I don't know enough," she said. "If that makes any sense to you."

He never got the chance to answer. Sensing an opportunity, as he stood there in shock, Diana ducked to the right, darting out of the path of the pistol. Her left hand already raised, she dropped the cuffs and grabbed the barrel of the Browning.

The sudden surge of movement startled Carter. He tried to pull the weapon back, but it was too late. Diana forced it up toward the ceiling, twisting until she managed to wrest it out of his grasp. He fell backwards, into his chair. She pressed the advantage, coming around the desk with the pistol in hand.

He gathered himself in a moment and jumped back up. But he ran right into her fist.

Her left jab seemed to come out of nowhere, cracking him in the nose and sending a stream of blood out of his nostrils. The impact sent him falling right back into his seat.

She didn't pursue him. Instead, she took a hankie from her pocket and she offered it to him. He held it up to his nose to soak up the blood as she secured the pistol in her belt.

"This doesn't need to get any uglier," she said. "That can be the end of it. We'll call it even. I just need to you to tell me what you know."

Carter moved his sight from the bloody hankie up toward Diana. He made a point of not answering though. Instead he just stared at her, defeated but not broken.

"I can stand here all day," she said.

Diana knew that was a lie. She suspected that Carter knew too.

"There's no point, believe me," Carter said. "You could stand here all day, all week, all year if you want. It won't get you anywhere."

"Why don't you let me be the judge of that, huh?" Diana said. "Maybe start by telling me what you've been doing these last few days. What did you do for Gregorian?"

"I can't tell you anything," he replied.

"Can't?" she asked. "Or won't?"

"What difference does it make?"

Diana lifted her red-sore eyes.

"Okay," she said. "I understand where you're coming from."

She turned her back and walked slowly toward the door of the office. But she didn't open it. Instead, she stopped and she slid the lock shut. Then she turned back toward Carter.

"What the hell do you think you're doing?" he demanded.

This time she was the one who answered with silence.

"Go ahead and arrest me, if that's what you're going to do," he said. "Get it over with."

"I'm not arresting you," she answered.

She took off her overcoat and placed it carefully on the coat rack. Then she removed her suit jacket, smoothed it over and folded it once. She set it down on the back of a chair.

"I want answers and I'm gonna get them, one way or another," she said.

"I've had enough of this. Even F.B.I. agents can't just do whatever the hell they want. There are rules and you have to follow them."

"You talk about rules. When I was a kid I played a lot with the boys," she began. "Mostly in the street. Not too far from here, actually. Stick ball in the summer and hockey most of the rest of the year. Have you ever played?"

"Not myself, no," he replied.

"Didn't think so. You don't strike me as the street game type. Anyway, when you play hockey there are the regular rules, the ones everyone knows—off-sides, high sticking and all that. Then there are the unwritten rules. Do you know what those are?"

He shook his head.

"There's a lot of checking, of course," she said, cracking her knuckles. "So you gotta learn how to take a hit. But you also need to know how to deliver one. You need to know how to fight. You know why?"

"This has gone far enough," he said, grabbing at his desk phone.

She reached his desk in an instant, snatched the phone out of his hand and yanked the entire thing off of his desk. It went flying against the wall, shattering with a clang of smashing bells.

"You need to fight because there are some cases where the rules don't work. Maybe the other team has a big guy and he decides he wants to throw his weight around and work over your best player. Well, the rules say he can do that."

She cleared a whole mess of books and papers off of his desk. Carter got up from his chair, blood still dripping from his nose.

"So the unwritten rule is, if you take a shot at our best player, you better be ready to throw down the gloves and fight one of our big guys. That keeps them honest, keeps them from hiding behind the rules and taking advantage—just like you're trying to do right now."

"Listen, this is not what I want," he said, backing away.

"So what's it gonna be?" she said. "Are you gonna be honest with me, or is this gonna get *really* ugly?"

Carter managed to get himself up from his chair, dropping the blood-soaked cloth, he tried to take a swing at her, but he was dazed and slow. She moved much quicker and without a wasted step. She had him by the collar before he could get far.

A second time she struck him in the face, sending more blood down into his mouth.

"That's strike two," she said. "Now talk to me, damn it! Where have you been the last few days? Who sent the letter to Luther Vayne? The post mark was from here in Boston. Was it you?"

A third time he tried to swing in defense, but he only flailed at her. Diana sidestepped the punch and caught him by the arm. She twisted it around and forced him down against the desk.

"You're gonna talk to me, I swear to you," she said.

He screamed as she twisted his arm almost to the breaking point.

"Did you send that letter?" she demanded.

"I don't…know about…any letter…" he replied.

She pulled him up off the desk and turned him towards her. Again her reflexes were fast. She landed a punch to his gut, doubling him over in even more pain. She pushed him down, spun him around and pulled his arms behind his back. Then she slapped her cuffs on him.

"That was a decent punch, I'll give you that," she said. "But this isn't a fair fight. I need answers and you're gonna give them to me."

He struggled in pain.

"You're working with Victor Gregorian, I already know that," she said. "I need to get to him. Your boss is in serious danger."

She was lying—*Victor Gregorian was the real danger*.

"Victor Gregorian? I doubt that."

The answer struck Diana. *He knew exactly what she knew.*

"Either way, every minute we sit here we're wasting time."

He looked back at her, down his nose with a glare that finally gave everything away. She decided to drop all pretense.

"You already know about Luther Vayne, don't you?" she said. "And the child of the demon. That wasn't just a story."

He nodded. It was the most she'd gotten out of him so far.

"The other day, everything you told me, about Sothoth and the old ritual," she said. "That was all true?"

He nodded again.

"Tell me the rest of it," she demanded.

He winced.

"That's all," he said. "That's all I can say."

She shook her head, grabbed him by the lapels and shoved him clear across his own desk. He went sliding, tumbling over it and landing on the floor. With his hands secured behind his back he had nothing to brace his fall and his face hit the tiles.

She heard the scuffling of security outside. No doubt alerted by the noises, they'd be at the door in moments. Even with it locked they'd get in sooner rather than later.

She needed leverage—fast.

Diana looked around. The office was already wrecked. On the floor was a mess of pens from the top of the desk. She studied the detritus until something caught her eye. She reached down and picked up the scissors from the pile. Then she held them up for Carter to see.

"Okay, so we know you can take a punch," she said. "Although I figure getting beat up by a woman like this is not exactly something you're gonna want to boast about at parties."

She stepped closer to him. With each click of her heels against the floor he tried to slink backward.

"I'm gonna ask you one more time, and then I'm gonna get wicked nasty—what are you into with Gregorian? What does he have on you?"

She heard voices shouting in the hallway. They were almost outside the door.

Carter was breathing heavy, blood clogging his nose and spilling into his mouth. He wheezed as he tried to talk.

Diana nodded.

"I don't think you realize how important this is to me," she said. "Maybe this will prove it to you."

She knelt down over him, put down the scissors and went for the belt on his pants. She unfastened it and just as quickly got the button undone, then the zipper of his fly. Though he tried to squirm in frustration and disbelief alike, she was relentless, and entirely dispassionate. She undid his pants with as little emotion as if she were untying a shoe.

"What the fuck?" he protested.

Without missing a beat, she reached up and yanked his pants down, pulling his trousers and his boxers to his knees and exposing him fully.

Then she picked up the scissors again.

"You know what comes next right?" Diana said.

Security was on the other side of the door, banging and jiggling the lock. She ignored it. For good measure she opened the scissors and then clamped them shut only inches above his naked groin.

"Now, tell me about Gregorian. Tell me about Azathoth," she said. "Or I start snipping."

She looked at him, a mess of blood and sweat half naked on the floor—humiliated and beaten. If he was hiding something, he was willing to endure anything to keep it under wraps. She grabbed him by the chin, pulled his face toward her. She stared into his eyes. He was terrified, but not of her. Something else.

"It's everything," he said, frantic. "Azathoth *is everything*."

Just then the door broke open. Security flooded the room. Director Quinlan was in the lead and when she saw what was going on—Carter handcuffed and half-stripped on the floor, beaten and bloody with an F.B.I. agent standing over him—she went ballistic.

"What in the hell is going on in here?" she said.

Diana refused to answer. She unfastened the handcuffs, grabbed her coat and went for the door.

"This is completely improper," Quinlan continued, as she ordered the guards to assist Carter. She got between Diana and the door. "I can have you arrested right here, right now. This is outrageous!"

Diana looked back at her, right in the eyes.

"Do whatever you want. Report me, file a complaint. I don't give a shit," she said. "I'm here on direct orders from Deputy Director Norris. So unless you're prepared to interfere with an active investigation, I suggest you get the hell out of my way—now."

Quinlan paused for a moment, then relented.

Diana pushed past her and out the door. Ariadne was waiting outside.

"I suppose there's no point in asking how it went in there?" the analyst asked.

"Let's just say, Richard's going to be getting some angry phone calls," she answered. "And you're right, I came up empty."

"Sorry to hear that. Now what?"

"Our boy Gregorian, it's time he got a return visit." Diana said. "I'll take the bureau car. I can be there before dark."

"Hang on, I'm coming with you," Ariadne replied.

Diana shook her head.

"Things are starting to get dirty," she said. "What I just did—what I might have to do now—you don't want any part of it."

Ariadne looked into the office and saw the mess. It looked like an earthquake had hit. She nodded slowly.

"Okay, I'll get a cab over to the field office, see if I can run interference with Richard for a while, maybe buy you some time," she replied.

"Thanks," Diana said. "I have a feeling I'm gonna need it."

FORTY-SIX

WHATELEY ESTATES
WILBURTON, MA

Daylight was fading by the time she pulled up to the massive outer gate.

No one answered her attempts to ring the call box up to the house. After letting it go for two full minutes, she got out of the car and stepped up to the railings. She fiddled with the gate for a moment, and much to her surprise, it was not locked or secured in any way. With no more than a push she was able to slide it open by hand.

Something's not right here, she thought. *Last time this place had tighter security than Fort Knox, now the place is virtually unguarded?*

She found her answer a few moments later.

The cobblestone driveway was totally empty. She drove up right in front of the main doors of the house without seeing a soul. No groundskeepers, no staff anywhere. There weren't even any other cars parked there.

The mansion itself was dark. Only a single light was on right over the front porch steps. Aside from that, every window seemed to have the curtains drawn shut. There did not appear to be any signs of life.

She hit the doorbell but also knocked, just in case.

Again, there was no answer. Hoping to luck out twice in one day, she fiddled with the door knob. This time however, she wasn't as fortunate. It was locked up tight. After a second round of knocking—harder this time—failed to rouse anyone either, she crept a little closer to the house, hoping to peek inside a window or through a space in the drapes.

Her last line of attack would be to try to pry one of the windows open, and she was seriously considering it, when the front door finally clanked and the hinges creaked open.

A feeble-looking elderly gentleman, half-dressed in a butler's uniform, stepped outside. Diana moved back toward her car, hoping to conceal the fact that she had just been nosing up to the windows. The gray-haired man was still unfolding his glasses as he came outside and did not appear to notice.

"Apologies," he began. "I was told there would be no visitors. Is there something I can help you with, young lady?"

"Yes, I'm here to see Victor Gregorian," she said. "I'm with the F.B.I."

She held up her ID. He barely looked at it.

"Mr. Gregorian is away, I'm afraid," he answered, with a tone that suggested he meant to say no more.

She looked him up and down, then gave the quiet, darkened house another once-over.

"Kinda figured," she replied. "When's he expected back?"

"I'm afraid I can't say," the man replied, maybe a little too fast.

"Well, where did he go?"

"I can't tell you that either, ma'am," he said.

Diana had been around enough to know when somebody was hiding something. He was too quick, too practiced. He was under orders not to say anything. She wanted to know why.

"Who exactly are you?" she asked.

"I'm the caretaker."

"No one else here?"

"When Mr. Gregorian is away the household staff either travels with him or is sent home until he returns. I am the only one who stays behind," he answered, seeming to grow impatient with the exchange.

"You won't mind if I have a look around then," she said.

"I'm afraid I'm not to let anyone in," he replied, stammering a bit. "Even the F.B.I."

Diana slowly pushed the door open all the way. Then she put her hand on the man's chest, and she pushed him back as well. He was rather frail and he put up no fight, letting her nudge him backward into foyer.

"If it makes you feel better, we'll say you didn't *let* me in," she said.

Though he stepped back, he didn't exactly yield.

"I can't allow this," he said. "Unless you leave now I'm going to have to call someone."

She grinned.

"Knock yourself out," she said. "Meantime I'm gonna have myself that look around."

The caretaker huffed and fretted, but made no further attempt to stop her. Instead he muttered something about the police as he receded into the front sitting room. Diana left him behind without much of a thought.

She toured the main corridor first, already further than the foyer she'd seen on her first visit. She was impressed by the rich tapestries and the millions of dollars of art hung from the walls. At the end of the gallery she came to a set of doors that opened up to a veranda and a stone patio behind the main house. It was all packed up for the winter. On the right side there stood a wide staircase and an archway beneath that led into something of a living room. There were several sectional sofas and a wide screen TV above a fireplace. None of it looked to have been used much.

Turning back, she went in the other direction, and passed through a second set of doors into the library salon. Immediately she knew this was a more important room. The faint odor of cigars lingered, and the furniture upholstery was worn in places. The massive desk at the far end was covered in documents and books, probably taken from the innumerable volumes lining the shelves on every wall.

She walked toward the desk, intending to see what was arranged on top, but she stopped halfway. Something else caught her eye.

The Persian rug that lay across the middle of the room was off kilter. Where the planks were exposed beneath she noticed the wood had been scratched up. Reaching down, she pulled back the rug and half-rolled it up to move it to the side. The hardwood underneath was completely marked up. She knelt down to run her hands over it. It was splintered. The wood floor had been gouged recently, as though something heavy had been dragged across it.

She followed the path of the scrape marks. They ended at a spot near the front of the desk. It took her a moment, but she eventually discerned the outline of the trap door built into the floor. Realizing that her hands alone were not enough to pry it open, she grabbed a poker from the fireplace and used that to get leverage on the latch. Once it came loose, the door flipped open, revealing the steps below, and the continuation of the trail of scrape-marks, this time dug into the stone.

She could hear the caretaker from down the hall. He was probably calling 911, which meant she only had a little time. Although it was dark and she could see no light switch under the floor, she ventured down anyway, using the light from above to get her as far as the first landing. There she felt around on the wall until she located an electrical switch. When she hit it, the entire underworld came alive.

"Holy mother fucking shit," she said, though no one was there to hear it.

The subterranean chamber was as deserted as the house above, but she marveled at the unparalleled opulence of it. A private museum hidden away from the public. She noticed that the scraping trail continued, and she followed it along the pathway that traced the outer edge of the complex, down each concentric level. Every time she came to a landing she found herself face-to-face with another piece of priceless art. The items were massive and staggering.

Nothing prepared her for the lowest chamber however, where the great tablet still stood in its place of veneration, its lower edge broken away but the remainder as magnificent as any treasure of antiquity she had ever seen.

Something about it made her pause. It was familiar, even though she had never seen it before. She got closer, she studied it. For a long moment she couldn't figure it out. She couldn't place it. *But she knew.* There was something she recognized.

A draft stirred in the deep chamber and chill ran through her. That was when it hit her. The markings, the script on the tablet. It was the same writing etched into Luther Vayne's body.

"Un-fucking-real," she whispered.

Then she noticed that the scrape marks continued. They led into the final chamber, the inner temple sanctum on the lowest level. She pressed forward, moving the heavy door aside to make her way through. But the moment she crossed into the ante-room she was hit with a stench. The air inside was different. It was heavy, thick and foul.

She recognized that too, and this time she didn't need a moment to place it. It was the odor of rotting flesh. A rancid stink she'd come across too many times, at too many crime scenes. It was something she never wanted to smell again.

The marks led to the black altar, where they stopped on the second of three tiers. She almost couldn't believe her eyes, despite everything else she'd seen, when she came upon the macabre statuary arrayed atop the pyramid. The horrific figure, more beast than man, slathered in what she guessed was dried blood, lording over a private hell.

The marks ceased at the edge of what appeared to be a sarcophagus. The lid to the long stone coffin lay cast aside beneath it, leaving the entire thing open. She peered in, and immediately pulled back.

The rancid stench was worse inside. She held her breath for a second look. The inner walls of the sarcophagus were rough stone, but they were not clean. Within the empty crypt the stone was slashed and cut with deep scratches that looked like the marks of claws. Black slime pooled on the bottom and spread to the far edge. When she looked closer she had a horrible thought—it looked as though something had crawled out of the coffin, leaving a trail of dried sludge across the floor. Within the slime were the outlines of something that might have been footprints. She knelt down to touch it, to run her fingers through the putrescent bilge. Before she could bring herself to do it, she heard voices, men shouting from outside, from above.

"Shit," she said. "The fucking cops are quick out here. Must be a slow day."

FORTY-SEVEN

WHATELEY ESTATES
WILBURTON, MA

Two dark sedans pulled up. One parked about thirty feet from the house. The second one continued on all the way to the front door, stopping right next to where Diana's car was still blocked in by a pair of local police cruisers several hours after they'd arrived.

Richard Norris got out. She could tell he was angry just from his posture, stiff and rigid like a cadet on parade review. He flashed his ID to the officers standing with her on the front steps.

The cops hesitated though, and one of them said something about waiting for their supervisor's permission. That only gave Richard an excuse to let out some simmering anger.

"Go away, gentlemen," he commanded. "She's mine now."

Diana knew very well that he didn't mean that in a good way.

The officers dutifully stepped back, retreating to their vehicles. That left the two of them alone on the massive front porch. For a long moment neither of them said anything. They just stood there in tense, awful silence.

"I'm getting angry calls from the field office in Boston, plus the local P.D. out here, and this fucking billionaire's lawyers. Christ, I had to jump in a car and drive all the way out here myself just to keep you from ending up in some Podunk local jail," he finally said. "Do you realize what you've done?"

"I did what I had to do," she answered.

"You threatened to castrate a witness!" he shot back, incredulous. "A witness that you brutalized while he was handcuffed. That's not only unprofessional, that's fucking criminal, Diana."

"He knows, Richard. He knows about all of it," she replied.

"Well good luck getting a goddamn thing out of him now," he said. "We'll be lucky if he doesn't sue the pants off us all in Federal Court."

"No pun intended," she quipped.

"Goddamn it, Diana!" he answered. "This is no joke. We're the fucking F.B.I. This isn't some back alley Boston street fight. We don't do things this way."

"I did what needed to be done."

"And you got what out of him?" he asked. "Nothing, right?"

"I know that he knows," she said.

"You know nothing!" he shouted back. "Then you come out here, you break in without a warrant, you tear the place apart and find what? An eccentric rich guy has a lot of weird old shit in his basement?"

"He's the thirteenth, I know you don't see it, but..."

"Will you stop? Just stop for a second," he said. "I was worried about you before, the lack of sleep, the bizarre theories, but now? You just put everything we're doing at risk and you probably cost yourself your job—if not mine too."

"You're firing me?" she asked.

"I'm suspending you, effective immediately," he said. "Firing comes later."

She pulled her ID from her jacket pocket and threw it at him.

"I'm gonna need your sidearm too," he added.

She groaned as she un-holstered it, turned it around and handed it to him butt-forward.

"What's happened to you, Diana?" he asked. "What did this case do to you? You look terrible."

"Are you saying that as my boss or as my...whatever the fuck else we are?"

He lowered his voice.

"Go home. Get some rest," he said. "I care about you. I don't like to see you this way."

"You care about me?" she asked.

"Of course."

"Tell me something," she said. "Were you ever really going to leave your wife?"

"Diana, this isn't the time…"

She put her hands on his suit, fiddling with his necktie.

"You fucked me once with that tie on," she said. "Remember that?"

He just stared back at her.

"It was the second time we did it," she continued. "In the back of your Explorer after that night we saw the Doors cover band play at Haggerty's. You were wearing this same tie. Then it was with a navy, three button suit. But you knew that, right?"

"Diana, what are you talking about?"

"I remember everything about that, because it meant something to me," she said. "What did it mean to you?"

"C'mon, not now."

"Was any of this real?" she asked. "I mean, I know it happened, I'm not questioning that. I'm not *that* unhinged. I'm talking about us. Was there ever really such a thing as *us*? Was this ever anything more to you than just fucking?"

He threw up his hands.

"What do you want me to say here?" he asked.

She smirked.

"It's amazing really," she said.

"What's that?"

"You spend your whole life trying to figure out what you believe—*what you believe in.* You think you have it, you've got it down. You know where you stand and then it turns out, you were totally fucking wrong. What you thought was real was just an illusion, and what you thought was impossible ends up being…"

"What?"

"I have no fucking idea," she said.

She turned to walk away, but he called after her. Not in the friendly voice, this time he was back to being a boss.

"I want you to go back to D.C.," he said. "You're done here."

She stopped. She heard Norris say something into his phone. A moment later, two agents got out of the second sedan parked further down the driveway. Both in sunglasses and dark suits, they marched right toward her.

She knew what that meant. She turned back to Norris.

"Seriously?" she asked, as the two men came up to her, one on each side.

"These two are under orders to escort you back," Norris said.

"Screw you," she said. "I don't need a chaperone."

"Don't make me do this the hard way," Norris said.

"Are you arresting me?" she asked.

"I'd rather not call it that," Norris answered. "Why don't you just get in the car, close your eyes and get some rest. I'll have your things packed up at the hotel and sent on after you. I guarantee you'll feel better when you're back in D.C."

Diana nodded. Then she gave him the finger, turned and got into the car.

FORTY-EIGHT

STATE ROUTE 2
CENTRAL MASSACHUSETTS

They had her sit in the back seat. She wasn't handcuffed and she wasn't on lock-down, but Richard had chosen his men well. The two Special Agents in the front were classic Bureau men, humorless and stoic to a fault—a pair of identical haircuts and dark suits. They might as well have been robots. If he ordered them to escort her all the way back to D.C., they were going to execute that command to the letter, every mile, and not an inch short.

But that couldn't happen. Not now. Not after what she'd seen.

The car wove through the winding hill country roads for over a half hour, as the two crew-cuts tried to figure out how to get back to Route 2. From the look of things, their G.P.S. was no better than hers, and they had to circle back a few times before they came upon a sign directing them to it. That gave her time to think.

Not only did she need to get rid of these guys, she needed the car and she probably needed a weapon. That wasn't going to be easy. She ran through her options.

Asking to stop for a bathroom break—they'd never let her get far and there was no way to overpower two of them at once.

Playing sick to get them to pull over, then snatching a sidearm while she pretended to puke—oldest trick in the book, they'd see that coming a mile away.

Faking some unspecified woman trouble and grabbing the car—always an option, but they'd probably see through that too.

It had to be something they wouldn't expect. She had to get them out of the car, but she also needed them to think they were in control the whole way, so that when she did make a move, they'd never see her coming.

Her phone was still in her jacket pocket. Richard hadn't thought to confiscate that. It was an asset. She glanced toward the front seat. The two agents were chatting, neither one paying her much attention. They'd probably been told to keep an eye out, but if Richard was true to form, not to go too hard on her. That was another asset.

As discreetly as she could, Diana slipped her phone out of her jacket and brought it down by her thigh. She clicked the sound off and opened her text messages. Ariadne was high on the list, and she fired off a quick one.

need ur help

The reply came back in moments. Ariadne always had her phone nearby.

whats up? :-)

Diana checked the agents again, keeping an eye on them as she tried to text with one hand. She could barely see the screen.

need a favor. off the books

U got it

might get u fired

figured as much

shoot

The two had shown her their IDs when she got in the car. It was a habit, all agents tended to do that, even when it was unnecessary. But that gave her their names. The moment she read them she fixated on both, just in case she needed them later. Now she did.

can u get number for SA Peter Jordan?

got it. whatcha need?

Diana looked up again. Still the agents were talking. Neither one had checked back on her in a while.

"Hey, can you guys turn the heat up a bit?" she asked. "Kinda chilly back here."

Agent Jordan, in the passenger seat, acknowledged her request, clicking up the dial a few notches. He turned to see if that was enough.

He seemed satisfied and turned back to his conversation with the driver. That would buy her some time. Her next message was long, and took nearly a minute to type out with one hand. Since she could barely see it, it was probably full of misspellings. She hoped Ariadne got the gist of it anyway. She sent one quick follow up after the long one.

can u do that? EXACTLY that way?

u got it boss.

A few moments passed, long enough for Diana to worry that she might have garbled the message. She was about to check her own text again, when she heard ringing from the front seat.

Agent Jordan looked at the screen of his smartphone before he answered.

"Looks like headquarters," he said.

He took the call and in an instant his already serious face turned absolutely determined. He nodded several times, listening intently for a long while. As he hung up he gestured to the driver, who nodded as well. Their conversation stopped. They sat in total silence.

"Hey, everything okay up there?" Diana asked.

Jordan didn't turn around this time, he answered without looking back at her.

"Nothing to worry about, ma'am," he said. "Need to make a little pit stop up ahead, that's all."

She waited patiently as the driver steered them off of Route 2 when they came to a rest stop. He by-passed the main area of the parking lot and continued to drive around the back, where there were no cars, just some storage containers and a few trucks parked without any sign of their owners. He stopped the car way off by itself, took the keys out of the ignition and got out. Jordan finally turned to Diana.

"I'm gonna need you to step out of the vehicle, ma'am," he said.

"Something wrong?" she asked.

"I need you step outside, please," he repeated.

She got out at the same time he did.

"Can you turn around, please, and place your hands on the top of the vehicle," he said, more like a command this time.

She saw that he had his handcuffs at the ready. The driver had joined them, and came around to the other side of her. His hands were empty, but one was hovering near his sidearm. She noticed that the holster latch was unsnapped, just in case he needed to draw it in a hurry.

Her phone was still in her hand. When she turned around to put her hands on the car, she let it drop. It clattered against the steel and the glass of the car, as it tumbled to the ground. Both agents jumped at the unexpected noise.

She turned around, with her hands up.

"Hey, hey, relax boys," she said. "Just my phone."

They both saw what it was, and after a tense moment they all exhaled. The driver lowered his weapon as he moved to pick up the phone. Diana saw her chance. She bent over at the same time, deliberately butting heads with the man. He recoiled as she pretended to apologize for her clumsiness, but she was on the move.

Before he could look up, she stepped forward, jamming the spike end of her heel into his foot. He squealed and doubled over. She had her eye on his gun the entire time. The moment he shifted, she reached for it, jamming her foot into his groin as she yanked it free from his holster.

Once she had it, she whirled. Agent Jordan had his out, but Diana had the edge. She got behind the driver, still wheezing from the sudden, unexpected attack. She held him by the collar with the man's own forty-caliber pointed at his head.

"You don't want to do this," Jordan said.

She smirked.

"Actually, I do," she answered.

"I'm serious," he replied.

"So am I," she said. "That call you got a minute ago. That was Richard's assistant, right?"

Jordan puzzled.

"How did you know…?"

"Telling you the team back at Wilburton discovered a body during their sweep, and that I was now a suspect in a murder," she said. "They told you to pull over quietly, and to take me into custody without alerting me, right?"

Jordan puzzled.

"I don't know how you know that," he said. "But this only ends one way."

She pulled back the hammer on the driver's gun, now menacing only inches from his ear.

"You're right," she said. "It ends with you throwing down your weapon and walking fifty paces backward, while I take your buddy's keys and he lays flat on the ground, face down with his hands behind his head."

Agent Jordan stammered.

"Trust me kid. I know how you think. *I used to be you*," she said. "Right now you're wondering if you can get your sidearm up and take the shot before I put one in your partner. *You can't*. You're also probably trying to remember how you did on your last firearms qualifications test, but your hand is shaking way more than you figured right now because this is real and you've never fired your weapon in action before."

He stared back at her.

"Plus you know that if you play this wrong, if you try to pick me off and your partner here ends up dead, not only do you have to live with that for the rest of your life, your career is probably over too. On top of all that, I bet you're trying to figure out from what little you know about me if I'm really the kind of person who would go all the way here."

Jordan was starting to ease up. She could see it in his eyes. Panic had already turned to concern.

"So you got a lot on your mind, and not a lot of time to stew over it. Let me save you the trouble," she said. "I'm giving you an out. Drop the gun, and step back. Once I'm gone you two will find a pay phone, or some random citizen with a cell and you'll call this in. You'll have a *bolo* out on the car in fifteen minutes and I'll probably get picked up by a Statie on the highway before midnight.

"No one gets hurt. No one gets shot," she said. "Yeah, you'll get busted down for losing the car and your sidearm, and you'll have a supervisor chew you out something fierce, but that's better than the alternative, isn't it?"

Finally, Agent Jordan gave in. He put down his sidearm and did as she ordered, stepping way back with his hands up. She took the keys from the driver, and had him lay on his tummy while she took Jordan's pistol as well

Then Diana Mancuso got in the car and drove off.

«««—»»»

She drove fast, but not too fast.

The last thing she needed was to get pulled over by some overzealous state trooper, or even worse, a bored local cop sitting by the road with nothing to do at midnight. So as she headed back toward Boston she pushed the speed limit, but only to a point.

Ariadne had forwarded her Carter Shaw's home address. Now it was her last hope. If he was there she was going to press him, as hard as she needed to this time. If he wasn't, she was going to tear his place apart looking for clues. He was her only remaining link to Victor Gregorian and Luther Vayne—although which one was the target and which one was the threat now seemed much different than she would have ever imagined.

Either way, she wasn't leaving without answers.

Carter lived in the Back Bay, a quiet, tree-lined stretch of nineteenth century brownstones nestled along the south bank of the Charles River that reached from near the Commons out west to where B.U. swallowed the neighborhood with student housing.

She pulled up once to get a bead on his unit, on the north side of Beacon Street. The lights were on in the main floor window, technically the second level, up the big front steps. She idled just long enough to see the silhouette of a man moving around inside, then drove a little out of her way, parking her stolen federal vehicle a few blocks down on Marlborough near Exeter—near enough to get back to it if she absolutely had to, but far enough that if Boston P.D. noticed it, she had some wiggle room.

Then she made her way back over to Beacon, slipping into the alley between Carter's building and the one next to it. The brownstones were mostly clustered right next to one another, but she knew that neighborhood. Once you got in behind the rows of homes, almost all of the structures had old-fashioned wrought-iron fire escapes in back. Carter's was no exception.

She had to climb a small fence to get in by his garbage cans and a tiny shed. It didn't take long though, and in short order she was up on the fire escape itself, right outside of what looked like a bedroom window.

The area was posh, but always noisy. She took some discarded newspapers from the recycling bin, wrapped them up in a wad around her fist and waited. It wasn't long before the scream of a siren from a passing ambulance or squad car drowned out every other sound in the area. She used the cover to smash the glass pane above the window lock. That gave her just enough space to reach inside, unlatch the window and draw it open, without shattering the entire thing.

The bedroom was empty, but she could see light spilling in from the hallway, and she could hear a radio or a TV going in the living room. A Bruins game, from the sound of it. More cover for her as she crept along, careful not to touch anything. Then she edged her way out of the room, trying her best to minimize the creak of the door. She saw a shadow moving at the end of the hallway. The floors were hardwood, so she took off her shoes again in order to get down to the end as stealthily as possible.

She got to the far side, just enough to peer around the corner into the living room, but oddly it seemed to be empty. The radio was playing, but the sofa and the lounge chair were both unoccupied. There was a glass of water on the end table and a half-eaten peanut butter sandwich on a plate next to it. But there was no other hint of the man himself.

Diana was about to turn, just getting up from her crouch, when a sharp pain erupted across the back of her head. She tried to reach out, whirling as the room started to spin around her, but a second blow sent an even stronger shock of pain through her.

Then everything went black.

FORTY-NINE

BACK BAY NEIGHBORHOOD
BOSTON, MA

The first thing she realized was that she was on the ground. The second was that her hands were secured behind her back—with the same cuffs she taken from her driver. Diana wanted to rub her eyes, to soothe her throbbing temples, but that wasn't an option. Instead she fought through the grogginess and the pain to see what she had gotten herself into.

It wasn't good, that was clear right away. She was not only cuffed, but they were locked around an iron steam pipe connected to an old-fashioned radiator. She managed to get herself to her feet, just in time for Carter Shaw to come back into the living room from the adjacent kitchen. He was sipping a cup of tea.

"Awakened by the smell of Darjeeling, I see," he said.

"What?" she replied, still foggy.

"You've been out for almost an hour," he said.

"Heard me coming, eh?' she replied. "I thought I got in clean. Must be slipping in my old age."

"Don't blame yourself, Agent Mancuso. Recent events have made me rather paranoid these days," he answered.

"That doesn't make me feel any better," she said.

"You are persistent, I have to say," he said. "I mean, after that scene at work. That wasn't enough for you?"

"I didn't come here to do that again," she said.

"Well, even if that was your intention, I'd say you're out of luck in that department."

She tugged on the cuffs. She wasn't going anywhere and she knew it.

"I need your help," she said.

"You want my help?"

"I said I *need* your help."

He put the tea down and got eye to eye with her, his voice lowered to a whisper.

"Maybe you shouldn't have threatened to cut my fucking balls off then."

She nodded. Then she smiled, just a little as he backed away.

"I wasn't really gonna do that," she said.

He just stared back at her.

"Okay, okay," she answered. "I'm sorry. You happy?"

"Not even close," he said.

"Look I get it, you're pissed off. You have every right to be," she said. "You have to admit though, it wouldn't have been much of a threat if you didn't think I really was gonna do it."

"That doesn't make it okay," he said.

"You're right, it doesn't," she said.

"Well, the shoe's on the other foot now, isn't it?" he said.

She tugged on the cuffs again, for whatever good it would do.

"I'm a federal fucking agent," she shot back. "How long do you think you can keep me like this? You could be looking at felony charges here."

He laughed.

"I think you played that card already today. By the way, I gotta tell you, that's about the least scary thing I've heard this week," he said.

She continued to struggle for a minute against the cuffs again, still it was no use.

"Goddamn it, let me go right now, or…"

"Or what?" he interrupted. "You broke into my home—after you assaulted me at work. You're an intruder, a stalker even. I'm well within my rights to hold you here until the cops come."

"What's your point?" she said. "You want some kind of revenge, is that what this is about?"

He got close to her for a second time.

"Revenge?" he asked. "Is that what you think? That I'm going to hold you here and make you suffer to get back at you?"

"You might," she said.

He smiled a sort of exaggerated, evil grin. He was near enough to smell the spicy tea on his breath.

"What is it that you think I'm gonna do?" he asked, getting right up next to her. "You think I might rip open your blouse, for starters? Maybe your bra too? Or how about just going right for the jackpot and yanking off those pants of yours?"

She sneered at him.

"You sicko."

"Oh wait, maybe that's not enough, maybe I should go to the kitchen and get a steak knife. I could cut every button off of your shirt one-at-a-time, and then slice through your bra really slow, make you feel every minute of it as you stand here, helpless to do anything. Is that what you're thinking?"

"You wouldn't," she answered, her heart racing.

He sighed, and he waited a long, slow moment before stepping back.

"You're right," he said, throwing up his hands. "*I wouldn't* do that. That's the difference between you and me...Agent Mancuso."

"So you're not gonna..."

"What? Deliberately humiliate you while you're handcuffed and then threaten you with serious bodily harm?" he answered. "No, I'm not a monster."

She nodded.

"Okay, point taken," she said.

He sat on the arm of his couch.

"But that doesn't mean I can let you go, either," he said. "Unfortunately you're going to be here for a while."

"How long is that?"

"You might just have to wait for the police to get here."

"Have you called them?"

"No."

She snarled at him.

"Then what…?"

"I can't do that, not just yet," he interrupted. "So you might as well get comfortable."

"What the hell are you and Gregorian up to?"

"I suppose there's no point in maintaining the façade any more—you're right, of course," he said. "I'm neck deep in this Azathoth business. That is exactly why I can't let you go. I can't have the cops here and I can't have an F.B.I. agent on my back. There are things I need to do. Like you, I have a job to do."

He turned back to look at her, really look this time. The rumpled clothing and the messy hair made her look like a drunk, or a bag lady in a second-hand suit. But there was something else. The look on her face, in her eyes. Almost like the old photos of combat vets who'd seen too much, the thousand-yard stare.

The same look he had.

"It's a shame, you know," he said.

"What's that?"

"You were close," he replied. "Honestly, you'll probably never know how close you came.

"To what?"

He looked at her, then looked away.

"To *everything,*" he replied.

She was about to answer, but something stopped her. The breath went out of her lungs in a rush. A horrific reek filled the air between them, a sudden surge of sulfur. Then the lights flickered. A moment later, they went out completely, plunging the entire apartment into darkness—but only for an instant.

When the lights came back on, Luther Vayne was there.

DAY TEN

"Let the wind carry him to places unknown."

Purported Excerpt from the "Tablet of Destinies"
Royal Babylonian Library of Ashurbanipal, Ninevah

The Priestess had come. Finally.

She stood over him, hands dripping to the elbows in human blood. Her red-slathered forearms were exposed to the starless sky. The elegant cowl and hood hid most of her head. As with her acolytes, it left only a faceless black façade, cloaked in shadow, denuded of any hint of humanity.

Chanting followed; the others were gathered all around, kneeling in rows on each side of his torture-dais, holding up tapers in the dark. Two of their number kept the pace with beats upon the tribal drums. To his untrained ear it sounded like nothing more than twisted nonsense. Just whispers at first, though they seemed to multiply in the telling, until the sound built itself up in a slow climb. A devotional hymn emerged from the jumbled mess of hissed and muffled syllables; a prayer of the oldest vintage.

"Ya'hya. Cha'hya. Sh'shaya Shoggoth chya'hath."

He watched as the Priestess passed her bare, red hands over his naked body. The evil woman ministered with delicate, practiced motions, her fingers tracing outlines in the air only inches from his skin. It soon became clear, as the strange words echoed in unison with the gestures, that the Priestess was following the tracings etched into his body. She was reading the scar tissue-symbols those silent, sinister witches had carved and burned and inked across every inch of his flesh.

He was the sacred text. He was the word made flesh.

"Ya'hya. Cha'hya. Sh'shaya Shoggoth chya'hath."

This time the gathered women answered, in zombie-like refrain.

"Yog Sothoth is the way."

The rite continued, with yet more strange and intricate verses read from the book of his flesh, each line sprinkled with drops of warm blood. Complex hymns and archaic words blended into the evening, until they began to echo as if reflected from somewhere in the distance.

Alone atop that sinister stone dais on that desolate barrow, that was quite impossible. But as the moments passed, as the verses swelled, the echoes only grew louder. It was as if the starless void above were answering. Soon it did more.

Clouds gathered from out of the clear sky. Emerging from the void, seemingly spawned by the verses themselves, they came together from every corner of the disturbed heavens, joining into a silent thunderhead. They roiled and churned until they had built a towering column, a captive, unnatural storm arisen where moments before there had been nothing.

The Priestess lifted her hands to it, she beseeched it, she prayed to it.

She commanded it.

It answered. From the swirling tempest a funnel cloud of mist descended. Reeking of sulfur and thick with fumes it lowered itself from the blackness overhead, coming down upon the hill crest in a spinning curtain of foul wind.

Still they chanted, even as the brimstone choked their lungs.

"Ya'hya. Cha'hya. Sh'shaya Shoggoth chya'hath."

Flashes of lightning began to scatter from within the mega-cloud, blood red and absent of thunder—or any sound but the constant droning chant of the women and their High Priestess. The swatches of eerie illumination soon revealed further peculiarities. Something was moving within the great, wicked cloud, something that was neither mist, nor shadow. Something else.

The swirl grew stronger, taking on a shape. A black whirlpool in the sky. Edges of the cloud spun outward in tendrils of mist, and even those grew into something else, something stronger, deeper and darker until they had morphed into claw-like pincers and fat tentacles, flailing and reaching from what was now a great maw of shadow and flame. The smoldering center belched stinking currents of smog girded by tongues of green and violet fire. Frost formed on the fingers of the Priestess. It crept over everything on the dais.

Chained and held in place by the hooks distorting his flesh, he could only stare upward at the abomination revealed, at the abyss opened wide above, spilling out a cold and putrid reek. He could hear it, calling to him. It was unlike any melody he had ever heard, singing in a thousand voices. A chorus of the darkest of angels. He now knew his purpose. He knew what all the suffering and the horror had been for.

When the Priestess called out again, he welcomed what he now knew was to be the final act of his awful drama.

"Keeper of the way between the worlds, we here offer this sacrifice. Take him for your pleasures, this strongest of men marked in your sacred words, this warrior of the highest order, this loyal servant, this soldier and killer who is truly the finest specimen of all that is pure in the dark soul of humanity."

Fingers reached out from the fractured sky, skeletal hands of mist and flame that stretched toward him. They stroked his ruined, ravaged skin with a soothing touch. Pain vanished. In that instant the agony was gone. As the way opened before him, as he looked up into an abyss without end, he felt something he thought he would never know again.

Luther Vayne was filled with joy.

FIFTY

BACK BAY NEIGHBORHOOD
BOSTON, MA

For a long moment, Luther Vayne said nothing. Diana stared at him, a familiar sight to her, and yet now somehow different.

Though his lanky limbs and his ravaged face were like stone, nothing else around him was at rest. As if disturbed by his very presence, the air and the light danced and broke around him. Brimstone fumes cloaked him in a translucent gray halo. He cast multiple shadows at once, all of them slithering and shifting like a nest of vipers.

She looked over to Carter. He staggered backward in panic, his sight locked on the intruder. His eyes were wide and unblinking. He looked genuinely frightened, scared silent at the simple sight of Luther Vayne.

The rune-faced figure pointed at Carter, aiming his bony finger toward him.

"You are Dr. Carter Shaw," he said, more a statement of fact than a question.

Carter's face went ashen. His legs quivered beneath him, forcing him to grab for the mantle of his fireplace to keep himself steady.

"I am," the doctor answered.

"You must come with me," Vayne said.

Carter stammered, unable to muster a reply.

Vayne pulled back his accusatory finger. As he did so, Carter was dragged across the room, reeled in by unseen powers. Though he made a flailing, desperate effort to grab hold of the mantle beside him, the inexorable force of Vayne's will hauled the doctor the length of the floor between them. He landed beside the frightful specter, brought down to his knees at Vayne's feet.

"What about me?" Diana asked.

Vayne turned to her, but his stoic expression did not change. He remained stone-faced when he set his gaze upon her, evidently not the least bit surprised at her presence. The runes etched into his skin barely moved when he spoke.

"You may accompany us," he said. She felt the handcuffs open by themselves behind her. "Is that not why you are here?"

"Figured you'd say something like that," she replied.

"Where exactly are you taking me…us?" Carter asked.

"To Victor Gregorian, I'd imagine," Diana answered, as she came to her feet.

"Correct," Vayne replied.

"You know where he is?" Carter asked.

"I do not," Vayne said. "I have but a suspicion."

He pointed his eyes at Carter.

"I believe you may be in a position to clarify things for me," he said.

Carter looked back the horrific, blind figure. He seemed almost dumbstruck with fear.

"Ghost Moon Hill," Diana asked.

Carter's head turned sharply, jolted from his torpor.

"How do you know that?" he demanded.

"So it is true," Vayne said. "Gregorian has chosen to bring everything full circle. Very well, we shall end this where it began."

"Which means what?" she asked. "Just so you know, I drove here in a car I stole from two Federal agents, so I wouldn't recommend taking that that thing anywhere. It's as hot as they come."

"Not necessary," Vayne replied.

"What's your plan then?" she asked.

He stepped back from the front entrance.

"We will open the door, and we will walk through," Vayne replied.

He looked to the apartment's front door, raised his hand again and waved his fingers once. The door responded. It unlatched and opened all the way. But that was only the beginning of the strangeness. What was behind it was not a street. It wasn't even Boston, at least as far as she could tell.

Diana looked at him. Then she looked at Carter. His face was still blank with terror.

"Shit, every time I think this can't get any weirder," she said.

On the other side was the dreamscape yet again, a tableau culled from a nightmare. A world that could not exist, and yet there it was, facing her one more time.

Vayne gestured toward the open portal. She knew he meant them both to enter. They did not walk. A current carried them forward, like riders on the wind. Whispering tendrils of green mist wrapped them in a foul-smelling web, guiding them across the unreal threshold.

The nightmare world seemed to move instead of them, fragments of images slipping by as they advanced through a parade of inversions. The sky ran in reverse overhead, clouds shifting backwards and the moon receding across the dark. The ground beneath their feet faded in and out of existence. Colors bled through the mist, showing hints of life beyond—glimpses of people, stolen hints of conversation, all broken and fractured. Light itself bent and twisted around them, like smoke in the wind.

Their ears betrayed them. Sounds echoed with a peculiar cadence. Some drew long, their pitch deepened by inexplicable stutters. Others squeaked and tumbled at speed, playing back upon themselves as though run backwards. It was as though time itself was indecisive there, a stream of thought plagued by seizures, stammering through a disconnected sequence of broken moments.

"Where are we? What is this place?" she said.

"It is neither a place, nor a time," Vayne said. "We walk now through the space between moments, through the shadow of the four dimensions you inhabit."

"This is all real?" Diana asked. "It's really…real?"

"Reality has many facets, only a few of which you can perceive," he said.

"But not you," she said. "You can *see* more?"

"The dreams of Azathoth altered me, gave me sight beyond sight. They opened my mind, broadened my vision to things you cannot imagine. To the threads that weave together time and space itself."

"That's how you walked out of Danfield?" she asked. "That's amazing."

"This is a means to an end, nothing more," he said.

"But I need to know," she said. "How did you…become this?"

"As I told you, Agent Mancuso, it was my loyalty that was my undoing," he answered.

"I don't follow," she replied. "You said you would tell me all of it, when the time was right."

"So I did," he said.

Once again the mist answered his commands, taking shape as he spoke, bringing to life memories of a time long past.

"For years I stood by Valeria Thorne's side, as she made effort after effort to invoke the dark ones," he said, the images playing out for them all. "On countless moonless nights we gathered in secret atop her private mountain, a torch circle of chanting and repeated invocations. She arranged and rearranged the rituals time and again, offering blood enough to fill buckets. But never with any success."

They saw the Tablet of Destinies, its dark magnificence pulled from the sandy ground by a host of workers, Valeria Thorne standing watch over them.

"It was only after she secured this ancient, long-lost tablet that she found more precise instructions. She learned the error of her ways. In order to open the path, the forbidden word must not be merely spoken, she realized. It must be made flesh."

They looked back at him, his entire body inscribed with the runes of Elder Script.

"*Your* flesh…" Diana muttered.

"In the ancient rites it was long considered an honor for the greatest of all warriors in the kingdom to be offered as the sacrifice, to bring forth the favor of the entity. In that moment, my fate was sealed. She ordered me seized in the night, drugged and chained to the altar beneath the black sky."

They saw it happening: the abduction, the inking, the scarification. The heard him scream. They felt his agony.

"She had her priestesses follow the horrific directions of the ancient text, using sharpened steel and flame to cut, sear and brand the runes of the lost tome into my skin. The process drove me to the brink of madness as every inch of my flesh was inscribed with the sacred writings.

"When it was finally done, Thorne once again performed the black rite. This time however, the abyss did answer her call, opening a pathway into the furthest reaches of the darkness. The Priestess called forth the demonic entity."

"Yog Sothoth," Diana said.

"My suffering opened the way for the beast to come forth," he said. "But that was only the beginning."

Carter and Diana witnessed it for themselves. Blood-red lightning tore a wound in the sky, bleeding into the New England night. The opening seethed. Steam swirled around the periphery, merging with the things that spilled out from the roiling ocean of dark flames beyond. Pus oozed out of the gateway, boiling in a toxic froth. Sulfur fumes choked the air with brimstone.

Something began to take shape within the heart of the noxious storm. It began to congeal from the cosmic bilge. Voices neither male nor female, or perhaps both, shrieked from a thousand mouths. Putrid winds swirled a mess of green-black tentacles all about its fat, blistered corpus. Jaws lined with pointed, jagged yellow teeth yammered in mindless hunger from the end of each one, slurping with purple lips.

A grotesque head dangled beneath a thorny carapace, hanging from a mass of slimy tendrils. Hundreds of dark, empty eyes peered out from its bloated, cephalopod form. The hideous entity manifested unlike any living thing, taking form within a ghostly congress of radiant globes, borne out of a bubbling lather suspended in a mist-like slime.

"The horror that followed turned the stomachs of all those who looked upon it," Vayne continued.

They saw the shambling creature emerge fully. Valeria Thorne was standing beneath it, naked but for her hooded cloak and ministering to it with shouted calls in dead tongues.

"Her spells ensnared it, bent the thing to her will," Vayne said. "Bound it to her demands."

Like a spider descending upon its prey, Yog Sothoth lowered itself from the sky. It extended its many spiny tentacles, wrapping them around Valeria Thorne, holding her fast. It drove its claws into the ground, rooting itself down. Then its terrible maw opened, and yet another dripping proboscis flittered into view. It searched around, sniffing, feeling and stroking Valeria until it found the opening it desired.

The beast roared. Valeria reared and screamed with the shock of something beyond ecstasy—a rush of pure agony and unfathomable pleasure at once.

"The beast mated with Thorne," Vayne said, as if to punctuate the abject horror they had just seen.

"She had *sex* with it?"

"The beast entered her, yes," he replied, without a hint of revulsion at the macabre display. "She welcomed him into her. That was her plan all along. She wished to become the queen mother to a new birth of demonic children, a new race to rule humanity. She almost succeeded."

"What about you?"

"It took me into its embrace as well, looked into my soul with a thousand eyes as black as the abyss itself," he said.

They both shuddered. What they saw next was even worse.

"I tore out my own eyes, for the dreadful horror of its sight," Vayne added.

They watched helplessly as the images played out. A tormented madman released from his bonds, only to claw at his own eyes, sinking his fingers deep into his own soft flesh and gouging them from his face.

"But that was folly. It invaded my very mind, infected me with sights and sounds and thoughts no words can describe," Vayne said. "Then, having served my purpose, when my screams and my agony amused Sothoth no more, it speared me with its pincers and cast me aside. Discarded like a child's broken toy, making final offering of my ritually scarred form to the void from which it came, to the endless laughter of Azathoth."

Diana and Carter watched as his broken, violated body tumbled into the sulfur-reeking whirlpool, screaming as he spiraled away into the abyss.

"What happened on the other side?" Diana asked.

"There are no words for it. What I saw...where I went...they are not places, and the entities I encountered are not beings as we understand them. Even time has no meaning there. A thousand years may pass by our perception, and it is but a minute. I drifted through those nightmares like flotsam upon an endless ocean, bandied about by impossible imaginings, twisted by the currents of ageless, tormented souls. No hell of Dante's conception could have compared. I was lost in the maelstrom for longer than the age of the world.

"Marked by the sacred texts I was somehow protected from the forces of that cosmic hell, left to roam for eons uncounted, until I was finally drawn into the orbit of the mad god. There I came to drown in the laughter of Azathoth."

"But you came back?" Carter asked.

"Not by choice," he said. "I would have stayed for all eternity, lost in the madness of the mad god. *I was sent back*."

"Sent back? Why?" Carter asked.

"That is not for me to question," he replied. "Azathoth commands it, and so I must obey."

"To destroy the spawn of Sothoth," Diana said. "That was your mission. That was what Azathoth commanded."

"Very good, once again you have followed the path perfectly," he answered. "When I did return, eons had passed for me—but it had been no more than a few months here. I found Valeria right where I had left her. She had already given birth to the demon spawn when I stepped out from the still-yawning abyss, but she remained there still, atop her lonely mountain."

"Alone?"

"Not alone," he replied.

"She was with him...*with it*?" Diana asked.

"Yog Sothoth remained under her power, yes," he said.

"But why did she stay? Why didn't she go with the others?" Carter asked.

"To consort in such a way with an entity from the abyss is to introduce forces into this world that do not belong here. Valeria took the demon seed inside her, she incubated his spawn. You cannot do that and remained unchanged."

"What does that mean?" Diana asked.

"The black currents polluted her, infested every corner of her bones. They began to turn her, to use her corrupted flesh for their own purposes," Vayne answered. "She kept Sothoth there, upon the old hill top, bound to her will, feeding off of his essence. She was already more beast than human by then. It was the only way for her to survive. She knew that if she lost her link to him, to the currents of power that fed her, sustained her, she would collapse into something else."

"Something inhuman," Carter whispered.

"Correct," Vayne said. "When I returned, I banished Yog Sothoth, sending him back into the same abyss from which he had thrown me."

Again, they saw it happen. They watched as Vayne emerged from the abyss in an explosion of shadow of mist, his rune-covered flesh swathed in dark flame. He reached out and snared the beast. It howled from a thousand mouths, spitting fire and slime.

Valeria was thrown down. The great tablet beside her collapsed. Singed by the flames and sundered by the fall, the whole lower section was sheared off. The stone facing crumbled, destroying part of the Elder Script inscription as Vayne wrestled Yog Sothoth, casting the entity back into the pit.

"Then I turned to Valeria," he continued. "She was doomed, and she knew it. I gave her one final chance to redeem herself, to undo the horror she had unleashed."

"She agreed?"

"No, she resisted," he replied.

"Resisted?"

"For a time. Eventually I persuaded her to tell me what she had done, and where she had sent all of her bastard children. By the end, she was entirely forthcoming."

"You tortured her?" Diana asked.

"Believe me, her suffering was a pale shadow of that which she once perpetrated against me," Vayne replied.

"An eye for an eye?" she asked.

"Far worse than that, if you truly wish to know. The power of Sothoth had changed her, had made her stronger in some ways, and rather tolerant of pain. It took quite a lot to convince her."

Diana remembered the old news clipping, how the forest had been burned all around the hill top when Thorne's family ventured out to look for her. It sent a chill through her.

"What did you do?"

"You have seen terrible things already, is it your sincere wish to hear more voices of suffering and horror?" he replied. "It should suffice to say that when the fire and the blood ended, she quite welcomed death, and so I left her to meet her end."

Diana shivered.

"It was more mercy than she deserved," Vayne said.

Diana puzzled. She raised a finger.

"Her body was never found," Diana said.

"I left her atop the hill, upon the altar where she fell," he answered. "I know no more than that."

Carter huddled to himself, staying silent and averting his eyes from either one of them.

"As you know, I next sought out all of the Disciples and their children, and I killed them—but Valeria had conceived one final deception," Vayne said.

"There was one last child," Diana said. "The thirteenth. Victor Gregorian."

"I knew the moment I killed the Dressler boy that he was no demon-spawn. Though I do not know how she accomplished it, Thorne managed to hide one final child, a demon born from her own womb whose identity she concealed from me."

"You couldn't go back," Diana said.

"My mission was left unfinished," he answered. "I could not return to Azathoth. I had no way to identify the thirteenth. I had only one final hope, one thing that would allow me to discover the answer—in time."

"The Convergence," Carter said.

Now it was Diana's turn to be confused.

"What is that?" she asked.

"The pathway Thorne had opened appears once every forty-some years, when the planes of Azathoth's realm and ours touch briefly," Carter answered. Then he turned to Vayne. "You were waiting for the cosmic alignment. You knew that if you bided your time, the demon spawn would reveal himself."

"I had only to wait."

"So you gave yourself up," Diana said.

"I surrendered myself. I offered no resistance to the law. For the next four decades I sat in prison, waiting—and watching."

"That's one hell of a wait."

"Hardly more than a moment in the view of eternity," he replied.

"But why?" Carter demanded. "Why would Azathoth want to destroy the children of Sothoth?"

Vayne appeared confused for the first time, as if the question had never occurred to him.

"To prevent them from doing what they seek to do this very night," he replied.

"To summon him?" Carter asked.

"Not only to summon him, but to rouse him. In order to beseech him, they must first awaken him from his endless slumber," Vayne answered. "That must not happen."

"I don't understand," Diana said. "Why would that be a problem?"

"Azathoth is the source of all knowledge, all power," Carter said.

"To rouse Azathoth is to court the fountain of wisdom and the deepest darkness at once," Vayne said. "Should his slumbering consciousness come to life, should he be fully roused from his endless dreaming, it could mean an end to all creation. Universes uncounted could be annihilated in an instant."

"Right, sorry I asked," Diana said. "Don't they realize the danger? If poking Azathoth risks destroying everything, why would they even attempt that?"

"Because to take that knowledge *without* awakening him would reveal the secrets of eternity," Carter replied.

"But can they do that?" she asked. "Is that even possible?"

"That does not matter," Vayne answered.

"Why?" Carter asked.

"Because Azathoth does not wish to awaken," Vayne said. "I have been sent to make certain he never does."

"There's still something I don't follow," Diana said. "If Azathoth slumbers, how did he send you to stop them?"

"It is true, Azathoth slumbers," Vayne answered. "It is also true that to awaken him from that eternal dreaming would be to court annihilation. But as with all things, there is a common understanding and then there is the more complex truth behind it. The true nature of Azathoth is even stranger than we might imagine.

"That which we can truly know of Azathoth is limited, and to learn much more risks madness. But this much is clear to me now—that which is Azathoth is vast, for it is not simply a single consciousness but instead many; multiples upon multiples uncounted.

"Much as we often say that "the nation slumbers" as night falls over the countryside, so too did the ancients tell us that Azathoth slumbers at the heart of his cosmic sanctum. But just as we do not mean to suggest that every flicker of thought, every spark of awareness in every sentient individual ceases to be upon the mere fall of dusk, neither than should we imagine that Azathoth's dreaming sleep means that he is not aware of what surrounds him.

"That his mind is vast and his consciousness is legion is impossible to deny. What became clear to me in the endless eons I spent drowning in his wake is this: Azathoth is always aware. He has many faces, and each of them has a kind of awareness, separate after a fashion, yet never cut off from the whole. Some fragment of his many, many facets is ever watching, pondering and thinking. Like the ebb and flow of an endless black ocean do his many splinter-selves rise and fall; ascending to great heights of thought beyond the contemplation of our poor minds, then collapsing back into the eternal dreaming sea.

"It is the threatened rousing of the whole of him that we justly fear. For should that multitude be awakened all at once, should that infinite ocean of darkness rise to a churning boil, the consequences would surely be dire. For all life. For all existence."

FIFTY-ONE

SHERATON HOTEL—NORTH END
BOSTON, MA

Fists banging on the door of her room called Ariadne out of the bathroom. She'd only been back at the hotel for ten minutes, long enough to drop her bag, take a shot of whiskey from the mini bar and start to run a hot bath.

She peered through the peephole before unfastening the lock, just to be safe. It was Richard Norris on the other side, flanked by two bureau men. His face was red, his eyes were huge and he was sweating in the middle of winter. His famous cool was gone, burned away by raw anger. She had never seen him that way.

The hot bath was going to have to wait.

He pushed the door open the moment she had it unlocked.

"Where is she?" he demanded.

"What?"

"Don't fuck around with me," he answered, stepping into the room and closing the door behind him. The two agents remained outside. "Where the hell is she?"

Ariadne raised her hands up as if surrendering.

"Look, I know you two don't see eye to eye right now," she replied. "I don't want to get in the middle of anything."

She backed away from him, letting herself fall into the office chair beside the desk. Her arms went limp and her head seemed barely able to stay straight. Norris didn't appear to notice her obvious exhaustion. He kept moving forward.

"Bullshit," he answered. "I heard what happened to the agents I sent with her. *I know that was you.* So don't act like you're innocent and don't tell me you want to stay out of it. You're already in too deep."

"Okay, okay. I was just trying to help," she said, rubbing her temples. "Fire me, if that's what you want."

"You're already fired," he said. "That's not even an issue. Now it's about whether you stay out of jail."

"Look, I honestly don't know," she said.

His fierce blue eyes narrowed, staring right at her.

"I swear to god, Ariadne, you tell me where the hell Diana is in the next three seconds or I'll have you arrested for obstruction."

She rubbed her fingers through her eyes and pushed herself back from the desk.

"I'm not lying," she said. "She asked me for help and I gave it to her. She didn't tell me where she was going."

He took out his cell.

"Come on in guys," he said.

A moment later, the two Special Agents entered the room.

"Take her into custody," he ordered.

They approached the desk.

"Please stand up, ma'am," one of them said.

Ariadne kept looking at Norris.

"Damn it, I'm telling the truth," she said. "I don't *know* where she is. Not for sure, anyway."

Norris stepped up, waving the agents back.

"But you have an idea?" he asked.

She lowered her eyes, as if she couldn't quite face him.

"Tell me," he said. "

She nodded, unable to look up as she said the words.

"Ghost Moon Hill," she said. "If I had to guess, I'd say she's going to Ghost Moon Hill."

FIFTY-TWO

GHOST MOON HILL
WEST LAVINIA, MA

A few minutes before midnight, Victor Gregorian summoned his disciples once again. Of the all the adherents to the Black Flame, only he remained atop the promontory of the hill. Under the dome of night, he sat upon the blood-slathered altar, the others having retreated below at the conclusion of Janet's sacrificial rite.

But he was not alone. Next to him lay the steel sarcophagus, opened and half covered in sticky red slime. Black tentacles curled up from within. They had wrapped themselves around his exposed, inhuman body, holding him in a tight embrace. Though virtually naked, the chill of the night did not appear to affect him.

Encamped around the base of the hill's peak, the others mustered to his call without delay. Wrapped in their parkas and hats to ward off the frost, the loyal followers emerged from their shelters and gathered into a line, climbing the steps to the crest of the rise, silent as they went.

None were shocked by the sight that greeted them—their half-human leader entwined with the dark and inhuman occupant of the crypt. Instead, it was what they *didn't* see that roused their concern. Krieger, again, voiced the thoughts of his comrades.

"Is it not time, Victor?" he asked, looking around.

Gregorian smiled, stroking the scaly tentacle nestled beneath his chin.

"Very soon," he replied. "Why else would I have called you forth?"

Krieger looked around. The top of the hill was just as they'd left it hours earlier. He looked up. The sky was as black and still as ever.

"I see nothing," he replied. "There's nothing above. No change here at all, despite all the blood. This cannot be why we've gathered."

The others bristled behind him, echoing his frustration.

"Patience," Gregorian answered. "The moment is very nearly upon us now."

Krieger threw up his hands.

"How can you say that?" Krieger replied. "After everything we've done, all of this—it's come to nothing?"

"Hardly," Gregorian said.

He used his good hand to push the lid of the steel sarcophagus all the way open. The tentacles that swathed him were then joined by a half-dozen others that emerged, slithering up and gripping the outside of the metal box. For a moment, they paused. Gregorian reached into the crypt, whispering encouragement.

"Come now, there is nothing to fear anymore," he said.

In answer to his urgings, the tentacles clenched, flexing as the main body of the thing raised itself up and into view. Drenched in viscous yellow slime, the center of it was slug-like. It seemed to have no fixed form, just a wet, hairy mass of oily blubber, pock-marked with swollen pustules and open sores. It undulated and shivered, moving to the stuttering rhythm of a hoarse cough uttered from an unseen mouth hidden somewhere inside it.

The cephalopod body expanded as it lifted itself up, until it had spread over the entire top of the steel structure. Even then however, it was not finished. A series of ripples disturbed the quivering pool of green-black flesh. They moved *inward*, multiple waves pushing from the edges toward the center, rather than spread outward like drops on a pond.

At the heart of the thing, the ripples piled up on one another, building a distorted bulge that soon towered over the entire creature. It extended itself as a kind of serpentine neck. Near the far end, glazed over in a layer of translucent slime, something like a face began to emerge.

Gregorian took it close to him, cradling the twisted visage and wiping putrescent globs off of it. His fingers revealed a pair of eyes, huge and set far apart. They glowed from within; black irises swimming inside globes of milky, blood-red luminescence. Wiggling between them, a beard of dangling peduncles extended over the whole lower half of the horrific face, only splitting apart when a great maw opened, yawning wide to show a set of dagger-fangs.

"Long have you waited, now for the final…"

A crash interrupted him, and with it a blinding flash.

One of the standing stones that ringed the altar dais shattered in that instant, broken apart as though bursting from within. The dolmen exploded outward, spraying the hilltop with an eruption of rock and ice. Fragments of weathered stone scattered in every direction, sending all the gathered ducking for cover.

The paroxysm of stone and flame faded just as quickly as it had come. In its wake there followed a long, dead silence. Dust settled on the cold ground. When all trace of it had gone, Krieger was the first to look out over the blasted hill.

The tumult had been only momentary, but came with an aftermath more startling than the Disciples could have imagined. Where the dolmen had stood, Luther Vayne now stepped out from the fading fog, as though spawned from the brief turmoil. Diana and Carter trailed in his wake.

The Disciples cowered, shocked at his sudden appearance. They huddled behind the rocks where they had sought cover as he stepped out from the mist. But Gregorian and the beast beside him did not. The tentacled creature reared, arching its long, scaly neck. It growled and hissed at Vayne with its forked tongue.

Vayne stared back with his empty eye sockets.

"Hello, Valeria," he said.

FIFTY-THREE

Ghost Moon Hill fell quiet.

Luther Vayne moved across the crest in his peculiar manner, sweeping through the midnight air with a flickering, disjointed gait; a specter only barely tethered to the world of the living. The Disciples gave him a wide berth, every one of them keeping their distance, crouched and huddled with hands raised. Carter and Diana remained behind him, standing amidst the ruins of the dolmen from which they had so inexplicably emerged.

He pointed at Gregorian and the beast beside him.

"You are the last of the thirteen," Vayne said.

Alone upon the hill, the warped billionaire did not shrink from him. He remained defiant, the tentacles of his exposed torso interlaced with those of the thing that had once been his mother.

"We do not fear you, demon," Gregorian replied.

"That is of no importance to me," Vayne said. "I desire only to complete my task, to answer the commands of Azathoth. I failed in that regard once before. I will not fail again."

"She was stronger than you thought," Gregorian replied, clutching the tentacles around him as though they were one single organism. "She survived."

Vayne smiled.

"I would hardly call this survival," he answered.

"We will not bow to you," Gregorian replied. "Far from it."

From his side, he lifted his silver-capped staff. He aimed it at Vayne like a weapon—and he began to chant.

"*Ya hi'ya. Ya hi'ya fylaah rytha,*" he said. "*Cha'yath shaa. F'thaam thathaam ry'leathaa.*"

Vayne smiled yet again. He had heard the incantation before. Once more the Rites of Domination and Control did not appear to trouble him.

"A valiant effort," Vayne said.

Gregorian continued. He issued the chant in furious fashion, all the while pointing the black staff as Vayne simply stared back at him.

"All for naught, however," Vayne finally said.

He bridged the final distance between them in a heartbeat, so fast that Gregorian stopped in mid-verse. Vayne wasted no time. He reached out, clamping his bony hand around Victor Gregorian's throat. The fat man choked, his distended neck squeezed like a balloon. The others looked on, helpless to intervene. He gasped as the air went out of his lungs, his bloated face turning pink, then red—then blue.

"You did not expect me to permit you to finish, did you?" Vayne said.

The Disciples shuddered at the sight of their leader ensnared, his gambit ended before it had even the slightest chance. But as Gregorian wheezed, he managed to turn his head. Not by much, and not enough to draw Vayne's attention. Just enough to steal a glance over at Dr. Shaw.

Carter leaped into action. Taking everyone by surprise, he pushed past Diana, bounding across the dais. He slipped between the beast Valeria and the struggling Victor Gregorian. Vayne only paid him any notice when he came around to face him, but by then it was too late.

He snatched the cuneiform-carved staff from Gregorian's hand, raised it up and aimed it at Vayne from the opposite side.

"*F'thay f'thah thulaam g'rel ryoth,*" he uttered.

The incantation took Vayne by surprise. He turned. The runes upon his bare skin pulsed with light, gleaming for an instant with a distinct, bluish hue.

Carter didn't let the moment pass.

"*Sha'shaal vuthim f'laast'ihkaah,*" he continued.

Each word seemed to stoke a fire beneath the old etchings, causing the pale light to surge through the stencils across Vayne's body, more and more with each passing second until the tattoos glowed like blue flame.

Vayne froze. Something took hold of him.

His grip on Gregorian faltered. His entire body stopped, struck cold. Then he began to shake, a slow trembling that came over him in wave after wave. Gregorian took a second to catch his breath, before he stepped away. He was smiling broadly by the time Carter completed the ancient spell.

"F'thaatah tha'laah dhum."

Carter raised his voice to a shout for the last line of the incantation, sending a quiver through Vayne's paralyzed body. His entire frame gleamed with the cold, sickly light.

"Apparently not for naught, after all," Gregorian said, taking the staff from Carter but keeping it pointed at Vayne. "The Rites of Domination and Control remain as effective now as they have ever been. Hold fast, you creature of the abyss. You abide by my commands now."

Diana tried to charge into the fray, jumping right at Carter.

"You son of a bitch!" she yelled.

She never made it to him. Logan intercepted her, drawing his side arm and stopping her in her tracks.

Carter looked back at her.

"I would offer an apology," he said. "But this was never any of your concern to begin with."

"You're helping them?" she exclaimed. "But you know what they're doing here! What will happen if they succeed!"

"If *we* succeed," he replied. "Yes, Agent Mancuso, I know very well what will happen. That is *exactly why* I am doing this."

FIFTY-FOUR

Diana looked at Vayne in disbelief. The fearsome, powerful figure had been immobilized, trapped somehow by the incantation issued by Gregorian and his disciple. Frozen like a bronze carving, swathed in a patina of pale blue light. The terrifying ghoul had been rendered helpless—and that frightened her more than anything.

Gregorian looked him over also, but not in awe. He admired the man like a prized trophy, studying his captive for a long, slow moment, scanning the runes etched into his skin as he stood there like a statue. Then he turned to look directly at Diana.

"Special Agent Mancuso, so good to see you again," he said. "Come closer, I have no intention of harming you."

She had no choice.

"I do apologize for misleading you earlier," he said. "This was the plan all along, you see."

She stared back at him, angry and scared at once.

"What plan?" she said. "He was hunting you. You're the one he's been stalking, all these years."

Gregorian smiled.

"Was he?" he replied, waving his distorted hand over the frozen figure.

"Or was it, perhaps, the other way around?" he answered. "You came to me several days ago asking about an envelope. You were right, of course. That was very much my doing."

Diana came even closer.

"You wanted him to find you?" she said.

Gregorian nodded.

"You lured him here," she continued, putting it together as she took it all in. "So the letter to the prison *did* come from you."

"It did," he said.

The reply put a jolt through the Disciples as much as it did through her. They grumbled and gasped, moving in closer to surround him.

"What is she talking about, Victor?" Krieger demanded. "What letter?"

Diana looked back, to the others closing in.

"They don't know, do they?" she said.

Gregorian cradled the tentacles of his mother's embrace.

"They did not need to know," he said.

"What is she talking about Victor?" Krieger asked.

"There is nothing to fret over, my friends," Gregorian said. "Everything is as it should be, as I always told you it would be."

Krieger and the others remained unsettled.

"Tell us," he demanded.

Diana stepped in.

"Vayne was alerted to you, to all of you," she said. "A little over a week ago he received a letter at Danfield Federal Penitentiary. It was a newspaper clipping about Roger Saxon's V.P. nomination—marked with a thirteen pointed star."

Krieger jerked at the notion.

"You sent him after Saxon, after one of our own?" he shouted.

"He was laying out a trail, a path for Vayne to follow…to bring him here," Diana said.

"But why?" Krieger replied. "We spent years preparing for this night. Why bring our oldest enemy here on the night of our greatest triumph?"

"That's the part I don't understand either," Diana said.

"Why else?" Gregorian replied. "Why would the hunted bring the hunter to him?"

It was Carter who answered.

"Because he has something we need," he said.

This time it was his turn to stand over Vayne, and unlike the others, he did not merely marvel at the horrific countenance or the glowing runes of the dreaded man's flesh. *Carter could read them.*

"He is the missing piece," Carter said. "This is what we've been after all along."

"What missing piece?" Krieger asked.

"The text Valeria used to make the summoning all those years ago, it was damaged. The stone tablet was broken the last time this rite was attempted," Carter said. "The only remaining copy, the only complete text of the ritual is here, inscribed in this living codex—Luther Vayne himself."

Diana nodded, astonished and horrified in equal measure.

"You needed Vayne…but you feared him too," she said. "You had to have him here in order to perform this rite, but if he'd simply be alerted to your location…"

"He would certainly have killed us all," Gregorian answered. "It was necessary to control the situation, to arrange his arrival on my own terms."

Krieger stepped forward.

"So you sent him to Saxon, knowing he'd point the way to the Reverend," the general said, finally understanding.

Bremmer was beside him, and she picked up his thought.

"And then to Dr. Shaw, and then here," she said. "You allowed Hayden to act as our leader, all these years, knowing that would make him the most likely target. It was all a diversion, everything."

Gregorian smiled broadly, raising his fat arms in triumph.

"Exactly," he said. "Everything I have done was aimed toward this moment. In order to open the gate, the word was once made flesh. Now, everything is in place for the rite to be completed once more—for the last time."

FIFTY-FIVE

The Disciples had set to work.

Krieger and Logan, strongest of the lot, took hold of the paralyzed Luther Vayne. They hauled him over to the stone altar and placed him down flat on his back. The sticky red slime that had once been Gregorian's assistant Janet still stained the flat platform. In the cold, the blood had congealed, turning viscous like used oil. It squished and oozed under Vayne's huge frame as they positioned him.

Where he had long ago been damned, he was yet again fastened for the ritual. Rusty manacles clamped around Vayne's wrists. Larger fetters secured his ankles. Though he could not move regardless, the adherents of the Black Flame took no chances. In moments, he was once again splayed out beneath the black sky, an offering to the abyss yet again.

While the two men secured Vayne, Bremmer did her part. Though Gregorian had forbidden torches or lamps until that point, he now reversed his order as the ceremony approached. She dutifully positioned a series of black candles on small stone outcroppings all around the periphery of the altar. They burned with a dull, red flame that painted the whole of the complex in dim crimson. The collected blood of their human sacrifice she took next, sprinkling it between the candles to link them in a series of glistening red lines, forming the shape of the sacred star.

As they performed their appointed tasks, Carter began the most significant one of all. A dark priest ministering the most sinister black mass, he tore off his shirt and exposed his bare skin to the cold. Reciting from memory, and supplementing his incantations with readings taken directly from the gleaming runes of Vayne's own flesh, he stood before the altar. Hands raised, beseeching the dark sky, he uttered the ancient phrases, calling upon powers unknown and places unseen.

Watching it all with something like joy, Victor Gregorian cradled the monster that had been his mother. Diana he kept close to him, and he laughed as he saw the abject horror played out across her face.

"Take heart, what is soon to happen will change the world as you know it," he told her.

She looked back at him, hatred and confusion in her eyes.

"You do understand what we're doing here?" Gregorian continued. "I was led to believe you had followed this trail perfectly. Quite admirable, in fact. Although, also quite unnecessary as well."

"I know what this is," she replied. "At least I think I do. But I still don't understand."

"What is that?"

"How?" she answered. "There were thirteen children of Sothoth, thirteen spawn of Valeria. But *fourteen* children were adopted."

Gregorian laughed.

"Yes, there was some subterfuge, of course," he said. "You can be forgiven for not knowing, for that was my mother's great triumph."

"Then how did you do this?" she asked.

Gregorian looked back to the incipient ritual. Clouds were beginning to form overhead, and a stray flash of lightning lit the sky.

"It won't be long now," he said. "But perhaps long enough to tell you what you wish to know."

Diana nodded.

"Valeria had seen how her father and grandfather and uncles had managed their power over many years," Gregorian said. "She learned from their mistakes. While she entrusted great responsibility to her inner circle, she reserved an even closer group of servants who stayed by her side at all times. Fiercely loyal only to her," he said.

Diana looked to Vayne, and Gregorian nodded.

"Yes, the first and most visible of these was her enforcer and protector—Luther Vayne," he continued. "The fearsome figure who kept her safe at all hours. A man who would kill without question if she gave the word."

Gregorian clasped his hands like a preacher in the crux of a sermon.

"But along with him, she kept close the loyalty of two others, neither one as high born or influential as the twelve disciples of the Black Flame."

"Anna Dressler and Victoria," Vayne said, the power of speech not robbed from him despite his paralysis.

Gregorian smiled.

"So you do remember them," he replied. "I thought they might not have been important enough for you to notice."

Gregorian looked to Diana then, as if to fill in the gaps for her benefit.

"These women were little more than hand maidens, you see. Long time servants of her household that she slowly brought into her fold. They were no less fanatically devoted as you, Mister Vayne, but even to those within the circle, they were always much less noticeable.

"While you walked beside her, always the gallant protector, always in the spotlight, these two were by her side as well, attending to all of her mundane needs and demands, rarely seen or commented on by anyone, but ever present and ever obedient.

"I still don't understand," Diana said. "What does this have to do with the demon? And with the children?"

"In the aftermath of the summoning, once Valeria had invited the entity Sothoth to breed with her, it opened her awareness in ways she had never imagined. Her senses broadened, she saw what others could not. Her mind and her sight expanded a thousand-fold.

"Her first discovery was a horror, of course. The black forces coursing through her flesh, the toxic energy of the demon impregnating her, had spread through every ounce of her. The power of Sothoth would bring new life, but it was also bound to destroy her—the host, infecting her like a fatal plague.

"She knew that her sacrifice would also be her undoing, that in order to bring life to the spawn of Sothoth she would suffer as her human form was twisted into unspeakable horrors, eventually ruining her entirely.

"Expecting her own demise, she entrusted the thirteen children to her trusted priestesses—one for each of the twelve. The remaining child, the thirteenth spawn, she entrusted to her handmaiden. Choosing between the two aides always by her side, she elevated Anna to the priesthood as her replacement, telling her and everyone within the Circle that she would be responsible for the child.

"But that was a lie," Vayne said.

"Indeed," Gregorian replied. "Valeria was always scheming, always plotting. She knew the dangers, and so she employed one last hedge. Her other servant, the one that all believed had been disfavored, cast aside and rejected for the post of thirteenth priestess, was instead entrusted with an even greater task. A wholly secret task.

"She was ordered by Valeria to find and abduct an infant from a local hospital, and she did just that. Then, Valeria instructed her to switch the newborn with her thirteenth progeny. No one was told of this, such that even the priestess who received the imposter child did not know it herself."

"So Anna Dressler didn't know," Diana said.

"But I knew it, the moment I killed the child," Vayne said. "By then it was too late. A mistake I have sought to atone for ever since."

"The subterfuge complete, and as one of her last acts before succumbing to the blackness within her, Valeria willed much of her estate to her last remaining loyal servant. Thus did she take the true thirteenth child away, raising him as her own. Even the other elders of the Black Flame were unaware of the trickery, believing him to be nothing more than her crippled, disabled son. It was a secret she took to her grave, many years later.

"But in the meantime, she protected him, watching over him while all the others of his brood were murdered. She taught him of all the things his mother had wanted him to know, never letting him forget his special place in this world as the only remaining son of Sothoth—and the only man who could one day reopen the path between the worlds, to restore Valeria and himself."

"You," Diana said.

FIFTY-SIX

A break had formed in the center of the clouds, directly overhead. The winds had begun to swirl there, spinning faster and faster, until a black vortex drilled a hole in the sky.

Diana looked at the fissure, and then to Carter. He was still standing before the bloody altar. His arms were held high, heedless of the storm lowering toward them. Where he had once whispered ancient verses, he now shouted the arcane words, raising his voice to compete with the thunder of crimson lightning and the howling of the cyclonic winds.

The candle flames around the hilltop surged as the tempest descended, lifting thirteen red columns of fire into the broken heavens. The clouds seethed when the flames struck them. Smoke from the blazing tapers swirled upward, spun into thousands of whirling tendrils, merging with far more exotic things that were beginning to spill forth.

In moments the edges of the clouds began to turn upon themselves, ripples collapsing upon one another until they solidified into something like bone. Soon, the space that had begun as a black hole in the clouds evolved into something more, an opening more akin to a mouth; a yawning maw in the sky.

Inside its depths, a starless void seemed to reach back forever, impenetrable and black—but not empty. Within that darkness, something even more foul was taking shape, congealing out of the cosmic bilge.

Feelers emerged first, antennae covered in wet cilia. Dozens of thin fingers moved in every direction, investigating and studying. But they were merely sentinels of what lay behind. A series of glowing, globular spheres followed; a rolling wave of pulsing, bloated flesh. Stalks crowned them with ghostly white eyes.

Behind, a swarm soared down on ragged wings, a toad-like multitude swimming amongst a bubbling lather of mist and slime. As they grew closer, Diana discerned more horrific details.

It was a conglomerated horde of flesh, crawling with swarms of smaller parasites. Encircling them were colonies of fat, pale worms, every segment writhing with slow contractions through slimy extrusions. Though it moved like a single entity, the throng was more like a living tide.

The reek of sulfur grew worse, and with it came a hissing. Larger, fouler things began to swim out from within the black sky. It was coming at them from every side now, a long slow march out of the darkness. Some vaguely resembled familiar beasts, though their bodies were warped in all manner of ways. A few walked on four or even three legs, dragging limbs and tails in hideous fashion. Not a one was the same. Some bore crooked horns sprouting from ruptured pustules, growing out of dripping scab-cocoons of blistered skin. Others were swollen lumps of skin, teeming with fungal lesions and festering sores, abscesses blackened around the edges and bursting with milky white fluid, leaving trails of organic sludge in their wake.

They moaned and they wailed, waving slimy claws and jagged tails. They moved with a purpose. They were closing in.

Gregorian stepped forward with his mother, extending his hands toward the steaming slime and the parade of apparitions crawling from the toxic effluent. Arms and tails and ghostly fingers touched him. Lightning and wind swirled from the storm-gate, spilling forth the chaos-born heralds of Yog Sothoth. Gregorian and Valeria drank it in, absorbing the noxious black fire into every cell of their bodies. They reveled in the spectral deluge. Their blood boiled, livened with the rush of unspeakable power.

The twin beasts surged under the waterfall of darkness, absorbing it, drawing strength from it. With every passing second, they grew larger. Gregorian's body healed itself, his once unhealthy human physique transformed, bulked up into a monstrous figure. His scabby skin hardened into reticulated armor. The tentacles of his mid-section sprouted new off-shoots until they flailed from his groin to his throat. His malformed limbs grew into crab-like claws. His goatish legs swelled to fully support his huge and grotesque frame.

Valeria's body took on a new and more twisted shape as well. The middle of her torso returned to something like a shadow of a human female, with breasts that were scaly and green. A crown of six tusk-like horns emerged from her pointed head. Her lower reaches curled under her like a serpent, but the furthest end looped back upward toward her mutant face with a great barbed stinger. Tentacles replaced her arms, reaching out to the blasted heavens to drink in the rushing waves of black energy.

Surrounded by the nourishing tide of horrors, they bowed in both sustenance and worship. But soon another figure drew their attention back toward the heart of the vortex. A final figure was beginning to emerge from the mist and the shadow.

"Guardian of the gate, watcher of the way," Carter chanted. "Come forth that we may hail you, great Old One!"

What followed was unlike that which had come before. It oozed forth, moving through the steam and the flame as though it were pure fluid. Greenish-yellow tentacles slithered around its bloated and ever-shifting center, edged with razor quills and reaching out with ragged, red sucker-mouths on the undersides. Tipped with talon-claws and maws snapping their fangs, they spread outward in every direction, only to vanish like pseudopods, drawn back into the formless host as others replaced them.

Its body was a rippling, lumbering mass; a thorny carapace of steaming, slime-drenched chitin, bathed in malodorous fumes. The bony plates merged with and blended into pale fleshy under-skin that dripped with phosphorescent pus.

Mouths champing with serrated teeth hungered from every corner of the shapeless thing, scattered as if at random across the corpus, wedged between bony spurs and fleshy peduncles. Glistening eyes as black as opals peered out from all corners of its wet, oleaginous form. It seemed to have no face, no single head or center.

"Welcome, keeper of the way, mighty Yog Sothoth!" Gregorian and Valeria shouted in unison.

It reached down with its pincers, answering with many squealing voices. Gregorian and Valeria lifted their arms to touch it.

The horrid behemoth groaned and flailed its fat, thorny limbs. They made contact, father and son, husband and wife, but only for an instant—Gregorian and Valeria both touching the outer reaches of Sothoth.

It did not last.

A shot fired across the hill crest, blasting apart one of the stone candle posts. A second followed right behind, this one hitting the altar itself.

Carter dove for cover. Diana turned, trying to locate the source. She glanced down, toward the lower reaches of the hill. For a moment she saw nothing, but then, much to her surprise, she caught sight of Richard Norris and Ariadne.

They had pulled up in a Bureau car, just on the edge of the campsite below. Diana called out, trying to signal them from afar. Ariadne saw her. She waved back, but before she could do anything more, another round of shots rang out. She and Richard both scrambled for shelter.

This time it was Krieger firing. He and Logan rushed across the hilltop, guns drawn. Krieger pushed Diana to the side, sending her falling down next to the altar where Carter was huddled. The two men raced to the edge of the platform, responding with a fusillade of their own. From the echo, Diana guessed that most of them clanged against the steel of the car.

A series of shots came back in return. Krieger and Logan ducked this time, and when they jumped back up to send a second volley, she heard an altogether different sound.

A shout and a gasp, followed by Ariadne's scream. Diana got to her knees, then climbed atop the edge of the altar. From there she was high enough up to see all the way below. Richard had been hit—she wasn't sure how badly—and Ariadne was pulling him behind the car for cover.

That was when she noticed the silver-topped staff. Resting beside the end of the altar, where Gregorian had laid it to rest upon the arrival of the entities from above. The beast that had been the billionaire now towered above her, heedless of his once-necessary cane. She looked across the platform, to where Luther Vayne remained shackled. He saw her. He spoke again.

"Release me," he said.

She and Carter reached for the staff at the same time. She got it first, wresting it from him with a twist and a hard tug. Carter didn't relent. He reached over and grabbed her by the arm.

"You know what happens if you free him," he said.

She looked back at him with a cold eye.

"Yeah, just like you, I know *exactly* what I'm doing," she said.

She got up, standing tall enough to lift the staff over her knee.

"I don't know if this is gonna help, but it's worth a shot," she said.

Bracing it with both hands, she raised her leg and brought the staff crashing down across it. The wood shattered through the middle, breaking into splintered halves upon her leg.

She did not need to wait long for her answer.

The break drew Gregorian's attention, turning him from the parade of apparitions above. But that was her concern for only a second. It was Vayne who answered next.

The pale light bleeding from his rune-scars faded. Once it was gone, he arose without impediment. The chains and the manacles tore like paper as he lifted himself. He called out to Gregorian and Valeria. His words thundered across the hill, drowning out the raging of the storm-gate above.

"Your time is at an end," he said.

Vayne raised his long, skeletal arms outward, and his body followed. He floated into the space between the altar and the descending gatekeeper, and his resurrection snared the attention of everyone. His words sounded like hammer strokes. His fingertips glowed white-hot. Wind surged all around him. It whipped the smoke and the shadows into a swirling black miasma, riven by shocks of lightning and the burning of dark flame.

Even Yog Sothoth took notice. Its slithering tentacles recoiled, struck by the shockwave of Vayne's resurgence. It screamed from a hundred mouths at once, shrieking in pain and terror. Gregorian and Valeria tumbled backward, thrown down from the demonic guardian. The connection between them was sundered.

"Return, gate-keeper," Vayne continued. "Return from whence you have come."

Yog Sothoth undulated and pulsed its huge, blistered corpus. It flailed its many arms and hissed with its multitude of mouths.

"*Summoned us, they have done*," it replied, only barely capable of producing anything resembling human speech. "*Do not interfere again*."

Vayne threw his arm toward the beast as if it were a weapon. A blast of white flames erupted, striking Sothoth across its entire form. The creature peeled in agony.

"Azathoth will not permit this," Vayne replied.

It was Valeria who answered.

"Curse you," she screamed, lifting herself up to face Vayne.

Her monstrous form was only barely human, a green-skinned blend of serpent, cephalopod and arthropod. Her coiled lower reaches unfurled beneath her, raising her up to the height of the hovering, otherworldly figure.

"You will not ruin my plans a second time," she hissed.

"I have not come to settle old debts, Valeria," Vayne replied. "I am here to end this."

"I will not allow you to stand in our way again," she said. "Yog Sothoth will show us the path. Azathoth awaits."

Vayne clasped his hands together. A shock of thunder erupted.

"*I am Azathoth*," he answered. "I am his hand. His will. It is he who refuses you."

"You are nothing. You are what I made you," she replied.

Victor Gregorian joined her in that moment, having only just recovered from the sundering. Coming around to stand at full height upon his massive, goatish haunches, he stood beside his bestial sire.

"You are a pawn, a pretender," he said. "We will destroy you."

Vayne was surrounded, at the center of a triangle, Yog Sothoth at one point, Valeria and Gregorian at the other two. He did not appear troubled.

"You will destroy us both," he replied. "Just as Azathoth desires."

The beast Sothoth launched an attack, whipping a dozen barbed tentacles toward Vayne, whose back was now turned to the demon. But they did not strike. Though Vayne remained facing Valeria and Gregorian, he somehow split away from himself. The ghostly, second aspect of him turned to face the keeper of the gateway.

This avatar of Vayne met the attack of Sothoth. He repelled it and in a flash of impossible movement, charged the beast. In an instant Vayne clenched hold of the monstrous apparition, wrestling with the demon in mid-air.

Valeria tried to press the perceived advantage, striking out against the side of Vayne that still stood before her—the figure somehow in two places simultaneously. Like her consort she tried to swipe at him with multiple arms at once. Yet again, he met the attack, bracing her and clamping down with his own counter-blows.

From his vantage, Victor Gregorian made a similar attempt, leaping and flailing his razor-edged tentacles. But he too was met by an utterly impossible defense—a third Luther Vayne stood against him, battling three adversaries, in three places all at once.

«««—»»»

On the hill crest beneath, Diana watched the unreal happenings playing out above.

"*Through the space between moments, through the shadow of the four dimensions you inhabit*," she whispered.

Carter grabbed her, tugging at her arm.

She looked back at him, almost too shocked to speak.

"So this is what you wanted?" he continued, pointing up at the tumult. "All of this?"

"Didn't we both get what we wanted?" she replied.

He stared at the chaos overhead.

"They're going to tear this place apart," he said. "You have no idea what's coming, what they're capable of up there."

"I did what I had to do," she said.

Bremmer interrupted.

"Now you're going to answer for that," she said.

While Logan and Krieger remained on the far side of the hill, she stood just to the side of the altar, her own Glock 22 drawn. Neither Diana nor Carter had seen her approach.

"This isn't the time," Carter answered.

"She violated the sacred rites," Bremmer answered.

"Don't you see what's happening?" Carter replied. "We can't waste time with pettiness."

"Is that what you think I'm doing?" Bremmer said, turning her gun toward him and away from Diana. "We've spent our lives preparing for this. Ever since we were children, we were taught to await this night. Now she's ruined it. I don't expect you to understand. Victor never should have brought an outsider into our fold."

Diana kept her eyes locked on Bremmer. It was obvious she wasn't used to using a firearm. She was pointing it without aiming, and she switched between the two of them haphazardly. She felt around her, looking for something—anything she could use. A stone, a piece of metal.

"Never mind her," Carter said. "I can still fix this, but you have to help me."

"You want to help?" Bremmer answered. "Fine, help me take her out, then we can talk."

Diana caught sight of something to her left. A pile of rusted, barbed chains. It was one of the shattered manacles Vayne had broken, fallen in a heap just a few feet away. She looked back to Bremmer, who was still watching Carter. She had only a moment.

She rolled out, diving through the cold dirt to cover the space between her and the chains. Bremmer turned in that instant, and fired off a round as she was moving. Just as Diana had guessed, she was inexperienced and her shot was wildly off target.

Diana reached the chains, spun them around in her hand and sent them flying. Bremmer tried to re-adjust, shooting again, but her second shot was no better than her first. The chains careened toward her, striking her as she tried to duck out of the way. The iron barbs slashed her arms and her midsection, knocking the Glock from her grip.

The commotion drew Krieger and Logan's attention. They came charging back.

Diana used the chance to get to her feet. She whipped the chains around, hitting Bremmer across the middle once more. That gave her enough time to close the gap between them. Diana landed a punch to Bremmer's gut, doubling her over. Then she looped the chains around her head, pulling them back around her throat.

Carter snatched up Bremmer's weapon. Logan and Krieger stopped about fifteen feet out when they saw that Diana had Bremmer in a chokehold. Diana tightened her grip on the chains. Bremmer coughed and wheezed as the links dug into her throat. She tried to speak but the words came out as a hoarse rasp. Diana edged backward, making sure to keep Bremmer in front of her as she held her from behind, a human shield against her brothers.

"Let her go," Logan commanded.

"Drop your guns and we can discuss that," Diana replied.

"Not a chance, honey," Krieger said.

Carter edged backward as well. He was off to the side of the altar, ten feet from Diana's right side, and just as far from Krieger and Logan and she was. Though he had picked up Bremmer's Glock, he wasn't pointing it at anyone. That did not go unnoticed.

"You know what you need to do Dr. Shaw," Logan said.

Carter nodded. Though his arm was shaking, he raised the pistol and aimed it toward Diana.

"Okay, let's think about this for a second, boys," she said. "I've got your girl here, and I'm not letting her go until I'm back down this hill and at the car."

Krieger and Logan shuffled just a bit closer. Carter kept the Glock pointed as best he could.

"Give it up," Krieger said. "You're out-manned and out-gunned."

"I think you're over playing your hand here, General," Diana replied. "You're not gonna shoot, not when you'd risk hitting one of your own. No, you're all gonna hang back while I very carefully get down this hill and get my friends into that car. Then she goes free. Not a minute sooner."

Logan called out again, but not to Diana.

"Dr. Shaw, it would appear that you have the clearest shot," he said. "It's time for you to do your duty, as we discussed."

Diana glanced over. The Brit was right. Carter had moved back even further, and off to the side he now had a much better angle on her, with an unimpeded line of sight. If he could muster a halfway decent shot, she was dead.

She stared him down for a moment, then switched back to Krieger and Logan. The next thing she heard was a shot, rapidly followed by two more.

Instinctively, she flinched. But she felt nothing. No bullets. No blood. No pain. The shots had come from Carter's direction. She looked over in that instant. He was firing, but not at her. He had turned the gun toward Krieger and Logan.

The two men fired back. Carter ducked and dove behind Diana, sliding down the hill. They kept firing, heedless of their fellow Disciple's exposure. Then Diana did feel the horrible impact of bullets, as a pair of them struck Bremmer in the chest. She felt the air go out of Bremmer's lungs right in front of her and the saw the blood coursing out of the wounds as she held her.

Stephanie Bremmer convulsed and trembled. She only took a moment to die right there in Diana's grasp. Krieger and Logan weren't done.

She looked below, to the rocky field beneath the hill crest, where Carter had escaped. Dolmen stones and cairns were scattered across the uneven terrain. He was there, waving at her.

"C'mon!"

She scanned the scene, then saw Krieger and Logan closing in.

"Mother fucker," she said.

She held Bremmer's lifeless, bloody corpse until the two men got close enough. Then she flung it at them, with as much force as she could muster. She didn't even look to see the result, she just turned and went sliding down the hill to where Carter was waiting, and they disappeared into the shadows of the great field of standing stones.

FIFTY-SEVEN

She landed in a heap at the foot of a stone monolith, at the base of the hill crest. Carter appeared beside her an instant later, springing from his cover behind it. Krieger and Logan scrambled to the edge of the rise, stopping short at the treacherous slope.

"Let's go, there's cover back there," Carter said.

They had no more than a moment. From above, the two old soldiers aimed and fired. This time, they didn't miss by much. Diana and Carter just barely managed to slip behind the giant slab of rock as the shots rained down.

On the far side, they found a maze-like path. The field was filled with gray slate menhirs and odd structures of various sizes, some stacked in classic trilithons to form henge-like circles, others built up into domes set upon earthen cairns. They saw an opening, where the alignment of giant rocks formed a winding corridor that led into the distance. That was their best bet. They headed down the stone path, soon finding that it curved and curled, branching off in multiple directions. Each one was guarded by more rows of eerie standing stones, many of which obscured the paths that lay behind them.

With only the moonlight to guide them, they made their way down and around a series of cromlechs, until they came upon a barrow that was larger than the others, that ended with a dolmen that held a wide, flat capstone big enough for them to crawl under.

"We can't stay here," he said.

"I know, but we need to catch our breath and figure out what the hell we are gonna do," she replied.

"If we can work together, I think I may have a way out—for the both of us," he answered.

He started to outline a plan, but she stopped him.

"First you have to tell me," she said. "You could have taken me out up there, but you didn't. You went for them. For your own people. Your friends."

"They are not my friends."

"But why show me any mercy?"

"Don't get all sentimental on me, Agent Mancuso. That wasn't mercy," he replied.

"Then why turn? Why change sides?"

"Because your interests are aligned with mine now," he replied.

"What are you talking about? You were working for Gregorian all along, for all of them, you said so yourself."

"I was doing no such thing," he said. "I may have been working *with* them, but that was only because my interests aligned with theirs, for a while."

"You wanted to open that gate."

"I did, very much so. Working with Gregorian was the only way to make that happen."

"And now?"

"Now you've made a mess of everything."

"So how does that put us on the same side?"

"You want to take down Gregorian, and his people? You want to save your friends and put an end to all the shit going on up there?"

"Of course."

"So do I."

"But you're the one who started all of that," she protested.

"Exactly," he replied.

Diana studied him, the determination in his eyes, the passion. She began to see what he was doing, what he'd been after all along.

"You want them out of the way," she said. "So you can have that gateway all to yourself."

He didn't reply. He just stared back at her, but his expression gave everything away.

A noise interrupted them. Footsteps in the dark.

They crept out from the safety of the capstone, crawling behind the cairn next to it. From the top of that dome, they could spy James Krieger. He was following the same path that they had taken, only slower and with the careful approach of a combat vet. He took every step with care, scanning the moonlit stones all around, his pistol held out in front of him.

Carter lifted his stolen Glock to aim for the man. Diana grabbed the gun and pushed it down.

"If you shoot now, he'll know exactly where we are, and so will the other guy," she said, her voice hushed.

"Not if I kill him," Carter replied.

"I've seen you with that thing, you're a horrible shot," she said.

"Thanks," he smirked.

"Do you have any idea how hard it is to hit a moving target, in the dark, from this distance with a handgun?"

"I'm going to guess *not easy?*"

"Not at all," she said. "But we do have an advantage. He doesn't know where we are, and *we do* know where he is. So if we can sit tight for just a bit, until he gets a little past us, we can circle back the way he came."

"What if he doesn't go past us? What if he turns like we did and comes right here?" Carter asked.

Diana looked at him, dead in the eyes.

"Hand me the gun," she said.

"Why?"

"Just give it to me," she ordered.

He handed over the pistol.

"Now what?" Carter asked.

"If he comes around this way, I'll kill him," she answered.

They kept their eyes on Krieger. He continued moving deliberately, every movement considered, every glance with a purpose. Diana held her breath as he got within a few feet, still unaware of their location. She clenched the handle of the Glock, making sure the safety was off.

Krieger kept coming, step by step, inch by inch. He was only a few feet from them now, creeping along in the night. They held their breath, huddled behind a pile of rocks, near enough to hear his breathing.

For an instant he paused, looking around. They froze, staring at each other for an agonizing moment as Krieger stood barely ten feet from them.

Then he turned, and he kept going, heading on away from them.

Carter was about to whisper something, but Diana stopped him. She motioned to the far side of the cairn and he nodded. Then she led the way, circling around the barrow and leading them to double-back.

They didn't get far.

Two shots clanged off the rocks beside them. They turned. Jack Krieger was coming at them, running and shooting. They scrambled, but there was no cover. They were exposed. Another round clipped Carter. He screamed as the bullet tore into his left shoulder. Diana took one in the hip, just above the pelvis.

She grabbed Carter and pushed him down behind her. Then she knelt down in a crouch, wheezing in pain as the wound in her side starting spilling blood. She aimed as best as she could in the dim.

"You thought you could get away that easy?" Krieger shouted. "You thought I would fall for that bullshit rookie crap?"

Diana fired back. She missed with her first round, but put one in the general's leg with her second. He returned fire, nearly hitting her as he charged. She refocused, trying to steady her quivering hands. She fired again, this time they connected. Two in the chest.

Krieger staggered. He went down on one knee. But he was still armed, and only about ten feet away.

"Drop it, General," she ordered.

He looked up. Blood was on his lips, but his face was as hard as ever.

"You'll have to kill me," he said.

"It doesn't have to end like this," she continued. "We can help you. Richard can help you."

"There will be no terms. No surrender," he replied.

Carter crawled up behind her, wincing in pain.

"He's not bluffing," he said. "These guys are devoted, fanatical."

Diana could see it in Krieger's eyes. He was determined to go down fighting. Every second they stayed there gave Logan more time to get to them.

Krieger raised his arm, smiling as he tried to lift his gun. Diana took a breath, blinked and fired. The bullet blasted out the back of his skull.

«««—»»»

They managed to get around the base of the hill crest, limping over to the far side without Logan catching up to them. Diana could see the Bureau car just ahead, parked at an angle. The hood was scarred with bullet holes. Steam vented from the broken radiator. The passenger side windows were broken out. A field of glass shards lay all around.

The moment they came through the last series of dolmens however, they found Ariadne blocking their path. She leaped up with her gun raised, but nearly broke down the instant she realized who it was.

"Diana?" she exclaimed. "What the fuck? What are you doing? What the hell is going on?"

"No time for that," she replied. "How's Richard?"

Ariadne looked back to the car.

"Not great," she said. "He got hit twice, both in the stomach."

"Show me," Diana said.

Ariadne led them over to the far side of the car. Richard was propped up against the wheel well, holding his gut with both hands. His shirt was soaked with red.

He looked up when he saw her.

"You're fired," he wheezed.

Diana smiled.

"No argument," she replied.

"I'm sorry," Ariadne said. "He wouldn't take no for an answer, I couldn't…"

Diana stopped her.

"You did the right thing," she said. "In fact, I'm glad you're here. You two saved my fucking ass up there."

Ariadne looked up. The top of the hill was exploding with smoke and flames.

"Doesn't really look that way from here," she said.

"Trust me, it was about to be way worse when you two showed up," Diana said.

"It still could get worse, if we don't do something," Carter added.

More gunfire intruded. Shots came at them from the other side of the car. They all ducked for cover. Diana managed to peer through the driver's side window. She saw Logan. He had staked out a position behind a toppled menhir about thirty feet out; good cover with an angle to shoot and very little exposure. He wasn't making the same mistake Krieger had.

Diana turned to Carter, as another shot shattered the windshield.

"Cards on the table here. What you said back there, that you could fix this," she said. "What did you mean?"

"If I can get back up there, I can take control of the gate," he answered.

She looked at him sideways.

"You said you could close it down," she said.

"I said *I can* close it, and once I have what I want—I will."

"And what's that?"

"Azathoth."

She grabbed his arm.

"Vayne said that's impossible, it's too dangerous," she replied.

"He said that to summon Azathoth was the danger, to awaken Azathoth. I just want to see, to see into the void. Even just a glimpse. That's all I've ever wanted, to know what lies beyond."

"No, it's too risky," she said.

He pointed at the chaos above them.

"If we do nothing, that will only get worse," he said. "I'm the only chance you've got."

She knew he was right.

"Are you sure you can do it?" she asked.

"If I can make it up there, I can."

"Even if you can close it down, then what?" she asked.

"The power coming through the portal is what fuels Gregorian and his mother," he answered. "Gregorian was a cripple before today.

Remember the story I told you, from back at Miskatonic. Hybrid beings like him can barely function in our world. Just like his beastly mother, he needs this power to regenerate himself. If you cut them off from that, they'll wither again."

"So they can be killed."

"Right."

"How do I know I can trust you?"

"You don't," he said. "But what's the worst that can happen?"

She looked to the burning sky again.

"Either you close it, or you die trying," she said.

"Something like that."

He put his hand out. She clasped it with her own.

"In case we don't see each other again, I must tell you, I did enjoy our little meetings," he said. "Most of them, at least."

"Yeah, sorry about that whole scissors and balls thing," she replied. "Always had a bit of a temper."

"No hard feelings, then," he said.

Diana smiled.

"Good luck," she replied.

He took a long, deep breath. She nodded to him, lifted herself just above the level of the front hood and squeezed off two rounds of cover fire. He jumped from behind the car, racing toward the top of the hill. Despite Diana's volley, Logan fired at him. His shots hit the rocks and the dirt at Carter's feet. Before he could adjust his aim, Diana sprang up from her cover a second time. She fired back at Logan, unloading her clip in a furious barrage. She got him in the left shoulder and the thigh, but he ducked to the side as he took the bullets, firing as he fell.

Diana's pistol clicked when the last round was expelled. She dropped back behind the cover of the wrecked vehicle, watching as Carter scaled the last few feet up the rise. Then he disappeared over the crest of the hill.

For an instant her heart sank. She'd done her part, but now she was pinned down and out of ammo. Two more rounds buzzed by overhead.

They were followed by the same hard clank, and then a shouted curse. Logan was out of bullets too.

She lifted her head above the car. Logan was already standing. She started to get to her feet. He tossed his nine millimeter to the side. Then he drew a long knife from his belt, and he smiled at her.

FIFTY-EIGHT

The heavens burned.

Carter clambered to the crest of Ghost Moon Hill, hustling out of range of Logan's last few shots. But the moment he got away from that first danger, he found himself square in the middle of something even worse. He had landed in the heart of chaos.

Though he'd seen it begin only minutes before, the surreal sight of Luther Vayne stole his attention once again. The rune-scarred figure continued his impossible dance across the night sky, battling three adversaries simultaneously. His every movement—multiple actions, in multiple places at once—was unreal. Carter couldn't discern whether he was simply moving too fast for his eyes to follow or if the terrifying figure truly was fighting in three places at a time.

The beast Valeria flailed at him with dozens of spiny tentacles and just as many razor-claws. She howled and snapped at him with giant mandibles. Vayne shifted like the wind, evading every attack and responding each time with one of his own. His devastating counter-blows sliced gashes across Valeria's inhuman form, spilling malodorous black and yellow ichor where blood should have been.

Gregorian fared no better. His armored hide deflected most of Vayne's strikes, but he could land none of his own. Each slash and hammer blow that Vayne did land however, pummeled the monstrous hybrid, weakening him and fueling his rage. As the struggle continued, Gregorian's senses lapsed, falling into a mindless, demented fury.

But it was against the entity Yog Sothoth that the true power bequeathed by Azathoth was laid bare. Vayne dominated the shadows. He commanded the darkness. The raging black sea that surrounded him both shielded his body and acted of its own accord, mustering a legion of horrors. The sentient dark energy manifested a parade of phantasms, unleashing a demonic host upon the unearthly entity, a spectral black horde attacking a thousand places at once. Even with a hundred arms, spines, tentacles and other weapons, even empowered by forces beyond measure, Yog Sothoth could not contend.

It screamed and it raged and it suffered, and the sky burned with it.

Carter climbed up atop the hill crest, dodging and weaving as he tried to slip through the edges of the three confrontations. Peculiar detritus rained down, boiling-hot slime and chunks of noxious, rotting flesh. Stone melted as flame blasted it from above, even as ice coated the ground beneath.

The combatants saw him, he was sure of it. But none could break free to stop him. He climbed upon the altar platform, standing with his arms held into the sundered clouds. The gateway itself, the yawning, swirling mouth of darkness in the sky, had lowered itself to that height. He was near enough to reach it, to dip his fingers into the cosmic soup, to touch the abyss.

It sent a shock into him. A chill unlike anything he had ever known rippled through his bones. Frigid and numbing, it swept over every inch of him. His head throbbed and his skin tingled, coated in a strange, dark frost. For a moment his sight failed him, his eyes went black. But then, the sensation shifted. The numbness faded, blending and then surging into a kind of euphoria. That was when his vision returned. And he saw beyond his imagination.

"Azathoth," he said. "Gamaliel, you old son of a bitch. You never told me it would be this...beautiful."

«««—»»»

Logan was in the open, standing alone among the field of stones. It was almost a challenge, daring Diana to come out and face him.

His dagger reflected the flashes of firelight from above. She recognized the blade from her days at Quantico: double serrated lower half, spear point tip, over six inches long. It was an MK II, a knife-fighter's blade. That meant he was a pro.

"I know your clip is empty," he announced. "I'll come back there and get you if I have to, but then I'll be certain to kill all of you slowly. Come out *like a man*, and I'll make it fast. For you and your friends."

Diana came around the hood of the car, her hands raised. Both were empty.

"Not exactly a fair fight," she said. "You've got that nice long knife there and I'm holding nothing. It's just little old me."

"This isn't about fairness," he answered.

"So you're just gonna kill me, then?"

He stared back at her, emotionless. He wasn't angry. Unlike Krieger, his eyes were cold and empty.

"You violated the sacred rites," he said. "You've earned your death sentence."

"I won't go down easy."

"Perhaps, but you will go down."

He leaped at her and took a swipe in a single swift movement. He was fast, agile and skilled. The blade cut across her right thigh before she could react. It burned. She forced herself to ignore the pain.

He came at her again, but this time she dodged out of the way, taking a swing at him as his arm went by. She landed her fist on the side of his head, only a glancing blow, but enough to let him know she was no pushover.

"You're not the first woman I've had to take a knife to," he said.

"That's shocking."

He re-grouped in that moment. A second round of attacks brought him in close, with a blinding series of slashes and swipes. Several of them cut her, ripping the flesh from her forearms and slicing across her navel.

He stepped back, leaving her to stagger a few paces, blood dripping off of her.

"With the S.A.S., back in Afghanistan, when we needed to know something, we got those ragheads to tell us. One way or another. Man or woman, didn't make a difference."

Diana clenched her fists, straining to fight through the pain of multiple wounds.

"So far you've been such a gentleman," she replied.

He snarled. He lifted the blood-drenched knife, waving the edge at her.

"I'm about to gut you like a fish," he said. "I'll show you your insides before you bleed out."

"You fucking Brits," she said. "All foreplay and no follow-through. Let's see you back that up."

It was nothing but bravado. She knew it and she knew that he did too. But she had nothing else.

"Don't you see what's happening?" she said, desperate to distract him. "You can't stop this. Even if you kill me, then what? What does that accomplish?"

He closed in.

"It doesn't matter."

She edged backward, trying to hold on to every second, to every step.

"How can that be?"

He didn't let her get far. He closed the gap between them faster than she could keep her distance.

"I swore an oath," he answered. "I serve the Black Flame."

His eyes told her everything. He was merciless, determined. He was going to kill her.

She slipped away as far as she could, until her back was against the hood of the car. He was still advancing, coming at her with the blade held high. Her arms were sliced open. Her hands were wet with her own blood. There was almost nothing left for her to do.

He rushed toward her. He swung the knife.

But he never got to her. From the side, screaming at the top of her lungs, Ariadne came flying. She had hustled around the back of the car, and hurled herself upon Logan. It was a wild, hopeless, mad attack.

She paid for it dearly.

Logan only needed a heartbeat to pivot. He dodged her bold, unfocused charge. One blow from his free hand, despite the shoulder injury, was enough to shatter her lower jaw. Once she was stunned, he turned his slash from Diana toward Ariadne, cutting her down with a single blow. His blade sliced her from shoulder to waist, sending her to the ground in a whimpering heap.

But his back was turned just long enough for Diana to take advantage. She threw herself into him from the opposite side, using her body and his own sideways motion to throw a hip check into him. The shock of it knocked the blade from his grip. He scrambled to recover, but Diana was faster. She was moving forward while he was reeling, and she got her hands on the knife first.

They separated, re-grouped and came around to face one another again. Only now she had the weapon, and he stood against her unarmed.

"Having the knife is one thing," he taunted. "Using it is quite another."

She waved it back and forth.

"You can't possibly want to die for *that,*" she said, nodding toward the tumult atop the hill.

"I serve Mr. Gregorian," he said.

"That *thing* up there?" she replied, pointing at the slobbering, beastly creature on the hill above.

Logan didn't take the bait. He didn't even look up. He didn't need to.

"Whatever he has become, I serve him, on my honor," he said.

"That's just blind loyalty."

He didn't give her any time. He came at her. Hobbled by his wounds but still mindful of his training, he attacked in a partial crouch, looking to get inside on her, past the knife and into grappling range, close in. She recognized the move. She edged back a step, drawing the blade down, pointed upward and held close to her. She let him move in, just near enough.

He got in on her, hot and sweating and close enough to smell him. She grabbed at his collar with her left hand, then brought the knife upward in a single stroke with her other. It punctured his abdomen, slicing right up under his ribs.

Logan wheezed. Blood drooled out of his mouth.

"I did not betray my oath. I did not betray what I believe in," he said, as the breath faded from his broken lungs.

Diana twisted the blade, then pushed him away, sliding it out of him. He crumpled to the dirt.

"Sometimes you have to," she said.

FIFTY-NINE

Ariadne was Diana's first concern. She'd fallen face-down next to the blasted out car. She wasn't moving.

Diana dropped down to her knees next to her friend. She tried to turn her over. That slight movement caused a moan and then a yelp—both were good news. It meant Ariadne was still breathing.

As gently as she could, Diana rolled Ariadne face-up. Her blouse was cut in two. Both halves were soaked in blood. The slash Logan had put into her was nasty. A deep gash ran from just above her belt, diagonally across her torso, all the way up to her collar bone. Thankfully, the blade had just missed her throat, but that was the only blessing. The cut was deep. She needed a doctor just as badly as Richard did.

"You saved my ass out there," Diana said.

Ariadne forced a smile, but it was clear even that pained her.

"Don't I always have your back?" she managed.

"Can you walk?"

Ariadne fought to take a deep breath, then struggled to get to her feet. Diana shouldered most of her weight, taking her by the arms and helping to lift her.

"Let's get you over to Richard, see if we can do something with this car here," Diana said.

Slowly, she helped Ariadne limp around the rear of the sedan and over to where Richard sat, still propped up against the back tire, holding his gut wound with both hands. He saw them coming.

"Goddamn it," he said. "I told her to stay put."

Diana carried Ariadne over, and set her down in a seated position beside him.

"I'm glad she didn't or we'd all be dead," she replied.

"Figures," Norris answered.

His voice was weak. His skin was pale and he was drenched in sweat. He was losing blood fast. They both were.

"We have to call in, get an ambulance and some back up out here," she said.

"Already did it," he replied. "Local sheriffs are on the way, I told them to send E.M.T.s. Kendrick is inbound with a full response team."

"How long?"

"Fifteen minutes for the locals, half hour probably for Kendrick."

"That's too long," she said.

"I can hold out," he wheezed.

"Me too," Ariadne added.

Diana looked up to the hill crest. The flashes and the clamor had not died down, but she couldn't see any sign of Carter. She looked back to her wounded friends.

"You two are gonna make it," she said. "Just hold on."

Norris glanced at the explosions above. The ground rattled with a constant quaking, swelled by every strike of crimson lightning and every blast of black fire.

"You want to go up there," he said.

She grasped his hand.

"Whatever's happening up there, in a half hour it'll either be all over or there'll be nothing we can do to stop it," she said. "We've got to do something now."

Norris looked at her, clutching Ariadne close to him.

"I'll keep my eye on her til the ambulance arrives," he said. "Get your ass up there."

He squeezed her hand tight and he looked right in her eyes.

"Whatever the hell this is," he said. "Finish it."

«««—»»»

Diana reached the top of the hill just in time to see the vortex change. It no longer hovered above the dais. Instead it had lowered itself, moving in response to Carter's commands. Now it swirled perpendicular to the hill, forming something like a portal before the sacrificial altar, a black door to the other side.

It was shifting in other ways as well. The edges were beginning to compress. The center was shrinking as Carter stood atop the platform, reciting his ancient words. The whirlpool of shadow and dark flame was narrowing, closing in on itself in answer to his incantation.

It was working.

Diana saw the titanic figures struggling in mid-air above, Vayne engaged in epic combat with all three adversaries at once. Thunder and flame erupted with every blow between them, screams and howls of agony from creatures who did not belong on Earth. Carter's efforts seemed to draw them closer, pulling them toward the gateway as he wove his spell, shutting the portal down further with every shouted verse.

She was about to cheer, to call out in joy as the nightmare looked to be ending. But then she saw something that made her shudder. Instead of stepping back from the whirlpool, Carter was moving toward it.

Her elation turned to shock.

"Carter! What are you doing? Get out of there!" she shouted, hoarse from straining to yell over the howling winds.

He ignored her. He kept walking toward the vortex, chanting louder as he went.

"Jump! Before you get pulled in!" she shouted.

Still he did not reply. He continued moving toward it. As she stood there watching, he did the unthinkable—he stepped into the black gate.

Carter had his back to her now, but he remained perfectly calm, despite the tornado of dark fire that now swirled all about him. He continued his chant, and as the vortex shrank, it closed in around where he was standing, *around him*, cutting him off from the world beyond.

Slowly, he turned to face her, now standing fully inside the gateway.

"What are you doing! You've got to get out of there!" she yelled.

"I can't do that," he replied.

"You can. You can still make it! There's still time!" Diana yelled back.

"It's the only way," he said. "The text makes it very clear. The gateway must be closed from within."

"No, there has to be something else we can do!"

"This is the only way to pull everything back in," he answered. "You have to draw the portal closed from this side, *from the inside*, or anything that has already escaped will remain on your side."

"My side?" she replied. "*Our side*!"

Carter shook his head. Amazingly, shockingly, he began to smile just then. That was when she realized it. She could see it in his eyes—*he didn't want to make it out.*

"Not anymore!" he shouted back.

"Don't do this!" she shouted. "You don't need to do this!"

He raised his hands as the edges of the vortex lowered near enough to touch.

"I do," he answered.

Vayne called out to him, even as he held back the squealing, thundering form of Yog Sothoth.

"To seek Azathoth is to court madness," he said. "You may never be able to return."

"I know," Carter replied.

"Very well," Vayne answered. "Do what you must."

Carter looked back at Diana. The vortex had shrunk to half of its original size. The door had become a window, just large enough to see him on the far side, half obscured by the whirling edges.

"Be ready," Carter said. "When the gateway closes, you must kill what remains there. Put down the beast that was Gregorian and his mother. Let no part of them remain."

Diana held up Logan's blade. She lifted her other hand, arm outstretched and palm up. Carter did the same, even as the mist and the darkness closed ever further down around him.

The whirling of the vortex swelled as it got smaller, increasing the speed of the winds until it raged like the eye of a hurricane. The force pulling everything near it grew stronger with each passing moment, sucking anything close into the abyss. Every creature and strange minion of Yog Sothoth was yanked inward, hauled in by some inexorable gravity toward the heart of the portal.

Vayne too was caught inside the event horizon. His figure was contorted, drawn out and pulled by the irresistible attraction. Clenched in his ruthless grip, the unholy entity of Yog Sothoth howled and screamed with everything it could muster, but it too was sucked inward. When Vayne finally released it, the being's shapeless, plasma-like body was stretched and twisted as the condemnation of the vortex drew it back into the eldritch dark. In moments, it was catapulted into the black abyss beyond, disappearing into the void.

His foil dispatched, Vayne seemed to surrender himself to the vortex. He looked back one last time, just long enough to catch the eye of Diana Mancuso. She saw him staring back at her with his vacant, eye-less face. He was somehow peaceful as he reached out his hands, fell backward into the darkness and faded into oblivion.

As the gateway receded with Vayne, the detritus of battle fell back to Earth; a rain of blood and bone and broken flesh. The brutalized remains of Valeria Thorne and Victor Gregorian came crashing down upon the stone dais. Valeria landed in a wet heap only a few feet from Diana. Vayne had beaten her into a shattered ruin. Her inhuman body was contorted in a dozen places. Her long reptilian neck was broken backward.

She wheezed and growled weakly through fangs dripping blood and slime. That was all she had left. One final breath escaped her maw. Then she died.

Gregorian had more fight left in him.

The wounded monstrosity turned his fury upon her, swinging its spiky tail at her head. She was able to duck out of the way just in time, but Gregorian pushed on. He bounded toward her on one remaining leg, half of his limbs hanging to the side, broken and useless. He threw his spiny tentacles at her in a whipping thrash. They tore through her shirt and cut deep into her skin, knocking her backward.

Even as she fell though, Gregorian tumbled down as well, unable to control his own momentum. He landed a few feet from her, squealing and huffing as he tried to regain his tenuous footing.

Diana didn't give him the chance. Just as Carter had told her, she jumped at the shambling mass. She hacked at him with Logan's dagger, chopping through bony armor and stinking, oily flesh. The beast squealed, flailing his last few tentacles in a desperate final effort. Diana sliced through them like fat weeds, spilling yellowish ichor and sulfurous fumes with every devastating slash.

The thing that had been Victor Gregorian put up one final stand, reaching for her with a broken pincer on the only arm he had left. Diana was merciless. She cut it down and then plunged the MK II right into the center of his fat body.

The dying monster moaned and then collapsed. His remains fell in on themselves, deflating like a dead balloon. His scaly hide broke in a dozen places, spilling a gusher of rancid muck out onto the hill stones. Everything inside bled out of him, until the only thing left was a steaming puddle and a pile of fetid, green-black flesh.

Diana collapsed beside him, exhausted.

She listened as she lay there, swamped in stinking slime and the remains of inhuman death. There was no sound. No noise from above.

The chaos was over.

The sky began to settle. Lightning flashes faded away. The ground stilled. The cold quiet of night finally returned to the lonely hill top. Then there was only the wind, whispering through the broken stone dolmens.

Diana came to her feet, slowly.

She wiped the viscous, reeking slime from her eyes, took a long breath and looked up. The sky was nearly tranquil, but a remnant of the gateway remained overhead. It was almost closed, nothing more than a porthole in the heavens. The edges were hazy, shimmering like fading candle smoke, but she could still make out one thing. She saw Carter, standing there, looking out into the cosmic abyss. He was gazing ahead, his eyes alive with wonder as he stared into the eternal black ocean that lay beyond.

"I hope you find what you're looking for," she said.

As the gateway vanished, the last thing she saw was Carter's face.

He was smiling.

Frank Cavallo was born and raised in New Jersey and now lives in Northeast Ohio. He is the author of *The Lucifer Messiah, The Hand of Osiris* and *The Eye of the Storm.*

Visit him at www.frankcavallo.com

39657761R00234

Made in the USA
Middletown, DE
22 January 2017